An Angel's Touch

"A wonderful magical love story that transcends time and space. Definitely a keeper!"
—Madeline Baker

TO HAVE AND TO HOLD

The man before Lauren clutching a sheet to his narrow hips was nearly smoking with restrained fury. This would probably not be a good time to mention how she got here.

"Who in the bloody hell are you?"

She must not look like an angel anymore. Somehow Lauren had expected his first words to be a lot softer and begin with thank you.

Wrong. Clearly Patrick Dugan had no idea that he was a lost spirit in need of rescuing. What had Aunt Lucy's "push" gotten her into? Very slowly, Lauren stepped out of the tub, vividly aware that she was covered only from just above her breasts to midthigh. Like bands of steel, her arms secured the towel.

"Lady," he said, his eyes telegraphing that he was really thinking of another term, "I'll be askin' only once more."

The hoarse, gruff demand in his voice screeched up her damp spine. She moved behind the too small expanse of water.

"I'm Lauren Sul—Dugan. Your wife."

Longer Than Forever

Bronwyn Wolfe

LOVE SPELL   ◆   NEW YORK CITY

LOVE SPELL®

Published by
Dorchester Publishing Co., Inc.
276 Fifth Avenue
New York, NY 10001

Copyright© 1995 by Bronwyn Wolfe

The name "Love Spell" and its logo are trademarks of Dorchester Publishing Co., Inc.

Printed in the United States of America.

It seems appropriate that the dedication in my first book should be to those first key relationships in my life.

Thanks and love to my parents, John and Bonnie Rosell, and to my five brothers and their families and to my sisters and their families—the Clarks, the McRaes and the Ballards.

Love also to my wonderful in-laws: Russ and Ida Wolfe, the Cunninghams and the Velts.

Finally to my own daughters—Elizabeth, Rebecca, Catherine and Carolyn—thanks, girls, for being my number one readers and the best cheerleaders. And to my sons—Mac, Joseph and Sam—thank you, boys, for cooperating even when you didn't understand what the big deal was.

Lastly to my husband, Russ, who always told me I could do it!

(And, yes, friends. It is possible that I have the largest immediate family in the publishing world. With this much support, how could I fail?)

Longer Than Forever

Every day more and more evidence comes to light supporting the idea of life after death. If indeed this life is not the end, can we say for certain that it is the beginning. . . .

Prologue

"Tell me truthfully, do . . . do you think it will hurt?"

Daeer could not look away from the serious eyes of his white-robed companion, sitting expectantly on the crystal bench. How should he answer?

"You were right next to me in class, Aiyana," he said with a mix of tenderness and humor. "You know as much as I do. But *truthfully* I think that what you imagine will always be worse."

"Is that supposed to make me feel better?" Aiyana shot back, and Daeer smiled. How he would miss the way she made him smile.

"It's just that I don't think I'll handle pain very well." She hesitated. "A form with substance, one that feels, is a difficult concept; touching flesh instead of sensing essence . . . I don't know. . . ."

"Stop trying to plan for what has not yet happened, angel."

"Daeer!" Aiyana cried with a hoarse croak, glancing around to see if he'd been heard. "You're not to use that title in such a manner and you know it. I'm certainly not an angel, and most likely will never be; especially if I fail."

"Aiyana, you are all that I will ever want just as you are now; an angel even before the journey begins." He gazed steadily into her translucent eyes and continued, "And as far as what lies ahead, the only way to fail is to quit, and we won't let each other do that, will we?"

"You're right," she affirmed with more strength. "We're each a half of the same circle, stronger together than we are apart."

Daeer stood, his brilliant robe brushing his ankles as he stepped toward one of the glittering paths that crisscrossed the waiting zone. Sometimes it worried him that he had such a powerful need for her, even though the instructors assured him that pledgers often felt this way. It was one effect of the bond. Maybe if he teased Aiyana a little, they would both relax.

"Frankly," he tossed back over his shoulder, "I can't wait to experience the wonders of the bodies we have been promised."

"Don't think I didn't notice how you concentrated on that lesson, Daeer," she warned, moving to stand beside him. "You had best not experience too many of those wonders without me!"

"I will try to wait," he deadpanned, then stopped abruptly at the look of anguish on her face.

"How will we find each other?" Aiyana whispered. "You know we won't remember more than traces about this place."

"We are pledged, love," Daeer assured her. "That gives us a link even the forgetting can't erase. Come now, it's time to go."

As they approached the transport station, lines of

many other white-robed individuals began to form. Only those to start the journey that day would enter past the recording terminals. Friends and family pledgers went as far as they could until the watchers gently, but firmly, led them away.

"Tell me one more time," Aiyana demanded, struggling to control her anxiety.

"Aiyana, no matter how we change, no matter what happens, you will look into my eyes and know. Our hearts will not forget."

Their line suddenly moved and, just as suddenly, Daeer was being processed. After the information was taken a watcher motioned for him to pass through the gold filigree gate. He shook his head; he had to wait for Aiyana. They were going to enter the power chamber together.

"What? That can't be right!"

The sound of her panicked words filled him with dread.

"I'm sorry, traveler," the recorder muttered. "Your marker is not valid for today's departure."

"No! Please try again."

"I'm sorry. It won't authorize transport."

"Aiyana," Daeer called from the gate. "What is the problem?" The watchers were not happy with the delay, and he knew they would not wait much longer.

Aiyana pushed past the terminal before anyone could stop her. If she could just reach him . . .

"Daeer!" she pleaded in a taut, strained voice. "They won't send me now."

One quick look at the number of controllers moving toward them and Daeer knew it was useless to argue. He leaned closer. "I'm afraid there's nothing we can do, love. Try to accept it." He spoke in a low, soothing tone, disguising his concern, holding her gaze with his own. "A little time between us won't matter, Aiyana.

You know the pledging cannot be broken. All will be well.''

Even as he uttered his last words, the door to the chamber opened, flooding the area with a pulsing, shimmering light. In awe, Daeer looked into pure energy and the uncertain future. For the first time the fear he'd been hiding nearly broke free. What if they couldn't . . . No! Pledgers were never separated, because their bond was too strong to be content with any other. They would be together. They *had* to be together. Theirs was a special balance of strengths and weaknesses; talents and abilities. Each needed the other to be fully whole. All would be as it should be.

''Remember, Angel.'' He spoke loudly enough that heads turned and some patrons gasped. ''We are meant to be together. I *will* find you!''

''Or *I* will find you, Daeer, since I'm sure you are the only one who will ever see the angel in me.''

As she had intended, the playful challenge pulled one last, warm laugh from her beloved. It was a gift, just as his declaration had been.

In the next instant he was gone.

Before Aiyana could step away from the gate she saw the male who had been processing her transport approaching hesitantly. A slight smile curved her lips. This poor worker had probably never had such a chaotic send-off. The tiny spark of humor lifted her concern over Daeer a bit. After all, she thought, it was just a little more time before they were together.

''I'm sorry, traveler, truly sorry,'' the recorder stammered. ''I don't understand how this kind of mistake could have been made.''

''Mistake? What do you mean?''

''Because your case is unusual. . . . I . . . ah . . . circumvented normal procedure and scanned ahead to give you a new transport date, but . . .''

His eyes shifted away, and the most terrible feeling swept over her.

"Yes?" she prompted.

"I scanned ahead more than seventy-five years. Your name did not appear. Not anywhere."

In a daze, Aiyana turned back to stare at the spot where she had just bid farewell to Daeer. Now he would learn the truth about physical pain without her. Now he would learn *everything* without her. Nothing to come could possibly hurt worse than this knowledge. Nothing.

Not even being born.

Chicago 1895

Holy Mary, Mother of God! It was so cold. As cold as death. Was he dead and this his own tailor-made hell of ice?

Patrick Dugan could not hold back the moan that sounded more like a wounded animal's than a man's. Sick and beaten, he curled into a ball on the hard cot, feebly trying to hold on to whatever warmth he could. Jolts of pain pounded through the side of his chest and head with the force of a smithy's hammer on an anvil. Each labored breath took more and more effort.

In lucid moments during the last week Patrick had cursed his idealistic stupidity. He should have known that Brown meant what he said. The Chicago Fair was McDonald's territory, and Harry Brown was his right-hand man. Neither one would tolerate some immigrant's noncompliance. They had told him they would break him, just as they had so many other Midway attraction hawkers who hadn't knuckled under to their demands.

He should have listened, but the promise of America had still burned so bright within him that he had thought he could find someone who would believe what was going on.

Sweet Jesus, what a green lad he'd been. Now he lay drowning in the putrid bowels of the Cook County jail, surrounded by McDonald's lackeys, with as much chance of surviving as finding the crock of gold under his sour-smelling cot.

"More the fool are ya, Dugan," Patrick rasped, forcing the words from his festering throat. The usual rolling lilt of his brogue sounded as scraped and raw as his body felt. "There's not a soul in this world who'll be ridin' to your rescue. You're a dead man, me boy'o."

The clank and grind of metal on metal sent an involuntary shudder ripping through Patrick's body. *Dear God, they were comin' again!*

"Hey, Dugan, move yer Irish ass!" sneered the huge guard swinging open the heavy iron bars. "There's important folks out here and they want ta' talk." A stream of black-green tobacco juice splashed against the wall near Patrick's head and caused his stomach to roil.

"Sit up, ya' lazy mick," the guard growled, jabbing his boot toe into Dugan's vulnerable belly.

He was too weak to utter more than a soft groan. Brutal, hard hands yanked him upright, sending arrows of agony plunging into his chest.

"Well, well, Mr. Dugan." A second officer entered the cell, dressed meticulously in full uniform. The brass buttons on his long, navy, double-breasted coat gleamed as if they'd been recently polished. "You'll be pleased to know that you are about to become the Chicago World's Fair criminal of the week. In fact, the *Tribune* wants a picture of you for tomorrow's edition."

Hansen might have a bit more pomp and polish than the other animal, Bates, but Patrick knew him to be just as crooked.

Thank God Ma was dead! Dugan slumped back heavily against the damp wall and tried to picture her face, but an image wouldn't form in his fuzzy brain. If only the angel would come. . . . Eyes, burning hot with fever, closed against the childish thought.

It was the sickness filling his mind with Ma's stories of guardian angels. The stories that had comforted them both so many nights when his uncle would rage over nothing. Patrick had never understood why they hadn't just left. It wasn't until the day after his mother's death that he'd learned the reason. She had signed away her inheritance on the false hope that her half-brother would guarantee a home for her fatherless son.

"Your ma was a fool, boy, and you're the bastard result of her believin' in fairy tales. For fourteen long years I've let the little slut think I'd hold a place for you. But it's finished now." He laughed and slapped the wide-eyed look right off Patrick's face. "I have it all. You're nothing to me, boy. Get out."

That was the day Patrick stopped believing in love. The day he had vowed to never let that foolish emotion betray him as it had his kind and gentle mother.

With tremendous effort, Patrick tried to shift onto his side and mask his turmoil. As he watched the *Tribune* photographer set up the equipment, Dugan's chest ached with the liquid pressure filling his lungs. His arms felt like blocks of stone pulling him back down into semiconsciousness, and he couldn't stop himself from falling sideways onto the cot.

"I . . . don't think Mr. Dugan is well enough for a picture, Captain Hansen," the young newsman stammered, attempting to angle out of the disgusting room.

"Hey thar, fella, why not take it like he is now? I'll stretch out his legs some, and in a few days you can run it in the paper on the obituary page," Bates snickered. "He shor looks dead ta' me."

"Maybe we should forget it, kid," Hansen bit out.

"A picture of a dead criminal won't sell as well."

Dead? Patrick's sluggish brain tried to untangle the words swirling around him. Sweet Jesus, if bein' dead would stop this pain, then maybe he should just let go and . . .

Patrick Dugan!

Ma? This couldn't be right! With his last burst of strength, Patrick tried to concentrate over the jumbled sounds of the other men in his cell. Then he heard it again; the soft voice of his dead mother.

Don't you dare let 'em win, Paddy. Open your eyes, son. Open your eyes and hold on.

From deep inside, Patrick felt a burning hotter than his raging fever. And he knew, he *knew,* that if he did not have this picture taken he would never live out the day. And, God help him, suddenly he wanted to live.

With a wrenching grunt, Patrick rolled forward to the edge of his cot and painfully levered up on an elbow.

"Prop him up, Bates. Hurry!" the senior officer ordered abruptly at Dugan's movement. "The citizens of Chicago are going to see just how well the police are doing their duty."

Patrick tried to brace himself. Steady, lad, no blackin' out now. He could feel his heart beating in his temples. Everything sounded muffled, and the faces around him started to blur. Nausea from the pain and putrid smells brought burning bile to the back of his throat.

The eyes, Paddy. For God's sake, OPEN YOUR EYES!

"Just take the damned picture," Hansen ordered. "We've wasted too much time as it is."

With one brilliant flash, it was done.

Patrick stiffened at the impact of Smith's boot to his side, but the suffering was insignificant compared to the irrational hope that filled his soul like the lush, green beauty of his lost Ireland.

He'd kept his eyes open.

Chapter One

Southern California 1995

Lauren Ann Sullivan could not keep her eyes open.

She'd been working non-stop since eight in the morning, on a Saturday no less, trying to finish a last minute assignment for Family Finders. Now, the draining heat of the late July afternoon had finally caught up with her.

With a half-hearted groan, Lauren pulled herself up off the floor and carefully picked her way around the genealogical mess to click on the air-conditioner. The old papers and documents floated deceptively like little ice caps on the sea of her living room's slate-colored carpet.

It would be wonderful to feel a brief blow from an arctic wind, she thought, as she stretched out on her sofa for a short nap. Her mind wouldn't work right anyway if she didn't take a break.

Lauren closed her eyes and curved her mouth into a

faint smile. Ahhh, the air was coming on . . . It felt sooo good, sooo cold.

Then, almost too cold.

And it grew steadily colder, until she felt so uncomfortable that she groggily stood to go upstairs. Trying to reach the stairs she instead found herself moving down a long, dark hallway, towards a foreboding shadowed entrance. A weak stream of light wavered ominously at the end, reflecting off the damp slime that shimmered in patches on the walls. Lauren knew instinctively that its glow did not lead to safety or sanctuary.

She tried to turn back, but her feet would not obey. The light drew her forward. At the door, snaking beams writhed towards her, wrapped around her hand, and pulled her through.

There was a man. A man lying on a cot in a cell. He was filthy. His collarless flannel shirt was stained with dirt and blood. There wasn't a movement or a sound. Unreasonable fear thundered through her like the roar of a passing train.

Oh God, he's dead! She dropped to her knees close to the stranger's face. A stranger whose suffering was tearing her heart to pieces.

Then she heard it; the halting hiss of breath. A sound so ragged and labored, her own lungs strained for air. He lived. Lauren had to touch him. Had to feel the truth of what she heard. She softly brushed her fingertips along his bruised cheek. With visible effort, the man opened his eyes.

His smile was liquid fire; purifying and bright, burning away all the ugliness around them. The longing in his eyes was so anguished, it nearly broke her heart.

"Ahhh, sweet angel," he labored to whisper. *"You've come at last."*

Before Lauren could react, the pounding approach of heavy boots shattered the silence. What could she do? What should she do? The man looked up at her with utter hopelessness.

"Too late again, love. God, don't make me wait much longer." The soft words formed on his cracked lips as the cell door burst open. Lauren jumped up to protect him, but the burly guard acted as if she wasn't there.

"This is yer last night, mick!" he laughed. Then in one smooth move, he swung a bucket forward and dumped freezing water over the still form on the cot. The wet body arched in agony.

"Stop! Stop!" Lauren screamed into consciousness, nearly jackknifing off the couch as complete awareness of who she was and where she was rushed back into the eerie vacuum. She sat hunched and trembling, her eyes clamped tight against the impossible images she'd seen.

"Okay, okay, Lauren. It was just a dream," she said, a little too breathlessly to give herself much comfort. She forced open her eyes and peered around the airy country living room dappled with fingers of waning sunlight. Everything looked completely normal and her taut shoulders slumped with self-conscious relief.

Her boss was right. It was time for a vacation. Her tired brain must be finally trying to give her the message. She'd been working too hard for too long and this bizarre dream had instantly done more to convince her of that than all of Mr. Clark's awkward concern for her apparently nonexistent social life. An employer whose fulfillment came from connecting fragmented families tended to be a lot more personally involved with his personnel.

Lauren wrapped her arms around herself and felt her throat work against the emotions still swirling inside. That man. No man had ever looked at her like that; as if he needed her in order to live. Why in the world had she con-jured him up? She would probably never know, but mercy, his agony had seemed so real she was still aching from it. And he called to her . . . called her love. . . .

Lauren shook her head, wishing she could shake away these lingering sensations as easily. She felt like she sometimes did after a good movie or a riveting book. The characters moved her, haunting her and mak-ing her feel foolish because they weren't real and yet she couldn't stop thinking about them. Feelings with nowhere to go. That was the story of her life; feelings with nowhere, no one, to go to.

She rose stiffly to her legs and blotted her damp fore-head on the dusty arm of her baggy gray sweatshirt. Boy, was she pathetic. Even in her imagination she couldn't manage to create a happy relationship with a man. But if only she could have helped. Even in the dream, if she could have done something. . . .

"This is crazy," she muttered, tunneling her fingers through her short wilted curls and heading for the kitchen. Great! Now she was regretting not helping a dream man.

With a quick twist, Lauren turned on the water and in a guzzling splash rinsed her gritty fingers. She leaned up against the white ceramic-tiled counter and studied the crossing lines of powder-blue grout. She didn't like to think of herself as lonely and one-dimensional, but the truth was, she was nearing 30 and pretty much liv-ing her whole life for her job.

A job Lauren normally enjoyed, true. Her friend Aunt Lucy, the godsend of her young life, had long ago taught her a love of the past. It comforted her to work putting together lost pieces of other people's families, since she couldn't mend her own. Not after her parents died. And as lonely as her time in foster homes had been, in the end, it had finally led Lauren to some of the warmth and comfort she'd lost so cruelly. It had come in the surprising form of her feisty, octogenarian neighbor and mentor, Lucille Walker.

Lucille Walker, who on her death bed had sworn to the stricken nineteen year old that heaven surely had to be planning something *mighty special* to make up for taking away so much.

"The powers that be try to give people enough hope and happiness to balance out the pain and disappointment, honey. It's just that sometimes we foolish mortals get ourselves into fixes that put everything off-kilter. Fear and anger will do it every time, child. But for you, it's fear. Don't let it stop you and don't think for a minute that I'm ever gonna stop lovin' you, Laurie girl."

Even though Lucy's fragile body had barely been hanging on to life, Lauren remembered her steady brown eyes and the vibrant spirit they had still reflected.

If I have to, I'll just take things into my own hands and give you a big push from the other side myself. You watch for it."

For a while, Lauren almost childishly had. But with the passing of time, she had seen Aunt Lucy's words for what they were—a loving attempt to help her not feel so alone and abandoned. They had done the job. Lucy's memory always made her smile. This time it was a small quirk of the lips.

Oh, Aunt Lucy would have had a field day with this dream. Made it into a real psychic event. And, she would have agreed totally with Mr. Clark, because doing something different was a perfect way to start looking for possibilities.

There was no doubt in Lauren's mind that Lucy would be disappointed to see how closed she'd become to people and the wondrous possibilities she'd loved to

23

speculate about. As a human, caring person, Lauren knew she was probably failing on a score sheet somewhere. There hadn't been a best friend since Aunt Lucy had died. And as for anyone remotely lover-like?

Lauren couldn't repress the shudder that rippled through her as she snagged a paper towel and dried her hands. The debacle three years ago with Jeff Reardon had stopped her caring stone cold. Lauren felt a sick laugh climbing up her throat. Funny, he'd told her in very unflattering terms that their relationship would never work because ultimately, she'd affected him the same way. Stone cold.

Abruptly Lauren moved to the small inspirational *Do you really want to eat?* mirror glued to the fridge, and forced the painful laugh. Brownish smudges ran along each side of her freckled nose; half her mascara was gone, giving her blue eyes an odd lashless look; and that hair! It resembled a haystack with a pencil sticking out of it instead of a pitchfork. She looked as wiped as she felt.

"A raving beauty you ain't, kiddo," she said a bit tremulously while using the damp paper towel on her face.

Well, if her poor stressed subconscious was desperate enough to try and send her a message about the tragic state of her life by conjuring up this tragic dream, it was time to make a change. Her forced vacation was right around the corner and this time she would really go somewhere; really look for someone.

She groaned as she looked back through the open doorway at the stacks of boxes in the front room and acknowledged that she wouldn't be going anywhere until she'd read that blasted journal and transcribed the pertinent dates.

"I promise, I promise, good old staid, reliable, Lauren Ann Sullivan is going to change." As soon as . . . Well, it was just so scary to think of being that vulnerable and failing again.

24

All right, Sullivan! Enough of the pity party. Get back to work and the real world.

Lauren debated for a second before opening a bottom cupboard and grabbing two chocolate chip cookies, another of Aunt Lucy's legacies. Maybe she needed a mirror down here, too? Oh, so what if her jeans fit a smidge tighter. No one was interested in looking that close any way. Besides she needed a little comforting and this was the only kind handy.

She marched into the living room and put her treat on the oak end table. With a whooshing grunt, she plopped down on her camel-backed sofa and flicked on the Tiffany lamp, creating a golden ring of light that pushed back the early evening gloom hovering outside her bay window.

So far, work *was* the biggest success in her life and Lauren wanted to keep that positive thing going. She vowed to work on better balance just as soon as the Harry Brown family history was out of her hair and out of her house.

Then, still a bit chilled but reluctant to turn the air off yet, Lauren pulled at a burgundy afghan draped over the arm of the couch and cozied in for a good read. She reached for the journal on the glass-topped table—and the life of Nancy Brown, a turn-of-the-century teenager, began to unfold.

May 17, 1895
What an amazing day! My 18th birthday cele-brated at the Chicago World's Columbian Expo-sition. Dina will be just green with envy. I wonder what Columbus would think of this anniversary celebration? Why, they even invited his last living relative, the Duke of Veragua.

The electric lights were awe-inspiring, sooo magical. Harry says there have never been so many lit up in one place ever before. The day was

25

perfect until I tripped on my skirt and the most glorious man at the Ferris wheel saved me from tumbling onto my head! But Harry got angry. I've never seen him look at someone the way he did that Irishman. I had the oddest feeling that they knew each other.

Harry ordered me to keep away from such trash and the day was ruined. Why does he always spoil things?

Poor girl, Lauren mused. Teens seemed to struggle with authority figures no matter what the era. The dramatic Nancy Brown was obviously caught in a profound first crush, and she had managed to get back to the fair unescorted a few times to find her "glorious man."

My man of mystery is so brave! I'm so lucky he works on the Ferris wheel, where I can observe him discreetly. I can't imagine ever having the courage to go up in it, why it's more than two hundred and fifty feet high. But I watch other people ride so I can be near HIM—only he won't say more than hello!

I'm sure Mr. Patrick Dugan (I found out his name from the concessionaire selling molasses popcorn—Dina can't believe how bold I've become) won't speak to me without a proper introduction and family approval. Harry would kill me if he knew what I was doing!

Nancy's entries went on in this vein for quite some time and Lauren hurt for the long-dead girl. Unrequited love was the pits. Here was yet another example of that emotion making things worse and not better. And on top of that, the poor kid had older brother Harry (a rigid late nineteenth century male if she'd ever read one) to contend with.

Then Lauren came upon the arrest.

Although nearly 100 years had passed since the words had been written, the despair and fury Nancy had slashed on the pages pierced right through Lauren's heart.

> *God in Heaven, Harry caught me! He said that Patrick was a thief and a cheat and that he'd get what he had coming. But I really didn't believe he'd do anything until a huge apelike policeman showed up at our door and told Harry it was all taken care of. Oh Patrick, I'm so sorry! When I tried to sneak out of the house to go to the Fair to warn him, Harry locked me in my room. I hate him!*

But the next page . . . the next page sprang out at Lauren. An oppressive weight seemed to hover in the air around her and she knew . . . she knew exactly what Nancy was recounting.

She knew it, because she had dreamed it.

> *It's been seven days now since Patrick was thrown in jail. I overheard that same ugly policeman tell Harry that the prisoner was very sick and would likely die after a few more wet nights in jail. Harry laughed, and said the plan couldn't be working any better. My brother is a monster, and there's nothing I can do! Not a soul in Chicago can help poor Patrick Dugan now.*

The rest of the journal was blank.

Lauren's hands began to shake so hard that the book fell and bounced on the carpet. A wave of dizziness swamped her as she rolled onto her side and pressed her fists against her racing heart. Something was very, very wrong. Oh, God, what was happening? Was her dream about something real? How could she have known?

Fighting against breathless panic, Lauren reached down for the journal and frantically flipped through it. Surely there had to be more information in it. Somehow. Somewhere. Reaching the end of the book in frustration, she was on the verge of giving up when she noticed something odd about the back cover. A small bit of one corner was unglued. Along the edge, the paper looked lumpy. Lauren hesitated, then pulled up the brittle lining, freeing a small square of yellowed paper.

The old newspaper caption was clearly legible.

It was a picture of Nancy Brown's unrequited love, Patrick Dugan.

It was a picture of someone in hell.

It was a picture of the man in Lauren's dream.

He was real.

"Oh my God," she murmured, pressing her forehead against her knees and wrapping her arms around them. The scrap of yellowed newsprint hung suspended between her thumb and index finger. Lauren lifted her head and studied the picture once more. As she held it up to the light, an odd shimmer seemed to flow across the grainy, sepia-toned photo. For a millisecond she saw colors and pleading, demanding green eyes.

Help me!

Lauren blinked rapidly and held her breath. Her stuttered gush of air was audible in the still room. Every muscle in her body coiled into knots and it felt like she had to consciously unlock each one before she could gingerly lay the ominous picture of Patrick Dugan back on the bed.

As soon as the paper left her hand the whirling in

28

her head began to slow. This was the man whose eyes beseeched her; the man who spoke as if he knew her; the man who asked her not to make him wait too long.

He was real.

Lauren began to shiver uncontrollably.

She could try to deny, explain and rationalize this until her dying day, but it would not change what she irrevocably knew in the rock bottom of her heart. Her dream man was real.

With incredible force of will, Lauren planted her bare feet in the carpet's soft pile and flattened her back against the cushioning upholstery. She unconsciously rolled her shoulders forward just a bit as if to protect herself, and dropped her head back, finally closing her straining eyes.

"Breathe," she panted. "Breathe. And do . . . not . . . think." A slow draught of forced air barely held back the panic attack that was shooting right up through Lauren's middle.

She *had* to get away from whatever was happening here.

Catapulting her quaking body up and off the couch, Lauren stumbled over the spill of purple-red yarn at her feet as she frantically headed for the stairs to go . . . to do . . . ?

To do? Something? Something normal. Something to drown everything else out.

In minutes, the biting sting of hot water was pounding a lethargic heaviness into her body. Lauren loved long, hot showers and she single-mindedly focused on the soothing sensation. Later, as she slipped on her sea-green robe and stood at the bathroom mirror her shoulders sagged. She was tired to the bone and unnaturally numb. Numb was good, though. It felt blank and blank was saving her sanity.

With a blow-dryer she began to methodically transform her wet look into a cap of frothy honey-brown curls.

If she just didn't think anymore, surely in the morning everything would be okay again; no longer a "Twilight Zone" outtake. Of course, that all hinged on her being able to sleep, or even wanting to sleep.

A nauseous, sinking sensation settled in her stomach, but she would not give in to fear. Lucy had warned her to fight against that in her life, and only now did Lauren realize that she'd just been avoiding it instead. Not fighting at all. So, she had to acknowledge what had happened and start looking at both these incidents from another perspective. Then, maybe, a reasonable explanation could be found.

She was, after all, a professional genealogist; trained to put together all kinds of different information to form a more clear picture of things. Hard, cold—make that dead, cold—facts were what professional genealogists based their work on.

It was true, however, that there was a growing faction who claimed much more was going on than met the human eye. On a number of occasions over the years Lauren had heard some very earnest stories documenting help and direction from the "other side." Although personally she had never even felt the tiniest twinge.

Until today!

Lauren headed for the thick cream-and-rose comforter on her bed. Even in her warm robe, burrowed under layers of covers, she shook.

That man. That desperate man had been shaking too! Curled on his side just like this!

She pressed her face flush into a pillow before releasing one primal scream.

30

This was crazy! It was too unbelievable!

But if this—she scooted up against the carved oak headboard of her bed—if all of this was a message or . . . Aunt Lucy's push, then what?

What was Lucy asking her to do? What could Lauren possibly do for a man who had died 100 years ago?

"He's dead, Lucy," she hesitantly whispered. "He's dead and there's nothing I can do."

For a long time Lauren lay very still, buried beneath her covers, vaguely aware of the deepening shadows slipping in through the paned glass, pooling on the window seat and then running out like splintered rivulets of dark water across the objects in her room. The monotonous ticking of her domed pendulum clock lulled her into a state of semi-awareness—her breathing and heartbeat timed to its unchanging rhythm.

Oh, Aunt Lucy, she thought to herself with a small sigh. Where are you when I need you? If this is your push, then what would you say about this . . . this mess? Smiling in spite of herself, Lauren remembered Lucy's final words.

"My love won't stop just 'cause you cain't see me, honey. Nobody with the brains God has would create this whole kit and caboodle just to have it all turn to dust. So you just remember that somewhere, somehow, I'm gonna have my eye on you."

Do you have that caring eye on me now, Aunt Lucy?

Suddenly sitting up with a start, she remembered something else Lucy had told her—something she'd shrugged off at the time. "Don't let anyone, includin' yourself, close your eyes to the wonder of possibilities, honey. You cain't see nothin' if your eyes aren't open. Lastin' love's waitin' and it burns as hot as an old bonfire, Laurie girl. But child, you cain't keep standin' outside the fire thinkin' the flames will burn like they've done before.''

Lucy had had a message for her, she was sure of it now. ''I'm tellin' you that when the time comes, and it's gonna come, you gotta jump in. Don't let your earthbound thoughts fool you. Let your heart tell you what to do. It's got the key. Listen, honey. Believe! Remember all our lives we're either choosin' fear or love. It's always one or the other.''

What key, Aunt Lucy? What are you telling me to do?

Lauren closed her eyes, and it was almost as if Aunt Lucy herself was speaking to her. ''You find the key, Lauren Ann. You find the key and Heaven will surely unlock the door. Help the boy, child.''

It was nearly dawn when Lauren finally decided to do it.

She'd spent a few difficult hours struggling with her fear, her demanding logic and her growing conviction that she was indeed standing on the brink of something that would never come again. She had almost slept a bit first. But as tired and unprepared as she felt, Lauren knew she could not wait.

Patrick Dugan was reaching out to her and Aunt Lucy wanted her to help him.

Lauren knew Patrick Dugan's death should not have happened the way it had. He needed her! And she had to try and help, or things in her own life would never come around right.

She *was* standing outside the fire; outside of life. Had been for a long time. Her fear had colored every decision she'd ever made. As a result, without noticing it, her days had become one long flat line.

Lauren folded her arms tight. Now, the question was, did she want the fire badly enough to take the biggest risk of her life?

But if Patrick Dugan's *need* was powerful enough to issue this cosmic call, could she turn her back on him? No matter what her fears, she couldn't. It was that simple. A strangled laugh burst out at that thought. Simple?

"Okay, Aunt Lucy," she conceded, leaning back and staring right up through the shake roof. "I've gotten your message loud and clear. I'm going for it."

Of course, there was only one way to help Patrick Dugan.

Go get him out of jail.

She could do it, if she would but believe in the impossible, and find the key to take her there.

Aunt Lucy said so.

After three days of research, phone calls and strange looks from people at the library, Lauren thought she'd found the key. Keys, actually.

First, she'd called the Chicago Historical Society. Patrick Dugan's picture *had* indeed appeared in the *Tribune* on August 2, 1895; coincidentally, his twenty-eighth birthday. He had been younger than she thought; a man in the prime of his life arrested for stealing a large sum of money from businessman Harold Brown.

A reporter had written that, after seven days in the Cook County Jail, the accused would most likely never make it to trial because he had developed a severe case of pneumonia. The newspaperman had been right. According to the microfiche of the old *Tribune*, Patrick Dugan had died two weeks later, saving the county considerable expense.

The hundred-year anniversary of this picture and Mr. Dugan's birthday had to be more than coincidence. The journal and the dream clearly pointed to that conclusion.

Then, later the second day, Lauren decided to read up on any information she could find about this "fair" Patrick had been working at. By the time she stumbled on an article detailing Chicago's centennial commemoration of the 1895 World's Fair, to be held in just a few weeks, she knew nothing more should surprise her. But it did.

The second key nearly sent her leaping out of her library chair. Lauren was gathering some things to copy when the magazine on the top of her pile fell off and open. The bold-faced title all but sucked breath right out of her.

Last Remaining Building of 1895 Fair Still In Use.

The centennial anniversaries and an actual place that Patrick Dugan could have gone into . . . one she could walk into today. . . .

But how was she to use the keys? How could she be certain where a time door would open—if such a door even existed. She struggled against her lurking doubts until early one morning, as she stood at the bathroom mirror putting on her make-up.

"I'm not crazy for thinking time travel is possible," she reassured her reflection. "I bet a lot of intelligent people would agree with me."

The instant those words left her mouth she remembered an intense former co-worker who had cornered her years ago and insisted that by using Einstein's theories it might eventually be possible to verify all genealogical data by traveling through time. That memory led her to the final key that linked the others together.

A little while later, Lauren read for herself Einstein's proposition that time was not a straight line, but one that curved back on itself. The famous scientist had not ruled out the possibility that at those points where the curves most closely came together, they might conceivably touch.

Lauren was staking everything on the hope that in a structure common to both times and on a significant anniversary, the veil of time might be thinner. That those curves might be closer then. Close enough to slip through.

It was wild, illogical, and she didn't tell a living soul. Luckily, living people were not involved.

She spent the rest of the week canceling commitments and getting ready.

The Brown records were turned over to an associate and Lauren asked her boss to extend her vacation for the full four weeks. She could only pray it would be long enough. How did one estimate the travel time anyway? At the last minute she felt compelled to keep Nancy's journal and Lauren decided she better follow every pushy hunch she had, and deal with the consequences later.

Shopping was fascinating but weird. Everything she chose was packed carefully in a worn carpetbag: money, clothes, medicine, even a history book and maps describing early Chicago.

She planned and researched as she always did when given a new assignment, except for one tiny difference: This project was a trip back in time!

At long last, the day was only as far away as the coming sunrise. Lauren knelt in the middle of the Chicago hotel bed and clutched a pillow tightly to her body. Could she find the way to 1895? Would her keys really work?

Possibilities.

As bizarre as the whole thing sounded, Lauren knew she had to try. Had to believe it was possible. If she could, she was going to right a terrible wrong, a wrong that she'd discovered had wiped out Patrick's particular family line. Nothing of him had passed on to the future. Maybe that was why this whole thing had happened. Maybe Lucy was trying to help both of them.

At this point only one thing was certain.

With her eyes wide open, Lauren Ann Sullivan was jumping into the fire.

Chapter Two

It wasn't going to happen!

Even though she was in the right place—the former Palace of Fine Arts of the 1895 Chicago World's Fair—and at the right time—one hundred years to the day since Patrick Dugan had turned twenty-eight and had his photo appear in the *Tribune* . . . It wasn't going to happen.

The keys she'd pinned so much on weren't working. What now, Lucy? Lauren thought discouragedly. What now?

Lauren leaned wearily against the museum wall, fully decked out in her Gay Nineties rig. The flat, straw sailor hat—so common to that time and so uncommon for a 1990s woman—tipped abruptly over her eyes. Perfect! At least it was cover of some kind. One lone tear slid undetected under the wide brim and one white gloved finger soaked it right up.

Any minute now, Lauren expected an official of the present-day Museum of Science and Industry to ask her what she was doing wandering around instead of working on "Yesterday's Main Street." The popular attraction had been the perfect cover for her transformation.

A few hours earlier, Lauren had entered a museum bathroom in jeans, sneakers, and a Bulls sweatshirt and exited dressed as a woman from the Victorian era. Not one of the patrons had thought a thing of it. Costumes were expected, accepted, and worked with her strategy of not standing out like a sore thumb if this unbelievable thing really happened.

But what if some official confronted her now? What could she say? *I'm sorry, sir, but this is the only building still standing from the World's Columbian Exposition of 1895 and I'm looking for a time door.*

"Well," Lauren sighed, taking a deep, cleansing breath and straightening up from the wall; crying under a turn-of-the-century hat would invite questions, too, so she'd better keep moving. Lauren shoved her headgear back and tried to look like an employee on a break.

Not one of the fantastic displays around her registered. For weeks she had been working toward this day, with every minute filled to overflowing. Now the waiting was shaking her. The foolishness of the whole plan rolled toward Lauren on a tidal wave of doubt.

It was a familiar feeling. She'd had it many times recently, and she knew what to do to keep herself from going under. Lauren smoothed her green-and-white-striped taffeta skirt as she bent down to grab a well-worn carpetbag. It wasn't quite accurate, as was the case with her shoes, but she had hoped both items had enough of the "look" to pass.

As nonchalantly as possible, she wove around some slow-moving groups, her tired, scratchy eyes scanning the area for a spot that could offer some quasiprivacy. A sensation of light-headedness roiled up through her as she climbed the stairs to the rotunda. The smells of so many perfumes, colognes, and just plain people unexpectedly hit her stomach like a brick.

Too bad she hadn't eaten any breakfast. A quick glance at a big wall clock confirmed that she'd missed lunch, too. Five hours were already gone. Time was running out.

At the top of the stairs, Lauren spotted a deserted area behind a wide column and made a beeline for it. She dropped her carpetbag with a thud and gratefully sank to the floor. Propriety be damned. In a flash, one glove dangled from clenched teeth. Almost purring, she unbuttoned the tight collar and cuffs of her white, multitucked, leg-of-mutton-sleeved blouse. The hat was the last to go.

"Ooh, ladies," Lauren muttered, gingerly using her fingertips to rub sore spots under the billions of bobby pins anchoring her fake hair piece. "How did you stand all these clothes?" The miles of fabric in her skirt and slips did give a certain cush to the hard floor, but then, she smiled wryly, most women circa the Gay Nineties would certainly never have used this one advantage. Proper ladies using their skirts as a bumper pad? No way!

At last she could feel a cool ripple of air-conditioning floating over her wrists and down her neck to the moisture between her breasts.

Lauren undid one more button and snapped open her bag at the same time. She rummaged a bit until the slick, laminated picture she needed to see brushed her hand. In a moment the image of Patrick Dugan filled her senses. Every time she looked at his eyes the compelling need to help him grew stronger and her logical resistance weaker.

"Oh, Patrick," she whispered with exhausted despair, clutching the old photo. "I don't know what to do now. It should have worked."

The admission, the failure, drained her. There had been too many nights in a row with too little sleep and too much uncertainty. That must be the reason, she acknowledged with her last coherent thought as she

tucked the photo away; the reason the room and objects
around her began to blur and shimmer like a heat-
induced mirage on a desert horizon.

Lauren's eyelids felt as heavy as lead. With one arm
wrapped protectively around the carpetbag, her head
slowly drifted toward her shoulder. "Just let me rest a
moment . . . and then I'll think of somethi . . ."

"Ma'am?"

"Nooo, tooo tirrrrrd," Lauren slurred.

"Ma'am, please!"

This time she heard the voice more clearly, and a
brief shove emphasized the unpleasant tone. As Lauren's cheek bounced against her shoulder, sharp stabs
of pain knifed their way up her stiff neck.

"Oooouch!" she moaned, clamping her right hand
over the protesting muscles. Someone gave an impatient
snort. Hesitantly, Lauren prepared to open her eyes and
face the laugh she was sure to see. She must look like
a fool. She certainly felt like one.

But the face Lauren Ann Sullivan stared into was not
laughing. It, or rather he, was glaring. And it quickly
became evident that looking like a fool was the very
best she could hope for.

"Ma'am, are you ill?" The grizzled face, stamped
with a bulbous red-veined nose trailing a drooping handlebar mustache, was not asking a question. Like the
snap of a whip, Lauren felt his disgusted gaze flick from
her arms, with the cuffs peeled back to the elbows, to
the swell of one breast barely exposed by the limp collar
of her blouse, to what appeared to be (by the horror
spreading across his features) the worst infraction of
all . . . her bare legs, revealed just past the knee.

Even with her head still cottony from sleep, Lauren
got the message loud and clear: If she wasn't ill, she
would be accused of being something else much worse.

Oh, brother, she thought, rubbing her sore neck and tucking the scandalous legs under her voluminous skirt, *I have to be found by some old puritan who probably thinks I'm a drunken employee.* She looked directly into the strange man's eyes and offered a weak but grateful smile. *Be cool now, Sullivan.*

"Thank you for esking," she said, lifting a hand to her forehead for effect. "I felt so hot all of a sudden, like I was gonna faint." He didn't appear to buy it, and that rankled. She would remain gracious, but darn it, that was the truth. "I think if I just get these heavy clothes off I'll feel a lot better. A good blast from the air-conditioner and that nauseous feeling will go right away." Lauren wasn't sure, but the man seemed to flinch. He took a full step back.

"Ma'am, I suggest you reclothe yourself immediately. And let me assure you that if any more clothes leave your person, the authorities will be called."

"Listen, mister," Lauren retorted in a tone vibrating with an odd blend of offended sarcasm and humor, "I don't normally *un*clothe in museums, so relax." Her fingers made short work of the undone buttons and she struggled to her feet. He stepped back again.

Someone this uptight shouldn't be working with the public.

"I suggest you leave the Palace if the condition of the air is causing these unsavory compulsions, ma'am."

Lauren's eyes rounded with righteous indignation as she jerked on her gloves. Her behavior unsavory? Did the man ever watch afternoon talk shows? She snatched her straw sailor hat trimmed with green and white ribbons off the floor and narrowly missed impaling herself with a hatpin.

For just a moment, as the sliver of silver rested in her palm, Lauren had the most uncharacteristic impulse to deflate this evil twin of Captain Kangaroo. The man was clearly dysfunctional and needed professional help. She decided to mention it to a museum official before she left.

Her plan was simply to walk away with regal dignity, head back to the hotel, and cry her eyes out. Nothing had gone right. She had churned up the craziest feelings for days, and now she was just plain drained and disappointed. Maybe she deserved this old man's contempt. Maybe she was the one who needed psychiatric assistance.

A small smile twisted her lips. With the kind of luck she was having today, she'd probably end up in the padded room next to his. Lauren reached for her precision-packed carpetbag, avoiding eye contact.

He pointedly cleared his throat.

Great!

"May I advise you to *stay* out of the Palace of Fine Arts for the rest of your *stay* at the Fair. This is not the place to sleep off your indulgences." His beady eyes narrowed. "Go back to the Midway for that."

That was it! Lauren felt herself readying to blow just like Old Faithful. He didn't believe her . . . the old poop thought she was drunk. She, Lauren Ann Sullivan, who had never even had an overdue library book. Her mind raced; her mouth began to form the words of a scathing set down; both gloved hands gripped the carpetbag to her heaving chest. Never in her life had anyone spoken to her in that tone of voice . . . as if she was some kind of degenerate! He might as well have said, go to hell. . . . Go back to the Midway! Not a chance, buddy!

WHAT?

The Midway? The Palace? Lauren swallowed a lump in her throat the size of a baseball; the bag dropped like a stone.

And she looked around her. Really looked.

The artwork in the room was different. The insulting, paunchy man before her was *not* wearing a costume;

41

that mustache was real. Lauren's eyes honed in on the newspaper wedged under his arm and grabbed it.

"Now you've gone too far! I must insist you leave!"

"Dorothy, my girl," she murmured with growing wonder, starring at the date next to the headline, "you are not in Kansas anymore." She'd done it. Lauren wasn't sure how it had actually worked, but Aunt Lucy had been right! Somehow, some way, the keys had opened the door. Later she'd have to figure out how to make it work in reverse. But now . . . now . . .

Patrick Dugan, here I come!

Moments later, quite a number of startled fairgoers watched a young woman dash down the back steps of the Palace of Fine Arts in an undecorous display of swirling skirts and undergarments. But none of them was more shocked than the bulbous-nosed guard up in the rotunda.

The one sporting mauve lip prints on his cheeks.

It was incredible! It was like watching *Life with Father* or *Meet Me In St. Louis* on a really, really big-screen TV. It was like walking onto a gargantuan city-size movie set, accurate down to the smallest detail.

But it wasn't until Lauren asked a man who looked a lot like one of the Smith Brothers of cough drop fame for directions to the trolley station that she truly registered that this was not, at all, pretend.

Not only did the gentleman seem highly agitated that an unknown woman was addressing him boldly, but when he asked to speak to her escort and Lauren made the twentieth-century mistake of saying she was alone, the look in his eyes was the same as that of the uptight guard in the museum.

The term "male chauvinist pig" was beginning to take on a whole new meaning. Lauren knew that women in the past had often been labeled good or bad with not a lot of gray area in between. However, knowing it intellectually was one thing; watching yourself be categorized and dismissed was another.

Oh, well, she thought, rushing down the walkway "Mr. Smith" reluctantly had pointed out; she wasn't here for consciousness-raising—although it would be fun to find Susan B. Anthony and thank her for kicking some serious hiney on behalf of womankind.

The male attitude she could deal with. She'd just play the game. The rest . . . Wow! Lauren decided to soak up everything she could. After she freed Patrick Dugan, who knew how long it would all last? However, her enthusiasm and attempts at small talk proved a bit too much for the reserved people at the trolley station.

Lauren realized her mistake when she started to tell a young family about the Fair "hot spots" she had researched. The moment she let "the Ferris wheel will blow your mind" slip, the barber-shop-quartet look-a-like husband straightened his celluloid collar and coolly thanked her, turning his wife and two children away.

Her quick, analytical thinking came through with flying colors: Zip the lip and when in Rome . . . imitate! Heck, she thought, while hanging on to a trolley strap heading to old downtown Chicago, if she could deal with the weird people in 1995, she should be able to do it here, too.

All of Lauren's initial euphoria drained away as she faced the harsh granite building. Suddenly her movie-set surroundings seemed far too real. An innocent man's life was hanging on her ability to pull off the acting assignment of a lifetime. Tiny tremors began inching up her legs, and she felt like a deep-sea diver with the bends and no time to stabilize.

Lauren's hands shook a bit as she tried to smooth a few wrinkles from the short-waisted, mint green jacket that had been folded in her bag. With nervous awkwardness, she pulled it on like armor. For dramatic ef-

43

fect she removed the glove on her left hand and slipped on a plain gold band. Then, pressing a fine lawn hankie to her brow, she bent her head for just a second, willing tears to come to her eyes. A vicious jab of a bobby pin to her tender scalp did the trick.

It's show time!

The stocky sergeant looked up at the thud of the heavy door. Anybody entering or leaving the Cook County Jail was his duty, and he took it very seriously. He sat elevated behind a tall mahogany desk that ran the width of the room. It was designed to keep what was in, in, and vice versa.

Well, well, well, he thought, twisting the waxed tips of his mustache; what have we here?

She looked as cool as the day was hot. Crisp as a green apple, and maybe just as sweet. The sergeant let the flicker of a leer cross his face. The woman seemed a little taller than most, but not by much. Had a good healthy shape. Somethin' a man could hold on to if she wasn't too proper.

As she walked toward him, he spotted the lip rouge. Holy hell fires! He smiled.

This wasn't going to be easy. Lauren hesitated in the doorway for a fraction of a second as the stuffy, sticky air wrapped around her. The shiny bald pate of an officer sitting high behind a desk reflected the weak gaslight, making the room seem even warmer. Sharp eyes peering out of his deceivingly soft face began a visual trek of intimidation.

Lauren could feel her blood pressure climbing as she approached the portly policeman in charge. She had always wondered what it would feel like to have a man really look at her with some kind of desire; but this was disgusting. Far worse than the neutral response she was used to.

Chill out and play the game. Deep breath. Here we go.

"Excuse me, Officer. I believe I need your help."
Keep it weak and needy. Dab those eyes. Atta girl.

"Ma'am, I'd be happy ta' help ya'. What can I do?"

"It's my husband." Lauren's voice cracked, partly from nerves and partly from discomfort. The man wouldn't stop staring at her lips. "I've just arrived from New York and I was told he's in here . . . in your jail!"

She had to make this look good. Of course, she'd never reveal that a journal written in the past, and read in the future, had given her the information for the present.

"What's his name, Mrs. . . . "

"Dugan, Officer; his name is Patrick Dugan." Lauren put twenty very expensive and authentic 1890 dollars on the edge of the desk. "I'm here to post his bail." She tried to sound firm, but not too pushy. This wasn't exactly the time for 1995 female assertiveness. "The article in the *Tribune* said he could be released if there was someone to pay." Her gaze never wavered, even though her stomach did.

"Ma'am, you won't be gettin' your money's worth outta that Irish thief now. Not in his present *condition.*"

His ferrety eyes were sending a message that Lauren wasn't quite sure of. Then, suddenly, his emphasis on the phrase "money's worth" and his sleazy stares at her mouth made perfect 1895 sense. In the rush and confusion of trying to be prepared for so many unknown contingencies, she had forgotten one very noticeable thing. Lipstick!

Not wanting to look like the walking dead, she had added a touch of color in the museum bathroom; and because that seemed like weeks ago now, Lauren had forgotten all about it.

No wonder every man who'd gotten a good look at her had acted so strange. Darn it! Subtly she began to gnaw off the incriminating makeup that marked her a floozy. Thank heavens the odious officer wasn't watching.

The sergeant felt a fine sheen of sweat break out across his forehead as he shuffled some meaningless papers. Holy hell fires! McDonald was gonna have himself a fit. Nobody was supposed to be able to post bail for that cursed mick. Who the devil even knew he was married? No way was he gonna make this decision. Captain Hansen was McDonald's key man in the precinct. Let him take the fall.

"Take a seat, ma'am. I'm gonna have to speak to my superior." The hefty officer ran a finger around the high collar of his snug navy uniform.

What should she do? Even though this man looked like a lecherous, Keystone Cop reject, he could cause a lot of trouble for her if he didn't believe her. That stupid lipstick had made him suspicious. Lauren licked her lips again as she turned and went to sit on a hard oak bench.

The handful of other people scattered about the room didn't look happy either. Tattered, mismatched clothes silently spoke of poverty; downcast eyes and hunched shoulders radiated fear. One older couple talked in whispers at the far end of the bench. Lauren could hear enough to know they spoke in German. This was no place to laugh. If doom had a smell, she would swear she was breathing its scent.

The men here had too much power. No matter how they appeared, she could not underestimate anything. Lauren prayed that the document in her purse would fool them. A professional had prepared it for her, thinking it was to be used to expose fakes. Nothing could be further from the truth now.

A tall, slender man somewhere in his early thirties burst through a side door behind the desk. With an abrupt snap of his fingers, he motioned for Lauren to come forward.

His brown hair was fashionably oiled; his mustache and wide sideburns, fastidiously neat. The cold eyes that searched her were very different from those of the other officer. Lauren knew he didn't really see a woman at all; like a hawk, he saw only prey.

For the first time she felt real fear; not worry, or doubt, or foolishness, or amazement. Fear. These people weren't actors, and heaven help her, neither was she. As Lauren stood, her grip on her life-line, her carpetbag, tightened. She could not show one sign of weakness. In the next moments she would have to convince this policeman, who'd no doubt already heard an earful from Ferret Face, that she was truly Patrick Dugan's beloved wife.

Of course, the only major flaw in the plan was that Mr. Dugan was not going to have a clue on God's green earth as to who she was. But it was too late to think of that now. The man who had identified himself as Captain Hansen wanted proof. Irrefutable proof!

"Well, Mrs. Dugan," he said, scanning the document in his hand, "this marriage certificate appears to be in order, but I will have to verify it first." The smooth, oily sound of his voice went well with his hair.

"But . . ." she pled for affect, "how long will that take?

"Possibly a week, or maybe two. The mail can be so unreliable."

Sure, just give them a few more days to finish their dirty job. Swine! No matter what she had to do, Patrick Dugan's life depended on her getting him out now!

"There must be *something* I can—"

"Well," Hansen paused meaningfully, "there is one other solution, Mrs. Dugan, if you are indeed who you claim to be."

"Yes?" The captain's gaze narrowed. His very stance left no doubt in her mind that his "solution" was going to be a test of some kind.

47

"You could marry him again, today, here in Chicago."

Hansen smirked, and the desk sergeant at his left failed to muffle a hoot.

"And, certainly," he continued, "a devote Irish Catholic like your husband would insist on a priest officiating at this little anniversary of something that has had such deep meaning for both of you."

The captain moved a step closer, and Lauren knew the man expected her to break. Obviously he was hoping that the threat of a legal marriage would do the trick; however, he was dealing with a woman from the future, where revolving-door marriages were the norm. Lauren squared her shoulders. Yes, she felt bad about involving an innocent priest, but saving Dugan's life was her first priority; and even a slight hesitation would tip off this creepy cop.

"Wonderful idea, Captain," she said in a sure, even cadence. Surely later she could explain to the priest that it had been a life-or-death emergency. "Send for Father Ryan at once."

For just a moment there was profound silence. Lauren thought Hansen was going to balk, and then an icy gleam returned to his eyes. She forced a smile, setting down the carpetbag next to her feet and giving her now less-than-white gloves a tug. In a most feminine move, she patted her hairpiece and straightened her ribboned hat.

"Well, gentlemen, on with the wedding."

The sense of déjà vu was so strong that Lauren felt faint. She was walking down the exact corridor she'd seen in her vision, only this time it was real. The despair seeping through the cold walls was tangible. She could smell the acrid, hopeless odor of fear.

"This is Dugan's cell, ma'am," the captain announced, waving away a hulking, apelike guard who stood blocking the barred door.

Lauren couldn't believe how large this new policeman was. His eyes were eerie, empty of any real soul. How long had this amoral subhuman been in charge of Patrick's cell? Every protective instinct inherent in her woman's heart and body jumped to battle-readiness. Adrenaline began to flow.

"I'll give you two a few minutes for a private reunion."

The big guard grunted and groaned with such disgusting lasciviousness that Lauren felt a slow burn heat her face and her tongue. If she were to open her mouth now, she would surely spit fire.

"That's enough, Bates," Hansen ordered mildly. "Unlock the cell and then go and get the good Father."

The small space was airless and shrouded in shades of gray. Only the diluted gaslight from the hall offered any illumination. Lauren stepped in as if she were about to walk barefoot on glass; carefully, lightly, knowing full well that no matter how she moved, pain was inevitable.

"Mr. Dugan?" She slipped off her gloves and stuffed them in her bag, which she set on the floor. Under a worn blanket riddled with grime, a long, indistinct form lay facing the wall.

"Patrick," she whispered, moving closer. "I'm here to help you."

A halting moan filled the room, and the body rolled.

Patrick kept his eyes closed defiantly. Merciful saints, not the dream again! God save him, but he didn't have the strength for the angel today. The Little People must be havin' a time of it with such a stupid lad. He would not look! He would not feel the salvation of her coming, just to have it disappear in his hands. Her caring was only an illusion anyway. The sickness was rotting his mind.

"Be gone, angel," he rasped. "I've not the heart for it today."

Lauren stopped, absolutely immobilized at his words, and watched the glittering green eyes close. His face was as gray as the sheet on which he rested. In the faint light she couldn't tell the color of his hair, but the limp stuff lay straight back from his forehead as if it had been tunneled repeatedly by frantic fingers.

Oddly enough it registered that Mr. Dugan must prefer to be clean-shaven in a day of almost compulsory male facial hair. Although a considerable forest of dark burnished whiskers grew evenly across his lower face to heavy sideburns, there were no denser areas indicating a beard or mustache.

Cinnamon, she decided, as she moved closer and studied him from a new angle. When his hair was clean it would be the color of cinnamon. With a start, Lauren realized she was reaching out to touch . . . What an idiot! Any minute the destructive duo would return, and things were definitely not ready.

"Mr. Dugan?" She sat cautiously on the edge of the cot and shook his shoulder with her right hand. "Patrick," she importuned more loudly in growing panic, "you've got to wake up. They'll never let you leave if you can't help me convince them."

His eyes opened reluctantly. "I didna know angels wore hats."

Damn! He was hallucinating. Her an angel? Not hardly. The term made her feel strange.

"No, Patrick, I'm not an angel." Lauren clasped both hands to his shoulders and tried to pull him up. Why did it feel as if she'd said this before? Everything was crazy, no matter what Aunt Lucy had thought of that word. It must be fallout from the time travel.

"My name is Lauren Sullivan," she puffed, straining to lift his ill but still muscular body. "You've got to help me now. . . . "

"No."

"What?" Lauren froze with his chest halfway off the bed.

"I'll not help you, angel, 'cause in the end you'll leave me. You always do." His pain-filled eyes looked straight into hers but didn't truly see. "Just let me sleep, colleen."

"No way, bucko! I'm not leaving!"

These were fighting words, but Patrick Dugan wasn't in any shape to realize it yet. She quickly laid him flat to reposition him.

Lauren swiveled to her knees, lifting and bunching her green-striped skirt and slips up to her thighs and shoving them over the side of the makeshift bed to the floor. With all the strength in her twenty-nine-year-old, four-times-a-week aerobicized body, she shoved her taffeta-covered arms under Patrick's back, locked her hands in a death grip, and *pulled.*

Her face naturally fell forward into the crook of his neck. The sailor hat rammed backwards, still speared by the hatpin. Lauren filled her lungs, even though he smelled of musty, stale sweat, and held her breath for one last mighty wrench.

"Now listen here, you . . . you . . . poor, unfairly treated, out-of-your-head stubborn man."

Her words made no sense to him at all, but the brushing of soft lips against the side of his neck did. Even near death, a man reacted when he felt a woman in his arms.

"Good! Come on, Dugan, move a little more. Helllp . . ." she tried to twist him toward the wall, ". . . me.

"Okay, great," Lauren huffed. "You're up and

51

your eyes are open.'' They were clearly on a roll.

"Now, Patrick," she said, slowly loosening her hands in case he toppled, then getting to her feet to swing his stiff, denim-clad legs over the side of the cot. "In a minute a priest is going to come in here with some policemen." Lauren crawled next to his now quaking body and wrapped the lame excuse for a blanket around his shoulders. She leaned forward anxiously, right into his face, to be sure he was getting everything she said.

"What's your name, angel?" Dugan formed the words slowly, gingerly working his cracked lips.

"Lauren, and I'm not . . ."

"Ah, a Laurie, sure 'n I should have guessed it. . . . " Patrick sighed. "But then, you've never stayed long enough to tell me your name before." Lifting one trembling hand, he stroked her cheek; then he let the hand fall like a dead weight to the bed.

Lauren felt as if she were caught in the power of the ocean's undertow. She knew that the gray-green eyes, dull as tarnished silver, didn't really see *her*. But the rough drag of his fingers across her skin suddenly seemed to be the most intimate touch she had received in years. So needy, so warm.

In this filthy, smelly room, in front of this filthy, smelly man, she was having the most moving and frustrating experience of her life.

The feelings she'd had when she'd first seen Patrick's face in that grainy newsprint photo were nothing compared to what was happening now that she was with him in the flesh. Oh, brother, time travel must have knocked something loose in her head. Why hadn't Aunt Lucy warned her?

It was getting so hot! Perspiration dotted Lauren's temples and her upper lip. Little wisps of short, moussed hair were starting to spring out of confinement. The oppressive surroundings were quickly draining her energy. She figured she had about two minutes to convince this man to cooperate or they were both doomed.

Time to fight dirty! Angel he wanted; angel he'd get. A strange shiver ran up her spine, but Lauren ignored it.

"Dugan!" The man was in la-la land. Lauren straddled his lap and grabbed a fistful of grimy shirt in each hand. When she sat back on his thighs she jerked his upper body off the wall.

"Dugan?" She shook him. "Do you hear me?"

"Aye . . . angel." He cocked his head to the side and leaned back, a wince tightening his features. "You're a mite loud for a heavenly bein'."

"Dugan, you're right, I am an angel, and I've come to take you back to Ireland." *Heavenly Father forgive me for lying to this poor, sick man.* "Do you want to go, Patrick?" Lauren shifted one hand to the back of his neck, grasping his chin with the other. "Do you want to go?" Desperately, she jiggled his face.

"Holy Mary, yes . . . to the open land and me horses, yes, angel!"

Lauren had never heard a voice so filled with longing.

"All right, then; open your eyes and listen." Such a lost, fevered soul looked out from the tiny windows of smoky green. Lauren blinked hard and fast to keep the tears from falling. "When I squeeze your hand like this," her fingers holding Patrick's chin dropped to his limp hand and curled tightly around it. "You tell the priest, yes. Okay?"

"And you'll take me from this place?"

"I promise. You just say yes when I squeeze."

"You . . . won't . . . leave me again . . . no more waiting?"

These were words he did not want to say. Lauren felt

his body tense and strain against the emotion behind them. The fever suddenly seemed to blow from his eyes like clouds pushed across a windy sky.

"I don't want to be needin' anybody, not even a dream angel."

The lucid moment bore a powerful message, defining this man to Lauren. She knew a lot about the kind of fear and hurt that drove a person to feel like this. But to be so ill and still hold the walls in place spoke of a hard core of pain that had been compressed into steel. It took a searing hot fire to melt steel, and a mistake would cause more than just a burn; but right now all that mattered was getting out of here.

Lauren swallowed the dry, aching lump in her throat. Somewhere, somehow, she prayed Aunt Lucy was still pushing.

Chapter Three

When Captain Hansen and the neanderthal Bates marched the withered little priest into the cell Lauren felt like a specimen smear on a microscope slide. She realized that both of the officers (and she used that term very loosely) were furious when they saw that she was not going to back out of the marriage. Yes, it would complicate things, but she'd face the consequences later.

They wanted Patrick to stand, but Lauren knew he would never make it. It was going to take every ounce of reserve strength he had just to get out of the jail itself and down the street to the cheap boarding house room she wisely had rented before entering this den of iniquity.

The worst moment came when Father Ryan asked Patrick, who sat motionless next to her on the cot, the all-important question. Dugan's face was devoid of expression, as if the energy to even shift his eyes was beyond him.

"Well, Patrick, son, what have ya ta say now? This fair colleen is waitin' most anxiously ta hear the truth of the vows ya've already made." The kindly face, wreathed with snowy hair, watched them both intently.

Lauren held Patrick's hand between their bodies, nestled completely under the green-and-white-stripped skirt and squeezed like there was no tomorrow. With Dugan's continuing silence, that was an ever-growing probability.

Finally, just as Captain Hansen cleared his throat, Patrick spoke.

"Yes," he drew in a rattling breath. "The angel promised. . . . ''

Lauren's eyes went round.

But Father Ryan chuckled. "Well, she surely looks like an angel ta me, lad, but only time will tell about her promises. Come now and give her a wee kiss, and we'll get the happy couple on their way."

Lauren had to do it. Patrick's lips were hot and dry, but she was too busy thinking about how she was going to haul him out of there to notice his soft sigh at their brief touch.

Thank heaven the good priest came to their rescue. Lauren knew she didn't have much undercover savvy. "Matlock" and "Murder She Wrote" were about her only claims to researching the criminal mind, but even she could tell that Father Ryan had some kind of influence over Hansen. The corrupted captain must have had a tiny spot of conscience still susceptible to religion. In a short time all the paperwork had been completed, and Bates lumbered back into the cell with a small bundle. Hansen followed and blocked their exit.

"The trial is set for September second, Mrs. Dugan. One month from today. Your husband had better be there, and you had better be with him! In fact,'' he added, his expression black with threat, ''we'll be keeping a close eye on both of you.''

His meaning was perfectly clear: They were only free technically. At that moment Lauren Ann Sullivan knew she was in way over her head. Because of her careful planning and the supernatural push from Aunt Lucy, she had never really calculated the people she'd be up against. They hadn't seemed real . . . and what harm could unreal people do? That had been a very big mistake.

Her hand in Patrick's was trembling. *Focus, Sullivan!*

Bates tossed the bundle onto her lap and both uniformed men turned abruptly and left.

''Where are ya goin', Mrs. Dugan?'' Father Ryan asked as he helped her get Patrick to his feet.

''I've got us a room close by,'' Lauren huffed, trying to hold the carpetbag and Dugan's stuff in one hand and balance the man himself with the other.

Dugan shuddered against her. He was heavy. Too heavy.

''Mrs. Du—''

''Lauren, please.''

''Let me help ya, Lauren.'' The priest glanced cautiously toward the iron-barred door. ''Ya both need to be leavin' here as fast as ya can, and ya won't make it a'tall, I'm thinkin', without some help.''

For the first time in what felt like hours, a smile spread warm and soft across Lauren's face. ''Why, Father Ryan,'' she said quite sincerely, ''I think you must be an angel yourself.''

Ahhh . . . the laugh of an Irishman. Pure sunshine.

After four endless days and nights there wasn't one corner of the small rented room that Lauren didn't know by heart.

Although a garish Victorian wallpaper in reds and pinks fairly screamed from the wall behind the plain iron bedstead, the sheets and wedding ring quilt that covered the lumpy mattress had been crisp and clean. The landlady's attempt at reproducing the style of the era, however, hadn't extended to the simple, serviceable rocker and slat-backed chair, nor the unfashionable shaker table that held a kerosene vase lamp, a pitcher, and a washbasin.

Lauren hadn't been outside the stuffy room for more than a few hurried trips to the outhouse—she wasn't ever going to grumble about cleaning toilets again—and getting fresh water from the pump in the kitchen. If Father Ryan hadn't been with her when they'd managed to drag Patrick into the boardinghouse, Mrs. Werner would never have let them stay.

Even though Lauren hadn't been much of a churchgoer, she promised herself that as soon as possible she would light a candle for the little priest with the big heart. The story he'd told Frau Werner was sure to cost him quite a penance. *They were a sentimental couple who'd come to be married and then honeymoon at the great Chicago World's Fair.*

Unfortunately, he'd explained to the grim-lipped matron, poor Mr. Kelly had taken a bit of a fever. Both the priest and Lauren had crossed their fingers and hoped the landlady hadn't paid a lot of recent attention to the newspaper. They were blessed, up to a point.

Dugan was not a cooperative patient.

From the first he had fought the pills. Lauren wished she could tell him how fortunate it was that she had developed a severe upper respiratory infection nine months ago and had misplaced an entire prescription of Suprax. Her doctor had had no choice but to refill it. Who could have known that finding the original medicine some weeks later would have turned out to be such an important event?

For an American living in 1995 pill-taking was so commonplace, one didn't even think about it. However, for a 1895 American it was a whole new concept.

"Don't make me swallow any more pebbles," he'd argued in a wavery voice. "You'll be killin' me for sure."

"Listen, Dugan," she'd warned, sounding tough as nails as she'd forced the antibiotic between his pursed lips. "I'm an angel, and God told me you have to swallow as many pebbles as I give you. Got it?"

Fortunately he did.

But last night, when the fever raged and Lauren had sponged Patrick's burning body yet again to give him some relief, the hard stance had crumbled to dust. With surprising strength he'd gripped her wrist, dragging it away from her cooling ministrations, and pressed her arm against the hard, bare rise of his chest.

"Faith, but I've missed ya so, Ma," he'd murmured in a rough, rusty brogue. "There's no one and nothin' for me now that you're gone. . . . Hell, but I'm so tired of being alone."

Like an erupting volcano, the suppressed emotions Lauren had been tamping down for days boiled to the surface and flowed hot and thick down her cheeks. She felt sure that Patrick Dugan had revealed feelings to her in the delirium of fever that wild horses normally couldn't drag out of him.

But he had, and she knew, now. She knew only too well that loneliness hurt the same no matter when, no matter where. It was something they shared, and it moved her unexpectedly. For one heartbeat a surge of self-protection had curled her trembling hands into tight fists. But the rare chance to comfort, to console, pushed past her insecurities.

Lauren had feathered her fingertips hesitantly across Patrick's strong, corded shoulders, finally cupping them and gently resting a wet cheek against the mottled green-and-blue bruise that marred his chest. Eventually she sank into an exhausted sleep as long-buried yearnings shifted dangerously in that fragile place of lost dreams.

Soft, pale pink streaks of light inched along the floor to climb the bed and tap like feathers against Lauren's closed eyes. Her body was fuzzily aware of the warm male length spooned so naturally around hers in this most unnatural of circumstances. For one foolish minute Lauren wallowed in the sensation with a tiny self-deprecating smile and let the sweet scent of lavender drift over her.

This old-world Irishman would no doubt cringe if he knew he was the source of the floral scent and also the cause of her ridiculous fantasizing. But any further rational thought seemed to be muffled, as if her entire brain was wrapped in cotton batting.

The small room was pin-drop still. Yet Lauren could hear the distant sounds of early morning activity pressing against the closed window and knew she had to let in the cool air while it lasted. Then, as she slowly straightened her cramped legs, she suddenly registered the one absent sound she'd been praying not to hear, and in its place was the even, easy, breathing of Patrick Dugan. He was finally turning the corner.

Lauren whipped up and around, quickly laying one palm on his forehead and another against his neck. He felt normal . . . and it was such a relief that tears welled and she bent her head low, almost touching his chest, breathing even more deeply of the lavender that clung to his skin from Mrs. Werner's soap. Two hot spots bloomed on Lauren's cheeks as she thought of Father

Ryan's quizzical look when she'd asked him to help her take off Patrick's clothes so they could clean him up as best they could.

Now she realized that if she'd thought to spare them both some embarrassment, she needn't have bothered. Bathing Patrick hadn't been that big of a deal, comparatively speaking. And in spite of everything, after the first bit of awkwardness it had seemed right that she should be the one to take care of him. Hadn't she been called across time to save him?

Lauren tucked her folded arms close against her ribs and visually trailed the peaceful planes of Patrick Dugan's face. Would there still be fire blazing in his eyes now that the fever had been put out? How long would he need her help? She'd probably be able to leave quite soon, her mission accomplished.

Slow, distinct heartbeats began to thud against her arms beneath her breasts. A red-brown beard shadowed the lean hollows of his cheeks and dipped in the cleft of his square chin. Perfectly arched, deep russet brows drew her eyes again and again. For some inexplicable reason Lauren wanted to trace them with her fingers. And those eyelashes ... geez! Without mascara hers were transparent, but Patrick Dugan's looked like a soft ruff of fur.

"You are sick, Lauren Sullivan," she muttered and pressed one palm over her heart, as if to control it somehow. "The poor man isn't even conscious!"

She tried, she really did, but her thoughts just couldn't be stopped. For the first time since the whole unbelievable adventure had begun, Lauren was seeing Patrick Dugan as a man; not a patient, or a victim, or a lonely child. This was very disturbing and definitely bad timing.

One hundred year's worth of bad timing, and she regretfully called up Jeff Reardon's harsh words to squelch her perilous feelings.

Their relationship had started at a research convention, and Lauren had hoped that the lasting love Aunt Lucy had told her about was finally going to be hers. Like a starry-eyed fool, she had jumped right into helping him and thought he was a gentleman because he hadn't pressed her for a physical relationship. Truth was, the man had never been interested in her physically. He'd only dated her to ensure her expertise on a difficult project.

Lauren wrapped her arms tightly around herself. Jeff's hurtful actions were something she needed to remember before she lost perspective of what she was doing here. Like a surgeon's scalpel, the memory of his cruel good-bye cut bone deep before the pain kicked in.

"Look, I'm sorry, Lauren. I needed that raise bad and I knew you could help me. And in the beginning I tried to make more of it. Really. But there's nothing about you that gets a man going, if you get my meaning. No heat at all. You left me cold, Lauren, and that's something a man can't fix."

No way was she ever going to put herself in that kind of devastating situation again. She was probably just reacting to one of those captive-captor, stress-induced, emotional-dependent syndrome things.

Get a grip!

And that's exactly what she forced herself to do.

The rest of the day was spent in pure pioneer pursuits. After straightening the small room and spooning some broth down a certain groggy Irishman's throat, she became very familiar with a washboard, trying to clean Dugan's filthy clothes.

Lauren almost bit her tongue when she opened her mouth without thinking and asked for a washer. Mrs. Werner was offended and quick to point out that only the very rich could afford those "new-fangled" machines. Besides, she'd continued, even the wealthy didn't like 'em, because they tore up more than they cleaned up!

Thank heavens she hadn't gone back to the 1600s, Lauren had mused. Her loose lips would have landed her in the fire for sure. Literally!

A few hours, and two ragged hands later, she had a revised definition of "the good old days." Her back and arms felt as twisted and wrung out as the fabrics she'd been wrestling with. However, she could not deny a surge of pride when she surveyed her accomplishment hanging on the laundry lines in Mrs. Werner's backyard.

Yes! She fisted her hand and pumped her arm once. Could Lauren Sullivan adapt, or what? Of course she'd almost made another blunder when the shocked landlady spied Lauren—and she must have been spying on her to have reacted so quickly—hanging up her "nightdress." It simply wasn't done! Heck, if Mrs. Werner got a gander at the underwear hidden in a roll in the cotton toweling notched under her arm, the poor woman would have burst her corset strings.

Quietly, Lauren opened the whitewashed bedroom door and shut it behind her. A light breeze tumbled through the small, open window, dancing with the lace curtains like a lover. The smell of roasting meat and muted sounds of laughter floated in with the rush of air, and off in the distance a trolley bell rang. She sighed with the wonder of it all as she walked to the bed.

Lauren could hardly believe this was actually happening. Four weeks ago she hadn't even heard of Patrick Dugan and now here she was, living a scientific, supernatural miracle.

While she'd been wrestling with the laundry, Patrick had rolled onto his side, facing the wall. The wrinkled cotton sheet resting low on his waist framed his broad, muscled back like white matting.

That slow, strong thud began again in her chest.

"This is ridiculous!" Lauren whirled around. No man had ever affected her this way. It was getting downright scary and totally stupid. Hearing the word *frigid* again in reference to her would be lethal.

In the last three years it had been so easy to shut down any attraction. Why was it such a problem now? She glanced back over her shoulder, following the length of his sheet-covered legs. The weird metaphysical connection she felt to this man must be sending a haywire message through her body. That had to be it!

Face it, my girl. The man has never even seen you as a real person, and yet you've got the hots for him. This is the stuff of which major humiliation is made. So cut it out!

With those stern words ringing in her ears, Lauren turned toward the quilt rack in the corner of the room and hung her bra and underpants on it. An inventive drape of cotton toweling hid the shocking apparel.

A sharp knock cracked against the door.

"Ma'am, we brung yer tub." The exaggerated male whisper paused until the door opened. "Oh, yeah; Ma said she's got some stew ready fer yer husband whenever he wakes up."

As Lauren nodded and stepped aside, she thought a ripple of movement came from the bed. Her eyes snapped back to Patrick, but he was perfectly relaxed, breathing slow and steady.

In a flurry of motion, Mrs. Werner's two teenage boys carried a slightly oblong metal tub and folding screen to the far side of the window. Its back was rounded high enough to lean against, and as the young men poured in pails of refreshing water, Lauren thought it looked like heaven. She was sweaty and dirty and had aching muscles that needed some warm, wet pampering. True, it was going to be a tight fit, and not as good as a shower, but she would wedge in and make do.

Lauren shot another calculating glance toward Patrick. His fever had been gone for hours now. Should she take the chance? She had to reason that if all the commotion in the past ten minutes hadn't roused him, she would probably be safe for a little while longer.

Dugan was going to be weak anyway, right? And it was time to be painfully realistic. It wasn't as if he would open his eyes and be so overcome by the sight of Lauren Ann Sullivan in a tub that he'd have to have his way with her. What man ever had? No doubt he'd prefer a solid meal.

Lauren maneuvered the wooden screen into position as quietly as she could, blocking the view from both the window and the bed. For just a moment her fingers toyed nervously with the small buttons on her blouse. It was an exact double of the other one, only this one was dark blue with tiny white dots. Between it and the heavy, navy skirt, Lauren felt as if she was wrapped in an electric blanket.

She looked at the inviting tepid water.

She looked at the deeply sleeping Irishman.

It was a land speed record for clothing removal.

The *ahhh* that swelled in her throat with the first slide of hot, sticky skin into clear, cooling water had to be physically swallowed. It was wonderful, but she would have been a lot more comfortable with a little bit more tub. Oh, well, with her knees up to her neck there wasn't much to see; though, of course, that would change drastically if she shifted her body. She'd better be quick.

In a move to rival Houdini, Lauren contorted to wash her hair and then soap herself. What was that noise? Was it a bedspring? It was so difficult to hear with water in one's ears. She felt too exposed. This would be the absolute worst time to come face to face with . . . Suddenly the whole bath idea lost its appeal. A dripping arm reached out to snag the grayed cotton toweling slung over the top of the screen.

Her cosmic rescue project would be awake soon and asking some very difficult questions. How much should she tell him? How could she possibly explain the possibility of time travel and mystic dreams to someone who'd no doubt think airplanes and televisions were notions of a demented mind?

Patrick Dugan was a stubborn, proud, very nineteenth-century man. Even sick, he'd tried to reject her help. It wasn't until she had pulled the angel thing, playing upon a weakness he'd not wanted to admit, that he had relented. Convincing him of the rest of her story wasn't going to be easy.

Lauren stood quickly and whipped the towel around her soaked body like a protective shield. She needed to be prepared for their first confrontation with as much propriety and dignity as possible. It was the only way she could hope to explain the unexplainable.

Her drowned-rat look didn't inspire confidence.

Unfortunately for the wild-eyed, wild-haired, half-naked Irishman that stepped around the screen, that was the look he got.

Lauren's eyes widened; her throat closed; her hair dripped. A mass of goose pimples covered her flesh in a wave. She was terrified! The man before her clutching a sheet to his narrow hips was nearly smoking with restrained fury. This would probably not be a good time to mention how she got here.

"Who in the bloody hell are you?"

She must not look like an angel anymore. Somehow

Lauren had expected his first words to be a lot softer and begin with thank you.

Wrong. Clearly Patrick Dugan had no idea that he was a lost spirit in need of rescuing. What had Aunt Lucy's "push" gotten her into? Very slowly, Lauren stepped out of the tub, vividly aware that she was covered only from just above her breasts to midthigh. Like bands of steel, her arms secured the towel.

"Lady," he said, his eyes telegraphing that he was really thinking of another term, "I'll be askin' only once more."

The hoarse, gruff demand in his voice screeched up her damp spine like nails on a chalkboard. She moved behind the too small expanse of water.

"I'm Lauren Sul—Dugan. Your wife." Well, what else could she say? One step out of the door and that's what everyone would tell him.

An almost undetectable tremor shook him and he blinked. "Why is it I don't remember you, Laur . . ."

"Lauren. You've been very sick Mr. . . . Patrick." She inched a little farther out of range.

"And just how long have we been enjoyin' the fruits of wedded bliss?"

He took a step forward and swept her body with a callous gaze that seemed to find the thought unbelievable.

So much for the tender, sympatico feelings she'd had for him when he'd been delirious.

"There has been no enjoying of anything, Mr. Dugan," she countered, returning the leer. "You have been flat on your back since I got you into this room." Unconsciously, she tucked the edge of the towel more snugly between her breasts, only to regret the move immediately when his accusing eyes zeroed in on the spot.

"You sound disappointed, colleen."

Before the bitingly sweet words had completely left his mouth, Patrick shot his free hand over the tub and grabbed the all-important knot holding up Lauren's towel.

"But you see, little wife, I'm feelin' ever so much better now. Come here." He grew very still for just a moment, and Lauren watched his eyes widen and then stare at the point where his hand touched her icy skin. She knew he could feel the pounding of her heart against the backs of his fingers.

He began to pull.

Oh, my God! The man was mad. Why in the world had she ever been attracted to him? The man had been in jail, for gosh sake! Even though Nancy Brown implied he'd been framed . . . what did she really know about him? Where was the sensitive guy who missed his mother? He was like a Dr. Jekyll and Mr. Hyde.

She had no choice but to follow as he shuffled backwards towards the bed. Her mind whirled, trying to come up with something to stop him.

Patrick Dugan sat heavily on top of the rumpled bedding, barely able to secure the sheet over his lap and still hold on to the woman who claimed to be his wife. He felt as if he'd been chewed up and spit out by the toughest thugs at the fair; and damned if he hadn't been. Those images were loud and clear. But how, in God's heaven, had he gotten to this place, and with this . . . this Lauren?

She was shaking, but her features were set determinedly. Patrick had to admire courage even from a liar. She was one, of course. Under no circumstances would he ever have consented to be married. It was a vow that had burned in his heart for so long that nothing but ash and a few precious memories remained there.

Only one person knew where he was and had the money to put up his bail. This little hussy must be workin' for the man himself: Michael Cassius McDonald! Sweet Jesus, this had to be a setup. Since the abuse in jail wasn't getting them the information they wanted, McDonald and Brown were trying another tack.

Leave it to pigs to use a woman's body. And what did it say about the woman who sold herself? Dugan stared hard at the bedraggled female standing taut as a wire with her hands just under his fist, gripping the towel like an Irishman holding the last bottle of whiskey on the Emerald Isle.

If they were countin' on this lassie to seduce the list of blackmailed hawkers out of him, the fools were in for a big disappointment. He'd never betray those folks counting on him to find someone powerful and honest to take up their fight.

Patrick was a man of amazing self-control even when he was tempted. Hadn't he proven his restraint with enough lassies in the past? For this woman he'd have to make almost no effort at all.

She was a liar, a sneak, and, most likely, a whore. Oh, she might be soft and smell like spring roses, but this was no great beauty to set a man's heart to poundin'. Hell, she still had a dirty face even after a bath and . . . his eyes narrowed in disbelief. Jesus, Mary and Joseph! The woman had no hair on the back of her head. He had to get a better look.

"*No!* no, no." Lauren's calm facade cracked when Dugan's big hands clamped onto her bare shoulders. As he jerked her down to his side, she completely lost it. She knew what was coming. How could she have been so wrong about this man?

"Don't do it, Dugan," she yelped frantically. "Please don't hurt me. I'm sorry."

Her plea rose and fell like her body pulling against his tightening hold. He could feel it the moment she changed tactics, but he didn't react fast enough. A small, panic-packed fist slammed into the side of his face.

"I'll fight you . . . you ungrateful swine."

Lauren swung again. Patrick dodged and toppled the vixen onto her back, immediately bracketing her flailing arms and legs with his own.

Everything froze. The sound of labored breathing filled the silence. Muffled noises from the other boarders trickled into his awareness; a door shut; footsteps sounded on the stairs. Patrick's weak body had just about reached its limit, and his weight involuntarily settled even more heavily on the gasping woman beneath him. Her curves felt good. Too good. Hell, this fight against McDonald had driven everything, including female company, from his mind for months. That must be the reason this unlikely woman was testing his control.

The blue eyes looking at him were swimming with tears. Pale lashes—though some were peculiarly black—and baby-fine brows added a softness to the oval face that made Patrick think of one of his newborn colt's silky coats. Her skin was like rich cream sprinkled with bits of cinnamon. He couldn't keep a small smile from curving the hard line of his mouth when he recalled his Ma callin' them angel kisses.

Whoa, Dugan. This so-called lady is no angel.

He was on to her tricks now. Maybe the woman wasn't a dazzler, but she had something as effective in its own unassuming way. This vulnerability he saw in her could be used just as cunningly as passion. Angels? Why did he think of that when he looked at her?

He shifted to move off her body.

"Wait!" The hands that had been pushing against his chest abruptly changed position and clung to his shoulders.

"This sickens me, woman. No matter what Mc-

70

Donald has paid you, you'll not get the list from me with this tired trick. I'll have none of it.''

The look of disdain on his pale, whiskered face was devastating. Lauren blinked, and one fat tear rolled down the side of her face and dribbled across her neck. Minutes ago she'd been scared out of her wits, and now she felt completely rejected, as if she'd done something unforgivable. This was totally perverse.

He was the bad guy here and he thought . . . he thought she wanted . . . And he couldn't have made it more clear that he wasn't interested. Period. As if she was!? As if she cared. As if . . . Mercy, she was losing it. Lauren lowered her red-rimmed eyes, willing herself to hold on to some small shred of dignity before she crumbled.

''No, I'm not trying . . . I mean—my towel has come loose.'' She took a deep, shaky breath to steady herself. ''Please let me fix it before you move.''

Dugan tracked the tear. Either his ''wife'' was a mighty good actress or she really was afraid. Why the hell should he care? Oh, his ma would skin him alive if she could see him now—for a number of reasons, truth to tell. The only light in his dark life had asked for just two promises: honor the Church and treat women with respect. So few men did, and his own mother had suffered at the hands of two perfect examples. Desertion and betrayal. They'd been his family's legacy.

God, was his father's and uncle's blood tainting him? What was he doing?

Patrick lifted himself up. Lauren watched and waited. The barest nod sent her hands slithering between their bodies, searching for the ends of the towel. His coarse chest hair brushed her fingers, sending a burning blush across her cheeks. If he thought about what else she was touching, he would spontaneously combust.

71

It seemed as if butterfly wings were beating against his bruised flesh. Such a flush of color could not be faked, he was quite certain. The soft nudges between them spread like wildfire through his whole being. He had to get up now!

"Woman! Are you finished?"

"Yes, I think it's okay."

Dugan rolled to his side and ordered in a flat voice, "I'm tellin' you to dress and get out then. Be sure to tell your boss that it didn't work. He'll never find those names."

"I have no idea what names you're talking about." Too puzzled to scoot to freedom, Lauren squinted against his penetrating gaze and considered.

"I have no boss, Dugan. I . . ." She willed him to believe. "I only came to help you for a few days."

"I haven't heard such damned blarney since I left Ireland. Get out!"

He lurched up, as if touching her was repellent to him, and Lauren skittered off the bed, rushing behind the protection of the wooden screen.

No one had ever, ever been so angry at her before. All right, then! Sayonara and arrivederci! Dugan was out of jail and she was heading out of this room. If some cosmic plan was goofed up, it was too bad! Aunt Lucy might not like it; Patrick's hopeful descendants might not like it; Heaven itself might not like it; but Lauren Ann Sullivan was hitting the road.

With her head bobbing up and down behind the partition, she tried to keep an eye on the big Irishman whose attitude so infuriated and hurt her at the same time. Ever since she woke up in the Museum, or the Palace, or whatever . . . she had been treated like some kind of Jezebel!

Lauren's gritted teeth held the towel in front of her as she tried to shove her still damp head through the

72

neck of her voluminous nightgown. No way was she going to give that pious chauvinist any more ammo. She would dress undercover and vanish. Luckily she had pulled the carpetbag behind the screen before her bath so she could make a quick getaway.

With her arms inside the floor-length gown, Lauren struggled to pull up a pair of plain cotton underwear. *He probably thinks I wear black lace, the pervert!* She bobbed to the surface for a quick peek.

Black lace would not be needed.

The pervert in question—the man who had called her across time; the man who had seemed so needy and tender; the man who had started such fragile, yearning feelings growing in her heart—was stalking toward her in an improvised toga. And from each hand hung an undergarment. A 1995 undergarment.

Uh-oh!

Chapter Four

"Just stay back, Dugan," Lauren ordered, raising a warning palm. "I'll be gone in a flash." These blasted slips! She couldn't watch and dress at the same time. "Damn!"

"What did you say?"

The words reached her just before his fierce green eyes topped the screen. His six-foot height afforded him a perfect, unobstructed view.

"Oh, pleeeeease! Does the double standard never end?"

"What are these?" Dugan swung the offending garments in Lauren's face.

"I'm not telling you!" The man actually looked stunned. *Big dolt.* She grabbed them out of his hands. Anger was blasting a hole right through her fear and hurt.

"Who are you?"

"What is this, same song, second verse?" Lauren's

fingers flew up the buttons under her nightgown.

"I'll not be singin', woman."

"You're telling me, Mr. Macho." A soft grunt escaped her pursed lips as she tugged on one black lace-up shoe.

Patrick thought she looked like she was wrestling a bag of monkeys. This Lauren was the most peculiar women he'd ever talked to. She spoke in a strange manner and called him such odd names. Where had McDonald found her? He hadn't even realized he'd spoken aloud until she answered.

"For the last time, Mr. Dugan," she said, crouching to stuff her tentlike gown into the bag at her feet, "I do not now know, nor have I ever known, a Mr. McDonald." The navy outfit was sufficiently in place, gloves and hat be hanged. Lauren picked up her bag and walked a wide circle around the ominously silent man staring at her.

"Prove it," he challenged.

"Why should I? I don't owe you anything, Mr. Dugan. You owe me!" She stopped next to the spindly table and picked up her hairnet. With her free hand she scooped up some bobby pins and began pinning the net in place. She had enough problems without flaunting a short hairstyle that wouldn't be acceptable for about twenty-five more years. These Victorian men would probably consider it yet another type of indecent exposure.

Patrick had never in his life been so angry at a woman. She'd changed from a scratching cat to a haughty lady in the blink of an eye. True, the clothes were not the apparel of a whore. She looked more like a schoolteacher now—and a shorn one. He hitched the sheet higher up on his shoulder.

It was actually a bit pathetic, watching her pin on the false hairpiece. Patrick knew that often aging or sick women had to use them, but . . . maybe that was why she seemed so different. Maybe she had been so ill that she had to work for McDonald. There weren't many ways to make money for a woman alone. Brown could be using her just as he'd tried to use him. Possibilities.

"And what is it that I'm owin' you, ma'am?"

"I got you out of that stinking jail," she challenged him, thrusting out her chin, then jamming the last pin into her hair and smoothing the short, feathered sides behind her ears.

Ah, the she-cat was back. He might get more information if he riled her a bit. Patrick needed to know at least part of McDonald's plan. It could mean the difference between life and death.

"That's my point, woman. McDonald had the power to get me thrown in that hole, and I'm thinkin' that only he had the power to let me out."

Hoping to coax her confession, Dugan kept his anger from strangling the words. In unhurried steps he walked to the rocker near the table and sat down. It put him in a better position, and the truth of it was, his legs were trembling.

"So you think I'm some kind of spy after this . . . this list?" Lauren planted her fists at her waist. Her lips pressed into a straight white line to keep them from quivering. *Don't you dare feel hurt, damn it! Get mad.*

Truthfully, he wasn't sure anymore; a bought woman who looked and acted so prissy? One who stood right up to him spitting nails instead of using her body to win him over? It made no sense.

She stood about two feet away from the door, ready to fly. Patrick was close enough to see pain shadowing the anger in her tempestuous blue eyes. That rat's nest of a hairpiece hung much too far to the right, and her cheek still had soot streaks on it. No, she didn't look like a conniving spy. The woman baffled him.

"How did you get me out, if McDonald had nothin' to do with it?"

"I paid the bail, and then Father Ryan helped us." Lauren felt a glimmer of hope. It seemed Dugan was listening at long last. "I think the police didn't dare make waves."

"What good would waves do?"

"No, no." She tried again. "I meant, when Father Ryan married us they had no choice but to let you go."

"What!" Patrick snapped to attention in the chair, the dangling sheet ends flapping between his legs.

"Father Ryan mar—"

Dugan broke in, in a voice so heavy with threat that Lauren felt a sinking pit form in her stomach.

"Are you sayin' an honest-to-God Catholic priest came into that jail and married us?"

She didn't have the answer he wanted to hear.

Lauren reached for her bag and propped it on the edge of the table. She'd make one last gesture and then get out of his life.

"He was a very kind man, Dugan. You owe him a lot, too." She didn't see Patrick's face go white. "Ah-ha; here it is." A small square paper was clenched in her hand. "I'm sure if you take this to Father Ryan and explain that it was the only way I could finagle the police into letting you go, well, he'll just tear it up or . . . something."

The back of her throat felt tight and achy. Lauren put the wrinkled certificate gently on the table and slowly drew her fingertips across their names. Patrick had barely been able to write it. Now that she'd changed his past, what would happen?

Sullivan! Just give the man his medicine and get going! He doesn't need you anymore.

She lifted her head to look at him for the last time.

And he was furious! Those sharp eyes drilled into

her. Oh, for heaven's sake! Every time she started feeling soft and mushy about the man, she got kicked for it.

Patrick held out his hand. "Give it to me."

Lauren slid the paper across the tabletop and shut her bag with a sharp click.

"I'm leaving this medicine here for you, Dugan. I know this won't make much sense, but please swallow one of these little round things with water every day until they're all gone."

He didn't acknowledge her at all. Zip. Nothing. *Nada.* Yet the air crackled like a brewing electrical storm.

Lauren swung her heavy bag down to her side and turned quickly, yanking on the faceted glass knob.

Wham! The door recoiled so unexpectedly, she couldn't stop her forward motion, and ran right into it. Hard. Automatically, she dropped her bag to gingerly cradle her flattened nose. The initial pain was so intense that Lauren didn't focus on the big, half-naked body closing in on her.

"Are you really thinkin' you can tear up a sacrament of the holy Church and it will be finished just like that?"

Patrick's lips were pressed against her ear, and she could feel moist puffs of breath as he spoke. His chest and thighs had her almost pinned to the door. He communicated with body language very well. His anger was palpable.

"Dugan!" she screeched, then paused, modulating her voice to reason with him. "This doesn't have to be a big problem."

"Just tell me one thing . . . are you Catholic?"

The lips pressed closer, and she could feel the drag of his whiskers on her skin as his jaw worked. A warm, musky scent surrounded her. Lauren felt herself becoming uncharacteristically woozy and shook off the feeling to answer.

"Technically, yes."

"How could you have done this, woman? How much money was it worth to you?" he demanded. Grasping her shoulders, he jerked Lauren around to face him, a horrible smile slashing his face. "Or did McDonald promise to untie this unholy knot by makin' you a widow soon?"

Lauren snapped her open mouth shut and hissed through her teeth. "Now wait a minute. I will not go through this again." She tried to twist away and managed to get her hand on the doorknob. "Let me go, Patrick! I promise . . ."

"Yes, my sweet, deceitful wife, that's exactly what you've done; made promises before God that cannot be broken without sendin' us both to Hell."

A sharp knock on the door brought them both up short. Their loud, angry voices had sent a violent message to stout Mrs. Werner, who was now demanding entrance.

Patrick pushed Lauren's carpetbag behind him with his bare foot. "Open the door, wife," he sneered the word, "and very carefully, if you've a hope of seein' your belongin's again." He lifted her treasure, knowing it for such by the way she'd kept it within reach every moment, and settled it beside him on the bed.

With one glance at Patrick's harsh expression and his arm slung over the lump under the quilt, Lauren knew she'd have to bide her time. She could not survive on her own without that bag. It was her time-travel survival kit, and she would have to play along until she got it back. Besides, there were things in it that she was just beginning to see could cause a lot of trouble. She'd have to stay on her toes. With a swish of her skirts, Lauren opened the door.

"I've brought you some supper and your laundry, Mrs. Kelly," the landlady announced, carefully looking Lauren over. She pushed a basket of folded clothes into the room with the pointed toe of her shoe.

Taking the still steaming tray from the short, prune-faced woman, Lauren couldn't help but admire her. This nineteenth-century stranger was worried about her and using the food delivery as a ploy to check things out. From the look in her eyes, her decision to intrude hadn't been an easy one.

She was a very brave lady in a time of such over-whelming male dominance. What did abused women do without shelters and support groups? Lauren saw her answer in the questioning manner of her gruff landlady. Most times, all they could do was listen and be there to pick up the pieces.

"Thanks, Mrs. Werner." Lauren smiled, warm and grateful, into the other woman's questioning eyes. "I hope my husband and I didn't disturb anyone. I'm afraid our discussion got a bit loud."

She turned from the door and set the food-filled tray on the spindly pine table. Brushing her hands together, she faced the landlady again.

"Men can just be so foolish, don't you agree?" Lauren impulsively decided to sink a few barbs so Mr. Macho didn't think he had her intimidated. "I told him he was too weak to get up, but would the big lummox listen?" Lauren lifted her hands palms up and shrugged.

Mrs. Werner's gaze skipped nervously to the scowling Irishman in the bed. Her pinched expression clearly indicated that she was not about to get any more deeply involved. This was as far as she would go. Running a fidgety hand over her white bibbed apron, she wished them a good evening and hurried down the hall.

As Lauren closed the door, her plan fell into place. Dugan was weak. The energy he'd just expended in anger had left him drained and pale. She almost rubbed her hands together with satisfaction. After a hot, heavy meal he would sleep whether he wanted to or not. It was simply a matter of waiting him out. So she'd act the part of a conquered damsel and then blow this joint when the heat cooled.

Right city. Wrong decade.

"So, Mr. Dugan," Lauren cleared her throat, picking up a crocker bowl of rich brown stew and carrying it toward him. "Are you willing to eat with a lying spy, bent on sending you to hell?" As she finished her sentence, she reached the side of the bed and extended the savory concoction.

Patrick ate without taking his eyes off her. He was too hungry and too shaky to get to the bottom of things just now. The luscious smell of simmered beef and onions had saliva pooling in his mouth, reminding him of how many days it had been since he had eaten a decent meal. Even so, at the moment he wasn't sure which he was enjoying more—the food or the nerves he was janglin' in the sassy-mouthed woman trying so desperately to seem unaffected by his relentless stare.

An uneasy smile rode her lips. She needed serious watching, but Lord he was tired. He'd have to do something right quick to keep her from sneaking away. The marriage certificate had changed everything.

Neither one spoke a word out loud, but thoughts fairly zinged through the air.

I'll eat and get stronger.

He'll eat and sleep.

Ah, good. She looks concerned, just as she should.

What in the heck is he doing? He looks like he's giving me the evil eye.

Now to hurry this along with a bit of shenanigans.

It's working; he's getting sleepy.

It's workin'; here she comes.

*   *   *

The heat of the day ebbed slowly from the little room as the cool darkness of evening edged in to take its place. Shadows flowed in and over the four walls so gradually that Lauren didn't even notice them. Oh, but she felt them; thick and soothing; blunting the things around her; blunting the ragged emotions inside her.

Dugan's eyelids were nearly closed, his head unnaturally bent up against the iron bed frame. Deep, steady breaths lifted his finely sculpted chest and then dropped into the curve of his belly. Up and down. In and out. Over and over. Lauren stepped closer, mesmerized, watching the play of muscles and hair undulating before her until her own body rolled in response.

Whenever she stared at him too long her common sense disappeared. Where in the world had this powerful attraction come from? For just a silence-soaked moment Lauren was actually sorry to leave the arrogant, narrow-minded, macho throwback.

Her sorrow lasted right up to the instant Patrick Dugan shot out a grasping arm and pulled her down on the bed. In a move she was becoming all too familiar with, he anchored her body beneath his. *Here we go again!*

"Hold your tongue, woman," Dugan growled in her ear. "Let me speak my piece or you'll be more than sorry."

Lauren didn't really think it was possible to be more sorry than she was right now, trapped under a good two-hundred irrational Irish pounds. The sharp edges of an old fear began to cut through her control.

"Don't hurt me, Dugan." The words escaped before she could call them back. Lauren grimaced and forced herself to look straight into those blazing green eyes without flinching. She would not freak out! An assertive modern woman would not lay here like a wimp shaking with fear; she'd watch for the main chance.

"You'll not be leavin'," he commanded, using the size of his nearly naked body to reinforce his command. Patrick shifted so only one sheet-tangled leg anchored hers and then grabbed a small wrist.

"I thought you wanted me to get out?" Lauren tried to speak in the most reasonable tone she could, hoping to calm him down. With great restraint she managed to keep her arm still.

"Everything's changed now," Patrick gritted out, nose-to-nose with this possible enemy, his wife. "Until I can get you back to Father Ryan you're stayin' with me."

"You can't...you have lost it in a big way, buster!" Lauren yelped and yanked simultaneously as his fingers tightened.

Dugan pressed her flailing arm down with one of his own until both rested between her breasts. "You're the one who'll be hurtin' us both if you keep carryin' on so."

"If you think I'm going to put up with—"

"Hush, woman!" he ordered, lowering his stony face toward hers. "You can't begin to know what I've lost, so don't even speak of it. I'm angry as hell and I'm not lettin' you go 'til I get some answers."

Patrick couldn't miss the shimmer of blossoming tears in her eyes or the effort she was exerting to keep them from falling. That took grit, and he grudgingly admired it. But they wouldn't manipulate him like some mewling lad.

"I didn't mean lost it like—"

Dugan slid his arm along Lauren's, brushing the inner curves of her breasts, extending his fingers until they pressed against her moving lips. The soft, tiny movements sent a ripple of awareness down his spine. He made himself keep talking.

"I've lost my job, my good name, my life nearly, weeks of freedom with maybe years to come if I live that long, and lastly, my mysterious little wife, I've most likely lost my matrimonial freedom for the rest of my mortal days."

"Bubbt . . ." Lauren arched and bounced on the sagging mattress, trying to free herself from the truth of his words and the touch of his body. The feel of his arm pressed so close to her heart; the heat of his fingers splayed across her mouth; the weight of his leg flush against hers . . .

"Holy Mary, woman, be still! I'm too tired tonight to try and wade through your crack-brained words and lies lookin' for the truth, so you'd best just accept this: The questions will have to wait 'til I get some rest. Don't make me do something we'll both regret in the mornin'."

At that exact moment Dugan's exhausted body began to feel the knife edge of desire more keenly than his desperate need for sleep. Damn! His illness had robbed him of his usual control. This had to stop now. Maybe a heavier hand and a bit more threat would settle the woman down and stop her soft, rounded curves from shifting against his.

"You're stayin', we're sleepin', and that's that." In one smooth move Patrick rolled fully onto his side, slid an arm around Lauren's twisting waist, and pulled her back snug against his front.

Lauren lay rigid, trying to control the huge gulps of air her body craved to cool her anger and fear. And something else—that disturbing something she would not examine closely enough to name but still made itself known with every movement of Patrick Dugan's body.

Patrick could feel her ribs expand and contract and he opened his hand, flattening it against her stomach. The motion stopped. *Hell, she's holding her breath.* The woman was too full of fear to relax. God, of all men he should have remembered what it felt like to be at someone else's mercy. A hot surge of guilt loosened his hold, and Patrick knew he had to distract her or neither one of them would get any sleep.

"How long have we been here?" he asked, moving his chin so it rested on the top of her head. A faint scent of roses drifted up toward him, blunting the scratch of her hairpiece, molded into the curve of his neck.

"It's been . . . four . . . days."

"Have you seen any police pokin' about?" Patrick continued, very aware of her short, breathless speech. He moved the hand resting on her stomach completely away and was instantly rewarded with the feel of her huge, deep breath against his chest.

"No. I . . . I really haven't been outside much."

"Well, they're most likely thinkin' I'm not long for this world, so they've only to wait. We've got to leave before those sons of Satan decide to come and collect the body."

Patrick's words rang through Lauren's head. Every other concern in her head shrank away to nothing, and the meaning of his words exploded to take their place.

"Oh, my gosh! I never though of that," she choked out, fighting to breathe and talk at the same time. "How could I have been so naive as to think that getting you out of jail would be all there was to this rescue?" She shook her head and unintentionally bumped Patrick's chin. "This lowlife McDonald you keep talking about—he won't give up until he gets those incriminating names, will he?"

Her words so startled him that Patrick balled his hand into a fist, fitting it beneath her ribs. He slid his mouth to her ear. "I'll warn you now not to repeat that to anyone else, lass. There's nothing in it for you but grief."

This time she felt no insult at his accusation. At last she was seeing this through his eyes. Patrick knew that someone wanted him dead; how could she expect him to trust a *strange* stranger? After all, she *had* tricked him into marrying her. How was he to know her motivations were righteous? The man had some heavy-duty reasons to distrust her, and she'd overreacted when she should have tried to explain.

Lauren realized she'd miscalculated the impact of her actions on him completely; especially the marriage part. She twisted around and looked into his weary eyes, glazed with fatigue and desperation.

"Patrick, I promise I'm here to help you, really." Lauren tried to infuse her words and gaze with total sincerity. It was important to her that he believe.

Dugan felt as dizzy and disoriented as he had after his first ride on the Ferris wheel. The guileless face so close to his was a stranger's, and yet . . . He couldn't deny all she'd done for him. Not once since his blurriest memories of her began had this woman harmed him, and she could have so easily.

But betrayal came in many forms, Patrick mused, watching the play of moonlight gild her solemn features and making him hesitate. For fourteen years he'd been guarding the meager ember of hope that faintly glowed within him. If one more harsh wind of deceit blew it out, would he be left forever cold, all needy emotions frozen?

What was he to believe? What was he to do with this woman? If she wasn't in league with McDonald, then who in the name of St. Joseph was she workin' for? They were married, for God's sake. What was he to do about that? Patrick rubbed the back of his neck and his shoulders slumped with exhaustion.

Lauren lay next to him so still, waiting with big solemn eyes. Half a lifetime of caution couldn't be undone so easily. Only time would tell, and Patrick would have to ensure that he got it. He'd have to keep her with him, but he didn't want to terrify her to accomplish that; on his mother's blessed memory he could not do that. What he'd done already was still burning in his gut.

Twice now she'd been afraid that he would hurt her, and he sensed she had used hard-won courage to fight back. Inexplicably, at that moment, it became more important than anything else to convince her that he was not capable of such actions. *Ah, Ma, forgive me. I'm not like them!*

"Laurie," Dugan said hesitantly.

Lauren sucked in a surprised gulp of air at that familiar form of her name on his lips for the first time since the jail.

"I have a bargain to speak of, a trade, if you will." Patrick shut his eyes, forcing himself to say the rest. Wanting this small bit of trust—*needing* this small bit of trust—shook him to the core. He searched twin pools of deep blue water for truth, only to focus on the false paint at the color's edge.

"My head is poundin' somethin' fierce and I've got to sleep, but short of tying you up, I don't know how to keep you from leavin'." Patrick could feel her body tense.

"So I'll promise to let you go if you'll promise to stay with me for a week; no more than two, for certain. I need some questions answered about the jail; the truth, mind you. And I need some time to get lost down on the South Side." And that's all he'd need from her, no matter what! "I promise I'll give you no reason to fear me. I'll not hurt you, Laurie." Patrick cautiously lifted his arm from her waist, expecting her to bolt.

A jumble of responses caught in Lauren's throat. The fact that he still thought she was lying didn't bother her anymore. Tomorrow, after they got someplace safe, she would prove herself to him; explain her mission. *And the poor man thought he had a headache now.* Lauren smiled as Dugan's eyebrows bunched together.

She could see he was at the end of his physical rope. It was also obvious that Patrick had asked for her promise, as if he had little hope of it being fulfilled. Someone had really done a number on this guy.

"Okay, Dugan, you've got a deal. I never planned to stay so long, but I'll do it." Under her breath, Lauren prayed that they both wouldn't regret this.

His head drooped forward in relief, a shock of chestnut hair tumbling down.

"And about the hurting thing," she continued hesitantly, scooting up toward the headboard by cautious degrees. "I'm sorry I overreacted." She shifted slightly, finally looking directly at Patrick's bent head. "I've always had this weird fear of pain that still gets away from me every now and then. My imagination makes it worse."

Searching green eyes shot up, drilling through red-brown tendrils.

Patrick felt the strangest pressure behind his eyes and opened his mouth as if to speak, but the thought vanished before he could form the words.

Seeing his distress, Lauren rushed on, hoping his bargaining mood would last. "I have something to ask of you, too." His beautiful eyebrows bunched again. "I have another kind of pebbl—pill—, ah, medicine. It helps with pain and . . . I want you to swallow two of them so you'll rest better. They're in my bag, so if you'll just let me get them, I—"

"You wouldn't be tryin' to poison me, now would you, lass."

Lauren took a deep lungful of air to cool her flaring frustration and saw Dugan's eyes rebound off her bodice buttons like a flubber-filled basketball. It tingled low in her stomach. This look felt so different from that of the lecher's, back at the jail, and it threw her for a loop, making her feel terribly foolish. Regret was going to flow fast and furious unless she got a grip on her heart and body!

"I'll take some first, all right?" Between Patrick's physical closeness and her stress, exhaustion, and three hundred razor-sharp bobby pins digging into the back of her skull, Lauren needed those Tylenols anyway. Bad.

Patrick was ready to agree to anything to get the woman to sleep. Lauren sat up and cautiously reached over him to get her bag. Sweet, warm breath eddied across his cheek, and he couldn't stop his eyes from flicking over her moon-kissed face. His lips began to tingle.

There was no doubt about it; his iron control was starting to melt around the edges. A hot flush ignited low in his body and slowly creeped up his neck. Hell, let it be too dark for her to see. He never let himself react like this. Dugan gathered up the sheet around his waist and lurched off the bed, padding to the table for water.

He was too tired to question her further.

She was too tired to cajole.

Lauren covertly took the pills out of the bottle; Patrick Dugan wasn't ready for any discussion of the origin of plastic. She put two Tylenols in the palm of her hand, reached for the water, tipped back her head, and swallowed them. Then it was his turn.

"I promise, Patrick," Lauren said soberly, sitting on the edge of the bed, holding his dose, "I'm not here to hurt you in any way." He hesitated for a moment, and she saw him struggle to believe. Was human kindness so foreign to him that any offer of help was suspect? Maybe he hadn't had anyone care in a long time. Maybe he didn't think anyone could.

With their eyes locked, Patrick raised his strong, work-worn hand to his lips and swallowed her offering. Lauren had rarely seen such courage. If she had been in his place, could she have done the same?

A wild rush of blood pounded through her veins as the faint light in the room painted his shoulders and chest with glimmering streaks of iridescence. Nothing seemed real or tangible except this powerful feeling building inside her like small whitecaps on the sea, pouring one into another until towering, they thundered to the shore.

She could not let him go on alone. Not again.

Lauren felt a little jolt streak up her spine at the odd jumble of words in her head. She shivered and quickly jumped off the bed when Patrick moved back to lay down. Hastily, she unbuttoned her tight cuffs and collar, then slipped off her shoes.

"Don't give me a Jezebel lecture, okay, Dugan?" she asked without looking directly at him, all the while primly spreading the sheet covering him out to the side of the bed and tucking it under. "I already feel like I'm sleeping in a straitjacket."

After rolling her towel into a ball she lay down facing away from him, hanging off the edge of the mattress, and mumbled some nonsense about mature adult behavior.

Long minutes seemed to stretch on forever until Laurie's breathing settled into a slow, steady rhythm. Patrick knew he should sleep, too. The night had reached its deepest shade of black, and every coming hour would only add more light until it gradually became the gray dawn. As much as his aching body craved rest from his illness and the beating Bates had given him, he was reluctant to leave the warm, sweet-smelling female cuddled up next to him.

It gave him more than a touch of the willies to admit to himself that for all that lay unanswered between them, she slept next to him as easily as if she'd always done so. Maybe it was those . . . pills.

Laurie had finally told a truth; the pain in his head was gone.

Very gently, he lay an open hand in the dip of her waist, carefully feathering his fingers over the silky fabric of her blouse. Even fully clothed her body felt oddly exposed. His palm grew warm.

Dugan drew in a gulp of air and held it. He ordered his traitorous body to relax as the compressed breath slowly seeped out. Wouldn't Miss Laurie be spittin' mad if he woke her and asked her to pretend with him that this really was their wedding night. After all, she had arranged their marriage, hadn't she?

The thought that he was legally wed sobered him immediately, and the light stroking of his fingers stopped.

Patrick had vowed never to leave a child on the earth the way he'd been left. Far in the back of his mind he had buried a dream that, someday, there might be someone who'd not care about the shame of his birth; then maybe there would be children . . . a family. But now even that small hope had turned to dross. His last foolish need had been torn away.

As he drifted finally into sleep his thoughts were confused. Was Laurie really helping him or luring him? She seemed at once a lady and a wanton; prim on the outside and wild on the inside. Like her clothes; on the outside she seemed proper, she fit; but on the inside . . . sweet Mary, what kind of woman would wear such undergarments? Just thinking about what she would look like in them made his body tighten.

Instinctively his fingers flexed, testing the pliable skin . . . the far too pliable skin. Jesus, Mary, and Joseph there wasn't an inch of whale-boned corset between his hand and that . . . Patrick's fever-dry lips curved into a rare smile. Come mornin', little Laurie was going to have herself quite a list of questions to answer.

Maybe he'd start with her underwear.

At the back door of the precinct house, Jones Bates stood almost docilely, waiting for instructions. His low forehead and straight brows gave him an oddly simian look. That, combined with the size of his body, illustrated Charles Darwin's theories to perfection.

"You'd better not slip up, Bates. The boss will have our heads if you do," Captain Hansen ordered, pressing a finger into the hulking man's chest. "He's put me in charge of this situation and I'll not pay the price for your mistakes."

"Ya don't hafta worry none, Cap'n. I know right where the bugger's hidden', and I'll not let 'im get away."

"Do whatever it takes," Hansen ordered.

"It'll be a pleasure, Cap'n."

Bates palmed a pistol and shoved it into the pocket of the civilian clothes he was wearing. A strange, excited expression spread across the ugly face, and even Hansen was unnerved by it as he watched the big man lumber away.

Bates left rubbing his hands together slowly. First he'd beat on that stupid mick, and then he would have himself some fun with Dugan's woman. Maybe he'd take her to Holmes's place. That man had all kinds of rooms for fun.

Pure pleasure!

Chapter Five

"Laurie," Patrick whispered in her ear. "Laurie, wake up now."

He gently nudged her shoulder and wondered if she would keep her promise or if he would have to fight her. Hell, he hoped it didn't come to that. They had a difficult day ahead of them, and even though he felt a lot stronger this morning, dealing with her seemed to wear him down fast.

"Laurie!" Holy Mary, she slept like a stone.

"What?" she muttered and coughed, eyes closed tight.

"It's almost dawn, colleen, and we've got to be goin' before folks are up and about. Hurry now, or I'll have to dress you myself." He thought that would do the trick.

It did.

Lauren jumped up. Last night had been the best sleep she'd had in weeks, and she could have used about twenty more hours. However, after Dugan's helpful offer she decided it could wait.

"I'll be ready in a sec," she said quietly, pushing her bag behind the screen.

"What?"

"Oh . . . never mind."

A few minutes later she poked her head around the side of the screen and unintentionally caught Patrick putting on his wash-worn flannel shirt. He looked up, and his hands stilled on the buttons. Lauren completely forgot what she was going to say.

He looked so healthy, so big, so male; the vulnerable patient was gone. Oh, he was still coughing and wheezing some, but the transformation disoriented her.

"Dugan, ah . . . could you please step out of the room? I . . . well . . ." *Oh, for pity's sake, Lauren. Who's acting the Victorian now? It's just a normal bodily function.* But a hot tide of embarrassment flooded her cheeks anyway.

"Now, wife—"

Patrick wielded that word like a miracle blade through a defenseless tomato.

"—it seems to me you must have tended to my needs, and yours, right here in this room while I was flat on my back. In fact, you've had quite the advantage, I'm thinkin'." He took a step forward and glared at her as the realization hit him.

"Now, Dugan," she soothed, waving him back. "You were very sick and I only thought about helping you." Well, most of the time, she added silently.

He kept coming.

Patrick stopped inches from her small oval face, framed with short wisps of honey-gold hair. For a moment he was distracted by the fluffy stuff he wanted to touch; the sprinkle of freckles any real lady would try to hide; the deep blue of her eyes, now surprisingly surrounded by a uniform ruffle of dark lashes.

By God, she was using paint! What kind of woman had he bargained with? Dugan screwed his eyes shut with a disgusted sigh and continued, clamping a hand on her shoulder.

"Now you'll listen, and answer either yes or no."

"But—"

"Only yes or no, wife," he warned.

Lauren stepped completely away from the screen and folded her arms, trying to shake off his touch. The scowling man would not be moved.

"First, you still claim you're not workin' for McDonald or Brown?"

"Yes. Get a clue, Dugan. If I'd been working for that man, I'd have done you in and rifled your belongings for that list you keep warning me about."

"You don't take direction well, do ya, lassie?" Patrick said, grasping the other shoulder and pulling her up onto her toes. "All I'll say about our trouble now is that the list just may have the power to stop the man before we're both dead." He felt her body go stiff and watched her mouth form a silent *o*. "McDonald's men won't be forgettin' your part in this, woman. You arranged the marriage and willin'ly paid a hefty bail, too, did you not?"

"Yes." More or less.

"And now, if this is the truth you're tellin' me, they're certain to be after both of us. So get yourself behind that screen and do your business, wife. We've got to be goin' *now*."

Lauren felt her face turn to flame. The man literally had his nose against her and she wanted to sink right through the floorboards.

"You've no call blushin', wife. After all, you've cared for me like a babe these last days, have you not?"

"Yes."

"Well, m' dear. In this case, what's good enough for the gander is good enough for the goose. You'll not use that flimsy excuse to bamboozle your way out of this room." Patrick leaned closer, and she felt the brush of his lips against hers as he spoke.

"You'll not be breakin' your word. You promised me time, and I'll have it."

The man had a point; fair was fair. Of course, he had been out of it during his time of need. *Well, Sullivan, here's trust lesson number one.*

"You've kept your promises to me, Dugan, and I have no intention of breaking mine to you." She jerked out of his grasp and disappeared behind the flimsy screen.

Chamberpots were the worst. The person who finally perfected the toilet should have been canonized. Perhaps she could look into that when she returned to the future. So much for the feminine mystique. Only women like Donna Reed and June Clever never went to the bathroom. *You, Lauren Ann Sullivan, can take it like a man. No big deal.*

Patrick took a peripheral peek at the she-cat's face when she hesitantly emerged from behind the screen. Foolish woman! She looked mortified at something everybody did naturally. Her stuck-up, speckled little nose didn't look quite so haughty radish red. Dugan's mouth twitched, and he turned to his clothes in the basket on the floor.

It was the most amazing thing that in the midst of all hell breaking loose he suddenly wanted to laugh. Patrick pressed his lips tight to hold in the chuckle. She wouldn't understand that he wasn't making fun of what she'd done. It would hurt Laurie, and he was surprisingly loath to do that.

Now why in hell would he care about her feelings?

"Would you be havin' room in that precious bag of

yours for a few things?'' Patrick stood and held out a small bundle.

Lauren gazed bravely at his neutral expression and felt the heat drain from her flushed cheeks. With a nod, she opened the brass clasp and reached for his stuff. In brief moments all their belongings were packed. She discreetly left the rest of the week's rent under one of the empty bowls on the shaker table for Mrs. Werner.

Patrick pulled on his brown brogans with a wry smile. The shoes looked battered; but they were sturdy, and he was grateful the scum at the jail hadn't made off with them. He had the distinct feeling that runnin' was going to fill his immediate future; and runnin' without them would be a mite uncomfortable.

"Come here, woman,'' Dugan ordered as he moved to the narrow window and pushed up the sash all the way. "Come,'' he repeated in a sterner tone, extending his left arm. "I've got to see if I can get you through this. I think it might be a bit of a squeeze.''

"Thanks a lot,'' Lauren muttered, coming alongside of him, at once self-conscious about the extra fifteen pounds she could never seem to lose. "You're not exactly Minnie Mouse yourself.''

Dugan gave her an odd, blank look that furrowed his brow. The expression was becoming quite familiar. Then, like the flick of an electric switch, the light dawned.

"No, Laurie, it's not so much you as it is the skirts.''

"Why, Patrick Dugan, you sweet-talker you.''

The blank look appeared again. He bent forward slightly to look in her eyes, as if trying to see behind Lauren's words. At the same time he curled his hand next to hers on the carpetbag's handle and pulled.

She pulled back.

Trust lesson number two. Lauren, let go.

Dugan saw fear and doubt flair and then tamp down.

She seemed to be trying to trust him as much as he was trying to trust her; or else she was a very good actress. The next few days would tell.

Patrick quickly leaned out the window and scanned the murky shadows. A fading sliver of moon still hung in the shifting night sky. The pungent smell of mist and earth rolled in off the lake, and soft, small chirps heralded the dawn with its inevitable power to dissolve their cover of darkness.

"Is the coast clear?"

The hushed words spoken so close to his ear nearly sent Patrick's head slamming up into the solid wood sash.

"And just how do you think I'd be seein' the coast from here?" he hissed, turning to pin her an inch from his nose. "I'm beginnin' to think you are completely daft and that McDonald figured I'd go to him just to get away from you!"

Lauren stepped back speechless as Dugan swung her heavy bag out the window and dropped it with a quiet thud to the ground.

If she didn't explain everything to him soon, she was going to detonate in a blast of righteous fury. Unjust accusations were so . . . well, unjust! She had definitely had enough of them.

Before she could even form a reply Patrick knelt on one knee and began to wrap the yards of fabric in her skirt and slips around her legs. It was obvious to Lauren that he was trying to condense her bulk; and it was equally obvious when he stopped, holding a bunch of cloth in his fist, that he didn't have a clue of how to keep her from unfurling like a flag in a stiff wind.

"Just stuff it between my legs, Dugan."

The look he gave her could have melted granite. Clearly the nineteenth-century male mind was far too literal.

"I can hold the fabric with my knees," she reasoned through clenched teeth.

His eyes bobbed to hers and then to her knees and back again. He seemed unsure of how to go about it.

"As much as I hate to remind you of this, Mr. Dugan, you have seen me in quite a number of, shall we say, compromising situations in our brief association. This happens to be one of the mildest in my opinion, so don't let it get to you. Okay?"

Lauren grabbed the wrinkled cloth out of his hand and pushed it firmly between her knees, which she clamped together. She felt a little bit like a too-full taco.

Patrick didn't move. Lauren's legs began to ache from the pressure.

"Dugan"—she tapped him on the head with one finger—"I know you men have this leg thing now, but I really can't stand this way much longer, so get me out of the window before I explode."

The woman had no shame! He had been ready for a fight when he moved close to her legs and she had told him calmly to touch her knees. Even through wads of skirt and slips, a real lady would never do that. *Careful, me boyo, or the lass'll have you twisted tighter than a seaman's knots.*

With a puff and a grunt, he lifted her rigid body and maneuvered it out the small window. Laurie might be a light skirt and a strange talker, but when push came to shove she seemed to understand what had to be done. She didn't simper and fidget, fearing he might drop her, even though she had to be able to feel his arms straining.

Patrick wondered, as her feet touched the ground, how many of her pills he would need before his full strength was back. Never letting go of Laurie's hand, his eyes swept the room for any forgotten items.

Answers! He needed answers. McDonald and Brown

could have men waiting anywhere; they probably did. The list he had stashed in the Palace of Fine Arts held the names of every Midway hawker under McDonald's control, and Chicago's well-known crime boss wanted that list no matter what had to be done. Patrick knew his only real chance was the hope that the scum thought he was already dead or dying and so weren't watching for a move at this time of the morning. He was counting on slinking right past any dozing watchdogs.

An impatient jerk got his attention.

Ah, yes, the she-cat was another big question that most definitely needed an answer.

Moving low and fast along the side of Mrs. Werner's boardinghouse, with one hand wrapped around Laurie's and one holding the bag, Patrick led the way back, past the little yard. A long row of buildings haphazardly butted up to the alley that he wanted to use as his route south through the city, forming a rabbit warren of twists and unexpected turns.

With Laurie tight against his back, he stopped at the foreboding entrance. Again, there was no choice. The end could be waiting behind any one of the undefined shapes or unseen openings ahead, but the dark was fast turning to dawn and with it their only hope of cover.

"Step where I step, and don't make a sound," Dugan shot over his shoulder.

"You got it; we'll be like two halves of the same person."

Her rapid breathing, fanning the back of his neck, belied the casual sound of her odd words. A dangerous current ran down his spine, and Patrick almost shuddered. This was no time to be feeling so . . . so strange. Hell! He had to be quick and alert. He'd be damned if he'd let her get to him. To reveal in any way that she moved him—intrigued him—would be like hammering the nails into his own coffin.

"I said not a sound! Can't you keep your bleedin' mouth shut?"

Dugan felt Laurie go still, her hand limp in his. Soundlessly, she took a minuscule step away from him. He could sense her pain at his words, and for a frightening moment he nearly turned to her.

No! Patrick gritted his teeth until the impulse passed, knowing anger was the only way he could protect himself.

With the night vision of a cat and the sure-footedness of a mountain goat, he carefully picked a path through the alley's obstacle course. Horrible smells of spoiled food and offal were overpowering in the deserted, narrow area, working effectively as a human deterrent. The rats, however, felt right at home.

Lauren twisted her hand out of his grasp. He spun around, ready to grab her, and ended up staring slack-jawed as she reached between her legs and pulled the back edge of her skirt through and then up over the front, tucking the fabric in her waistband. She resembled one of those scandalous women who were starting to wear bloomers.

Why was he surprised?

Not once had she made a sound; not once had she looked at him.

Lauren was determined never to speak again. Since it was clear that Mr. Dugan was going to blame her for any and all noise she had to do everything in her power to prove him wrong. After agonizing minutes of steering her voluminous skirts around a number of hazards she had come up with the only possible solution.

Take that, you pompous, straitlaced, ungrateful man!

Lauren worked diligently at stoking her anger. As she lightly placed her quasi-old-fashioned lace-up shoes where Dugan's clodhoppers had been, she concentrated

101

on silence and self-righteous recriminations. Listing Patrick's offenses one by one in her mind was like adding logs to a fire. If she could keep it burning hot enough, she might be able to ignore the icy lump of pain that had settled around her heart at his cutting words.

Why couldn't he accept that she just wanted to help him? All her life Lauren had kept a certain distance from people for this very reason. Somehow they always let her down; never needed what she had to offer. Except for the short time with her parents and Aunt Lucy, she had never felt truly wanted.

With Jeff's rejection on top of everything else, Lauren had carefully built emotional dikes to hold back the ocean full of caring she dared not risk on another person. The real problem was that, with no more than a name and a young girl's words, the battering of Lauren's protective walls had begun.

Oh, God, what if she turned into one of those pathetic women who traveled the talk-show circuit: *Women who care too much and can't keep it to themselves!*

She knew enough pop-psychology to identify the desertion phobia that fueled her I-must-be-unlovable syndrome; intellectually, Lauren had a handle on it. Knowing that, it made even less sense to hope for acceptance from a man who already had a slew of his own troubles, and didn't seem to like her much, besides.

But as Lauren trudged along after that very man, her hand locked in his, she admitted to herself an even more telling weakness. As irrational as she knew it was, she was hurt because somehow, deep down, she had expected Patrick Dugan to recognize her sincere caring . . . and respond to it. Instead, he had latched onto any negative about her he could find.

It was terrible to discover, one hundred years away from home, that one was a hopeless romantic in rational, analytical clothing. Lauren squared her shoulders and rubbed away the lone tear trailing through the dust on her cheek.

Patrick had been concentrating so keenly on their ominous surroundings that it took some time for him to notice the unnatural behavior of his companion.

Any other woman of his acquaintance would have been balking or crying by now. They were in a filthy, dangerous part of the city, heading to a place not much better. Killers were likely dogging them at this very moment, and he, himself, had been acting like the bastard he was.

He glanced back over his shoulder and caught Laurie's expressionless eyes with his own. One fair brow lifted and Dugan noticed that, once again, she had soot on her cheek. Absently, he realized it must be her eye paint, another contradiction. Was she a lady or a wanton?

Why was she so calm? Unconsciously he squeezed her hand tighter. Did she know what lay up ahead? Damn! He couldn't stand this. One way or the other he had to be sure of her motives. The hollow, empty look on her face made him feel guilty for doubting her word; automatically, he covered the sympathy she sparked in him with anger.

"You seem to be cooperatin' a mite too easily, colleen. Are you hopin' a friend will be along in a bit to save you?"

Lauren felt her eyes sting with unwanted tears. He couldn't have hurt her more deeply if he'd slapped her. Furiously staring him down, she shook her head no.

Patrick set down the carpetbag and gripped both her shoulders just as a huge shadow snaked across a pile of trash stacked behind him. A bright stream of early morning sunlight pierced the murky alley, reflecting off something in the stranger's hand. Somehow Lauren knew it was a gun.

"Well, if the dirty, thievin' mick didn't survive after all."

Dugan froze, his fingers digging harshly into her flesh. Gray-green eyes filled with fury and betrayal blazed into hers. It's hopeless, she thought. He thinks I dragged him into this. The stranger was Bates, and the minute Lauren heard his voice she knew why he had followed them. Both he and Captain Hansen had all but said it in the jail, only she'd been too naive to get it.

"Look at it this way, Irish; ya had a right purty nurse for yer last days." Bates lumbered up behind Dugan and pressed the tip of the steel barrel into his back. "And maybe ya got a taste or two of the best damn medicine a man can get." The officer snorted and gave a nudge with the gun. "Not a bad way to go, eh, mick?"

Reaching one beefy arm over Patrick's shoulder, Bates ran a dirty finger along Lauren's jaw and down her neck to hook inside her high navy collar. He smirked when she flinched and pulled away.

"Well, now, little wife, me and Cap'n Hansen shor have a score ta settle with ya. Mr. McDonald nearly strung us both up for lettin' ya waltz right outta jail with his prime example here." He cocked his head forward, his mouth closer to Patrick's ear. "McDonald wants that list, mick, and you're gonna take me ta get it now, or this whole thing's gonna be more messy than the boss likes."

Bates's fingers gouged more deeply, cruelly twisting the fabric at her neck, raking the skin, pulling her flush against Dugan's chest. Lauren's eyes lifted to Patrick's, and she watched the anger drain from his expression. At last he believed her. Too bad it was too little, too late.

"I know just how ya can pay for all the trouble ya've caused, girl. After I finish with Dugan we'll have ourselves a party, and you can doctor me up real good.''

The fetid breath blowing across Patrick's face made his stomach roil. The look of stark terror on Laurie's face made his gut twist into knots. The feel of cold metal through the thin shirt covering his back made his heart pound.

Never in his life had he felt so helpless; not when his cursed uncle had stripped him of his birthright and declared him a bastard; not even when he'd first been locked in a jail cell; because this time it wasn't just himself who would suffer. Hell, if he was gonna die, he might as well make it count for something. Maybe Laurie would know how sorry he was for accusing her when she had only wanted to help.

He tried to tell her without words to follow his lead, and she seemed to understand, giving him the barest nod.

''Bates, I'm turnin' around.''

''Fine, mick, I want ta see the look on yer face if you make me pull the trigger.''

With one last squeeze to Laurie's trembling shoulders, Dugan slowly swung to face McDonald's henchman. He felt a small hand shove between his shirt and pants, curling tight on his belt. Holy Mary Mother of God! Don't let the she-cat come out now!

As if he'd taken a slam in the gut, Patrick abruptly bent double, erupting with the loudest wracking coughs he could summon. Since he'd been suppressing them from the minute they'd entered the alley, it was easy to be convincing. Bates only dropped his guard for a second, but that was all Dugan needed.

''Run, Laurie!'' he yelled as he rammed his shoulder into the bigger man's paunch, at the same time bringing both arms up and slamming them viciously into the brawny one holding the gun. If he could just give her enough time to get away, it wouldn't matter what Bates did to him. Bloody hell! Let her run fast. His fever-sapped strength wouldn't last long against this ox.

Lauren froze when she realized what Patrick was doing. At the sound of his fierce command, she fell backwards for a moment, watching the terrifying scene unfold in slow motion. Bates had been surprised, but already his size and power were wearing Dugan down. If he got his hand firmly on the gun, they wouldn't stand a chance.

For almost the first time since she'd taken her century-wide jump Lauren Ann Sullivan's practical, logical brain kicked into complete control. She was a 1990s woman who knew that danger stalked the physically weak, and she had prepared for that possibility in her own time. It had made perfect sense to bring some protection with her, and, boy, was she glad she had.

Lauren prayed that Bates was so focused on Dugan that he wouldn't notice her lunge close to their legs and drag the carpetbag a small distance away.

Patrick, however, caught the movement out of the corner of his eye. Laurie was crazy! If she didn't run now, there would be nothing he could do. He couldn't even catch his breath to warn her.

Practiced fingers flew over the contents of the precious carpetbag. No way was she going to cower in a corner while her man—scratch that—a *good man* paid the ultimate price.

I am woman, hear me roar!

With her body humming from a surge of adrenaline, Lauren clutched the compact spray bottle snapped securely in its brown leather pouch. Thank heaven she'd taken self-defense training from the County Sheriff's department. After all the talk of gangs, burglars, and rapists in the criminal hotbed of Southern California, it seemed ironic that her first use of Mace would be on a policeman in the "good old days."

Lauren scrambled to her feet and held the small bottle firmly in her hand. Two of the good things about Mace were its instant effect and the fact that it could be used on an individual target without affecting people nearby. At least that was how it was supposed to work.

"Dugan," she screamed, "hold your breath and duck!"

He did so instantly, registering briefly that after all his doubts concerning this woman, he had trusted her instinctively.

She caught Bates full in the face for a good three-second blast. His screams slashed through the new morning like violent hands rending fragile silk. The gun fell from his grasp and the huge man stumbled to the littered ground, ramming balled fists into his eyes in agony.

Patrick couldn't take in what he was seeing. Just moments before he had accepted the inevitability of his death and then, like a banshee, Laurie had run around him and right up to the animal who could have snapped her neck with the flick of one hand. Without laying so much as a finger on that human mountain of worthless flesh, she had dropped him to his knees, writhing in pain.

Stumbling away together, Patrick hooked his hand on her elbow and scooped the amazing bag off the packed earth. Bates was bellowing like a gutted bear, and Dugan knew that it was just a matter of time before some brave soul came to see who was making such a ruckus.

"Go . . . now . . . woman," he huffed and coughed with exertion.

Lauren jammed an arm around Patrick's waist and shoved her shoulder up under his arm. It took two sharp tugs before Mr. Macho, Doubting Thomas, released her trusty carpetbag. The man was so stubborn that for a moment Lauren thought he wouldn't lean on her, but then she felt his deep, rattling breath against her arm, stretched snug across his back, and they staggered forward, weaving like drunken sailors down a small side opening, winding back and forth until they reached the street.

The normal sights and sounds of early morning traffic and bustle burst upon the two escapees as they entered the thoroughfare. Furniture vans and vegetable wagons lumbered up and down the rutted dirt road, stopping randomly for deliveries, heedless of the confusion behind them. Shop owners were busy rolling out awnings and setting up their goods on makeshift display tables that jutted out to the narrow walkways, purposely designed to slow shoppers. Harness bells jingled in the cool morning air; friendly haggling floated on the summer breeze.

Hidden for the moment between the cramped walkway separating a general mercantile and a dress shop, Lauren briefly reconnoitered. When a hasty glance over her shoulder confirmed that they weren't being followed she started to propel them into the safety of the hustling crowd.

"Wait, Laurie." Dugan stopped, slumping against a dress shop's whitewashed pine siding. "We need to fix ourselves up a bit. Sure as you're born, somebody's gonna come askin' folks what they've seen this mornin', and right now I'm thinkin' we stand out a mite too much."

His long, weary look at their tangled bodies sent a clear message. She quickly stepped away from the warmth and comfort his closeness had given her. Had he pulled in tighter just before letting go, or had she?

Lauren pursed her lips and bobbed her head once. With spare, deft movements, she shook out and smoothed her dust-powdered skirt, finger tucked the polka-dot navy shirtwaist, and pulled a slightly bent straw boater from the carpetbag. In a flash she had anchored her sagging hairpiece and pinned the hat in place. Standard-issue white gloves lay across the open clasp. Hesitantly, she peeked out from under the wheat-colored brim and studied Patrick.

Mercy, Dugan needed help badly. At eight o'clock in the morning he was not a reassuring sight to see. His haggard face alone would prompt enough second looks, but the grimy streaks making the bruises look worse had to go. Although the screams from deep inside the alley had dropped to a muffled moaning, Lauren knew they had to move.

She pressed a black plastic comb into Patrick's dangling hand. *Please let him be too distracted to notice it's not the heavy rubber kind he's used to.* While Dugan straightened his middle part, raking his wavy auburn hair into order, Lauren crouched and discreetly opened a couple of moist towelettes. The cool, refreshing bite of alcohol and moisture felt wonderful gliding over her dusty, flushed face.

Now to help Mr. Gratitude.

She snatched away the comb, even as Patrick began turning it over in his hand. Standing and lifting herself up on her toes, Lauren gently rubbed at the sweaty grit dusting Dugan's skin. Once across his high forehead, barely brushing those perfect brows; then down his straight nose and over the pads of his cheeks. The backs of her legs began to get shaky . . . probably from standing on her toes too long.

A sharp smell, vaguely reminiscent of the scent of a hospital he'd been in back in New York, rose from his skin. The woman had just saved his life. Again. And was taking care of him. Again. He had to stop this before . . . Hell, he hadn't even been able to protect her, and she had been terrified of Bates.

Dugan's eyes traced the long red welt that disappeared under her collar. At least her motive on that count was clear now. Whatever else she was, she was not an employee of Mike McDonald. Her soft, caring touch against his face tortured his battered body.

Why this woman? He sighed, ignoring the rough wood prickling through the back of his gray flannel shirt. After fourteen years of holding himself apart why did this strange woman have the power to make him feel things he had never wanted to feel again? Was that the reason he'd been hurting her?

Oh, maybe in the beginning he'd had some cause, but now? After what just happened in the alley? Still, why . . .

Her feather-light dabbing at the blood on his swollen bottom lip brought Patrick's curled finger up under Laurie's chin, tilting her face to his.

"That's . . ." she paused and swallowed as Dugan's gaze bored into hers . . . "about the best I can do. We better get moving." Rats! The man's eyes were like the last bit of green on an autumn-cloaked tree. They completely broke her concentration. Her body began to twist away in self-defense, and he grasped her chin between his thumb and index finger.

"I find I must thank you, Laurie." He was at least man enough to admit that. Dugan could feel the subtle tightening of her jaw. She started to look away, so he lifted her chin a notch higher and bent low over her face.

"I'm sorry I couldn't keep that animal's hands off you." It bothered him to think of her in pain. Almost against his will, one finger gently grazed the wound on her neck.

Lauren stiffened her wobbly knees and reached up to unlock his hold on her. *Remember, Sullivan, only a few more days and you will be a historical footnote in the man's life. Keep your dignity, and don't forget that this Irishman can turn on a dime.*

Her hand rested on the back of his and slipped down to bracket his wide wrist. Patrick's whispered words brought his battered mouth so close to hers that for one shocking moment Lauren actually parted her lips to soothe his hurts with the tip of her tongue.

The instant he knew he wanted that silky, pink tip to touch him, Patrick Dugan bounced away. One brush of those sweet lips and somehow he knew he'd be down for the count more surely than if he tried to hold his own in the ring with the great Irish-American boxer, John L. Sullivan. Hell, the woman had a fair right cross.

"What's the fastest way to get where you want to go?" she demanded.

"Hmmm?"

"We've got to get out of here now, Dugan. Which way do we go?"

He was watching her mouth very closely.

Now was not the time to notice how different a woman's body looked without a corset, for pity's sake! But he did, God help him. He did. Laurie moved and shimmied and jiggled in the most distracting way.

"*Mr.* Dugan?"

He dragged a weary hand down his face.

"Takin' the elevated train to the southside stockyards would be the fastest, but hell and damnation, I don't have any money." Only after he finished did he realize what he'd said. A surge of heat climbed up his neck. "I'm sorry. I didn't mean—"

"A little cursing won't send me into a swoon, Patrick, so don't get your knickers in a knot. Let's go." Lauren stepped out between the buildings and turned. "*I* have the money we need." She smiled condescendingly and opened her gloved hand, displaying four weathered nickels.

It had taken six dollars of 1995 money to buy twenty cents' worth of coins minted in or before 1895. The portly man at the antique coin and currency shop had become very interested in Lauren's purchases. Old money was surprisingly expensive, and it had taken quite a chunk out of her savings. However, Lauren had decided that if she managed to find the key to Patrick's time, she'd need some way to protect herself. She'd need some kind of power, and for a nineteenth-century woman, money was about all there was.

And now, after seeing the stunned expression on Dugan's face, she felt every cent had been worth it; if for no other reason than her self-esteem. Evidently, having a woman pay his way and refer to his underwear was a very difficult thing for this nineteenth-century male to take. Little did Dugan know that the twenty cents for the train fare was just the beginning.

Bite the bullet, bud! You're in for a wild ride.

Chapter Six

"Sit."

"What . . . here?" The wooden crate Patrick indicated was propped against a steel beam under the elevated train and tracks they'd just been riding on. It didn't look too sturdy.

"I've waited for answers as long as I intend to, lass. We won't be takin' another step until I hear the reason why you got me out of jail." Dugan punctuated his statement by cupping Lauren's shoulders, forcing her bottom down onto the crude box.

"Listen, Patrick, I told you I keep my promises, but . . ." She eyed the scraggly weeds and debris that littered the deserted area canopied by the crisscrossing girders over their heads. ". . . do we have to have this conversation in such a grungy place?"

Although, now that she thought about it, maybe being confined in a small room when she broke the news wasn't the way to go.

"It's only a bit after eight in the mornin', Laurie. No pubs or beer halls are open, and I won't be goin' to any eating establishment without a cent in my pockets."

He nailed her with an accusing glare.

Lauren schooled her traitorous lips into a neutral line and fussed with her skirt, and then the carpetbag plopped at her side. The rumbling on the elevated tracks above her head began again, rising to a crescendo as a cinder-spraying train roared by, trailing an acrid, smoky smell.

Their noncommunicative ride to the 29th Street Station had made her think of Disneyland and all the workers who dressed in costume there. The brass-buttoned, blue-coated conductors were the most authentic. *Idiot! Everything here is authentic.* She was still struggling with the whole time-travel thing. Ever since they'd left the alley the reality of her situation had been impossible to ignore. It had been easy to put it in the back of her mind in Mrs. Werner's little room, but, judging by the intensity of her companion, the time to face the music had arrived.

Boy, she hoped Dugan had more whimsy in him than she'd seen thus far.

Laurie's silence made Patrick angry and embarrassed that he had nowhere better to take her. Harry Brown would have runners watching his lodgings at the working man's home on the fairgrounds, so he dared not go there. Molly and Stephan would take them in, he was certain. Damn! How he hated to ask his only friends for this favor. The young couple had problems enough in their new marriage. Laurie had to answer his questions now!

Dugan paced, flipping open his cuffs and folding back gray flannel to expose his corded forearms to the barely stirring air. He came to an abrupt halt and asked himself if he really wanted to know what she had to say. Part of him felt sure that letting her leave now would be for the best . . . but he just couldn't do it.

"All right, Dugan, let's get this over with." Lauren plucked off her confining gloves and gestured to another box. "Pull up a seat."

He just stood there, curling his shaky hands into fists.

"This is going to be difficult enough without you towering over me. Please, I really think you're going to need a little support." She lifted one palm in supplication, and he reluctantly dragged another crate into position and sat down.

Lauren licked her dry lips, took a deep breath while tangling her fingers in her lap, and looked directly into the steely eyes not a foot from hers.

"I wish I could do this a better way, Patrick. Just dumping it seems to make the whole thing even more unbelievable. I mean, if I could explain it to you scientifically or metaphysically—well, maybe it would be easier to accept. I think I haven't had such a problem with the concept because where I come from people have seen the impossible become fact, and here . . . I . . ." Her words ran out with her breath.

"Laurie," Patrick interrupted with growing concern, "I haven't a clue as to what you're talkin' about." He covered her fidgeting hands with one of his own. "But the truth shouldn't be so hard to speak, lass."

"Oh, fine," she sniffed indignantly. "Don't say I didn't try to warn you. The stark truth is that I'm from the future . . . 1995, to be exact!"

Dugan jerked back as if he'd been mule-kicked and slapped his palms over his knees.

"Woman, in case you've forgotten we've been runnin' from thugs since before dawn; we've had nothin' to eat and I'm still not too steady on my feet. This is not the time for blarney!" He leaned forward, gripping her upper arms, and pulled her up off the splintery wood. "Who are you and why have you come to me?"

"I'm Lauren Ann Sullivan, and I . . . I came to save your life. Although . . ." Her gaze skittered off to the side for a moment, and then swung back to his. "It *has* gotten a wee bit more complicated than I had originally planned."

Poised as they were, almost nose to nose, Dugan couldn't help but see every flicker of emotion dance across the face he was beginning to know so well. Laurie's voice was low and sincere, with no trace of deceit. Unnatural, spiky black lashes emphasized the steady gaze of her eyes and made him think of the puzzle pieces that didn't fit: priss, paint, and deluded paranoia all found in the same woman.

Good God! What had he gotten himself into?

"Look, Patrick," she said softly, with just a touch of anxiety, "think about it; the medicine, the stuff I sprayed at Bates . . . and my hair, for gosh sakes. Do you know any other woman with hair like mine?" His eyes were like clear pools beneath his symmetrical brows; flat as glass, reflecting nothing.

"Okay; I have it. My underwear! The underwear you found. Doesn't that prove something?"

As if her words were stones dropped in a pond, Dugan's response finally rippled to the surface. He *had* been planning to question her about that. It would explain . . .

"How did you know someone was goin' to try to kill me?"

His fingers were cutting even deeper into Lauren's aching flesh, if it was possible. Very slowly, she brought her hands up to soothingly stroke his cinnamon-hair-dusted forearms; partly from a real desire to comfort him and partly to relax his painful grip.

In the simplest terms possible she explained her genealogy work and how she had stumbled upon the diary of Nancy Brown, knowing full well that he was comprehending only a fraction of what she said. Again she marveled at his courage and composure. In a day of such narrow thinking on so many subjects, this had to have the impact of an atomic bomb.

The whole conversation would have been a lot easier if only H. G. Wells's book, *The Time Machine,* had been published a year or two earlier. It could have given Patrick some kind of frame of reference.

"I have the barest acquaintance with this Miss Brown," he murmured in a daze, loosening his death hold but not breaking away from Laurie's calming touch. "Why in God's name would she be concerned enough to write about a poor Irishman her brother hated?"

"Why, Mr. Dugan," Lauren teased, attempting to ease the strain of the moment. "Maybe you're underestimating your impact on the female of the species."

"That's bunkum, woman."

"No, really. I've read her very words and it *was,* or would that be *is,* now? Well, whatever: the girl had the hots for you." Ooops!

"The hots?"

His eyebrows arched, and Lauren's fingers stilled with her thumbs pressed against the ridged tendons of his wrists.

Great going, Sullivan. Try to handle this with some modern sophistication.

"Well, let me try to rephrase this for Victorian sensibilities." She pondered for a moment. "I suppose one might say that Miss Brown found you desirable." Lauren sighed, quite pleased to have extracted herself from a potentially embarrassing situation so skillfully.

Patrick Dugan, on the other hand, found himself in a most unusual predicament. It was becoming increasingly evident that being close to this woman scrambled his thinking like breakfast eggs. Any other man who'd been as sick as he had been, with killers on his trail, hearing the story he'd just been told, would be up and gone before the next train passed overhead.

But here he stood, chained by small fingers, watching a slow blush wash the freckled cheeks of a woman who, if he believed her, wouldn't be born for almost seventy years.

Shamrocks and shillelaghs! This was the outside of reason. She behaved like no woman he had ever known, and that fact only strengthened her claim. Yet, instead of demanding some tangible proof—which Dugan felt certain he'd find in her carpetbag—he wanted to push her off balance, off kilter. He was tired of being there alone.

"Desirable?" Without breaking her grasp his hard hands slowly slid across her cloth-covered shoulders and laced themselves behind her neck. Both thumbs lay flush against the high navy collar, with just the rough pads touching the delicate flesh under her chin.

Lauren was suddenly aware of the rhythmic surge of Dugan's blood, pumping through the veins in his wrists. A pounding thunder seemed to shut out everything around her, and she wondered vaguely if this man was calling up the sound from inside of her, or if it was simply another train.

"Surely—" She squeaked, swallowed, and tried again. "Surely, even in 1895, that word has the same meaning." Like a lightning strike, she felt a bolt of knowledge illuminate her mind; if too many of her protective barriers fell to this man, she would be the one who ended up a lost soul.

"Desire may have the same meanin'," he said, pressing closer, "but, judgin' from your paint and underclothes, I'm nearly certain you act on it differently."

"Okay, we do get physically intimate . . ." Patrick's

eyebrows shot straight up. "Closer, closer," she sub-
stituted hastily, "faster when we're dating,
er . . . courting, but take my word for it, Dugan," she
rushed on, stepping backwards and out of his hold.
"Nancy Brown was dealing with something beyond her
control, and it works just the same in the future."

Never in her life had she felt such longing for a
man's touch. It had been all she could do to break away
and sternly remind herself that she was not some flighty
young schoolgirl with a crush. Romance and physical
attraction weren't subjects Lauren had had a great deal
of experience with. She couldn't keep a small, self-
deprecating smile from lifting the corners of her mouth
as she circled the discarded crates and reached for the
black leather handle of her bag.

This was actually the one thing with which she had
more in common with the women of the past than the
women of her own time. Twenty-nine-year-old virgins
were probably not nearly so rare here.

*Watch out, Lauren. This time isn't for you, and nei-
ther is this man.*

Patrick watched Laurie struggle for composure. What
was happening to him? How did she do it? She wasn't
typically beautiful, yet the woman tempted him like a
Celtic siren. Good God! Maybe she was one. This was
past believin'. Crazy. By all the saints—craziness might
explain this whole thing.

"All right, Miss Sullivan," Dugan said defensively,
lifting one foot to a crate and bending foreword, resting
an elbow on his raised knee. "If I'm to believe that
some kind o' fairy wind blew you back a hundred years
to rescue me, then I ought ta be thankin' you, I suppose.
Of course, you have pushed your painted face smack
into my affairs without so much as a by-your-leave.
And now I have your Irish butt to look out for as well
as my own."

119

Patrick unconsciously ran a hand over his bristling whiskers and added sarcastically, "Although it seems we of the Emerald Isle don't sound quite the same in the future."

"Oh, yes, Dugan, there's lots of Irish brogue in 1995. It's just that my family has been in America for over a hundred and fifty years. So I . . ." Lauren ran out of steam as the rest of his words registered. He thought she was painted and a pain in the . . . ooooooo!

"I can look out for my own . . . fanny, Patrick Dugan." She stiffened. No one had ever made her feel so many strong emotions, and, frankly, the onslaught was wearing her out. For the first time since becoming an adult, Lauren saw her need for logic and order as the protective wall it was. Even when Patrick had been no more than a name on a page, he'd begun blasting her shell all to bits. This was a horribly vulnerable feeling.

"Bates won't be forgettin' what you did to him in that alley, woman. The man takes far too much pleasure in hurtin' others to let it go." No matter what she said, he couldn't let that monster get his hands on her. He owed Laurie that much at least for saving his life twice. Patrick grimaced as he straightened up, rubbing one hand absently over his abused ribs. "Whether you think you can look after your own butt or not, you'll be keepin' the promise you made and give me the time we agreed on."

Lauren tracked his unconscious move with concern. She knew that her presence would only make things more difficult for him. Promise or not, it would be best for both of them if she disappeared.

Damn, what he wouldn't give for a shot of good Irish whiskey. Maybe a dram would clear his aching head and dull the affect this woman had on him. Her story sounded unbelievable, but considering the evidence he'd seen, felt, and heard, he was nearly convinced.

As an Irishman, how could he deny the possibility of the unexplainable? The mystical? Hell, even in that cursed jail he'd felt something happen. His own ma had always been sure of guardian angels. Her stories had comforted him when he was a child, especially after she'd died and he'd been so alone, without even his treasured horses to care for.

With dawning insight the hazy memories of the past few days shifted and cleared. An incredulous Patrick Dugan recognized that somehow the angel of his fevered dreams was standing before him. It rocked him down deep. Holy Mary! What did this mean?

Lauren sensed that Dugan had tuned her out. No doubt he was planning a quick way to dump her now that she'd spilled the bizarre beans. But how could she fault him, even though it hurt? What else was there to say, except to be the one to say it first? She stuck out her right hand in a very 1990s move.

"Good-bye, Patrick. I'm sure you'll want to call off our deal now, so take care and . . ." Damn! Her voice quivered.

Surprised by the manly gesture, Dugan was slow to respond. The pain of his unintended rejection flooded her eyes with embarrassment before she could hide them beneath her hat brim. As Lauren's bare hand hung awkwardly between them, he latched on to it and instantly knew himself to be the biggest of fools for not turning—or running—away.

Instead he found himself holding tighter and saying, "So you're plannin' to leave your husband once more."

After her crack-brained story about coming through time he ought to be glad to see her go. Hell, the woman knew too much and had no sane reason for that knowledge. She could get him killed or get herself killed. . . . And that was the very devil of it. He couldn't abandon her to McDonald's men; yet how could he stop her? The only solution was to ensure her willing compliance.

"Now, Dugan, let's not argue about this again," she reasoned, pulling slightly against his hold. "Since I've explained everything, I'm sure Father Ryan can straighten out this husband wife technicality."

"Bein' that we're both Catholic, you must know there's but one way to straighten out this tech . . . whatever you said." Patrick paused for a moment before plunging on. He lifted the brim of her hat with a finger, and Lauren had no choice but to look up.

"One of us dies."

"What?"

"That's the only way out of this marriage, Laurie, and it doesn't matter where you came from or where you're goin'. A priest heard our vows, and in the eyes of God we are one *'til death us do part.'* " Their clasped hands trembled.

"Come on now, Patrick, that's just too old-fashioned and rigid for wor—" Oh, good gosh! Of course he was old-fashioned. No wonder he'd been so upset when he realized how she'd gotten him out of jail. In 1895 people didn't change spouses like their shoes. Divorce was beyond the pale.

"One of the only things my sainted mother ever asked of me was to honor the Church that gave her tortured soul peace. And while I've seen little evidence in my twenty-eight-years of God and His Heaven, I'll not be castin' aside her wishes."

"But—" Lauren jerked hard to loosen his grip. It didn't work.

"This marriage was your doin', woman, and I'll not be ex-communicated just because you've realized your mistake." His powerful hands surrounded and dwarfed her own. "Besides, even if there was something Father Ryan could do, he'd not do it on my word alone. And we've not got the time to find the man now.''

Lauren felt like the lock of a safe when all the tumblers suddenly fall into alignment and click open. No wonder Captain Hansen had been so shocked when she'd agreed on the priest. No wonder Dugan's anger had flared so unreasonably. Her actions had forced his future onto the rocks, just as wreckers of old had lured unsuspecting ships off course with false lights that promised safety—only to doom them to the reefs of destruction.

One side of Patrick's whiskered jaw ticked and an unruly sideburn undulated with the movement under his skin. Trying to explain the 1990s view of marriage would most likely deal the final blow to his already low opinion of her.

It was pointless anyway. She'd be gone in a week.

During the long days at Mrs. Werner's, waiting for the antibiotic to do its work, Lauren had methodically traced every move she'd made in the Museum of Science and Industry to find the key that had finally unlocked the invisible door. Aunt Lucy had been right. Heaven must have helped, because, Lauren realized now, it had been pure chance that she'd taken Patrick's picture out of her bag at the right time in the right place and held it.

She knew without a doubt that the time door was in the modern-day museum old Palace of Fine Arts. The centennial anniversary must indeed have brought Einstein's time curves in line. But it hadn't been until Lauren had held the authentic document printed with the date she was trying to reach that the miracle had actually happened.

Lauren, lost in thought and barely aware of Patrick's hand on hers and his puzzled expression, shook her head in wonder. She had to give Aunt Lucy credit for this adventure and the nudge she'd felt in the museum to pick up their brochure detailing the one-hundred-year celebration of the Chicago World's Fair.

If it hadn't been for that little push, she wouldn't have a way home now; a way to virtually cease to exist in 1895.

And, with no trace of Lauren Ann Sullivan left . . . no evidence, in fact, that she had ever been born, she should qualify as dead—certainly the best solution. Patrick Dugan would be perfectly happy and relieved, and she would be perfectly happy, too . . . in a depressed sort of way.

Overhead, the thunder of a passing train filled the uneasy silence between them with noise and oily fumes. Lauren's shoulders slumped as it occurred to her that, in her effort to save this man and to go with Aunt Lucy's push, she had only created more problems.

Okay, so *dead* was about the most serious problem a person could have. Just now, arguing that point wasn't much consolation. Her only legitimate solace was in the fact that none of this had been her idea in the first place. She had been following a cosmic call for help, and Aunt Lucy would simply have to use her clout to set things right.

Dugan dropped her hand and rested his palms on her shoulders. Lauren lifted her solemn face at his unspoken command.

"We've got to go, Laurie, and I want some things clearly understood."

She nodded her compliance. It was the least she could do. Besides, the man liked to lecture; a sign of the times.

"I've a friend, Stephan Polaski, and I'm sure he'll help us. We won't stay long 'cause I don't want to be leadin' danger to his door, but I don't think there's any way Brown or McDonald could know about him. I'm sure we haven't been followed, so this will give me some time to get a wee bit stronger and find out what sort of donnybrook Mr. McDonald has stirred up.''

Lauren blinked and shifted her weight.

''Your story about the future is not one I want you passin' about, do you understand?'' This was certainly not the time to give her wild notions any encouragement. Patrick tightened his hold to prompt her response. Laurie was acting too composed again.

''I understand. No matter how I must appear to you, I'm not a fool. I certainly don't want my actions to cause you any more problems.''

Holy Mary! Miss Priss was spewin' her two-bit words like water again, and he could feel the tension in her body through his hands. Laurie seemed to be going along without a fuss, but where was she hiding the she-cat?

Patrick pulled the carpetbag out of Lauren's fist. He handed her the gloves and waited soundlessly until she had tugged them into place.

''The man carries the bags,'' he replied, when she arched a fine, honey-brown brow. ''The farther we get into the tenements, the more likely we'll be watched, and I don't want to give any old biddies grist for their gossip mills. McDonald will eventually send ropers down here, so we want to be attractin' as little attention as possible.''

Smoothly, Patrick swung one of her gloved hands to the bend of his elbow and pressed it into place.

''I don't know what to believe about you yet, lass, but for now you must act the part of a proper wife. Surely *wherever* you've come from, you know the way of a *proper* wife.''

The expression on his face was so condescending that it cooled the hot coals of guilt over which Lauren had been roasting herself since she realized she'd locked him into a loveless marriage. After all, the man *could* be dead! The barest glimmer of rebellion crept into her docile gaze.

Now, who was the most perfect little ol' wife she could think of? It would have to be sugary-sweet Melanie Wilkes from *Gone With the Wind*.

"Whaay, sirrah," Lauren drawled and batted her lashes, "you wound me."

Jesus, Mary, and Joseph! The she-cat was back!

"All right, Hansen, how many beers have you had?"

"None, Mr. McDonald, I . . . I swear it." Captain Hansen's normally impeccable uniform was noticeably rumpled. A rivulet of sweat ran down his left temple.

"Are you tellin' me, boy, that some slip of a woman brought Bates to his knees?"

"Yessir! When a runner dragged me from the precinct house I couldn't believe it either. But honest to God, sir, that's what he said happened."

The tall man, dressed in solid black relieved only be a stark white shirtfront, turned in his chair behind an imposing cherry desk and effectively dismissed the off-duty officer.

After the door had shut with a quiet click Michael Cassius McDonald leaned back in his reclining chair and stared out the second-story window at the twilight activity on Clark Street. Two steepled fingers tapped twice against his chin.

"What did you find out, Harry? Is Hansen lying?"

A balding, snub-nosed man stepped from behind one of many side doors, blotting his shiny face and drooping handlebar mustache with a large linen handkerchief.

Mike wasn't going to like what he had to report. Raking a nervous hand through thinning, salt-and-pepper hair, Harry moved his considerable bulk to the chair at McDonald's side. Although hard living accounted more for his appearance than actual age, tonight thirty-eight seemed mighty old.

"Hansen ain't lyin', Mike. I talked to Bates myself, and he still don't know what hit him. One minute he had Dugan covered and then the next he was screamin' on the ground. He says this wife of Dugan's squirted some mist on his face that burned like the very fires of hell. It's been hours now and he still can't see right."

"So the bastard got away!" McDonald's fist slammed down on the desk like the crack of a rifle. "We've got to get that list, Harry," he insisted, standing and bracing his flattened palms against the expensive polished wood. "Send your sister back to the fair to watch for him. Maybe she can lure him in."

Brown nodded, prudently masking his reluctance to involve Nancy further. What in the world could he come up with to make her cooperate again? Maybe he'd make her think he'd dropped the charges against her precious Dugan. Yeah . . . that might do it. Nancy was a twit, but she was still his baby sister. Damn, he'd have to be careful. McDonald could sniff out sentiment like a blooded hound dog. The faster he tracked that worthless mick down, the better it would be for everyone.

"I want him, Harry. No young punk is going to think he can hold Michael McDonald over a barrel—not that I think he'll find anyone with power enough to cause us trouble. Who'd listen to the bastard anyway?" The imposing crime boss pointed a finger at Brown for emphasis. "Bring me that meddling whore, too," he said, his tone dark and ugly. "She has something I want almost as much as that list. Do whatever it takes."

Harry Brown tugged on his felt bowler and walked out the back door of Mike's saloon. He wasn't too worried; with enough money, *any* needle in *any* haystack could be found. Chicago was filled with rats who would be more than happy to sell out their own mothers for a hunk of cheese. It was just a matter of time.

*   *   *

If Lauren didn't keep her mouth shut, it was going to be filled with flies.

As Dugan pulled her down increasingly narrow streets, she couldn't keep her jaw from dropping open. The coolness of the early morning had been burned away by a fierce August sun, heating the air to a cloying thickness. Her legs felt as if they were encased in a portable sauna. The dark fabric of her clothes drew the blistering rays like a magnet.

Over and around the fetid smells that ripened under the heavy humidity, a few whiffs of coffee and bread painfully reminded her that the last food she'd eaten had been Mrs. Werner's stew. How was Dugan staying on his feet? The man had to be starving and exhausted. Lauren peeked up at his blank face and wondered what it cost him to keep that neutral expression there. The longer they walked, the more he leaned against her. Did he even realize it?

Once again, Lauren had to remind herself that everything was *real* and not a movie set. Rows and rows of undulating laundry swung limply above their heads, casting distorted shadows on the objects below. Small children sat listlessly in the battered doorways of deteriorating tenement buildings, jammed one after the other with no end in sight. Jumbled piles of trash seemed to be the only embellishments.

Dark, dirty, and depressing . . . how had millions of immigrants survived the disillusionment that must have come after their first joyous look at the Statue of Liberty?

Here and there, as they walked along the uneven pavement, Lauren spotted hopeful splashes of living color against the dreary brick, struggling to bloom from crude flower boxes.

"We're nearly to Stephan's building," Dugan announced, and bent over a bit to see under her hat.

Her paint-framed eyes watched him with a steady calm that both reassured and disturbed him. How could he hold her? What kind of powers did she have? He clenched the warm leather handle in his hand, testing the weight of her mysterious bag. Powers! Leapin' leprechauns; he sounded as daft as the old croakers at home.

Come on now, man, she's just a woman.

Oh, sure, Patrick, me boyo. The day Lauren Ann Sullivan proves to be 'just a woman' is the day old Will Vanderbilt claims you as his long-lost son! Dugan quickly shoved back the pain of knowing that no man would ever make that claim.

What in the hell was he goin' to tell Molly and Stephan about his outlandish wife? Her speech, her actions, her hair, and that cheap paint . . . If Molly ever saw those undergarments! Damn! If he had any other choice at all, he'd take it.

Maybe if they thought this was a flaming love match, it would work. Love was supposed to be blind, wasn't it? Well, this would surely test the saying, then. His friends would have to believe him blind, deaf, and dumb.

"Here we are." Patrick stopped at another set of trash-strewn steps. He set down the bag and pressed his free hand over Laurie's fingers, nestled in the curve of his arm. "Molly Polaski is a fine woman, Laurie, and for the time you're here I'll not be havin' you upset her or treatin' her like a servant."

"Now just a min—"

"Don't try tellin' me that you aren't used to a soft life, 'cause I'll not believe it."

He showed her the flat of his work-scarred palm, clearly daring her to do the same.

"You've fine clothes and money and you're . . .

129

well . . .'' Dugan shifted uncomfortably as he tried to
see her as the folks here would. ''No one's goin' to be
quite sure what kind of woman you are.''

Oh brother, here we go again! Lauren fumed and
yanked her fingers away.

''Now listen here, buddy, I—''

''Hush up, woman, so I can tell you my plan.'' He
cupped her elbow and whisked them around the side of
the steps and into a shadowed corner.

Lauren's damp shirtwaist came up flush against the
wall and she leveled Dugan with her most disgusted
look. The man probably wouldn't trust the Pope either.
Ooooo! but Patrick Dugan made her mad! She used the
cotton-covered heel of her palm to blot her moist forehead and prepared for his lecture.

''I haven't known Stephan very long, and when we-
've talked it's been mostly about his problems and such,
so I think he'll not find it too strange that I've not mentioned my own marriage. Surely not as strange as I do.''

His eyes clouded like a sudden squall on Lake Michigan. Lauren took a slow, deep breath and pushed back
a little against the lumpy mortar. Not a happy camper
here!

''If I tell him I've been missin' you so bad, I couldn't
even speak of it, he'll think me a lovesick fool just like
himself and understand. And he'll have no problem
with our separation, since money's so precious. Why,
Stephan told me that he and Molly had to save for two
years to get married. Faith, but it'll be a blow to my
pride to have him think me a slave to a woman—
ouch!''

The pointed toe of Lauren's black shoe connected
solidly with his shin.

''All right, Patrick Dugan, you've gone too far!''
Lauren hissed as he bent to rub his abused flesh. ''I'm
sorry you're married to me, too, but it was the only way

to save your ungrateful hide. From the first all I've tried to do is help you, and I'm sick of your macho, scum-sucking attitude.'' She finished with a sharp finger poke in the center of his chest, blinking rapidly to clear her bleary eyes. Holding on to the fury; hiding the hurt.

Hell, he'd riled the she-cat, and at the very worst time. Someone could walk by or come down the steps at any moment. Patrick knew he had to be completely honest now or she would bolt at the first opportunity. ''Macho scum-sucking attitude'' was not an expression he was familiar with, but her meaning was easy to discern. Patrick figured out right quick that some of her anger was born of hurt. What he'd said hadn't come out right.

''I'm sorry, *Miss Sullivan;* you're right. As far as I can tell, you've been tryin' to help me at every turn, but you can't be holdin' it against me that I've a few reservations after the pie-eyed story you've told.'' Dugan saw her mouth open to speak and he quickly pressed a finger to it.

Soft, soft lips. *Not now, man!*

''We'll talk more about it, I swear, but we've got to get inside and out of sight. So please, colleen, follow my lead and try not to let your . . . ah . . . unusual differences show too much.''

Soundless puffs of air soughed against his finger, and Patrick gently rubbed her parted lips closed.

''There's too much danger for me to be thinkin' of anything else except the men who are after us, Lauren. McDonald wants that list of names that I've gathered—names of those willin' to testify against him. They're all countin' on me to find someone who'll listen and help, and I need the time to do it.''

The seriousness of their situation rang in his formality. Unconsciously, he lifted a finger to one fine, fair brow and traced down a satiny cheek. ''I'll not have anyone hurt for the likes of me, woman; not you and not my friends. We've got to work together or there'll be hell to pay.''

Lauren knew her poor heart wasn't going to be able to take the strain much longer. Just the touch of one finger dragging across her skin had every nerve in her body at rigid military attention. Why, after all this time—after finally accepting she would never, could never feel this way . . .

''I understand how important this is, Dugan. Please believe me—I won't intentionally do anything to make things more difficult or hurt your friends. I'm normally a very calm, even-tempered person. It's . . . it's just all so . . . you seem to make me . . . oh, damn!'' She lifted her hands, palms up, and shrugged.

He had to tighten every muscle in his face to keep from smiling. What had sounded shocking coming out of this woman's mouth yesterday seemed amusing today. Why shouldn't she say just what she felt? Good God, he was thinking like a man he'd heard recently supporting the suffragettes. Was he being corrupted?

Laurie was turning him upside down. And damn if she didn't seem to be as affected by his touch as he was by hers. But Patrick couldn't think about it now. Those thoughts could very possibly be as dangerous to his heart as McDonald and Brown were to his body.

''Nancy, honey,'' Harry Brown called with deceptive sweetness as he knocked on his sister's hand-carved bedroom door.

''Get away from my door, Harry.''

''Nancy, I've had about enough of your hissy fit. Open up right now or I'll change my mind and let that stupid mi . . . Irishman rot in jail.''

There was a sharp click, and the oak barrier was gone. Nancy Brown, a full twenty years younger than her brother, waited with wary calm, draped in a diaphanous silk robe. Her pale face and hair enhanced her fragile aura.

"He's free, honey," Brown lied easily, promoting his own purposes.

"Oh, Harry," she gushed and surged forward, then caught herself and stopped. "Do you mean it? Really?"

"I've dropped the charges, Nancy, but I don't know if he'll go back to his job." This was the tricky part. He had to say it just right. "So I was hoping you'd help me straighten out this whole misunderstanding."

"Of course, Harry." She smiled innocently. "Just tell me what to do."

Chapter Seven

Molly Polaski was a beautiful young woman of about twenty. Her midnight black hair poofed gracefully around her face in the most popular style of the day: the Gibson Girl. Up close and personal, it was even more feminine than it had been portrayed in the pen-and-ink drawings of the American illustrator Charles Dana Gibson, who'd made the look all the rage.

When Lauren had been doing research on the time period she hadn't been able to help but be impressed with this man who'd captured the first real visual picture of the new emerging female, racing into the twentieth century: athletic, stylish, involved, and intelligent. Quite a change.

Even though her clothes were obviously of a better quality then Mrs. Polaski's faded pink muslin blouse and gray poplin skirt, Lauren felt self-conscious. She was thankful that her pathetic little head of hair was hidden. No wonder Patrick had looked so aghast at her barbered locks.

His friend's wife surely fit the definition of ''Black Irish'' to a *T*. Molly's dark hair and crystal light blue eyes completely overshadowed her worn clothes and stark surroundings. The smile that lit her flawless face when she opened the door at Patrick's knock sent a surprising jolt of pain to the bottom of Lauren's very empty stomach.

Just hunger pangs, she told herself as she followed Dugan into the tiny room that served as the living, cooking, and eating areas. The woman is married, anyway.

What? What was that last light-headed thought? Jealousy? Oh no, not an irrational, jealous response over Patrick Dugan. Her blood sugar must be dropping.

Lauren took off her hat and stood perfectly still, watching the two before her as they moved closer to the small iron stove and square oak table in the far corner of the drab room. She felt like an intruder, left out. It seemed as if it had been just her and Patrick for so long; his having a relationship with someone else caught her by surprise.

Yes, of course, that was it. Not the green-eyed monster at all, just the captive/captor dependant thing again. Besides, this gorgeous girl was married to the only man Dugan could turn to for help in all of Chicago. Would he mess with that? *Ah, ah, ah, Sullivan, watch the slip, my girl.*

Mrs. Polaski darted a quick glance at Lauren. Patrick was no doubt filling the lady in on the situation, and their story, whatever that ended up to be. Lauren drew her threaded fingers in tighter against her middle and nervously tapped her thumbs together. She felt so out of place, so out of time.

She eyed her precious carpetbag, resting next to Dugan's feet, and then the door. Bag. Door. Bag. Door. As if he could sense the wheels turning in her head, Patrick casually nudged the bag with his shoe until his long legs blocked it.

The man was clearly a control freak.

"Laurie, darlin'," he said warmly, turning to her.

Oh ho, the wolf dons sweet, sleazy sheep's clothing.

"Forgive me for leavin' you standin' there." Patrick couldn't help but notice the pinched look on Laurie's face. With his back to Molly, he sent a glaring warning to his willful little wife and hoped she would behave.

It was the first time Lauren had ever seen two eyebrows say so much. Okay, she'd play along with the lovey-dovey stuff and send him a body language message, too. When he circled her waist and pulled her close it felt for a moment as if he'd pinched her there. Ooooo!

"Why, Patrick, honey pie, don't you worry yourself." *Oops; too much Melanie. Watch it, Sullivan,* she thought batting her Maybellined lashes.

Holy hell! The she-cat!

"Molly Polaski, this is my bride, Laurie Ann Dugan."

Lauren's head snapped around like a sprung rubber band. She was! She really was Lauren Ann *Dugan.* Involuntarily, her knees buckled, and instantly Patrick tugged her closer.

"Ah, Laurie, I'm happy ta meet ya. We've been so worried about Patrick since those animals locked him up."

The black-haired beauty spoke with such honesty, the music of Ireland in her every inflection, that Lauren couldn't help but respond.

"Thank you, Mrs. Polaski, for letting us stay here. We—" Dugan pinched her again.

"Think nothin' of it. After all your man's done to

help Stephan and me, providin' a safe port in a storm is the least thing we can do.'' Molly came forward and took Lauren's free hand to give it a squeeze. ''It'll be some hours before Stephan's home from his job at the fair—the job he has thanks to your husband—but I'm sure he'll have some news.'' She said the last with a hopeful nod in Patrick's direction.

''Mrs. Polaski—''

''Molly, please.'' She gave Lauren a shy smile.

''Molly, is there someplace where D—Patrick could sleeeep—'' Lauren hissed out the word on the tail end of a firm pinch.

''Why, Patrick Dugan, forgive me for not thinkin'.'' Molly waved one hand toward the closed door in the opposite corner. ''You'd best be gettin' yourself right in that bed and rest while I go out to do some shoppin'.''

''There's no need, Molly,'' he said firmly.

''You're not standin' there askin' me *not* to see what me own eyes tell me? Ah, Laurie.'' She sighed, shaking her head. ''Why is it that big, strong men have such a hard time admittin' to a weakness now and then?'' The girl winked.

Lauren felt the most surprising response. Somehow she had found a kindred spirit. They both laughed, that special laugh of comrades and confidantes. It was karma.

It irritated the hell out of Dugan that the two women were actin' like bosom bows; as if Laurie didn't need him. Couldn't Molly see all the strange things about this woman? He retaliated, uncharacteristically so.

''Well, now, Molly, if you're goin' out anyway,'' Patrick said with a sly smile, splaying his fingers out wide along Lauren's side and sliding them forward just under her breast. ''We *both* might sleep for a bit.''

Molly's sky blue eyes rounded, and a bright blush stained her ivory cheeks. Lauren was furious at Patrick for causing her new friend embarrassment. The macho manipulator was about to get a dose of lovey-dovey, 1990s style.

She turned into him a little, hoping her full skirts would shield her actions. The lesson was for Mr. Dugan's benefit, not to make Molly feel even more awkward.

At the first touch of Laurie's hand on his bottom Dugan's entire body went stiff as a board.

"Patrick, honey pie," she sweetly scolded, squeezing the firm flesh under her fingers, "you shouldn't tease Molly so." Now a fierce little pinch. "Apologize right now." Lauren could feel a slight trembling in the leg pressed next to hers.

Caught in the crash of so many feelings and urges, Patrick was utterly immobilized. That small hand touching him the way it was, and where it was, was starting a chain reaction in him that would soon have him flushing redder than any woman he'd ever seen. Holy Mary, what must the future be like if this was how women behaved?

He had to get to that closed door or he'd not be able to look Molly Polaski in the face ever again.

"I'm sorry, Molly." Dugan tried to smile, but it came out more like a grimace. He jerked forward from Laurie's side, heading quickly for the bedroom, grabbing up the carpetbag as he moved.

"Don't wait up for me, dear," Lauren called as he twisted the knob. "I think Molly and I will have a nice little coze."

"Wife—" both his face and his voice were taut with strain—"*remember, I have your things.*"

Dark, turbulent green eyes held hers, sending an undeniable message. Lauren knew a threat when she heard one. Apparently so did Molly, who bustled out of the line of fire to the old black stove.

"Of course, husband." The word stumbled off Lauren's tongue. "It's fine with me." She offered him the small concession, hoping to thaw his icy anger. He scowled. She tried another. "I'll bring you something to eat after you sleep for a while."

The raw pine door whooshed shut before she finished speaking. Maybe her move hadn't been the best way to handle him. *Handle . . . stop thinking about it, Sullivan!* But the longer she thought about it, the more mortified she became. What in the world had possessed her? *The devil made me do it* would cut no slack here.

Hell to pay popped unpleasantly into her mind. Well, at least she'd face him next with some food in her stomach. It wasn't much of an advantage, but she'd take anything at this point.

Lauren sat on one of the mismatched chairs circling the oak table; praying for courage, grateful for a woman to talk to, and wishing for some chocolate chip cookie dough ice cream. She was a firm believer in Mary Poppins's sage council: A spoonful of sugar helps the medicine go down.

In this case, a half-gallon would do the trick.

Think, Sullivan! Come on, come up with a story quick! She really should have known what would happen the minute she was alone with Molly.

"I'm sure ya must be starvin', Laurie, so get some biscuits out of the saltbox and sit right down while I tend to the tea."

Help! What was a saltbox? She would never be able to stay in such close quarters and fool this woman. The lies on her lips tasted bitter, but the truth would cause too many problems. Too many to handle right now.

"Molly . . . I . . . have a confession to make." The naturally dark lashes of her new friend fluttered at the

139

forbidding sound of Lauren's words, and Molly sank onto one of the chairs.

The story sprang fully formed into her mind, and she crossed her fingers in her lap, hoping that Dugan wouldn't have a fit.

"You see, Patrick and I have had a few problems since our marriage." Talk about the understatement of the year.

"Oh?"

"Yes, truthfu—" Not! "Let me just come right out and say it. I'm rich, and Patrick didn't know it until after we eloped."

"Ah."

"Ah what?"

"That explains your clothes and your . . ." Molly cut off her words abruptly, but Lauren knew the rest of the sentence as she felt the other woman's gaze shift from her hair to her eyes to her shoes. The young lady before her, who most likely didn't have more than a sixth-grade education, was as sharp as a tack.

"Molly, Patrick and I have been separated because he just can't handle the money thing."

Her baby blue's opened wide.

Ooops!

"I mean," she rushed on, "he was the iceman . . ." *Yes that's the ticket.* ". . . who came to my parents' home in New York, and I never met him before because . . . because I was traveling." *Molly seems to be buying it. Good.* "But after they died I was so lonely that I went home to live in the family house. One day I was sitting on the back step in an old dress when Patrick arrived with his delivery. I was smitten and he thought I was a servant." *This had to be a stretch even for an enlightened Irish girl married to a Polishman.*

"Aye," she nodded cautiously. "Patrick is a fine figure of a man, and book smart, too."

"Well, it was love at first sight, but I knew he was so proud that if I told him about the money, he'd leave. And—" Lauren took a deep breath to fortify herself in order to finish this travesty—" when he found out that's exactly what he did. The foolish man thought I would rather have wealth than his love."

Lauren couldn't help thinking, as the impassioned words poured from her lips, that if she ever found herself in such a situation—if real, honest-to-God lasting love was within her grasp—she would have no trouble making the choice. It would be worth losing every material thing she had.

"So, I hired a Pinkerton man." *Mercy, this just gets worse and worse.* "And when he reported what had happened to my darling Patrick, I came without delay to sprin—uhumm . . . liberate him. I swore to give up my fortune to prove my love, and as you can see, so far he's kept me with him."

Lauren felt like a top that spins wildly at first and then gradually winds down to a jerking halt. She simply couldn't put any more romantic sentiment into Dugan's mouth.

"And . . . ?" Molly sat forward on her chair, clasping her hands tightly.

"I want our marriage to succeed, but I'm not sure how to be a good—er, proper wife." That at least was true; of course she hadn't ever really intended to be— a wife. "While we're here, would you be willing to teach me, Molly? I've had servants all my life so . . ." Not necessarily the human kind—washing machines, dryers, microwaves . . .

"Say no more, Laurie." Molly stood, reaching for her new friend's gloved hands. "This will make me old chores seem fun." She laughed excitedly, pulling the cotton-clad fingers free. "Your Patrick is goin' to be so happy when he sees all you're tryin' to do to make things right between the two of ya." Molly set aside the formal wear as easily as she set aside their differences and stepped to the stove for the tea.

"Fat chance," Lauren grumbled.

"What?"

"Oh, I said I'd fancy that, Molly, I truly would." A deep ache began to swell, pressing against her heart. It would be so sweet to see Patrick Dugan happy. If he was capable of it.

"Come on over here then, me friend. Tea will be your first lesson."

They sat for nearly an hour, sipping strong honeyed tea and eating the best biscuits Lauren had ever tasted. The fruity smell and summery flavor of Molly's strawberry jam made the warm, sticky discomfort of the little room bearable. Listening to the struggles that her friend had faced because of her marriage to Stephan Polaski reaffirmed the ghastly results of prejudice in any time.

The poor girl had been completely disowned, but she had willingly risked everything for the man she loved. Lauren couldn't help wondering if anyone would ever love her fiercely enough to do that.

"When my parents refused to give their approval it was either them or Stephan." A few tears slipped from the corners of her eyes and she sniffed, wiping her face with the backs of her hands. "But though I've lost, I've also won. Just wait 'til you meet my big, handsome . . ." The black-haired beauty pushed away her sadness and celebrated the love that was in her life. She smiled, suddenly shy. "It's wonderful havin' a woman friend to talk to again."

Lauren reached out and patted Molly's hand. It did feel good to have a woman to talk to. Back in her other life she had been friendly, but not a friend. Why had she cut herself off from people after the warmth she'd shared with Aunt Lucy? Why hadn't she ever stopped and questioned her actions? For as long as she was here Lauren vowed to nurture all the friendships she could, especially this burgeoning one with Molly, and even the on-again, off-again one with Patrick.

Molly's last-minute invitation to go shopping was very tempting. Lauren wanted to see, hear, and taste what it was like to live in 1895 Chicago. This young Irishwoman could teach her so much. But marketing would have to wait for another day; resolving things with Patrick was vital while they had the small apartment to themselves. Heaven only knew what would happen when Stephan Polaski got home and heard their traumatic love story from his charming wife.

After Molly left, Lauren crossed to the closed door with the enthusiasm of a condemned prisoner marching to the gas chamber. Dugan was probably waiting and steaming. Maybe the tray of food would distract him from the tongue-lashing he was no doubt rehearsing. She wrinkled her freckled nose and fluffed her dropping bangs.

Oh, what she wouldn't give for a long, hot shower. It was a bit past noon, and Lauren felt as if she hadn't slept in weeks. The emotional toll of the last few hours had drained her energy reserves to an all-time low. How could she possibly deal with an enraged, offended Irishman?

A whiny creak sounded as she pushed open the door. Lauren held an anxious breath until she realized that he was completely sacked out. Like a log. She ran her eyes over his relaxed body, from his wavy cinnamon hair to his oddly vulnerable stockinged feet. A small hole was beginning in one heel. Too bad she didn't know how to darn. Geez! What an archaic, domestic thought. Betcha Molly would know. Maybe . . .

Get real, Sullivan; the man is more likely to ask you to stuff it than mend it.

The rich, warm tones of a carved walnut bedstead gleamed with loving care, and although the walls were unadorned, the room was colorful and clean. Covering the bed was a quilt of bright, primary colors, which were repeated in the embroidered dresser scarf spread across a small chest of drawers. On top of the scarf was a simple rose-glazed pitcher and basin. One square window bracketed by clothes pegs on either side offered the only air and light.

Directly beneath it was a plain, squat bench on which Patrick must have put the lacy, heart-shaped pillow. No doubt it normally rested in the middle of the Polaskis' bed. Lauren set the tray on the dressertop and tiptoed over to raise the cloudy glass, opening the stuffy room to any available breath of air.

As she struggled with the warped wood frame, the delicate stitching on the lemon-and-lace pillow caught her eye. *Molly and Stephan—Two hearts became one April 23, 1895.* Lauren scooped it up and sank onto the hard seat. So much hope, she thought, tracing the letters with her finger. Here in a place of such poverty and ugliness, a young girl had created a lovely spot in which to nourish her soul and her love. The only treasures she had were in this room.

Molly had responded intuitively to a profound truth that women always seemed to know: The human spirit needs beauty to survive. What a lucky man Stephan Polaski was!

Lauren gently set down the sweet momento and moved to the side of the deep, soft bed. Would Patrick Dugan ever find someone to make him feel as loved as Stephan did? The thought of some laughing lass in his arms brought such a sharp, swift pain to her chest that she instinctively folded her arms in against it.

Don't do it, Sullivan; don't you dare let yourself fall for this man. The ache crawled up her throat, making it difficult to swallow. Maybe if she got a little rest, these wild emotions would be controllable again. They both would have to have clear heads to come up with a plan that would keep Patrick safe and free.

Lauren quickly unbuttoned her collar and cuffs, but regretfully decided that her itchy hairpiece would have to stay put. She was a light sleeper, and she reasoned that Molly's return would wake her up long before Dugan's depleted body stirred.

You're really pushing it this time, Sullivan, Lauren thought as she unlaced her shoes and eased on to the not-quite-double-sized mattress. Here she was in the same bed with Patrick Dugan again. No wonder he kept alluding to her morals. After her grab earlier how would she ever convince him that she was basically as pure as the driven snow?

But oooh, it felt so good to stretch out and sink into the plump, slightly crackly bedding. A faint buzz of outside noise drifted up through the second-story window, and though it was humid, the fabric beneath Lauren's cheek was sleek and cool.

Dugan's whiskered face angled toward hers. In repose, it was easy to picture the boy he'd been somewhere below the tough surface. His steady, easy breaths pleased her, and she reminded herself to make sure he took another dose of antibiotic when he awoke.

As a languorous, syrupy feeling of exhausted wellbeing settled over Lauren, she succumbed to a long-suppressed impulse. One feather-light fingertip ran the length of one silky russet brow and brushed the barest fanned edge of thick lashes. Perfect addition to her gene pool . . .

*   *   *

Lauren was dreaming again.

On one hand she was very aware it wasn't real, which both relieved and alarmed her. Even in this abstracted state, she acknowledged that her dreams had become very precarious things lately.

However, on the other hand, the sensations she was experiencing were so sharp that she told her unconscious self to go ahead and enjoy them. It didn't want to, but her logic-hampered subconscious let go, allowing Lauren to indulge her fantasies.

A warm, secure weight rested against her, protecting her from head to toe; circling her with strength. Moist, sweet lips softly sucked on her mouth, first gently and then with more pressure, more need; deep inside her body an unknown thread pulled taut.

This was absolutely the most realistic kiss she had ever fantasized. Lauren pressed into the feeling, wrapping her dream arms around the pleasure, the acceptance, the passion. She knew that all too soon it would dissolve like smoke on the wind.

Again the warm mouth covered hers and coaxed her to open. A silky tongue feathered the tender inside of her bottom lip, and for the first time in her dreams she answered. Tiny, light strokes that began to grow harder and faster; hotter and hotter until she was going to . . . just one more second and she'd feel . . .

When Dugan's rumbling stomach was awakened by the smell of food his consciousness was quick to follow. He lay for a moment without moving, testing his bruised and fever-weakened body for stiffness. Relieved that he felt better, Patrick opened his eyes, intent on eating and setting a certain little hussy straight.

But the little hussy in question was curled up, kitten-like, just inches from him. He couldn't reconcile this woman, who looked so innocent and fragile, with her smattering of honey-kissed freckles and her wispy short curls springing out every which way, with the one who had touched him so suggestively, and in public, no less.

It was time to teach her a lesson. Woman from the future or not, she would know that Patrick Dugan could give as good as he got. Maybe it would make her think twice before she tried the likes of that again. A warning flickered in the back of his mind, but it was firmly ignored.

He scooted over until their faces were a hairsbreadth apart. With the arm farthest from Laurie's relaxed body, he reached behind his head and pulled away the goose-down pillow, dropping his head a few inches. The soft rhythm of her exhalations and the sudden pounding of his heart closed out any other sounds.

Tentatively, he brushed Laurie's mouth lightly with his own. Only a small catch in the cadence of her breathing followed. Dugan moved a bit closer, the weight of his head and shoulders tilting her body more fully toward his. Petal-soft pink tinged her slightly parted lips, and Patrick hesitated at the thought of his scraped mouth hurting her; but he stepped hard on those traitorous feelings. Was he or was he not man enough to take this lady down the notch she so justly deserved?

With a tiny tug on the corner of her pillow, he let gravity bring their lips together. Laurie's mouth warmed and melted under Patrick's searching kiss. Heat roared through his body like a brushfire, consuming his detachment as if it were dry tinder.

When he felt her resistance give way Dugan unwisely rolled her pliant body onto his. An involuntary moan sounded deep in his throat at the press of her breasts against the hard wall of his chest. One needy hand burrowed under the false hair to capture the small bastion of exposed skin at the back of her neck; the other, finding no bustle in the way, spread wide at the base of her spine.

Patrick felt as if the revolutionary new power of electricity was flowing unchecked through his veins. The moist, full, feminine lips moving so responsively above his seemed to be asking for more. Merciful saints! He was starved body and soul for the taste of this woman as he had never been for any other.

Dugan opened his mouth wider, sucking sweet, strawberry-flavored lips inside the harbor of his own; dragging the slightly nubby texture of his tongue across her sensitive flesh.

His motion spun a web around them both, binding their bodies closer and closer, until subconscious barriers could not hold up against the force of his desire.

Laurie opened to him like a flower in the morning sun. The first touch of her tongue nearly brought him straight up off the bed.

Home! It felt like he was home and welcome and wanted. Sweet Jesus, he felt wanted.

Dazedly, Patrick realized the nature of the lesson was changing, and his rational mind tried to warn him to stop before it was too late. *But it was already too late!* Every moment of awareness that he'd fought to deny the last few days flashed before his eyes, sinking him like a gunshot.

Not once in the last fourteen years had Dugan allowed his emotions to blaze beyond control like this. Needing someone, loving them, left the heart wide open to the worst kind of pain and betrayal. His uncle had taught him the truth of that long ago with a cruel laugh and a harsh fist.

In a panic, Dugan reared back, pushing his head as deeply into the mattress as possible. Not for all the fairy gold in Ireland would he let Lauren Ann Sullivan see the effect she had on him. If he weakened, if he cared . . .

Her seeking, glistening mouth nearly pushed him off a treacherous cliff. Feeling raw and vulnerable, Patrick scrambled for something to nullify the tender, soul-binding passion he'd just ignited.

Laurie's delicate blue-veined eyelids fluttered.

The lesson, man! Make her think you were handlin' her body to prove who has the power. She has to see it means nothin' to you.

A muffled voice in the back of his head tried to tell him he was cheapening something rare and fine, but he slammed the mental door before the thoughts could escape.

Disgustedly, he shoved aside a wad of navy skirt and angrily whacked Laurie a good one on the curve of her bottom. Then he rolled her onto her side and onto the mattress again. For a fraction of a second Dugan's hand hovered over the rounded swell he'd just swatted, then dropped to it. Damn! He could feel the heat through her clothes. This should make her madder than a wet hen, and that would keep them both a hell of a lot safer. *Wouldn't Ma be pleased to see the fine man you've become now, Patrick Dugan?*

After allowing himself one last longing glance, Patrick steeled himself and waited for the ax to fall.

It wasn't a dream.

Lauren instinctively hesitated before opening her eyes. The dream that hadn't been a dream was still wrapped around her in the guise of Patrick's strong arms. A swirl of heavy air danced across the moisture his mouth had left on hers, and she savored the sensation. It felt so good to be held as if she was something precious, but as Patrick's heavy hand fell on her buttocks the fragile feelings splintered. Every ounce of feminine intuition she had prompted Lauren to pull in her emotions and batten down the hatches.

Green eyes met hers with disgust. What had felt so beautiful and shared had clearly been a calculated set down. The man had somehow sensed her greatest insecurity and used it: It never seemed to be enough, no matter how much she gave.

Little pinpricks from the scrape of his thick beard began to sting around her mouth and across one cheek. Lauren slowly lifted a hand to the burning and pressed her fingertips to the grazed skin above her top lip.

Because it was her nature to be honest and fair, she had to admit she'd pushed the man too far. But it hurt; it hurt so bad to see his total disinterest in something that had felt so special to her.

"Okay, Dugan, you've made your point." Lauren's normally low voice sounded even deeper. It was all she could do to hold it steady, inflectionless.

"And what is that, me darlin' wife? Isn't this what you were tellin' me you wanted a while ago in front of Molly?" He laced the words with blatant sarcasm to cover his reaction to the kiss.

"Listen, we're not going to get through the next few days if we're looking for ways to trip each other up." She never flinched as he flexed his fingers on her hypersensitive rear end.

Business, Sullivan; get this on a business level fast before you break down and cry.

"Trippin' you is not what I have in mind, lass," he said with a leer.

Lauren tried to sit up, but he shifted his branding hand to her shoulder.

"Just drop this whole sexual intimidation thing, Dugan. You're not really interested in me physically. You wanted to pay me back for touching your . . . ah . . . well, for touching you earlier, and you did. Believe me, I've gotten the message loud and clear."

"Woman, you make me feel like I've tipped one pint of stout too many every time you speak. What must females in your future be like to talk so bold and brassy? Faith, but I'm not sure what you mean half the time."

"So, you believe me," she said flatly.

"It must be so; I can think of no other explanation. Although I'm not leavin' this room 'til you've shown me that bag."

Lauren wrenched out of his hold and twisted to get off the narrow bed. Her lips still tingled from his feigned attention. Ridiculously, it made her feel pitied and pitiful. It wasn't as if any of this whole crazy thing was her real life anyway.

The sight of Laurie's whisker-burned skin actually made Patrick ache. Moment by moment, it was becoming more difficult to defend his heart against her surprising tactics. But by God he would! Any damn way he had to. Now that he'd admitted she was from a hundred years in the future one thing was perfectly clear: Laurie didn't belong here with him, and she wouldn't be staying.

"Wait," he said, resting a hand on her turned shoulder. "We've got to come to an understandin' before Molly and Stephan get here. I can see that the way of it in your time has men and women speak more plainly to each other then I'm used to, so I'm promisin' to try and let you explain before I lose my temper."

Lauren swiveled around at his sincere tone and he sat up, facing her, hands draped between his crossed legs.

"I agree that neither one of us should use . . . sex," he continued firmly to mask his awkward use of the word, "to make things more difficult than they already are. Although we must act the happy couple in front of others, as a husband and wife would in this day, I think we'd best keep the touchin' to a minimum.''

''Agreed, Dugan. I'm sorry I started the whole thing.''

Laurie looked at him with her great indigo eyes mirroring the apology in her voice. Holy St. Joseph, what a cad he was! It was he who'd accused her from the start; and he who'd embarrassed both women with his indelicate remark about *sleeping*; and he who'd taken those lips . . .

He had taken; she had given. Merciful God, was he becoming more like his cursed uncle and his faithless father?

Patrick swung off the end of the bed and abruptly moved to the small dresser. He spoke as he wet his handkerchief with tepid water from the rose-colored pitcher.

''Let me just say that I've not had much reason to trust people in my life. Stephan is the first in a long, long time.''

Stephan he trusts, not you, Sullivan. Lauren let her head fall forward to hide the hurt in her eyes. She was beginning to think that her trip back in time had left her a trifle slow-witted. The shock of the cool, damp cloth against her stinging cheek brought her unguarded face up to Dugan's view.

Her shaky fingers reached up and tangled with his as she tried to maneuver away the soothing material; tried to maneuver herself away from his haunting touch.

Now that Lauren knew the power of Patrick's mouth on hers any contact was just too difficult to endure for long. Besides, she needed to get in a little better defensive position before she came clean about the story Stephan Polaski was going to hear from Molly.

As Laurie scooted out from under his hand, Dugan felt the muscles roped across his back knot and bunch in his effort to keep from reaching for her. The look on her face was wounding, but he'd put it there with his own actions and words. She hadn't expected any kindness from him, and it had surprised her. She who had been infinitely kind to him . . . except, of course, for a few random hissy fits. The corners of his mouth hitched up at the thought of his she-cat.

His! Sweet Jesus, he was diggin' his own grave.

Chapter Eight

"Look, Dugan, whether you trust me or not is your problem. Truthfully, I've given up on that whole issue."

The man's face had that blank expression again, but Lauren continued.

"I have a lot to tell you in a short bit of time, so if you'll sit . . . Sorry, I seem to be saying that too much." She shrugged sheepishly and gestured to the squat bench under the window. "I know the tea is probably cold, but the sugar will give you some energy and the biscuits are really good." Lauren ran her still shaky fingers through her tangled curls and waited for his acquiescence.

Patrick nodded and pulled the bench closer to the food. The bright pillow drew his eye like a bee to a spring flower. A silent curse framed his lips, and he wondered if his friends knew their chance for lasting love was about as strong as this delicate lace. *Right now they seem to have a bit of heaven on earth, even in this hole. . . . Dugan, ya fool, soon you're gonna be too deep in it to climb out.*

Angrily, he reached for the tray. Eating would give him some time to harness his wild reactions and bring his bucking heart into line with his mind.

"In eight days another time door should open and I will leave," Lauren began as he took a bite of biscuit. "But in the mean time I want you to know that I truly like Molly and I won't do anything to harm her, okay?"

Dugan stretched out his denim-covered legs and crossed his stocking feet at the ankles. The sweet flavor of sun-ripened strawberry preserves sent his hungry gaze seeking the place he'd just tasted. Laurie's lips were infinitely sweeter.

"Okay?"

Nod, you bounder! He barely managed the move.

"Once I'm . . . gone," Lauren faltered so slightly she hoped he wouldn't notice, "I think all your problems will be solved." An assertive plan to enlist the aid of the most powerful woman in Chicago, Bertha Palmer, was the one tiny detail Lauren chose to leave out. Given the historical evidence of this outspoken lady's commitment to the Fair, Lauren felt sure she would be very interested in Patrick's information. Surely Mrs. Palmer and her influential millionaire husband could do something about the list. All she had to do was get it. Ha!

The big Irishman, who appeared to be getting larger as he got stronger, sat unresponsive as a marble statue, sipping his tea.

"Of course, if that doesn't work for you . . ." she said, worrying the corner of her lip.

"What about our marriage, Laurie?" Patrick asked, his intensity broadening the Gaelic brogue.

"I . . ." Lauren swallowed the lump her thoughts had formed as she forced herself to speak the words. "I think that since technically . . . ah, in reality . . . Oh, hell" she mumbled, dropping her head in the cradle of her hands. "Shoot. I'm sorry, Dugan, I just can't tiptoe around you, always worrying about what I'm saying." Lauren gave him a defiant glare and moved to the edge of the bed, planting her feet firmly on the plank floor.

"What I'm trying to say is that since I haven't been born yet, as soon as I'm gone I think you can truthfully tell people that I'm dead. So, even though you'll end up a widower, you won't be stuck in a loveless marriage, and the Church shouldn't have a problem with that."

"Yes. That will do." Patrick paused to take a deep breath and relieve the pressure Laurie's words had driven into his gut like a hammer. Why he felt such distress at her solution he would not allow himself to dwell on. The woman didn't belong here and she wasn't staying.

Maybe his mother's faith and love *had* somehow sent an angel to save him. Now it seemed vital to remember that not once, in any of the Bible stories he'd been told, had any angel stayed on the earth.

If he could keep Laurie locked out—just ignore her and for damn sure not kiss her again—then maybe he would be able to get through the next week.

The woman obviously didn't have much experience with men or she would have realized that the kisses they'd shared meant he was about as interested as a man gets. Thank God for both their sakes that she didn't. Guilt and the threat of passion seemed to hold her at bay, so those were the weapons he'd use.

Weapons, aye! This was a battle that he would win by staying as neutral and cool as possible.

"Yes," he repeated, leaning forward to rest his elbows on his thighs. "That shouldn't be too long to manage our wee farce, but you'd best tell me what you and Molly were gabbin' about for so long if we're to keep our stories straight.''

To her horror, Lauren discovered that she was both furious and hurt that Dugan was reacting just as she had hoped he would. If it killed her, she wouldn't wallow in romantic delusions.

Practical, L. A. Sullivan came to the fore, quietly and confidently repeating the outlandish tale she'd spun for Molly. The only indication that Patrick had any opinion at all came from the widening and narrowing of his emerald eyes.

''I know that the detective part was a little much, Dugan, but the rest of it . . . well . . .'' She shrugged. ''For the spur of the moment it was the best way I could think of to explain my lack of daily living skills, my unusual grooming habits, and the fact that I have money. Unfortunately, Molly thinks that she's going to help me become a proper working-class wife now, but I'm sure I can handle it.''

''All right, then,'' he said, standing and placing the empty tray back on the dresser. Dugan deftly raked his tousled hair into order, tucked in his bagging collarless shirt, and picked up his old hard-knock shoes off the floor. ''Molly and Stephan won't be alarmed at my actin' a bit reserved with you because of your money and my problem with McDonald. I'll be gone a lot durin' the next few days and nights, so we won't be performin' all that much anyway.''

Lauren nodded in agreement and bent to struggle into her own tight, black ankle-high shoes.

''You need to take another pill.''

''Fine. I'm wantin' to see what you used on Bates, too.''

A quick swing dumped the well-traveled carpetbag on the bed. Okay, Lauren thought as she rummaged for the Suprax, Patrick clearly wanted nothing to do with her emotionally or physically, but this . . . some of the wonders of the future they could share.

"Is this the only weapon you've got in there?" Patrick asked after she had explained the way to use Mace and its effects.

"Uh huh; here's the medicine."

It was amazing that the small white pill in his hand had so much power. Dugan allowed himself one question. "Is there still sickness where you come from?"

A.I.D.S. popped into her mind, but it wasn't something she wanted to explain to a Victorian male. "Yes, but so many diseases have been conquered, and scientists are discovering new cures all the time." Lauren was glad he'd finally shown some interest. This at least was safe ground on which they could meet.

"I've got some more stuff to show—"

"No."

His sharp command cut her off. Dugan crossed the distance that separated them in two long strides and pulled Laurie off the bed, then dropped her arms like they were live coals.

"I've decided that I'd be better off not knowin' much about you or where you come from." Her eyes, framed by fair, arched brows, were round and bewildered. Dugan heaved a breath and dropped his head back on his neck, resting his hands on his hips.

"The more there is to remember, the more I fill my head with images I'll never see, the harder it will be to return to normal, everyday livin'. A few days of questions and fanciful answers isn't worth it, lass. I'd have the leavin' as unencumbered as possible. Thank you for savin' my life, but I don't want to know a thing about yours."

I don't want to know a thing about yours.

Protectively, Lauren stepped away from his sweeping rejection and bumped the backs of her legs into the Polaskis' beautiful, hopeful, loving bed. It was absolutely revolting how schlocky and sentimental she was becoming. Actually, Patrick hadn't been mean or unkind, just freezingly honest. And she should be used to that. Not even knowledge of the mystical future was alluring enough if it came with her as part of the package.

Smile and nod, dammit!

Patrick winced as a flicker of surprised hurt flared for a moment in the dark pools of Laurie's eyes. With painful dignity she closed away the little mysteries she'd been so eager to display. This is how it had to be!

"I trust you'll not burden Molly and Stephan, either." He forced a hard edge to his voice that hurt them both.

"Dugan, my friend," Lauren's righteous frustration was simmering dangerously close to the boil, "don't ever use the word *trust* like that to me again. You don't mean it, and it's the worst kind of insult you could give me. Say *command* or *demand* or whatever! And don't worry; I won't contaminate your friends with wild tales of the future that could drive them over the brink of sanity."

Try to throttle down, Sullivan, or he's going to guess you're a touch upset about this.

What was that old commercial—never let them see you sweat—or cry, a little voice of self-pity added.

"There is one thing, however, that I don't intend to keep hidden from the Polaskis, and I guess you should know it up front." Lauren's low-pitched voice was smooth and businesslike.

Patrick fisted his hands on his hips. He couldn't think of one saint who'd have qualified if they'd been dealin' with the likes of Laurie Ann Dugan. Hell! *Sullivan.*

"You'll be tellin' me right now, colleen, not up in front of anybody else."

It was profoundly immature of her to gloat over the man's misunderstanding, but, heck, she was grabbing

159

at straws. If she didn't focus on the laugh here, she just might humiliate herself beyond belief.

"It's my hair, Dugan." She lifted a hand to the scraggly mass. "At least at night, I've got to take this thing off. Tell them whatever you want to."

From the other room a loud *thunk* indicated that one of the Polaskis had returned home. For a long moment Lauren hesitated, hoping in vain for something she couldn't define. Not a trace of the tender passion she'd felt in Patrick's arms showed in the hard face before her. Carefully, she edged past him and picked up the tray on the dresser. With every tick of the clock, time was crawling right on by. At this rate her stay in 1895 would seem like a mere eternal sentence in purgatory.

"Well, husband," Lauren said flippantly, opening the door and turning her head toward him, "let's get this show on the road."

"Wait!"

But it was too late.

Holy Mary, he hoped he could keep the lies and the truth straight. Using Laurie was the truth and lovin' Laurie was the lie . . . or was it the other way around?

Don't answer that, Dugan!

Chapter Nine

Patrick was freezing her out!

In fact, he hadn't even smiled at her since that first night when they'd been preparing to sleep on the pallet Molly had made for them in a corner of the combination kitchen-sitting room. When she had handed Lauren a chipped chamberpot Patrick's grin had been open, familiar. For just a moment their eyes had met, and they had shared something warm and lighthearted; then he had turned his back on her.

The last time he had touched her had been to lead her down to the row of unkempt, tin-roofed latrines called "school sinks." With a sharp warning to latch the door, he had gone, not to return to the Polaskis' until she was fast asleep, as he had done each succeeding night.

The only thing Lauren could think was that their kiss had disgusted him to the point that he could barely keep up his end of the performance. Being gone was easier than being with her. And thank God he was acting this way. Otherwise . . . otherwise Lauren was horrifyingly afraid that she would do something to get him to kiss her again, even though she knew he'd felt worse than nothing afterward. Dugan's rejection would be a hundred times more devastating than Jeff's, and that scared her to death.

This very morning, when even Stephan Polaski had sent her a sympathetic look, Lauren had known that the next five days couldn't pass quickly enough. Molly's broad-faced, broad-shouldered, flaxen-haired giant of a husband hadn't spoken more than a handful of words to her since they'd been introduced three evenings earlier. However, at six A.M., when he and Patrick had finished breakfast and prepared to leave to scout out the Fair and McDonald's movements, his hesitant, puzzled smile had communicated directly to her heart.

Each of the last three mornings had been exactly the same, and Patrick's behavior had become more and more noticeable. Lauren got up the minute she heard Molly stirring in the bedroom. She washed quickly at the dry sink, tacked on her hair, put on some mascara and a touch of pink lip gloss. Not even to fit the social mores of the time would she appear in her lashless state. Fortunately, the Polaskis didn't seem to be offended by it. After that she quietly went downstairs to the row of weathered outhouses at the back of the building's small courtyard.

By the time she returned Molly was starting breakfast. The two women then worked companionably, cooking what had proved to be the daily fare: mush with just a touch of cream and sugar and a huge pile of hot biscuits. Lauren had already memorized Molly's pinch and palmful recipe.

After each of the first two breakfasts the Polaskis had stepped into their room for just a moment before the men had left, and Lauren was pretty sure they weren't in there sorting dirty clothes. But yesterday they had made their farewell quite public. Frankly, Lauren couldn't tell if it was because the young couple felt so comfortable with her and Dugan or if Stephan was trying to give his dim-witted Irish friend a lesson in husbandly affection.

The smile he'd given her as Patrick stood stiffly at the door and uttered his morning endearment, "Have a good day, wife," was reflected in Molly's face, too. Suddenly her eyes went round and her mouth flattened into a look Lauren had come to know meant her beautiful, tender-hearted friend was about to do some fast maneuvering.

"Wait just a minute, now, Mr. Patrick Dugan," Molly said sweetly, sauntering toward him with one arm still wrapped around her husband's waist. "Stephan has told me that nothing unusual has happened at the Fair these past few days . . ."

Lauren's heart lurched in her chest. Patrick had told her nothing.

". . . so", Molly continued, "you'd best be here with Stephan this evening, because me and Laurie have somethin' special planned."

She turned to Lauren who sat pinned like a collector's butterfly to the kitchen chair, and winked.

Lauren didn't have a clue as to what Molly meant, but she was tired of being complacent. Oh, she would still be careful, but there were only five days of her adventure left, and she had yet to experience it to the fullest.

She watched Patrick's eyes narrow and his finely shaped lips flatten into a straight line. Ever since she'd seen that mouth clearly revealed sans whiskers she'd had a heck of a time keeping her eyes off it. With a clean-shaven face his kisses would be even bet . . .

Lauren winked back at Molly. *Stick that in your pipe and smoke it Dugan!*

The big surprise was turning into a cooking marathon. Molly had left her two hours earlier with detailed instructions on how to make an authentic, layered Irish Mutton stew. Peeling and chopping in the sticky heat wasn't very pleasant. Lauren wished she had even a tiny electric fan, and her spoiled 1995 body wasn't handling the humidity very well. No wonder so many folks of the day loved to stroll near Lake Michigan. No doubt it was one of the reasons the World's Fair was so popular, sprawled as it was along the shore.

Molly told her that on really bad nights people went right up on top of the tenement roofs to sleep. Unfortunately, too often, folks rolled off and were killed.

A sharp slam made Lauren drop a knife and a potato from her hands. One look at Molly and she knew something was terribly wrong.

"Molly, are you all right?" Lauren asked as she dried her hands on her apron and quickly poured a cup of water for her friend, whose face was white. Molly's dark hair, usually poofed so gracefully on top of her head, was mussed and dangling.

"Sweetie?" She slipped her arm around the trembling body and led Molly to one of the slat-back chairs.

After a long gulp of water Molly focused her luminous sky-blue eyes on Lauren.

"She didn't care, Laurie." The sob hovered in the small room, filling every corner with abject sorrow.

"Who, Molly? What happened?" Instinctively, Lauren clasped her grieving friend's hands, giving her a caring lifeline to hold on to.

"Me ma." The tears began to fall.

"Oh, Molly, I thought you weren't going to try again for a while."

"But . . . I thought that this . . . time . . ." She tried to catch her breath. "Oh, Laurie, she said she never wanted to see me again or my . . . my . . . baby!"

Molly rested her head on the table and cried as if her heart was broken.

It had taken almost an hour to get Molly calmed down and asleep. Lauren had finished the stew and made some soda bread while waiting impatiently for Stephan Polaski to get home. She had to talk to him before Molly woke up. If only Patrick were here, she thought, as she absently arranged a blue gingham napkin in the middle of the table and placed a blue enamel water pitcher in the center.

"Molly, darlin', I'm home."

Lauren jumped and whirled at the booming greeting.

"Good evening, Laurie," Stephan said as he hung his cap on a peg by the door, his eyes sweeping the room.

Boy, was this going to be a doozy of a first one-on-one conversation. Lauren pulled out a chair and prayed the gentle Pole would be able to give his little wife what she needed. The next few minutes weren't going to be easy for either of them.

". . . so you see, Stephan, I think Molly was hoping that her wonderful news would soften her parents' hearts, and when her mother reacted so horribly, well, she was pretty strung . . . umm, upset." Lauren quickly fixed her slip, but the stocky young man in front of her hadn't noticed. Actually, he hadn't seemed to register a thing she'd said.

"Stephan?" She reached for his thick, bare forearms and shook him hard. Molly absolutely could not take another rejection. The man had to gut it up and come through.

"A baby? A baby?" His soft words filled the air with

wonder, leaving no room for sadness.

"My darlin' is . . ." Stephan's deep voice broke, but a smile spread across his face.

"Oh, Stephan, I'm so glad you're happy. Molly needs you so much."

"I'm much more than happy, Laurie," he whooped, scraping back his chair from the table and pulling her into his arms. "How can I ever thank ya enough for bein' here for Molly?" He whirled her around until they were both laughing.

"What the bloody hell is goin' on?"

Patrick Dugan stood braced in the doorway, seething with anger. His hard eyes fixed accusingly on Lauren.

"Patrick!" Stephan shouted, dropping his hold on Laurie to extend an open palm. "Laurie has given me near the finest news a man can hear."

"And you believed her?"

Stephan Polaski came to a dead stop and watched as the color and life drained from Lauren's face.

"Dugan, ya great fool, what the hell—" Stephan growled, curling his open hand into a fist.

"No! No, Stephan, it's all right," Lauren insisted, touching his shoulder briefly from behind, forcing the hurt out of her eyes. This was no time for more stress. She was leaving in just five more days, and she didn't want to come between these two friends.

"I'll check on Molly." She smiled falsely and escaped in a swish of green-and-white-striped taffeta.

"Are you crazy?"

Stephan's quiet roar finally seemed to penetrate Patrick's jealous haze.

"Sit your sorry butt in this chair, Patrick Dugan, before I knock you down to do it!"

Patrick rubbed a hand down his face, wishing he could wipe out the last few minutes as easily. He sank bonelessly into a chair, thunked his elbows on the table, and speared the hair on either side of his head with trembling fingers.

"Of all the cockeyed, addlepated, crack-brained . . ."

"You're right, Stephan. I don't know what came over me," Dugan mumbled. But heaven and all the saints help him, he was afraid he did!

"Well, I do, friend."

Patrick lifted his weary gaze at Stephan's confident claim.

"You found your woman in the arms of another man and saw red," the big Pole stated with absolute certainty and a satisfied smirk.

Bloody hell! It showed! Dugan's head fell like a lead weight into its previous position as he tried to deny the truth of his friend's words. For the last few hellacious days he had forced himself to stay away from Laurie; to forget the kiss that still smoldered in his memory; to find an answer to his problems before McDonald found him. And all his efforts had burst into flame as easily as a lucifer striking sandpaper. God, he was tired!

"Honestly, Patrick, even though you've dug yourself quite a hole, I'm mighty glad to see you've got some strong feelin's for your wife. Because . . ." Stephan paused and flattened his huge hands against the kitchen table, ". . . Nancy Brown was askin' for you today at the Ferris wheel."

Men normally didn't have these kinds of conversations, and Stephan was reluctant to continue, but too much was at stake here. It was only a matter of time before someone in McDonald's pay picked up Dugan's trail, and Stephan felt a prickle of fear, mostly for his Molly and strange little Laurie.

Nevertheless, he'd not turn his back on the man who'd gotten him out of the detestable slaughterhouses at the stockyards and into his present job on the maintenance team of the Ferris wheel. That alone was the reason he and Molly had been able to marry, even without her parents' approval.

Stephan shifted uncomfortably and continued. "Now mind you, I'm not tryin' to tell you what to do." One square hand rubbed absently at the back of his neck. "Hell, I didn't even know you had *any* women in your life, and suddenly you've a wife and a very interested young woman buzzing like starving bees around the same flower."

"What did she want?" Patrick leaned back and folded his arms across his chest. The soft cotton sleeves of his shirt were rolled up to his elbows, like Stephan's. With a quick twist he unbuttoned a portion of his snug collarless shirt, trying to cool his body and his mind. If what Laurie had told him about Nancy's journal was true, Harry Brown might be behind her questions.

"According to Hank, she wanted you! Anybody that might know where you were was to deliver the message that she *needed* you urgently!" Stephan pushed back his chair, reached for the pot of tea on the iron stove, and poured two cups. "I know I may be oversteppin' the bounds of friendship, Patrick, but with your wife becomin' overnight like my Molly's long-lost sister . . . I . . . well—"

"Just say it out, man." Dugan didn't know whether to be amused or irritated at his friend's discomfort.

"Well, I understand that you and Laurie have had a time of it with her money and all, but blast it, Dugan, the woman is your wife and she's here, now, tryin' to learn to please you. I hate to admit it, but I've been watchin' the two of you, and you never even touch her, let alone speak a sweet word or two. So, if there's somethin' between you and this Miss Brown, aside from it bein' hellfire dangerous, it plain isn't fair to Laurie."

Patrick didn't think he'd ever heard Stephan Polaski

say so much in one breath before. It didn't feel right, having another man defend his wife. Holy Mary! He couldn't stop thinkin' of her as *his,* no matter how hard he tried to stay away. Well, he'd be damned if he'd let Stephan think she had him hog-tied.

"Believe me, Stephan, Laurie Ann is more than enough trouble for me to handle, but pretty little Nancy Brown definitely has somethin' I want."

A sharp gasp from behind him sent his heart crashing to the floor.

"You're in for it now, Irish!" Stephan mumbled out of the side of his mouth as he rose from the table to greet his speechless wife, standing in the bedroom doorway.

Lauren recovered first; maybe because she'd already been dealt such a blow that she was still partially numb. Come hell or high water or a broken, bleeding heart, nothing was going to ruin the evening she had planned for Molly. She quickly turned the shocked girl and gently pushed her back inside the bedroom.

"Stephan, if you'll step in here for just a bit, I'll finish getting supper on the table." Lauren felt as if her pleasant expression had been put on with a trowel, and that any sudden move would cause it to crack and fall apart like brittle plaster. Not for all the shamrocks in Ireland would she let Patrick Dugan think he'd affected her at all.

If she were a *real* wife, it would hurt terribly, but both she and Patrick knew it wasn't so. By acting as if nothing had happened she would be able to sweep this whole awkward mess under the proverbial rug.

"Well, husband, you're going to be so glad you've made it home early today." She bustled right past him to the dry sink.

A joyous shout shook the paper-thin walls. Lauren's hands clenched around the bread board and a sharp, swift dart of pain shot through her chest. Soft laughter followed by a deafening silence made her feel like a balloon being filled with too much air; the pressure was unbearable. How could someone be so happy and so devastated at the same time?

Please, God, let them come out before I have to turn around.

"Patrick!" Stephan yelled, swinging open the door and stepping through, holding a blushing, radiant Molly in his arms. "We're havin' a baby!"

Lauren's prayer was answered, and the ecstatic couple's conversation filled the deadly quiet.

Maybe the Polaskis were fooled, Patrick thought as he sat watching Laurie springing up and down like a jack-in-the-box, fetching and serving, but he wasn't. She hadn't looked him in the eye or spoken directly to him in hours. Come to think of it, Molly hadn't been too friendly either.

When the meal was finished Laurie forced the expectant mother to sit and rest, then worked tirelessly to put the kitchen to rights. Patrick couldn't stop the misplaced pride he felt at her accomplishments over the last few days. Whether he'd seen Laurie doing things himself or not, Molly had pointed out each and every one.

All she'd done since he'd discovered her, wet and nearly naked, was help, and all he'd done was hurt her.

Molly worked with her for a moment, demonstrating a nuance in regulating the heat in the wood-burning stove, and he thought he heard Laurie mutter something wistful about a Mike Rowave. A flush of hot anger rippled deep in his belly. Damn, it was true. Just hearing the name of another man on her lips was twisting his gut. Bloody hell; it was getting worse. Five days . . . five days . . . He repeated it in his mind like a litany.

"I'm sorry, Laurie and Patrick, but I'm just so tired, I think we'll be turnin' in early tonight." Molly stood up, and Stephan followed. "I was hopin' my surprise was goin' to involve more folks." Her bright eyes dimmed.

"Now, don't you worry, sweetie. We're happy enough for a whole building full of people." Even as Lauren was offering her support, she had a great idea. There was something real and tangible she could do for Molly before she left.

For the first time that night she smiled with genuine warmth and waited for Dugan to add his best wishes. The man was clearly as dumb as a stump when it came to sensitivity. Geez! Seeing it from this end, most men in the 1990s had really come a long way.

She knew people were generally more prudish about discussing pregnancy in the nineteenth century, but Stephan had been speaking so openly that Lauren had just now realized that Patrick hadn't said a word. Nothing. She kicked him once under the table.

"Congratulations."

The word barely reached the happy young couple before the unfinished bedroom door closed.

"Well, don't get carried away." She couldn't help it; the words just popped out.

Lauren blew out the kerosene lamp, plunging the small living area into semidarkness. Soft light from other buildings and apartments filtered in through the two tiny front windows. She hurried to their pallet in the far corner, where her trusty bag waited, and pulled out a tentlike nightgown.

She was getting really good at shucking her 1890 trappings undercover. The sense of freedom she felt each night when all the cloth layers and phony hair came off could only be topped by an all-over, water-up-to-the-neck bath. But, according to Molly, that was impractical more than once a week.

When her green-and-white dress hung neatly from the peg next to the navy—was she ever getting tired of those two outfits—Lauren ran her fingers repeatedly through her short, flattened hair, releasing the natural curl. The Polaskis had been told that a doctor had recommended her hair be cut for health reasons, and Molly had been very sympathetic about Lauren's loss.

A quiet moan slipped past her unwilling lips as she lifted her linked hands high above her head in a bone-cracking stretch and then dropped them to press them to the small of her back.

Patrick hadn't been able to take his eyes off her.

If he had to witness this little routine once more before she was safely gone, he'd never be able to control himself.

"I need to leave for a few hours," he blurted breathlessly into the semidarkness.

"Fine, Dugan." Lauren sighed, moving out of the corner toward him. The door opened before she stopped speaking. "Run; it would probably be the best for both of us."

"What are you accusin' me of?" The soft snap of wood on wood punctuated his question.

"Now don't get your male pride all bent out of shape," Lauren said, modestly arranging her nightgown around her legs as she sat at the table. "We all have fears, Dugan, and I just happen to agree with the way yours is manifesting itself."

"Woman, I promised some days ago that I would try to allow for your strange ideas and words before takin' offense, but I'm thinkin' you'd best explain yourself quickly."

As Patrick sidled into the chair across from her, Lauren wondered if he realized she had stopped him cold. There was no time for gloating, however. Given his penchant for disappearing, this might be her last real private time in which to speak with him.

"I think . . ." She hesitated for just a second, knowing her next words could leave her wide open to his ridicule. What the heck; as Aunt Lucy used to say, in for a penny, in for a pound. The longer she was here in 1895, the easier it was to simply go for it.

"I think you're afraid to be around me since that kiss. You're always leaving, and now with what we overheard about you and Nancy Brown . . . well, it really upset Molly. So please," she leaned forward a bit, "if you're worried that I may have read too much into our . . . encounter, or that I'll spill some deep, dark future secret before you can shut me up, believe me, I haven't and I won't."

Patrick sat back in his chair and desperately searched for the right response. The pale ribbons of light that streamed in through the windows seemed to add a mystical glow to the darkened room, making him think of fairy rings and magic. But they had no time for such fancy. Laurie wasn't playing coy games. He knew she was making a tremendous effort to speak honestly to him instead of continuing the acting they'd done in front of the Polaskis.

What would she do if she knew why he was really leaving? How would she react right now if he told her that he had his hands clenched into fists to keep them from unwrapping that innocent-looking nightdress? He couldn't stay much longer. Soft, short, honey-gold curls framed her intent little face like a halo, and once again Patrick caught himself thinking of her as an angel. His angel. Hell!

"That kiss could hardly amount to much in the future you come from, Laurie," he said, purposely testing his will by stretching his cramped fingers out flat on the table. "You flatter yourself a bit, lass, to think that's been weighin' on my mind with all else that's bubblin' in my pot.''

Thank heavens it's dark, Lauren thought. Her hands, resting lightly across from Dugan's, crept together, as if seeking something to hold on to. She had been right! Even though she had experienced such warm and wonderful feelings, Patrick hadn't felt the same. Jeff had told the truth; she just didn't have it in her to ignite a man's desire.

''Well, t-that's good to hear, Dugan,'' Lauren managed to get out, hoping that the broad-shouldered Irishman in front of her was buying it. What would it have been like if he had felt what she had felt? To her surprise, Lauren realized that she would have been very tempted to forget everything else but this man.

''Really good to hear,'' she forced herself to continue, ''because you're going to have to put in a few more appearances for Molly's sake.''

The vertical line that formed between his brows arrowed toward the middle part in his thick auburn hair. Lauren glanced down at her hands and consciously relaxed them.

''I'm worried about Molly and the baby, Dugan, and I need you to help me.'' The events that had occurred earlier in the day were succinctly stated. ''Because I only have a few more days here it's vital that she knows you're on her side, too.'' Lauren hesitantly reached out toward one of Patrick's large hands that lay splayed against the table. ''Don't you think we could work together to help Stephan and Molly?'' For only a moment two of her fingers curled around his thumb.

''You truly care about the Polaskis.'' His words were a statement, not a question.

''I realize that you have reason to think I'm cold. But, yes,'' Lauren swallowed with difficulty and drew back her unwanted touch, ''I truly care for them.''

Laurie Ann had to be as blind as a newborn kitten. Just sittin' across from her made his blood boil. And good God, after his ranting at Stephan, he knew that what he was feeling was dangerously close to burning him alive. No matter what he'd thrown at her, no matter what she'd come up against since landing back in his time, the woman didn't stop caring. She warmed up a room like few people he'd ever known. Patrick lifted the hand that sizzled from the press of her soft skin and tucked it under his arm.

The man was obviously put off by her touch. Why couldn't she remember that? Lauren squared her shoulders, determined to salvage her pride.

"First, is it true that McDonald and his men haven't been spotted anywhere?"

"Yes, as far as Stephan and I can tell."

"Have you found anyone to help with your list yet?"

"No."

"Could you hang around here a little more for the next three days?"

"I'm assumin' that hangin' has nothin' to do with a noose."

Unexpectedly, awkwardly, they both smiled.

"Why, Patrick Dugan, I believe you just made a joke."

Her dark eyes gleamed in the moonlight. *Too close, Dugan.*

"Sure'n I don't want anythin' to happen to Molly and her b-baby." He crossed his arms over his chest and scraped his chair back from the table, away from Laurie. "But it's a shame to be bringin' another innocent into this hard life."

"That's exactly the kind of thing Molly doesn't need to hear!"

"Don't fash yourself lass, I'll not be sayin' it to her. But look around you," Patrick ordered, throwing out his arm. "What will a child find here?"

"Love, Mr. Dugan," Lauren whispered fiercely, getting to her feet. "That old argument is still being used a hundred years from now. And, yes, this world isn't the most wonderful place for every child. Love isn't always a birthright, though God knows I wish it were." She wrapped her arms tight around her, trying to hold her walls in place.

"You've the truth of it there, colleen," he said, pushing to his feet. "I for one never want a child because of it!"

Lauren stared through the shifting shadows at the strong back that had just been turn to her. His bleak tone had revealed more than his cryptic words.

"But, Patrick, for those that are born to love it's worth it. Worth the risk. I . . . I lost my parents when I was very young, and you're right; for a while it hurt so bad that I couldn't remember anything else. But lately I'm realizing how much that love meant. How much it still means."

Slowly Patrick wheeled about to face her, his expression hard as stone in a wide shaft of moonlight.

"And what about those who aren't fortunate enough to be born to love, Lauren? Those children who find that by their very bein' their mother's life is torn apart! What perfect words would you offer to a child who'd been forced to beg on his hands and knees for his birthright from an uncle who professed to care for him? A child who discovered in the cruelest of ways that his own father had heartlessly duped a trusting girl and left her in humiliation? A lad who had felt the eyes of a whole village pity his tears and stupidity when his mother was renounced as a whore and a liar?"

Lauren clenched her hands into fists until her nails left prints in her palms and forced her yearning arms against her sides. So this was the pain and betrayal that defined the word *love* to Patrick Dugan. His angry words hung in the air between them.

"Did you think it was your fault, too, Patrick?" He cocked his head a bit, as if he didn't understand. "When my parents died and left me I wondered if I'd done something to make them stop loving me. Everyone I've really cared about has left me, so maybe I know a little bit of how you're feeling. It's hard to find lasting love, isn't it?"

Patrick stepped back as if she'd struck him. How could she know he'd carried such guilt? This strange, strong woman seemed to be able to look straight into his heart, and the comfort of her understanding terrified him. He would not, could not, let her touch him this way.

"Lasting love and leprechauns are both childish fairy tales I left behind in Ireland," he growled.

"Your mother's love wasn't a fairy tale, Patrick." Lauren saw him flinch at her words, but she had to go on. "Have you ever thought that having you, loving you, was worth it to her?"

Dugan's body snapped to attention, and Lauren could almost feel his tension. She got to her feet and took a hesitant step closer. "She could have left you. She could have gone on with her life, but she didn't, did she?" Lauren felt her tears pooling and gathering, making a soggy web of her lashes. "I bet it was just like my parents. Only death had the power to make them leave us, Patrick."

The truth of her words began to flow over him. Yes, it was true; his mother *had* loved him. But the blood of faithless men ran through his veins. What did he know about the gut-deep commitment he saw between Stephan and Molly? He knew nothing about loving that way.

"It's been too long for me, lass, and I've not had the

most reliable teachers on the subject. My life is best left the way it is, so don't be wastin' your tears on the likes o' me. It's the Polaskis we're talkin' about.'' Laurie's quiet acknowledgment of his pain forced him to deliver his words with the hard-edged off-handedness that he hoped would protect him and keep her at a distance.

But Lauren couldn't let him retreat yet.

"I won't tell you it's not harder, a lot harder.'' Her bare feet didn't make a sound as she moved across the smooth wood floor to the spot where Patrick stood. He *needed* so much. "But I truly believe loving is a learned thing.'' Lauren reached out, as if to touch his arm, and then pulled back. "And I think under the right circumstances it can be learned and received at any age.''

She watched his hands curl into tight fists at his sides. It seemed to her that he was fighting some deep inner battle.

"What would you have me do?''

The man looked braced for a physical blow. His eyes wouldn't settle on her face, and Lauren knew he was regretting the emotions he had revealed to her. Never in her life had she wanted to hold someone so badly. Just hold him. But he couldn't handle that now. Do-not-touch signs all but appeared before her eyes when she looked at him, so she would have to ease him with her words.

"Just be a bit more friendly, okay? So poor Molly isn't worried about you running off with Nancy Brown on top of all her other problems. She needs to see you as a good guy, you know, a White Hat.'' Her focus on the Polaskis eased the concentrated intimacy vibrating in the dark room.

"I'm supposin' that a bad *guy* would be sportin' a black one.''

"You're fast, Dugan,'' Lauren sighed with a smile. "You'd adjust fine in the future.'' The words spilled out before she could call them back.

"I've no reason to go there, lass."

"Of course not; your friends and Nan . . . well, your life and your friends are here." This time Lauren was the one who turned and hid, moving to their folded palette, readying it for bed.

"What will I tell her when you've gone, Laurie?"

For a moment her hands faltered as she smoothed the coarse blanket. Still not facing him, she answered, "I've planned to leave Molly a letter and tell her that I just can't survive without using my money. She'll see that I've left you and then, in a few months, you'll have to leave town and mail another letter. Coming as it will from some distance, I hope she'll believe I caught some terrible illness in my travels and died."

Lauren waited, nearly motionless, for Dugan's response. She heard nothing.

"I . . . I know this is a big favor to ask, Patrick, but if you could keep that second letter until after the baby is born, I think it would be best for Molly. If you're discreet, it needn't hold up your love life too much."

The weight of Patrick's heavy hand on Lauren's shoulder nearly stopped her heart. She froze like a child playing statue. Ever so slowly, both on their knees, he pulled her around to face him.

"Why, Laurie, lass?" His voice rumbled low and gruff. "Why would you leave lettin' Molly think the less of you?"

"You're the one staying, Patrick. She needs you to be there for her and Stephan and the baby. I'm . . ." Lauren tried to look away from his piercing gaze but couldn't. "I'm just passing through."

And what kind of hole would her passing leave in all their lives? Bloody hell! He couldn't stop thinkin' these morose thoughts. Not with those sweet lips so close; not for this woman who cared so much about an unborn child. She'd love a baby so much. What a lucky wee one he or she would be.

Before Patrick could stop himself he looked down at the soft rounding of her stomach. With undefined emotions blazing in his eyes he sought hers again.

"We're both afraid, aren't we, Laurie girl?"

"Y-yes, Patrick, we are."

His fingers began to pull her closer, then abruptly let her go.

"Then, yes, I'll help with Molly till you're gone." Dugan got to his feet and slowly moved toward the door.

"I've got to leave now, lass."

"It's all right. I understand."

"I'll wait for the baby."

"Thank you for your sacrifice."

" 'Tis no sacrifice a'tall, Laurie," he returned with a strong Irish burr. "I'm not a man made for a life like Stephan's, nor am I one to pay for a lady's favors, if you take my meaning. Right now the only 'hold up' I'm worryin' over is this wait for McDonald's next move."

With a sharp snap of the door he was gone.

Lauren lay down on the flat layer of bedding and tuned out the myriad noises and smells filtering through the thin walls. Now she knew why she had come; why cosmic forces had drawn her to this time and this man. Aunt Lucy must indeed be watching out for her, or else have a powerful "in" with some post-life bigwig. Until meeting Patrick and the Polaskis she'd all but erased the good, loving memories she'd had in her life. The hurtful ones, like Jeff, had taken far too big a chunk of her storage banks.

Leave it to feisty little Lucy to kill two birds with one stone. Lauren already knew she would never be the same once she returned to her own time. She had let too much living and loving roll right on by, but it wasn't too late to change. This was the truth she could leave with Patrick Dugan. Understanding his code of honor, she knew he would do all he could for Molly and Stephan. The longer he saw what they shared, the more he might come to believe he could have it too; deserved it too.

And the baby would do the trick.

If she could just get him to hold the Polaski's baby . . . Suddenly Lauren's vision blurred and her chest felt tight.

Molly would have to see to it. She'd be gone.

Michael Cassius McDonald sat in a dark corner of his sumptuous saloon, waiting for Harry Brown. The comforting feeling of power and accomplishment settled over him like the heavy layer of smoke hanging in the air. Faux gold gilding and red-embossed wallpaper gave the room a rich glow in the gaslight. It was his. The whole damn building was his, and no two-bit mick was going to chip away at the empire he had worked so hard to build.

The cool, lead-crystal shot glass in his hands soothed his nerves, but the bite of aged Scotch burning a path to his churning stomach soothed them even more. The plan he had helped put together for controlling crime at the Fair had been carefully laid out. No one group, be it thieves or confidence men, was to go out of the approved boundaries.

Even good old Mayor Harrison had agreed that they had to keep out-of-towners from taking over. The Fair managers themselves had negotiated a deal to ensure that no pickpockets would hit a mark at the entrance gates. After all, if patrons had no money to spend, everyone lost.

He had worked with Eddie Jackson, dean of the Chicago pickpockets, and Tom O'Brien, king of the bunko men, to present a proposal that had garnered the support of politicians and police alike. And dammit, it had all been rolling right along until that bastard Dugan had begun stickin' his nose into places it didn't belong.

A round of loud laughter erupted from the bar, and Mike sank back even farther into the tufted leather booth. A lazy curl of smoke trailed up from his cigar, and he felt his patience coming to an end. The profits so far had been excellent. Not only did he get his cut from his own people, but he charged a very nice fee for coordinating the combined collection and payoffs to the men on the supposed right side of the law: those politicians, police, and judges who kept the workers in the field, so to speak.

Truthfully, there weren't many men left in the state who had even a chance of stopping him. Oh, one or two of Chicago's wealthy do-gooders might be able to get the govenor involved. But, hell, what were the odds that a dirty, broken immigrant could get anyone with enough power to listen to him? Mike pressed his mouth into a thin smile. No, in this case, the house would most definitely win.

McDonald rested his elbows on the linen-covered table and steepled his fingers. The real damage Dugan's cursed list could do lay elsewhere. Too many of the players in the game of crime in Chicago wouldn't hesitate to kill him if they had proof of his plan to take even more control and money for himself. Damn! Other lesser bosses might even band together to get him. Enough jackals hunting in a pack could bring down an animal many times their size.

Double-crossing professional double-crossers could be fatal.

At last! Harry Brown's square body lumbered out of the shadows. If the man didn't have something to go on tonight, the screws would have to be put to the girl, post haste. And if Harry didn't have the guts to make his sister talk . . . well, McDonald would have to see to it himself.

Chapter Ten

"Hush, ladies! She's on the stairs! All right, get ready. . . . "

"Surprise!"

Molly Polaski was flabbergasted. Stephan had taken a rare Saturday off, and they had spent half the day at the Fair. She had felt so guilty leaving Laurie behind, but they all agreed she couldn't afford to be seen there. And now this! Her sweet, strange friend had made her a party.

"Thank you, Stephan," Lauren called, rushing to the door. "You timed it perfectly." She linked her arm through Molly's limp one. "Would you like to stay?" she whispered to the gentle blond giant. Stephan blinked once at the room packed full of chattering femininity and began to back away.

"No, Laurie, I'm meetin' Patrick." He gave his glowing wife a swift kiss on the cheek and beat a hasty retreat.

The baby shower was a booming success.

It had taken two days of sneaky trips to invite the women Stephan had listed, but they had all been happy to accept. Lauren suspected they'd also been quite curious. Molly had introduced her to a number of her friends in passing on the street, but no one had come for a visit since she and Dugan had arrived.

Patrick had even gone begrudgingly to the corner store and used her money. Lauren suspected he'd agreed with her plans so easily because they were both using the party as a safety zone. Neither one wanted to look too closely at the emotional connection they had discovered. Any more personal revelations would only make things tense again.

"This is my gift to Molly and the baby, Dugan," she'd told him yesterday morning on the dirty front stoop. "Please just get what I've written down."

"But, merciful saints, lass, what could you be needin' with chocolate bars and so much pink and blue ribbon?"

Well, he'd see soon enough, Lauren thought, watching Molly circle the small room that a week ago she would have described as poor and crude. Oh, it was still poorly built. Only just now, with a new blue cloth spread on the table and a rainbow of fresh flowers gracing the steelware pitcher and yards of pink and blue ribbon looped across the ceiling . . . it looked fantastic. Full of every good thing.

Yes, Lauren was used to more creature comforts than these women could possibly imagine. But none of those things made friendships any richer, or love any dearer.

"Ladies, we have a game to play now."

Some of the gifts she'd gotten for the baby were arranged on a tray, then covered. While Molly counted to thirty, they each looked, and then the one who remembered the most items won. Lauren was going to have them write their list, but a discreet shake of Molly's head spoke volumes to her in seconds. Reading and writing! She should have known.

Not for the world would she have wanted to embarrass any of these fine women. If only they could realize that they all had valuable things to teach each other. Every skill was important.

Lauren presented the winner, Greta Olsen, with a tissue-wrapped gift. Ten pair of eyes waited expectantly. A few lengths of yellow ribbon spilled across her lap, along with a scented bar of soap. Enthusiastic clapping filled the warm afternoon air.

"Can we give Molly our gifts now, Laurie?" Greta asked.

"Oh, but I told you all, you weren't to . . ." Lauren's navy skirt stirred up a small breeze as she spun around. Little by little, Molly's lap filled with small treasures, some wrapped in newspaper, some in cloth, some not at all.

Lauren stepped back out of the tightening circle of smiling faces and thought she had never really seen such giving before. That old biblical story about the widow's mite had popped into her head. Which, indeed, was the greater gift? Suddenly she wanted to give that way, too. Deeply and more meaningfully than she had ever done. What would make a difference? What would last? Hope!

"Why do you call this a baby *shower,* Mrs. Dugan?" an older woman asked as Lauren served her big surprise.

"Why . . ." The name was disorienting for a second, and she floundered for an answer. *Great, Sullivan! When will you learn to think before you speak.* "It's . . . because we're showering Molly with good wishes." Lauren sighed as the woman's nod quickly turned into a smile when the lady took a bite of the dessert.

"Saints above, Laurie, what is this? And how did ya make it?" Molly spoke eagerly for all of them.

Lauren hoped some horrible long-term effect wasn't going to blight America for introducing the chocolate chip cookie to this small group of immigrants. But it was Aunt Lucy who'd gotten her hooked on them in the first place, and it was the only treat she knew how to make by heart. So, she'd reasoned while mixing the dough, since she hadn't gotten any instructions on what not to do on this time trip, Lucy would just have to smooth out any ripples she inadvertently created.

Besides, with the handicap of that monster iron stove, it was a miracle the cookies had turned out at all.

Lauren had read years ago that the chocolate chip cookie was credited to a woman who had bought the Toll House Inn back in the 1920s. For some unknown reason this Massachusetts baker had laboriously diced a Nestle's chocolate bar and mixed it into her basic butter cookie dough. Eventually, the company gave her a lifetime supply of free chocolate in return for printing her recipe on the wrappers of their bars.

Thank heavens, Lauren had thought this morning, as she frantically chopped chocolate, Nestle had finally wised up and started selling the familiar morsels in 1939. The cut-it-yourself method was for the birds.

Lauren's cookies looked a little odd, but Molly's friends loved them.

"It's not a family secret, is it now, Laurie?" Molly managed to ask while chewing.

"Well, no." After all, somewhere, in some other dimension, there were millions of people who already knew. "I'd be happy to write down the recipe for all of you." Lauren noted a few frowns. Hope! Wasn't that what she wanted to give—to leave.

"Ladies, I know that on such short acquaintance my idea may seem a bit pushy, but I think you should form a self-help gr . . . er . . . a Ladies League," Lauren finished in a rush, flushed with possibilities and fearful that she might have embarrassed Molly. She tugged nervously at the cuffs of her polka-dot blouse, then smoothed short, straying wisps of hair behind her ears.

"You mean like Mrs. Palmer and Mrs. Pullman?" Greta Olsen spoke the names of the leading ladies of the high-toned Gold Coast, with near awe.

"You all have as much to offer each other as those ladies have." Lauren's words scarcely left her mouth before the snorts and giggles commenced. She couldn't lose them. Two days was all she had left; the old ball had to start rolling now.

"Okay, let's just see." Lauren crossed the circle to stand by Molly's chair. "In five years the world will enter a new century, the twentieth century; the century of the woman, if we are prepared to make it so." Would this qualify as plagiarizing? All eleven faces looked as if she were speaking a foreign language. Well, maybe she was.

Who can read? Who can write? What about music? Does anyone read the paper? Have you thought about teaching your children to read? Who could use help? The questions went on and on. After a while Lauren noticed that Molly was writing down the rapidly spreading ideas.

Before the party ended the day and time of their first meeting had been set. As each woman left, the enthusiastic words of thanks and laughter seemed to float out the rough-hewn door and pour down the littered street like beautiful music.

Molly and Lauren stood in the doorway with their arms around each others' waist.

"Sure'n this day will forever be one of me most

188

treasured memories.'' Molly sighed, sweeping her free hand up the back of her drooping chignon.

''I'm so glad,'' Lauren replied with a slight catch in her voice. Without warning, she felt the sting of gathering tears.

''You've been farther than France, have ya not, me friend?'' Molly turned and looked into the eyes three shades darker than her own.

The strong, mystic sound of Ireland in Molly's question surrounded Lauren with loving acceptance. As before, words and explanations weren't necessary between them.

''I'm thinkin' the coast should be clear by now, Stephan.'' Patrick tossed back his last swallow of stout and set the heavy glass down on the shiny bar of O'Malley's Pub.

Polaski had the oddest look on his face. Dugan knew his friend was happy, but he almost felt sorry for the man, emotionally dependant as he was on his wife. After the next few months poor Stephan was going to feel like a rowboat caught in the riptides.

''What coast?''

Holy Mary! He was talkin' like Laurie. Patrick slapped down ten cents for their drinks, grabbed the bug-eyed Pole by the arm, and steered him out the door. Suddenly the clear picture of a two-seated rowboat formed in his mind.

''Did you see anything this mornin' I should know about?'' Patrick wanted the information, but he also wanted to distract Stephan.

Polaski gave Dugan a knowing smile and shoved his hands in the pockets of his denim pants. ''Just as Molly and I were comin' up on the Wheel, I saw Miss Brown again.''

''Did she see you?''

"No, I'm nearly certain she didn't. She was talkin' real serious with Hank, and after she left he told me she seemed desperate to find you; cryin' this time."

"What did he tell her?"

Stephan continued down the sidewalk, bustling with people and crowded with shop wares.

"Stephan?" Patrick demanded.

"He told her my name."

"Dammit to hell!"

"Just my name, Dugan, and when I work next. The man couldn't stand her pleading."

"We're runnin' out of time. I suppose I'd best talk to her before she tells her brother." Patrick wove around a vegetable cart and unconsciously lowered his cap on his brow.

"Good God, man, you know as well as I do that this could be a trap. Not even a disguise is safe. Let me see her first."

"It's more than just Nancy Brown, Stephan. How can I get the rest of the signatures I need if I'm not there?" Dugan raised his hand to stop the words he knew his friend was going to say. "No, I'll not involve you in that part of it. 'Tis bad enough that I've told you where the list is. Besides, I gave the others under McDonald's thumb my guarantee that their names would be protected. Since my arrest I'm thinkin' that some may change their tune if they don't soon see the emerald green of me own Irish eyes."

Stephan laughed and raked blunt fingers through his hair. He knew Patrick was trying to downplay the seriousness of his situation, so he would go along with him for now. But the other hawkers and peddlers on the carnival-like Midway, the Fair's greatest money-maker, had no idea what kind of risk the man was taking with his own life to protect them. From the food vendors and Hagenbeck's Animal Show to the dancer,

Little Egypt, on the popular "Street in Cairo," no one was exempt from McDonald's reach.

"Two days, Patrick," Stephan said, laying a hand on his friend's shoulder. "Give me two days."

Two days left for Laurie; two days for Stephan. As they climbed the stairs to the Polaskis' digs, Patrick felt as if he'd been given the exact date of the end of the world.

"Molly! Help me!"

The front door cracked against the wall like a gunshot. Patrick's heart was poundin' in double time as he ran into the room just in time to see Laurie losing the tenuous balance she had with one foot on the table and the other on a chair.

"What in the bloody damn hell are you doin', woman!" he yelled as he snagged her around the waist and shifted until she was cradled in his arms like a baby.

For just a moment Lauren let herself sink bonelessly into Dugan's safe, snug embrace. With her nose jammed tight in the notch between his neck and shoulder, she couldn't help but breathe in the warm, musky smell of man and bay rum. It felt so amazingly sweet to be held this way. This is what she'd wanted to do for him a few nights before.

"Thanks for saving me, Dugan," she said softly, raising her face until it was about an inch from his.

Patrick was angry, and he wanted to stay angry. Was determined to get angrier. However, one by one things were starting to register. Low against his stomach he felt the press of Laurie's hip. One soft breast nestled next to his chest, and her hand tangled in the hair at the nape of his neck. The arm wrapped around her back had extended just far enough that his fingers were cushioned by a stirring fullness.

And she was dripping with ribbons. They ran like

small, colored streams of water over her head, across her shoulders, and down her arms. He even felt some trailing down his back.

Patrick's expressions shifted, out-of-control. Anger. Surprise. Passion.

"Get a grip, Dugan," Lauren whispered in his ear. "Here comes Molly. Remember your promise."

That hot, sweet breath was the last straw. Any better grip and he'd be throwin' the woman on the closest bed and tanglin' with her until they were tied up in hopeless knots.

"Now this sight surely does me old heart good." Molly laughed, walking in a circle around the decorated pair. "Stay just as ya are so Stephan can see."

Stephan was still laughing two hours later. Evidently Patrick Dugan in ribbons was too, too funny. Lauren had to bite the inside of her cheek to keep from joining him. As she looked across the table, cluttered with the remains of their meal, she tried to memorize the moment.

The old-fashioned, middle-parted hair and sideburns seemed normal now. She couldn't even imagine what Patrick would look like with a blown-dry style. Stephan's mustache and Molly's Gibson Girl . . . they wouldn't be right any other way.

In a rush of loss, Lauren foolishly wished she had brought one of those disposable cameras. Oh, sweet heaven, for just one picture. Of course, she would have started a riot, but she could care less about that right now.

Dinner had been festive and funny. The four of them had laughed and laughed as Stephan told a story about a young boy he'd seen throwing beans up in the air by the Ferris wheel. Some older woman had gone hysterical, convinced that using electricity was hardening the rain before it could fall.

Then Patrick would say something, and Stephan would get that look in his eye and start chuckling all over again.

She was going to miss this for the rest of her life.

Sitting at the table, safe because she couldn't let her emotions run free here, Lauren openly admitted it to herself: Not once since leaping back in time had she missed the TV or even her music. They had been noises in her condo that kept the loneliness at bay.

Yes, she felt isolated to some degree. It was strange to realize how long it took for the world to relay information in 1895 . . . but so what? Maybe having so much information at one's fingertips was the problem. After a dose of world news a human being could feel so overwhelmed, so steamrolled with monumental problems, that fighting back seemed impossible. Lauren guessed that many people in 1995 felt as unconnected as she did.

But in this small corner of the world community was everything. It was all there really was. Washington was too far away. You needed your neighbors to survive. Street by street, people made a difference.

This was another truth she wouldn't forget.

Patrick wondered what Lauren was thinking. Every now and again, between the laughter, she got the saddest look in her eyes. Hell, it was for the best that she'd be gone soon. This whole evening had felt too damn good. *Admit it, Dugan, ya craven coward, she felt too damn good in your arms!*

"Are you listenin', Patrick?" Molly asked again.

"What?" He blinked and turned to the black-haired beauty who was passing a plate in his direction.

"These are just the best cookies I've ever had, and Laurie made them for my party."

As the men each took a tentative bite, Molly brought some of the gifts she'd received to the table and related the plans for a Ladies' League.

"Laurie, m'girl, you are a gem." Stephan stood and bent his husky frame at the waist, lifting Laurie's hand to his lips. "You bake with fairy magic and you've made my darlin' wife feel like a queen. I'm makin' it my solemn duty to help this dull-witted Irishman to realize the prize he's got."

As the Polaskis started toward their bedroom door, Molly turned to face Patrick and spoke.

"Just remember, me friend, the Fair will be over the end of October. All those grand buildings, the whole White City, and none of it built to last. Most of what you find at the Fair is that way."

Lauren cringed. She knew exactly who her loyal friend was referring too.

"You might consider buildin' somethin' permanent, like me and Stephan."

Molly's red-faced husband pulled her behind the door, and muffled voices immediately seeped through the cracks.

Lauren felt terrible about the whole situation. She was deceiving her friends and putting Patrick in the most awkward position, especially knowing how he felt about love and babies.

"I'm so sorry," she murmured, clasping her hands together on top of the table. "I never meant for any of this to happen."

Dugan sat silently across from her as if he hadn't heard a word. A number of small pieces of clothing fanned out over the blue tablecloth, and he seemed mesmerized by them.

"I'm worried that after I leave Molly will give you a hard time if you and . . . well . . ." At her hesitation, Patrick lifted his eyes to hers, waiting. "If you and Nancy Brown start dating, er, courting."

"Nancy Brown is nothing to me but a link to her

brother. I'm sorry the girl is distressed, but you don't have to worry about me keepin' company with her.''

"No, Dugan, you've misunderstood me. It's not my place to worry about whomever you choose to 'keep company' with. I just don't want Molly making things more difficult.'' Lies upon lies upon lies. One look into his hooded green eyes and they both knew it.

Maybe she should tell him. Tell him about all the wondrous feelings careening around inside her. Feelings that made it seem as if she'd known him much longer than the handful of days since they'd met. That would be honest and up front and cleansing. Besides, she'd only have to be humiliated for a day and a half, tops.

Patrick couldn't keep his finger from tracing the fragile baby shirt before him. Maybe Molly was right. Some people had to be builders, or else what would become of the world? And if Lauren was right, too . . . If loving was something a body could learn, then why not him?

Two days. What if she . . .
Two days. What if he . . .

They both heard it at the exact same moment: a gentle squeaking rhythm muffled by the closed door.

A blush the likes of which Lauren had never known heated her entire body.

Patrick's fist closed fiercely on the tiny shirt.

"I'll be back," he said hoarsely, shoving back his chair.

Lauren didn't open her eyes until she heard the door click shut. Then she got to her feet and quickly followed. She wasn't trying to catch Patrick; he'd no doubt started running the minute his feet hit the stairs. And it wasn't that she didn't feel like running herself. She did. There was simply nowhere to go.

She slipped out the door and leaned back against it, giving the love behind her the respect and privacy it deserved.

There was only one night left. One more chance to feel what Molly and Stephan were feeling right this minute.

How much pain could she stand?

Patrick stopped halfway down the block to rest his back and mop his shiny face. Holy Mary, he was hot and tired. After leaving—no, running—from Laurie last night, he hadn't dared return and so had spent a very uncomfortable night on a bench at O'Malley's.

Although it wasn't yet noon, the sizzling summer sun was bright as a lemon and making folks just as sour. Heat and humidity seemed to bring out the worst in lots of people. Maybe if he tried hard enough he could convince himself that was what was bothering him.

"Well, me friend," a passerby exclaimed, clapping Patrick on the back. "It looks like congratulations are in order."

No, Dugan thought, slumping his broad shoulders, the heat was not a good excuse for his irritability. With a grunt he hefted the cherry cradle. This was a day for tying up loose ends, and he meant to do it cleanly. His plan to hold Laurie at bay was full of more holes than a sieve. Too much of what he felt was leaking out.

God almighty! Last night he'd almost burst like a cracked dam. Patrick swiped his forehead with the back of his rolled-up sleeve. As long as he lived he was afraid he'd never forget the sound of that bed creaking, the baby shirt in his hand, and the look in Laurie's big blue eyes. Just before the embarrassment he'd thought he'd seen envy, longing.

But the worst of it was, now he knew exactly what Stephan Polaski had . . . and what he didn't.

The spicy smell of roasting smoked sausage wafted down from an upper window, and Dugan mocked himself with a sardonic smile. First he tried to blame the heat, and now it was hunger givin' him this pain in the pit of his stomach. *Tell yourself whatever you must, me boyo.*

He shifted his burden a bit on his shoulder. At least his strength was back. He'd taken Laurie's final pill this morning: another ending.

Patrick spent the next few minutes gathering that very strength as he hiked the last block to the Polaskis' building. He was keeping his promises even though he was afraid it might kill him. Afraid? Aye, she was right about that, too. Hell, the woman was driving him mad.

He took the corner in full stride, unreasonably anxious for her to see the evidence of his commitment to helping the baby.

His jaw dropped.

Beneath the canopy of hanging laundry, a small army of long-skirted ants were swarming the street. The normal routine for a Saturday morning had clearly been discarded. Aprons of every style and color adorned the group like mismatched uniforms. Patrick lowered the cradle to the sidewalk.

Around piles of trash already mounding in front of five or six buildings, he could see women scrubbing steps. Old barrels cut in half sat to the side on each front stoop. Goggle-eyed, Dugan watched feminine hands planting flowers in them. A sharp whistle cut through the heavy air like a knife, drawing the attention of the worker ants and the growing gallery.

"Mrs. Dugan? Mrs. Duuugan!" the whistler yelled.

His heart picked up its pace, and Patrick waved the young man over. "I'm *Mister* Dugan, boy. What is it you're needin'?"

"If you'll just sign for this stuff, mister, we can deliver it to you." The strapping lad shoved a pencil and paper into Dugan's hands and motioned to the crew behind him.

Bronwyn Wolfe

Patrick compressed his mouth into a thin white line. It seemed *Mrs. Dugan* was takin' things into her own bossy little hands again.

"Laurie? Laurie Ann Dugan, where in blazes are you, woman?" Hell, that name came to him so naturally now.

"Patrick, is that you caterwaulin' loud enough to wake the dead?" Molly smacked his arm, at the same time blotting her face with a corner of her pink gingham apron. "Oh, Paddy," she laughed, waving her hands right and left. "Isn't this a sight!"

"You're sure to be seein' an even more amazin' sight if your husband catches you workin' like this in your . . . ah, condition."

"I'm havin' a baby, Dugan, not dyin'," she challenged him, her hands on her hips. "Besides, Laurie is watchin' me like a hawk. Mostly I'm relayin' information for more effective produc . . . ah, productivily."

Patrick's eyebrows pulled together, pleating his forehead like a fan. Laurie was affecting them all. Molly stepped back with a devious smile spread across her porcelain face and pointed over her shoulder.

Still carrying the cradle that Molly had totally ignored, he zigged and zagged toward the Polaskis' front steps. A voluminous circle of skirts blocked him like a wall. On the other side of the fabric barricade he heard the voice he'd been searching for.

Dugan peered over a brace of feminine shoulders. What did she think she was doing, spending money like this; getting these women het up like this; wearing men's pants like this?

Men's pants! In public! Jesus, Mary, and Joseph! He almost fainted. The she-cat had gone too far this time.

Like the Red Sea, the women in front of Patrick parted instantly at his muttered curse.

"So, ladies, if you'll prepare the next stoop—"

Bend. Flex. Wiggle, wiggle. Bend.

"I'll finish with the paint here and move right over."

Wiggle, wiggle. Bend. Flex. Tilt.

A suspiciously familiar groan met Lauren's ears. Slowly she set down her brush and rubbed a dribble of paint on Stephan's old coveralls. With incredible composure she reached up to straighten the bandanna tied on her head.

"Mrs. Dugan, may I have a word with you?"

Both sides of the Red Sea melted instantly into the crowd.

When had she become so beautiful? Patrick shook his head as he set down the cradle yet again. Paint—real paint, this time—and dirt streaked her cheek, but a wide grin parted her shiny pink lips.

The best defense is a good offense, Lauren repeated silently. Not even this Irishman's righteous indignation was going to ruin her last day.

"Doesn't everything look wonderful! I'm just so pleased that all these wonderful women are getting involved and making a difference." Lauren stopped for a breath and spotted the cradle. "Oh, Patrick!" She clapped her hands. "You got that for the baby, didn't you?"

He arched one brow.

"Well, of course you did. It's just that I'm so surprised, and Molly will be so happy." Lauren blinked fast, twice, to beat back the tears that had been threatening on and off all day.

"I'm fillin' all my promises today, lass."

No! The word burst through her like a bazooka blast. All the hopes she'd been bricking away inside her heart rushed right up her throat, barely stopped by her sealed lips. She wanted to plead, *don't make me go*. But she couldn't risk it. If he didn't want her enough, it was hardly his fault. She felt so much whenever he was

199

close that it was difficult for her to read his reactions. If Patrick would just give her one little word: *stay.*

Lauren had reluctantly begun facing it last night, but the truth really hadn't hit her until this very minute; looking her absolute worst, standing in the middle of a dirty, crowded street.

She loved him.

From the peak of her discovery she was free-falling to endless agony, and there was nothing she could do to stop it. She had already been here too long and asked too much from a man who felt he had nothing to give. The cradle at his feet represented a huge personal concession.

With one strong, brown hand Dugan reached out and grabbed a fistful of Lauren's shirt.

"Do you realize that your back end is on display for every man jack on this street to see?"

At that instant she would have swallowed her feminist pride and let the man drag her by the hair if his concerned anger was fueled by love and not propriety. But no matter how she felt, Lauren could not let him stop this project. It was her gift of hope. *Nope! He didn't see what she was trying to accomplish here. Try again.*

"This is certainly not the time to get into the whole issue of repression and male ideas of modesty, but suffice it to say, *husband,* that we are being watched!" She wrapped her green-spattered hand around his at her throat and planted a brief kiss on his cheek. It hurt.

"You're making my friends nervous, Patrick," she cautioned, sliding her lips over to his ear. Lauren felt his deep inhalation. *Thar she blows.*

"The paint would ruin their dresses. Ruin my dress. Admit it, Dugan, it just didn't make sense to do it that way. And I have to do it. I have to leave something of me here."

*   *   *

Because she was standing on the step her eyes were even with his. And just as so many times before, they reflected total sincerity and asked for his understanding.

He did understand. Patrick knew exactly what she meant. That was why he had made the list in the first place. To make a difference, to leave something better behind him. To prove he wasn't like either the man who had spawned him or the man who had raised him.

She had tried to help him and now he could close the circle by helping her. There was just one compromise they would have to reach.

It was very possible that Stephan Polaski was the first completely unprepared person to witness the results of the South Side Ladies League's first project. The original group had doubled as the day progressed and more helpers volunteered and pitched in. Reading classes were to begin the following week.

Eight buildings, four on either side of the narrow street, had freshly painted, deep green stoops and gray front doors. Each stoop boasted a half barrel of blooming flowers with nary a speck of trash to be seen anywhere.

Sitting on his front steps were the obvious leaders of the miracle. Molly's long black hair hung in one thick braid over her shoulder. Her head was resting in Laurie's lap, and Stephan saw that his wife's friend was covered with paint and dirt. But the face that surprised him most was Patrick's. The man looked like a pine tree dusted with gray snow. Even his eyebrows had paint on them.

Molly stood at his approach and flung her arms around his neck with a happy shout. It seemed Laurie was taking them all out to dinner and they were waiting for him to help with the bath water. Stephan laughed when Dugan shrugged and blamed his wife for wearin' him to the bone.

Polaski noticed right away that Laurie had on his old coveralls, and he couldn't help but wonder at the sight of her climbing the stairs. He knew the woman was eccentric and held to a lot of city-fancy ways, although her hair and face paint didn't even bother him anymore. She was a light in his sweet Molly's life and that was all that mattered.

But surely even a woman who'd been to France knew that you didn't wear an apron over your behind.

Nancy Brown was frightened.

Harry had insisted she go to the Midway every day, looking for Patrick, and each time she had returned without information he had gotten angrier. His ruse of helping the Irishman hadn't lasted long.

If only she could leave, she thought, standing in front of her mirror-topped chiffonier braiding her hair. Maybe if she took some of Harry's money she could make it to wild Aunt Claire in California.

But before she could do that she had to get word to Patrick. Harry had offhandedly mentioned a trip out of town he was taking with McDonald next week, and she hoped her news would help. This time she would not fail; not get caught. She might be young, but she was not as big a fool as she had allowed her brother to believe. She'd have to give him something tonight, and she did have a name. That name would buy her a little bit more time.

A loud slam downstairs signaled Harry's arrival. Hurriedly, she scooted to the center of her lace-covered bed and manufactured a guileless smile. She prayed she could reach Patrick before her brother did.

Chapter Eleven

"What did you call that supper again, Laurie?" Molly asked over her shoulder as the two couples strolled home through the ebbing light of the day. Dusky relief from the summer heat had finally arrived, and every window and roof lining the crowded streets sported fanning faces.

"Spaghetti and meatballs!" Lauren returned, happy that her final surprise had been so well received.

It had taken more than a good hour for them to scrub off the paint and dress in their finest. When she had led her followers out of their familiar domain and across three blocks to the Italian restaurant she had heard about a few days earlier, Lauren was very aware of their hesitation. Polarization was a real problem in this time; not that the 1990s had it handled. She knew too well how far people still had to go. But learning to appreciate the differences was a good place to start.

Watching Stephan trying to corral the slippery pasta

and keep it from dangling off his wax-tipped mustache had them all giggling like children. Lauren couldn't keep her gaze from straying to Patrick again and again. The flickering candlelight on the table bounced off his shiny hair, darkened with Madagascar oil for this special occasion. A celluloid collar and tie completed the formal look, and Lauren thought she had never seen him look so handsome, nor so clearly a hundred years away from her.

All during their long walk home she had soaked in the things around her, especially the Irishman cradling her arm next to his side.

She began to pretend that she and Patrick were as much in love as Molly and Stephan. That they, too, had their whole lives ahead of them. Oh, the little voices in her head tried to talk her out of this craziness. Logical platitudes pounded uselessly at her heart's door, because tonight Lauren wasn't going to listen. Tonight she was going to reach out for wonder.

She would surely die a little more each day if she didn't take this risk. This might be her only chance to discover if she could fan the flame of desire into the roaring inferno she'd heard so much about. Somehow, as they trudged up the stairs, Lauren knew she would never know if she didn't act now.

Playing femme fatale wasn't in her seduction repertoire. In fact, she grimaced, taking off her hat and glancing at Patrick out of the corner of her eye, she didn't have a seduction repertoire, period. But the man felt something for her; that was undeniable. If it all blew up in her face . . . well, she would just leave a bit sooner than planned.

"Ah, Laurie." Molly laughed as she gave her hand a squeeze. "This has been a golden day. It's made up for so much."

Stephan came up behind his wife and pulled her into

his arms. "We've a favor and a blessin' to ask of you two Dugans," he boomed with a smile.

Patrick's heart sank like a stone in an icy lake, knowing the exact request his friend was about to make. He moved closer to Laurie and lightly placed his hand against the small of her back. This had been a long, hard day for her, and knowing how much she cared for Molly and this baby she would never see . . . Well, he just thought she might need someone to lean on.

"We want you two to be our baby's godparents," Molly burst out.

Dugan felt Laurie stiffen, and he slipped his hand securely around her waist, waiting.

Lauren should have known. Should have expected it. But the happy words pelted her with sorrow. For an imperceptible moment she lost the strength in her legs, but Patrick caught her. A soft pinch at her waist made her smile and gave her the power to respond the way she needed to.

Patrick will be there. He'll stand up for the baby. Lauren kept repeating the litany as they all took turns hugging each other. Yet, as hard as she tried, she couldn't keep an anguished expression from shadowing her eyes.

"Now, Laurie girl," Stephan soothed, wrapping one beefy arm around her shoulders, "I can see you're worryin' about this problem Dugan's got himself into. But don't fret; it'll be over and gone long before the baby gets here. I won't let anythin' happen to your man."

"I'm holding you to your promise, Stephan Polaski," she answered with a fervor that no one else in the room would understand.

Stephan let her go and walked to the saltbox to grab the few remaining chocolate chip cookies. In a solemn flourish he handed one to each of them.

"With nothin' stronger to seal our promises and toast

this grand occasion, we'll have to settle for Laurie's special recipe. To friendship.'' He raised his cookie and his voice, waiting until they all had taken a symbolic bite.

''Come on, wife.'' Stephan ambled to the bedroom door, dragging Molly behind him. ''With tomorrow bein' Sunday, we're likely to have folks from all over comin' to see our beautified street. We'd best get some rest.''

As soon as the door shut, Lauren put the rest of her cookie on the table and turned her back on Patrick. She marched to her bag in the corner, all the while holding her breath to control the sound of her ragged sighs.

Leave! Get out the blasted door, she screamed silently, tearing off her fake hair and pulling on her nightgown. Hot tears rolled down her cheeks and soaked into the tucked cotton bodice as she forced herself to pack for her departure in the morning. Everything was in place, her letters and money ready.

''Laurie?''

Oh, no! Why tonight of all nights wasn't he running?

''Hmmm?'' She scrubbed the backs of her hands across her wet cheeks and dried them on the pallet blankets as she rolled them into place.

''These truly are grand cookies.''

''Good,'' she mumbled, bending over her task.

''I'll take care of the christening no matter what happens.''

''Good.''

''And . . .'' Patrick paused, wishing she would turn around and look at him so he would know she was all right. ''And I want you to know it hasn't been half bad these past days, actin' the part of your husband. Why, with the Irish magic you've worked in this neighborhood, I've become quite the favored gent.''

''Will it cause problems?''

The shadows in the darkened room concealed Laurie's face, but Patrick started at the sound of her raw voice.

"No, lass, don't fash yourself. I'll be takin' my leave tomorrow also, just for a bit, to take care of McDonald and Brown." No need to tell her how difficult it was going to be to find someone willing to listen. "Before you know it, this will all be just an unpleasant memory."

Word by word, his statement sank into her body like individual, razor-sharp blades. Lauren could actually feel the impact.

To her eternal mortification, she couldn't hold back a strangled sob.

Dugan watched in horror as Laurie folded in on herself, until her tender mouth nearly pressed into the scratchy covers. Holy Mary! Whatever he'd said had cut her down like a tree. Not again, by God! Not again would he hurt her and turn away.

Strong, determined arms pulled her crumpled body into a warm, safe haven. Then, as Lauren felt Patrick lean back against the wall and settle her across his lap, she began to struggle.

"Hush, Laurie," he whispered, stroking the tense curve of her spine, willing her to understand what he couldn't say; couldn't define. *After all you've done for me . . . chased away the loneliness for the first time in years, let me do this for you. Take back some of the hurt. Ease this strange leave-takin' for the both of us.*

Slowly Lauren relaxed and uncurled her legs. Every protective instinct she had screamed for her to move, to leave before she was wounded far more deeply than Jeff's rejection had ever gone. But the love, spreading through her with each beat of her heart, won out. For this night she would risk it all.

It seemed he had waited for years to hold her again.

Gently he tipped her face up to his and splayed the fingers of his hand wide, covering the whole of her cheek. With his thumb he swiped at the damp patches under her eyes and chuckled at the tiny trails of paint.

"You've the look of a raccoon, lass."

"Oh!" She tried to move.

"No, Laurie. Tell me why."

He showed her the black smudge on the pad of his thumb and then rubbed it on his dark twill trousers. She was leaving the next day and Patrick realized that he was starting to throw caution to the wind. He'd be alone again in only a few hours, and suddenly he couldn't make himself end this hazardous moment too soon.

It was the first personal question he had ever asked her.

"I have unattractive, thin, light eyelashes. In my time women try to . . . umm . . . mask their inadequacies." She attempted to duck his scrutiny until he anchored her face back into the crook of his shoulder.

"I think you've lovely eyes with or without the paint, lass." He saw the denial forming on her puckered pink lips and thought of all the good she'd done since her mystical arrival. She was leaving, but she deserved to take something back. Something important to remember about herself. Holy Mary, but sometimes the memories of his mother's words of love were the only things that made him feel worthy. He could give her the vision of the Laurie he honestly saw.

"Real beauty comes from what's inside, Laurie girl. It's the heart of a woman that makes her beautiful. Meanin' you, of course, are beautiful inside and out." Her eyes opened wide in surprise, then darkened with a longing Patrick knew she wasn't aware he could see. Now was the time to stop, to change the intimate mood in which the night and the tears had wrapped them. He tried.

208

Patrick rested his thumb over her pursed little mouth, rubbing lightly, and continued, "But I suppose a touch of help here and there wouldn't hurt."

Lauren was lost in sensual sensations and missed the man's little joke for a heartbeat as she concentrated on the feel of his touch on her lips. Then it hit, and before she could stop herself she bit him. And before he could pull his injured thumb away she drew a tiny, moist line down the firm pad with her tongue. He trembled; she was sure of it. Maybe she had a seduction repertoire after all!

Patrick couldn't stop the groan that rumbled up from his chest. This was wrong. Stupid. Pointless. One day! One more damn day and she'd be gone and he'd be safe. Safe from a fate worse than the damage McDonald could do to his body. It was his heart stirring to life again that should be making him run, but all he could think of as he watched her blue eyes go soft was what she tasted like.

Strawberries? A sweet, light memory on his tongue. Something he had to have again.

The shifting pools of light in the room glinted across Lauren's shiny lips, and Patrick crossed the line. He'd lived empty for the last fourteen years and he could do it again; would do it again, starting tomorrow. But now, this moment, he was taking, and damn the pain.

"I have to know, Laurie," he said, his husky words forced out on a tight, compressed sigh. "God forgive me, and Ma too. But I have to know."

Sweet heaven, he was drowning. She opened to him as every man dreams his woman will; as he'd never dared to hope to find blossoming in his arms. The fire she ignited roared through his body once again, demanding he quench the flames as he had never done before. Permanently. Forever. She tasted as dark and

209

luscious as the candy in her cookies; rich, rare . . . exotic.

Hungrily, he lifted his mouth and pressed it again and again, back and forth across her own, rocking unconsciously to a primal rhythm. His hands gathered huge fists full of confining cotton as he tried to rein in the passion scorching him to dust. He held on for dear life; held himself rigid against the need to touch her bare flesh.

The first jolt of his mouth on hers shook her to the core. Lauren felt her breath evaporating until harsh demand bade her open to receive all he had to give; all he would ever give her. She trembled, too, as he swept her tongue with his, washing every bit of tender flesh he could reach with the taste of desire and chocolate and man.

Lauren could barely lift her eyes and register that he had stopped. Taking deep, shuddering, involuntary gulps of air, she forced herself to meet the consequences of her actions.

He burned; flames shot sparks in his emerald eyes.

He burned for her.

The joy left her speechless.

For the first time with a man she was going to reach out to take what she wanted and needed, empowered because she saw real need for her in return. Lauren's fingers curled against the straining muscles in his neck and tangled in his thick hair, pulling him back to her.

"Wait, Laurie," Patrick made himself say. "You're leavin', lass; this isn't right. I . . ."

The minute the words were out of his mouth Patrick felt the power of the lie in them, and it stopped him cold. It had to be the loneliness and the danger . . . the knowledge that he'd likely not live out the next few weeks that made this woman, whose hands running through his hair sent lightning streaking down his body, feel more right than anything he could ever remember.

"No! Please. I've waited forever, Patrick, and I can't wait any longer." When he still hesitated she added, "No regrets; I promise."

No regrets, but she couldn't promise not to hope. To hope that the feelings that had started back in her little condo as she stared at his picture—and grown day by day to fill her entire being—would communicate to him now, in this most intimate of ways.

Patrick had never had a woman look at him the way Laurie was. Oh, there had been a few who might have really cared if his heart hadn't been a stone in his chest. And yes, there were some who had wanted only for the moment or the money and had let him know that with their bodies and their eyes. But those forgotten invitations had always come with demands he could not meet. It had not been difficult to walk away.

Laurie's steady gaze spoke only of giving, and for the first time he couldn't deny his need to feel wanted. To push back the loneliness that never left him and feel real arms hold him against the night. It was weak, God help him. But if it was only their bodies touching, he'd not be giving away much; not damning himself as his mother had. He would be wiser because he knew there could be nothing more than this one night.

He watched as Laurie chewed her bottom lip, as if trying to make a decision, and then tentatively lifted her hands to the buttons on his shirt. As much as he wanted this, he had to make the situation clear. He'd not be guilty of what his father had done.

"We've only this night, lass. This one night out of time before we each must finish the journey to which fate has called us." With a sinking heart he felt her hands grow still, and he levered himself up to move away.

But Lauren circled her arms around his neck and

pulled him down until his chest rested flat on hers. "One night is more than I've ever had before, Patrick. It will be enough. Show me."

The last she sighed against his lips, lifting herself to him. Waiting for another mind-blowing, honeyed kiss that left her breathless and limp.

"I—I'm not sure I can . . ."

He faltered and looked away. The gnawing ache surging through Lauren twisted painfully to awful embarrassment, and she closed her eyes because it was the only way to hide.

However, Patrick was still so close that when he awkwardly cleared his throat, she chanced a tiny peek. Even in the dappled shadows of the Polaskis' small room, Lauren could see that the look on his face was one of chagrin, not rejection.

"I'm not sure I can give you the night you deserve, lass."

"What? You mean . . . you never? A man of your age?"

He couldn't decide if she sounded frustrated or amused. Hell, he felt like a green lad with a woman of the world; a world far and away from the one in which he had grown up. The rush of passion began to leave his body as he thought how he must appear to her. Not enough, again.

With a tentative touch, Lauren tapped the chin of the shuttered face above her. Patrick reluctantly looked down.

"I don't have any firsthand experience myself," she admitted ruefully. "We'll just have to help each other."

"What? A woman of your age? And wearin' such underwear?" Patrick attempted to carry off the teasing banter because she had taken his inadequacy and made it theirs: something to share and overcome together. Not a lack at all.

"I wondered if it had ever occurred to you that I was older," she said shyly with a self-conscious moue. "A dyed-in-the-wool old maid, especially in your time."

Patrick heard the joke, but he also heard the insecurity beneath it. The woman in his arms wasn't old; she was ripe and ready. She wasn't cold, but bubbling with the most welcoming heat he had ever known. And if this ended up being the worst mistake of his life, he'd still make it, trying to erase that who-could-want-me look from her face.

He would call on every word of advice and every fantastic recital of lovemaking he had ever heard and give her the proof that she was everything a man could want. This time he would give and not take.

"You're like a fine wine, lass; the best ones just get better as time goes by. Besides," he said quietly, dropping his mouth back to hers for a light, lingering kiss. "I'm thinkin' between the two of us we've enough years to get this right."

As if they both saw a giant clock ticking away their precious hours, inhibitions and fears were cast aside. Patrick rocked back on his knees at Lauren's insistent shove so she could sit and strip off his shirt. Boldly, she ran her shaking hands up his muscled arms, measuring the width of his corded shoulders. The freedom to touch and taste left her almost light-headed.

Patrick wasn't prepared for the slide of her tongue across his nipple. Surely smoke would soon begin to fill the room from the smoldering fabric of his pants. Tender, sucking kisses crisscrossed his chest like a branding iron until he thought he would lose his mind.

"Woman," he paused, swallowing to soothe the rough edge in his voice, "I thought you said you had little experience." His hands stopped her hungry mouth and pulled her up so that they faced one another on their knees.

"You inspire me, Patrick." Lauren laughed softly and then faltered. "It's all right, isn't it?"

"I'm not certain."

"Oh?" She tried to shrink away.

"I'm thinkin' I'd best test this on you, Laurie," he said, and he gathered her pooled nightdress in his hands and lifted it over her head.

For an instant all of Lauren's insecurities threatened to destroy her courage; her one chance with Patrick. But then she heard his ragged gasp and raised her downcast eyes to his. That she, Lauren Ann Sullivan, had inspired such a look on the face of a man like Patrick Dugan was more than she had ever dreamed of. For the first time in her life she felt truly beautiful.

Deliberately, Patrick trailed his fingers lightly up Laurie's smooth thighs to her arms, crossed protectively over her breasts. He tangled his hands with hers and gently tugged.

"Ah, lass. Let me."

Never taking his gaze from hers, he unfolded the barrier and placed one small hand on each of his trembling shoulders. Laurie's eyes grew round.

"Aye, Laurie Ann Dugan. This is what you do to me."

He rubbed his callused palms from her silky waist up to under her arms, over and over again, until she breathed with the motion . . . and waited for more.

Oh, for a thousand electric lights, Patrick thought as he strained in the shifting shadows to see every nuance of the woman humming under his touch. How had he ever thought her less than spectacular? He opened his hands wide and moaned as he finally covered her breasts, dropping his forehead to hers.

It was more than either of them had ever hoped to find, ever hoped to feel; a connection so deep it bordered on reverence.

Then needy arms clung and needy mouths opened and Patrick's clothes melted away until they rested naked in each other's arms. Hard against soft; rough sliding over smooth.

Patrick threaded his fingers through the short, honeyed hair he had longed to touch until he held Laurie's fragile head in the cradle of his hands; just as she held him in the cradle of her body. Braced on his elbows, he watched the play of light and emotions moving across her face. Such a tender and wildly passionate woman she was. He angled her head back, offering her mouth to his, and he took it; long and deep, as a man lost in the desert would drink life-giving water.

With a subtle shift he brought their bodies closer; so close that it took all his force of will to manage a final word of warning.

"I'd not . . . hurt you."

"I'm not afraid, Patrick. Not in your arms."

Then his mouth drove all rational thought away. Everywhere he touched Lauren burned, making the sharp, tearing pain first bearable and then sweet. Nothing in her life had prepared her for the intimacy of another's body, covering hers so completely. Nothing had prepared her for this overpowering hunger to be filled with all the love she had ever dreamed of, and she sobbed at the glory of it.

Patrick froze.

"No!" She arched up and hugged him fiercely. "I love you, Patrick! Love me, too."

The words! Those words he'd thought never to hear again drove him past all reason and beyond his vow to spill his seed outside her warmth. Sweet Mary, she held him so tight and promised such love until it flowed over, around, and through him, and he could not stop until he touched her very soul.

"Angel, my wife," Patrick breathed brokenly in

215

Gaelic before he could stop himself. His body still pulsed from the force of their joining.

Sweet Jesus, what had he done?

It had been like nothing he'd ever expected, and he felt a dank and treacherous pit opening all around him. Weakness had blinded him; his loneliness had driven him, and now wrenching misery began to unfurl in his chest like the petals of a black rose.

He rolled to his side, ordering himself to let go and yet unable to stop from pulling her snugly against his shaking body. Fool! Trying to find comfort from the source of the problem. Concentrate. Concentrate on surviving the next few minutes without giving anything away.

Lauren burrowed deep in Patrick's strong arms, not understanding the words he had gasped in her ear but sure of their meaning. He'd made love to her. He wanted her. Even with her limited experience she knew this had been something shattering.

Patrick couldn't deny it. Not now. Maybe she could even stay! Any second he'd ask her. She'd stay here with her husband and her wonderful friends—have his babies and grow old and never, ever be alone again outside the golden circle of love.

The emotions swamping her heart and simmering in her blood were going straight to her head, making her bold and possessive. His mouth, his arms, his body were hers whenever she needed it. And she was his; gloriously, deliriously his. Lauren turned until she could trail hot, wet kisses over the muscled rise of Patrick's chest. He trembled.

Oh, thank God. He does feel it, too.

Oh, God, no. Not again. Never again, or I'll be destroyed by my own cursed heart just like Ma was.

The magnitude of what he'd done and what Lauren had made him feel began to roll over Patrick in crashing waves of fear and denial. This had been about making Laurie feel desired and chasing away his demons for a night; that was all. Bodies, not souls. He would not love. He would not give his heart to the wrong person, as his mother had, someone destined to leave just as his father had.

He'd asked her once, after an ugly scene with his uncle, why she had ever loved. "The heart doesn't always choose wisely, Paddy. Perhaps some can call back their love once it's been spoken, but I could not. My words were my bond, and I couldn't break it. Even in the face of pain, I couldn't break it."

Never. Never would he allow himself to love that way. There simply wasn't enough trust left in him.

Patrick felt Laurie shift in his arms, and he cursed his greedy body for making a mockery of all his thoughts by wanting again what it could not have. Passion always muddled the mind, or so he'd been warned years ago by more experienced lads.

And poor lass; she'd called it love, this comfort they'd foolishly shared for a moment when there could never be anything lasting.

Nothing but the physical between him and a woman who belonged somewhere else; *sometime* else. That's all he would ever let it be from this second on. The kindest thing he could do for this woman he'd unintentionally wronged again was make that clear. Nothing had changed.

He had to prove that to Laurie and to himself quickly, before her intoxicating kisses pushed all rational thought from his mind. Thank heavens he had spoken his passion-hazed confession in words she could not understand.

"Patrick?"

He steeled himself against the hint of hurt vibrating in that one word. There was nothing he could say to explain what had just happened, and no way to go back and undo it. Damn! It would be best for both of them

217

to just get on with the leave-taking.

"Where will you wait for your time door tomorrow?"

The sound of his flat, quiet voice rang obscenely in Lauren's ears, building to a deafening howl.

Oh, God. He didn't want her. Once had been enough. What? What had happened? Without moving a muscle, she felt herself falling, falling so fast it left her gut-punched, as if the wind had been knocked out of her. Lauren slowly, gingerly pulled away from him and covered the gaping wound of her unwanted body with the folds of her crumpled gown.

"I'll . . . wait . . . at . . . the . . . Palace." Each word was separate and distinct from the others. In the dark, Lauren closed her eyes tight and willed her breaking heart to hold against the blow it had just taken.

She had gambled and lost. People did it every day. And though she had not been able to sustain the warmth for long, it *had* been there, for a few minutes at least. The risk hadn't been completely worthless.

She was, after all, still excruciatingly alive.

Patrick watched her strained movements and forced himself to lay motionless. The cloth barrier she labored to slide between them felt like a thousand needles pricking his skin; still, he let her go.

"I'm thinkin' I'll take you to the time door myself, Laurie."

"To make sure . . . it works?" *To make sure I really go?* she amended in her mind.

"Yes."

"Fine," she answered and rolled to her side, as far away as she could get and remain on the pallet. There wasn't a chance in hell that she would ever see him in the light of day again. Pride counted for something, after all.

"Laurie? About this . . ." Dugan lay a hand on her shoulder and felt her flinch, as if he'd given her the slap he deserved. Every muscle in his body screamed to hold her again, to make her his and never release her. For fourteen years he hadn't let anyone have this kind of power over his heart and mind. He'd sworn after he'd seen what it had done to his ma that he never would.

And now here he lay on the brink of making the same damning error.

With his mother's death, Patrick had discovered the true cost of her heart's mistake. All he'd known of his life had been a lie. His father had deserted them both before Patrick was born, and his uncle had barely been able to wait for the last clods of earth to fall on her grave before taking away Dugan's legitimacy and his horses.

Experience had taught Patrick a hard lesson: Love eventually came to betrayal or desertion. If he didn't close off now, pull back fast, she'd leave him cut to the bone and bleeding 'til the day he died. For leaving she was; not once had she even mentioned the possibility of staying.

In the morning she would be grateful that he hadn't allowed this situation to become more difficult through useless conversation. There was no future for them. In fact, she already seemed remarkably calm after so recently coming apart in his arms. For both their sakes he'd best remember he was a bastard in fact and deed, with nothing to give her.

"I told you it was for just one night." Patrick forced the cutting accusation from his lips, aching body and soul.

"And I agreed, Dugan, so you're off the hook. Let's sleep now." The cost of those smooth, steady words almost killed her.

Thank heavens tears could drop without a sound.

Just before dawn Lauren was ready to go. As on the day she had arrived in 1895, she was decked out formally in

219

her green-and-white-stripped taffeta skirt with the matching short walking jacket detailed with leg-o-mutton sleeves. Everything was exactly the same except, of course, her heart. That poor thing would never be the same again.

Two letters and a small pouch of money rested just to the side of Patrick's inert body. He slept so soundly that she blushed in spite of herself when she considered the reason for his exhaustion. But no more tears! Not one! She was taking far more with her than she had started with. Good memories of wonderful friends, a fantastic adventure, and the knowledge that her life need never be as empty and sterile as it once had been.

Certainly there were people in her present for whom she could care and love. There had to be! Even her feelings for Patrick . . . agonizing as they were right now, they had taught her a lot. And just maybe, if she was very, very lucky, she might be taking a part of her old dream, a little someone to love, with her.

At the bottom of the rickety stairs Lauren froze when a heavy hand fell on her shoulder.

"Pat—" She whirled.

"Laurie?" Stephan yawned, smoothing his wild hair back from his face. "Where are you off to at this ungodly hour?"

"I've a breakfast appointment with Bertha Palmer, Stephan. I think she and her husband can help Patrick." Since this was the basic thrust of her plan anyway, it only took a moment to gild the lily.

"How do you know such a high-toned la—"

"My parents and the Palmers have a mutual acquaintance." It was fortunate that mortifying humiliation wasn't slowing her down a bit. "But now that I'm thinking about it, having the list in my hands could save a lot of time."

"Yes, Patrick has been mighty concerned about timing."

"Stephan, do you trust me?" Laurie asked sincerely, laying a gloved hand on his arm.

"After all you've done for me and mine, you know I do."

"Do you know where the list is?"

Stephan hesitated for a few long minutes, balancing the scales of loyalty in his mind. Patrick didn't stand a chance of finding another couple in Chicago with a greater position of power than the Palmers. Time *was* running out, and something had to be done before the fool got himself murdered.

In a few succinct sentences he described the hiding place in the Palace of Fine Arts, and Lauren couldn't help but wince at the irony of it all.

"I think I'll just come along," he added at the end of his disclosure. "Molly will have my head on a platter if anything happens to you."

"No way . . . I mean, certainly not! That's all you and Molly need, to get more involved in this whole problem." Lauren reassured him with a pat on the hand, "I promise that Patrick will understand. You'll see; he won't be upset at all." No doubt he'd be dancing a jig upon hearing the good news of her departure.

"So, he knows what you're about?"

"Well," she paused, "not exactly—" She threw up a hand to halt Stephan's reaction. "I mean, you know how mach—stubborn the man is, and I just can't have him interfering because he thinks he should do this on his own."

Stephan reluctantly nodded his agreement. That was just what his hotheaded friend would think.

"How long do you need, Laurie?"

"Oh, I'll be back in the late afternoon, most likely." She lowered her traitorous eyes to her bag and continued the lie. "If there's any delay, I'm sure Mrs. Palmer will send a message for me."

"All right, then; I'll stall your fire-breathin' Irishman as long as I can," Stephan promised with a quick squeeze of her shoulder. "He won't be happy that you took this risk, Laurie, but I'm sure with the way he looks at you, he won't stay angry long."

"No doubt you're absolutely right, Stephan. Before you know it, I—this will all be just an unpleasant memory." She lifted a hand in farewell and headed around the corner of the building. Just before she was out of sight, she called back one last request.

"Take care of Molly and the baby."

Stephan stared after her at the sound of those words, then stopped and shook off the strange feeling they'd given him. For a moment there, it had seemed as if she was sayin' good-bye. Ridiculous.

Chapter Twelve

During the course of her life Lauren had never encountered a real honest-to-God butler. She almost felt as if they were the human prototypes of the answering machine. In the last hour she had come to realize the two had a lot in common. They gave a repetitive, unchanging message and never revealed what was actually going on.

Her wait in the Palmers' small French sitting room was now approaching one full hour, and the lingering coolness of early morning had been replaced with a syrupy heat. Apparently the dynasty that had founded Chicago's Gold Coast didn't rise on Sunday until brunch was served. However, she had been told that if she cared to wait, there was a possibility that she might be received. Lauren quickly seized the opening and stated emphatically that she had vital information for Mrs. Palmer.

She'd then crossed her fingers behind her taffeta skirt

and cinched it by linking her message to the women's building at the Fair. Lauren knew from her research that this project had been Bertha Palmer's baby from beginning to end. The woman was recorded as being so amazing and so farsighted that Lauren had put all her eggs in this one fragile basket.

A fragile basket that was about to shatter.

She shifted on the silk brocade settee and irritated the tender part of her body she'd been ignoring for hours; the tender flesh that conjured excruciating memories of the night just past. A paralyzing pain hovered ever closer to Lauren's heart and mind, compelling her to firmly clamp down on the thoughts trying to push her over the edge. This was the last step, and then she could leave.

As if by magic, her unspoken prayer was heard and the inlaid double doors of polished mahogany glided open across a intricate rose, green, and gold Persian rug.

"I am told you have news that is only for my ears."

A woman of great consequence swept into the room in a cloud of lace and lilac voile. Lauren knew Bertha Palmer to be somewhere in her mid-forties, but for her age was irrelevant. Her light hair seemed to be arranged like a crown on her head, and Lauren thought it perfectly fitting for the lady of the castle.

The limestone-and-granite-turreted mansion was one of the city's finest showplaces. It even boasted the first completely authentic Louis the Sixteenth salon, complete with furniture from that French monarch's palace. And yet the regal Mrs. Palmer didn't remain in her ivory tower; she believed in helping people, or so Lauren had read in numerous history books.

She was counting on that historic perception with all her heart.

"Thank you for seeing me, Mrs. Palmer. My name is Lauren Dugan." Her voice wobbled for only a fraction of a second as she leaned over to retrieve Patrick's list from the carpetbag. She took a deep breath to dislodge her heart from her throat, mustered all her 1990s-empowered feminine confidence, and continued. "And, yes, I do have some information I'm praying you'll be able to help me with."

An hour later Lauren sat silently sipping tea from the most gorgeous silver tea service she had ever seen. Bertha Palmer had interrupted her story only twice with keen, incisive questions, and now she seemed to be contemplating the truth of the whole affair. Lauren's hastily scrawled copy of Patrick's list lay next to a paper-thin hand-painted china cup. The original remained hidden in the cracked pillar in the Palace of Fine Arts.

"I must tell you, Mrs. Dugan, that I find you to be a courageous woman and a devoted wife." Bertha Palmer folded her hands in her lap and scrutinized Lauren with an intense look. "My interest in maintaining the excellent reputation of Chicago's World's Fair is deeply personal, and I know my husband will be able to make effective use of this information."

"Truthfully, Mrs. Palmer, my main concern is for the safety of my hu-husband and our friends."

"I shall send for Potter immediately, and we'll begin . . ." She paused and furrowed her brow, as if searching for the right word.

"Brainstorming," Lauren finished without thinking, and then choked on her own tongue.

"Why, yes, Mrs. Dugan. What an unusual but descriptive expression." She rose gracefully and walked to a bell pull. "I like that very much," Bertha mused, tapping her chin with one finger. "The committee will love it."

"Somethin's wrong, darlin', I just know it!" Molly muttered for the fifth time in as many minutes. With a clatter, she slapped her knitting needles and yarn down on the oak table and fingered the decaying flowers Laurie had arranged in her water pitcher.

"I told you what she said, honey." Stephan crossed the small room and hunkered down in front of his worried wife. "But I promise that if we haven't heard anything in an hour, I'll go to the Palmers' myself."

"I don't understand ya, Patrick Dugan! This is your wife we're talkin' about, and as sure as green is an Irishman's favorite color . . . I'm tellin' ya, she's in trouble!"

Patrick was hard pressed to ignore the accusation in Molly's voice. Even Stephan had begun giving him long, pointed glares as the morning had turned into afternoon. With a grunt, he shoved back his chair and stalked to one of the small front windows.

"Stephan is the one who let Laurie go off on this wild goose chase to the gold doors up on Lake Shore Drive. That just shows you how truly dim-witted the woman is. As if Potter Palmer would give a flyin' fig about the likes of me."

"By God, she was right!" Stephan said, dumbfounded. "Laurie was right."

"What?"

"She told me you wouldn't care and I let it go—let her go because *we* both care so damn much for you, ya stubborn jackass, and I couldn't think of another plan that had half as good a chance of workin'." Stephan stood up and fisted his huge hands. "I feel bad enough for my part in this, but you should feel lower than a snake's belly. She's probably givin' her entire fortune away this very minute to keep you safe, and you're already hopin' she won't come back, aren't you?"

Patrick whirled away from the window, fury burning like liquid fire in his veins. Bloody hell, he was mad—mad at Stephan for siding with his wife; mad at Laurie for leavin' him without one word; and so blasted mad at himself that he was walking right into the punch that Polaski was a push away from delivering.

"Stephan! Patrick! Stop it, the both of you! This is just our fear talkin', and I won't let you come to blows over it. Come on." Molly grabbed her husband by the arm and tugged him out the door. "We need a bit of hot, fresh air right now."

With one last scowl Stephan stomped out.

What was she doing? Patrick winced as he slammed his hand against the windowframe. Why hadn't he heard her this morning? *You know why, you bastard!* No matter what he'd tried to tell himself about last night, his body had reacted like a well-satisfied man's. Damn fool! He'd slept!

For the first time in his life, Patrick knew he'd acted like the men whose heartless blood ran through his veins. Responded as if their lovemaking hadn't meant a thing, hadn't changed a thing; and it made him sick with shame.

She'd given him the two most precious gifts a woman had to give and he'd made it clear as the freckled little nose on her face that he wanted her gone as soon as possible.

What's all this carryin' on about, Dugan? niggled a quiet voice inside his head. *You've been waitin' days for the woman to leave, and clearly she has. So be happy, man.*

But he wasn't happy. He was empty as hell and twice as desolate. And the real fear he'd been denying as fast and furiously as he could was that this feeling, this bottomless pit of tangled emotions, was never going to go away. Dugan slumped into a chair at the table and jammed the heels of his hands against his closed eyes.

Just remembering that last moment of utter closeness, utter completion, seared like acid in his belly. He knew she had been waiting for something, anything, to let her know what her gifts had meant to him. Wasn't that what he had arrogantly thought he could give her? The knowledge that she was worthy and wonderful and all woman. God curse him for the bastard he was.

Even now he could feel the clammy cold after her soft body had pulled away to curl into a small protective ball. And he had just lain there, unable to stop the withdrawal. Unable to stop the fear that he'd felt as a lad on the edge of manhood, stripped of everything he had, everything he thought he was.

The same fear he had buried deep in his heart next to his ma's memory; that his black-hearted uncle was right, that no one would ever again love someone as unworthy as he. That love was a fool's game, and he and his mother stupid pawns.

On pain of death, Patrick could not let himself believe for a moment that Laurie had meant what she said. It had just been the passion. The woman had never meant to stay; never even talked of staying. She had another life, and she'd gone back to it. This was the pattern. Oh, desire might blaze bright enough to trick poor souls into thinking love was real and would last. But after the fire burned out there was nothing left but worthless ash.

As bad as he felt about hurting Laurie, Patrick knew he should be grateful that she'd left before she had realized her mistake.

Molly would believe Lauren had left him, all right; but not for the reason Laurie had dreamed up. These past two days had brought the end of the world, just as he'd suspected.

"Patrick?" Molly called, opening the door so quietly that at first he hadn't heard her. He lifted his head.

"A messenger just delivered this note." She cautiously handed it over and moved back to lean against Stephan for support.

"Holy Mary, I can't believe she did this!" Dugan exclaimed, skimming the card. "It's from Bertha Palmer herself, lettin' me know that her husband is very interested and committed to helpin' me with my problem. The list will give him the tangible proof that he needs to take to the governor. . . . What?" Dugan stood in one smooth movement, dropping the hand that clutched the paper and staring bug-eyed at Stephan. "Tell me you didn't do it," he demanded.

"I'm sorry, Patrick." Stephan shrugged. "At the time it seemed for the best. You can see that Palmer agrees."

Patrick continued reading, mumbling a variety of curses under his breath and ignoring Molly's gasp.

"Bloody hell!"

"What!" the Polaskis asked together.

"Listen,"

Although your charming wife asked that I notify you of her intention to leave town, I fear I cannot simply leave it at that. Knowing it is none of my business to interfere in your intimate disagreement caused me to consider this carefully, as I know you are in a certain amount of danger. However, my butler has informed me that it appeared your wife was being followed by a very unsavory man when she left here.

She seemed adamant about protecting you and keeping you in your "safe house"—the term she used—until my husband has positive news. But I cannot, in good conscious, concede to her wishes. Please ask Lauren to forgive me: she will agree that as women we must not turn a blind eye to the wrongs we see. I could not close my eyes to her possible danger.

The woman is a jewel, Mr. Dugan, and most definitely ahead of her time. She is not a female to wait and wring her hands, but I fear she is a bit naive in this situation. My husband will meet with you in four days. Present this card at the servant's entrance and you will be admitted discreetly. You must be quite a man to have such a crusader in your corner. I hope to see you both at that time.

"It's Bates! That animal's out there somewhere after Laurie!" Patrick fell into his chair and pounded his fist on the kitchen table. "Mother of God, what if he already has her?"

Stephan Polaski felt his blood run cold at the anguished sound of his friend's voice. The man would have to be tied down before he would listen to reason. With a loud crash, a ladder-backed chair hit the floor. Patrick's heavy shoes slammed against the wood planking and he lunged for the door.

"You're not goin' anywhere, my friend," Stephan said harshly, moving directly into the path of a raging bull.

"Get the hell out of my way, Polaski," Patrick roared. "That's my wife out there, and nothin' will stop me from going to her. If they find her with that list and know she's shown it to Palmer . . ." He swallowed, nausea crawling up his throat. With one swipe he snatched his cap off a peg by the window and pulled it low on his head, missing Stephan's move until it was too late to stop the fist from connecting with his jaw.

"Forgive me, Patrick," Stephan murmured, still shaking his throbbing right hand. He and Molly levered Patrick's limp body onto their bed; then he opened his arms and gathered his worried wife close.

"Whatever you do, love, don't let this hardheaded

Irishman leave.'' Stephan could feel her tears seeping
through the worn cotton of his shirt. ''I'll find her, darlin'. Remember, our Laurie is a very unusual woman.
She won't be easy to corner.''

Later, Molly Polaski stood at the foot of her beloved
walnut bed and literally watched the bruise on Patrick's
jaw swell and darken. She crossed her arms tightly under her breasts and prayed like there was no tomorrow.
Please God, help Stephan.
Please God, help Laurie.
Please God, don't let Dugan wake up too soon.

Lauren was stalling.

After two hours she had to face it. She had left the
Palmers assuring herself that it was reasonable to wait
for the Sunday crowds to thin so she wouldn't send
some poor, unsuspecting 1890s' tourist over the edge
by disappearing into thin air. She quickly supported this
thought with a perfect back-up excuse for her lollygag-
ging (an expression she'd learned from Molly.) Having
come all this way, it was only right that she see a bit
of the famed Columbian Exposition, the costly event
that lasted only six months but impacted the world in
so many ways.

Grounds by Lake Michigan that had once been virtually uninhabitable were now covered with an incredible mix of lagoons, gondolas, an island, and buildings
of every description, including the famous White City.
Excited patrons witnessed a literal preview of the new
scientific age that was dawning. Electricity boomed. Edison's Kinetoscope, the first long-distance phone call,
and a moving sidewalk were only a few of the wonders
to be seen. Even the word *midway* had gone on to ever
after denote the carnival-type attractions found at any
circus or fair.

Lauren's initial relief at Bertha Palmer's warm re-

ception and her husband's promise had lifted her heavy
heart for a while. The wonder of dwarf elephants, cam-
els, and whole foreign villages (including sixty African
tribesman), brought to this one spot without the benefit
of twentieth-century technology, had occupied her mind
for at least an hour, crowding out the pain she held at
bay.

Then she'd found herself at the Ferris wheel. It really
was incredible, she thought, tipping her neck back as
far as it could go. Each car was the size of four railroad
coaches and held sixty people; 2,160 people when fully
loaded. Nothing at any of the modern-day amusement
parks Lauren had heard of seemed scarier. What would
G. W. Ferris think if he could see how far others had
taken the thrill ride concept?

That was when Lauren admitted the real truth: She
couldn't bear to leave. Here she was, at the one spot in
the six hundred acres around her most connected to Patrick Dugan, and she had homed in on it like a trained
pigeon.

The confounded sting of tears threatened for the first
time since early morning. Lauren tugged on her gloves
and used a hankie to blot her moist forehead, composing
herself. The long line of wheel riders shifted, and she saw
a popcorn concession stand. Maybe something in her
stomach would help with the wobbling in her knees.

She almost laughed in spite of her turmoil when she
got close enough to read the sign. *First Time Anywhere—Candied Popcorn and Peanuts—It's Cracker
Jack!* Even as an adult she had loved the sweet, molas-
ses-flavored treat. Who would have known! This clever
entrepreneur was about to make a fortune.

A big lady with an even bigger hat thrust herself in
front of Lauren and asked for her money back.

"I don't like the peanuts in this a'tall, mister," she
bellowed.

The poor man behind the wooden counter paled as numerous passersby stopped and gathered around.

"Vell, ma'am, ve don't vant unsatisfied customers, so here you go."

Lauren watched the obviously German gentleman hand back a coin, and as the big but-bustle waggled away, she thought she heard him mumble something about peanuts staying at the circus.

"Oh, Mister . . . ?"

"Rueckheim," he supplied.

"Mr. Rueckheim, please don't leave out the peanuts; that's what makes your recipe so unique." Lauren was very aware of the interested faces around her, and she raised her voice as she accepted her bag. A sweet, tangy smell rushed up to meet her as she took a deep whiff. "Ummm, this is totally awe-fantastic. A fair wouldn't be complete without it!"

"Vhy danka, Missy," the bewildered but grateful man beamed.

"Papa, pleeease!"

The plaintive, childish whine caught Lauren's attention just as she stepped out of line to make room for the next customer. She struggled to chew with her mouth closed and smile at the same time. That poor parent had a long day ahead.

"Now, Franklin Delano, I will purchase a bag, but you will not have a single piece until after luncheon."

Lauren executed a world-class double take and watched the boy and his father disappear into the teeming masses. Franklin Delano Roosevelt? Naw . . . it couldn't be.

Talk about grasping at straws to avoid doing what you have to do. Get moving.

With a quick stoop and a snap, the popcorn was stuffed in her trusty carpetbag and Lauren pointed herself in the direction of the Palace of Fine Arts. Luckily, her favorite guard hadn't been on duty early this morning when she'd cautiously searched the rotunda for the cracked pillar Stephan had described.

"Please, Mr. Hank! I'm begging you."

Lauren froze at the woman's frantic plea, as if an arctic wind had just swept away the humid summer afternoon.

"Oh, all right, then! You tell Patrick or Mr. Polaski. Tell them about McDonald. Swear it! I don't dare come again!"

Improbably or not, Lauren knew exactly who was making the impassioned plea. Nancy Brown. Beautiful young Nancy Brown; a picture-perfect postcard. For the briefest moment Lauren felt crushing bands of jealousy snaking around her chest.

Pretty little Nancy Brown definitely has something I want. . . . And what she, Lauren Ann Sullivan, had given, he hadn't. Not for long, anyway. But whether Patrick really cared for this girl or not didn't matter. Protecting him and the Polaskis was her priority.

"Miss Brown, I believe I can help you."

The wide, startled eyes that rounded on her were the color of dark, wet, earth. A large-brimmed, soft-crowned hat dripping with pink plumes and roses, overwhelmed the pinched pale face it framed. Bloodless lips formed a tiny *O*.

"I'm Patrick's wife, Lauren." She extended a gloved hand to the stricken girl.

"Harry told me . . . but I didn't believe . . ." Nancy visibly shook herself, plumes bobbing, and continued, "I'm sorry for getting your husband into this trouble, Mrs. Dugan. Of course, now that I know he's married, it explains why he acted so, never would . . ."

A vivid blush stained the embarrassed girl's cheeks, and Lauren took pity on her awkward attempt to handle the situation.

"I admire your courage, Miss Brown," Lauren said sincerely, and squeezed Nancy's hand before releasing it. She had read the journal, after all, and knew what Harry Brown was capable of.

"Please tell Pat—Mr. Dugan, that my brother and McDonald are going out of town next week. Maybe that will help." Nancy's eyes filled with tears. "This whole thing is my fault."

Dropping her bag, Lauren placed both her hands on the young woman's quaking shoulders. "Nancy, I want you to listen to me very carefully." She pressed down a bit to ensure the emotional Miss Brown's attention. "I swear to you that this problem between your brother and Patrick has absolutely nothing to do with you."

"But—"

"You stumbled into something that was already happening. Truly. Neither Patrick nor I blame you in the least tiny bit."

"But Harry's my brother," she choked out. "I have to do something."

As Lauren looked into the imploring mud-brown eyes, she had an amazing, desperate idea. An idea that popped fully formed into her head. Almost like a push . . . It was just possible that she might be able to read some kind of message, have something of Patrick back in her own time, if this girl would agree to her strange request. She grabbed the worn leather handle of her bag and cupped Nancy's elbow, steering her over to the side of a mock Parisian store.

"Do you have a journal—a diary?"

"Yes," she answered tentatively.

"I can't explain now, but it would help so much if you would record anything you hear or read about Patrick."

"All right."

Nancy looked unsure.

Come on, Sullivan, come up with a reason! Anything that sounds remotely sane.

"It might be useful later, as evidence . . . and if anyone named Polaski," Lauren saw her look of panic but continued, "comes to you with a message, write that down too. Just stay out of your brother's way. I've got someone working legally for Patrick, so don't cause problems for yourself."

The trembling girl squared her shoulders and took a deep breath. "I'll do it, Mrs. Dugan, never you doubt it, but I'd better tell you one other thing."

Lauren's stomach knotted into a hard little ball.

"This one really is my fault." Nancy bravely held her gaze steady. "Harry knows about Polaski." When Lauren gasped, she quickly added, "Only the name; that's all."

Before Lauren could muster an answer, Nancy Brown darted around the store's corner, dragging her along.

"Oh, my stars, Mrs. Dugan," she wailed. "One of the horrible men who work for my brother is coming our way."

The danger that Lauren had romanticized and minimized over the last week with Molly and Stephan exploded into breath-steeling reality.

"Is he big?" *Please God, not him!*

"He's huge and ugly, Mrs. Dugan. He's the one who was hurting Patrick in jail."

Bates!

He'll not be forgettin' what you did to him, lass.

"Did he see us?"

"I'm not certain. I don't think so."

"It was so stupid to come here!" Lauren pounded the heel of one hand against her forehead. "I want you to leave very discreetly, Nancy, and don't ever come back to the Ferris wheel. There,'' she pointed. ''There's a big crowd to duck into.''

''I won't forget to write, Mrs. Dugan,'' Nancy promised. ''If ever you need my diary, just ask or send for it.'' With a brief wave she merged into the human river.

''Be careful,'' Lauren whispered as Nancy was swallowed up. For a fraction of a second she pictured Nancy's journal in the post office box she'd arranged for in Chicago. Shoot! There was no time and no point in wondering what it all might mean. Following promptings was something she was learning to just do, and figure out the reasons later.

Right now she had to get gone, and fast. Lauren warily pulled down the brim of her straw boater and couldn't help but wish she'd worn her navy blue outfit; she'd blend in better. But it was too late—too late for so many things. Lauren sneaked a quick peak around the corner and wedged into the middle of a human stream going in the opposite direction.

The late Sunday afternoon crowd had dwindled down to nearly nothing. The fair itself hadn't been slated to be open on the Sabbath, but in an effort to offset the stock market crash of 1893 the directors had overruled the detractors. In the end, it really hadn't helped at all, and Lauren desperately wished for the safety of numbers.

Very soon now the Palace of Fine Arts would be closing, and she needed to get inside. Restlessly, her eyes swept the open area. For tense hours Lauren had circled the pavilions and shops, feeling more and more like a hunted animal. Exhausted, hungry, and frightened, she had finally felt safe enough to wait out of sight in this small bunch of trees and shrubs.

The museum brochure with the 1995 dates had to work. Holding the printed date of the centennial leap she was trying to make must be the key. After analyzing each step of her experience traveling back to 1895, it was still the only thing that made sense. But now, with a monster on her tail, a strong hypothesis wasn't at all reassuring.

Lauren looked down at the blue paper in her hand. August 14th and August 31st. She had to go today. No way could she face Patrick Dugan again and, truth to tell, her old battle with fear was winning. Bates was out there somewhere, and she just didn't know what she might reveal if he caught her. To bring any kind of harm to Patrick or the Polaskis was horrifying. She had to go, and go today. The 31st was too long to wait.

As Lauren tucked the brochure deep into her skirt pocket, she mentally girded her loins. One more exposed run to safety, and then it would be over.

Wearily, she leaned against a lumpy tree. Her burning eyes closed and she released a shaky sigh. Even though the air was heavy, the musty, earthy smell of water and greenery was not unpleasant. Fewer and fewer footsteps echoed in the deepening twilight.

For the first time she dared to open the tiny closed door in her heart that held back the memories of last night. If she only cracked it a bit perhaps just the sweet would seep through, and she could slam it before the bitter followed.

Silent tears slipped from between her lashes as she remembered the honeyed taste of those deep, delicious kisses. Just like a tender movie she had seen months ago, Lauren prepared to stop her reverie at the happy part. Why in the world would a screenwriter, who had the power to end his work any way he wanted to, finish it with heartbreaking sadness?

But as the image of Patrick's powerful body formed in her mind's eye, she lingered a moment too long, feeling protected and cherished. Warm all the way through. The words she had not been able to understand became words of love, and the pounding of her heart roared in her ears, rushing past her defenses to the moment . . . Oh, it hurt! The pain was terrible. Crushing.

And, God help her, real.

"Well, now, ain't this nice of ya, Mrs. Dugan," Bates drawled in her ear, locking an iron arm around her waist and twisting her right wrist cruelly behind her.

"Please . . ." She struggled to breathe. "Please don't hurt me." As soon as the words escaped her, Lauren despised herself for allowing her fear such control. Bates tightened his hold and her agony grew, but she'd be damned if she'd go easy.

"Now there won't be no reason to hurt ya, ma'am, if you'll just give ol' Bates some sugar."

Bile moved up her throat as the huge, hairy arm moved up her chest. When hurtful, pinching fingers fastened onto her breast Lauren felt her whole body lurch. Get away! She had to get away!

Bates must have felt the scream coming, for he clamped the offending hand hard over her mouth.

"This ain't the way to please me, woman. You're a mite too stubborn to take outta these trees right now." With a quick jerk, he snapped her head back to his shoulder and lifted her right up off the ground. "Behave, or you'll be sorry!"

Lauren almost gagged when she felt him nuzzle his scratchy face down the side of her neck and lick her. The rancid smell of his breath and body was awful enough, but the touch of his slimy tongue promised such horror that she would rather die than endure it.

Lauren kicked him with all her might.

Bates bit her savagely, and she could feel something warm trickle down under her collar.

Her hard rubber heels rained blow after blow before

239

he hurled her to the ground. Lauren tried to scramble to safety, but he caught her skirt and quietly laughed as he dragged her toward him. With a yank, he pulled her to her knees and backhanded her twice when she opened her mouth to scream. Lauren's head exploded in pain. Her ears rang and she couldn't focus. Even then she wouldn't stop fighting. With one desperate lunge she dove for her carpetbag.

"Now, now, missy," he cackled, kicking it out of her reach. "Ya won't be using no witch potion on me again. But I'm obliged for the reminder. Yer gonna pay for that, woman. And wait till ya see the place I'm fixin' to take ya. My friend has some real interestin' toys that'll teach ya right quick. But here's a starter."

With that, he hauled back and punched her squarely in the chest, laying her full out.

Shallow, shallow, shallow breaths; deeper hurt so bad. More oxygen began to clear her head, and Lauren felt cool air on her legs. That animal was exposing her. *God in heaven, help me! Help me!*

Lauren blinked rapidly and saw her opening. The arrogant bastard was totally vulnerable as he fumbled with his pants. With her last bit of strength, she kicked him viciously right where it counted. She dropped him again.

Adrenaline fueled her escape. She rolled awkwardly to her feet, grabbed her bag, and kept to the trees.

Every gulp of air, every step brought fresh agony until sweat rolled down the sides of her face, followed by tears.

Hide! She had to hide! This time Bates would surely kill her. Lauren emerged from the little grove just in time to see a guard locking the Palace doors. Her chance was lost! She stumbled and roused the attention of a passerby. Quickly she yanked off a filthy glove and used it to wipe away the red trails coming from her mouth. Since it was almost fully dark she pulled her hat forward and tried not to limp.

The panic-induced energy was flowing out of Lauren's body just like her blood. A dangerous stuporlike sensation began numbing her limbs. Steps. Up the steps she staggered. Up the steps and back into a welcoming black corner, willing herself to become invisible.

Her last action was to clutch the can of Mace before dropping her head to her bent knees.

Patrick sat bound to the stoop steps as surely as if he had been harnessed by an iron chain. The dusky twilight settled peacefully over the buildings and street, making a mockery of his violent emotions. All around him he saw Laurie's handiwork . . . and the beauty of it, the kindness in it, pummeled away at his damned pride.

On the sacred life of Molly's unborn child he had sworn not to leave and then had almost unmanned himself when the blood rushing from his head left him in a near swoon. Baby! Babies! What in God's name had he been using for a brain? He had ordered Laurie right out of his life; shoved her right out of his life, and maybe his child, too. Molly had *shoved* him out on the stoop at that point, for some air.

Where the bloody hell was Stephan? Was Laurie hurt? Gone? He couldn't stand this!

Patrick began pacing restlessly across the steps. He raked a handful of hair out of his face and cautiously fingered the lower right side of his jaw. Polaski had one hell of a lot of nerve.

How long had it been since he'd let anyone get this close? Even this new relationship with Stephan and Molly he owed to Laurie. Because of her he had been forced to depend on them, forced to give and take; forced deeply into their lives and they into his. He wasn't alone now.

Patrick sunk his hands into his pants' pockets and looked up at the darkening sky. Tiny pinpoints of light were flickering to life . . . but weren't they always there? he mused. They just couldn't be seen except under the right conditions. Was that true of him, too? Had his desire for love and friendship always been there, only invisible because the white-hot flames of anger and fear blinded him to any other need?

He dropped again to the painted green step and ran his fingers over the same place Laurie's had been; *his wife's* had been. What if this was all he ever had of her? If Stephan didn't find her, it might mean she was gone . . . back to the future. Out of his reach forever.

Patrick's heart began to pound. He hadn't heard the words *I love you* since the day his mother had died. His poor ma. Deserted and betrayed by the scoundrel who'd fathered him and the brother she'd been forced to turn to. But she had never stopped believing in love. Never stopped believing in the watchful help of heaven. Never stopped loving him . . .

Only death could make her leave you.

Dugan jumped to his feet and curled his hands impotently at his sides. In all the years since her passing, he hadn't really looked back at that time clearly; not until a few nights ago when he'd so rashly spilled the sordid story of his youth to Laurie. The stunning truth in her words brought memories to light that had been lost in a dark cave of hate.

"I want you to know, son, that I've always thought of you as an angel, sent to me when I needed love the most."

His mother's energy had been draining out with every word she spoke, and Patrick sat, watching helplessly; knowing he could do nothing to stop the ravaging illness.

"I've not been able to give you much, Paddy. Your

uncle is a hard man to understand, but I'm counting on . . ." She had lowered her fever-bright eyes, and Patrick realized that even then she had been uncertain as to what her brother would do when she was gone.

"You've given me the world in your books, Ma," he'd assured her.

"You keep reading, Paddy, and going to church." She had lifted a trembling hand to stroke his cheek. "And no matter what happens, no matter what you hear, remember, you have been the best thing in my life." Her arm had dropped to press against her chest. "Don't ever believe it wasn't worth it. Lasting love is worth whatever the cost. A life without it is wasted. So don't horde your heart away, lad. When you find love again don't be afraid to hold on tight."

The last time he had held on tight to love had been that night, grasping his dead mother's hand until it grew stiff and cold in his own.

Patrick forced his aching fingers open and sat once more on the step. While he'd been lost in the past, the darkness had rolled in. Unconsciously, he began to rock forward, rubbing his cramped hands along his thighs. Lasting love, leprechauns, and angels were fairy tales! Stories to make the bitter facts of life go down a mite easier.

Until Laurie Ann Sullivan Dugan dropped into his life, he'd been able to keep that straight in his mind and his heart.

Dugan tipped back his head and studied the star-studded sky once more. Against the black curtain of night they shimmered like countless diamonds. For days now, there had been a precious jewel glittering around him, but the glare of hate, fear, and pride had hidden her value. The one time he had held her in his arms he had not done so long enough, tight enough.

He'd hurt her and maybe destroyed, maybe lost forever the wonderful thing in which his mother had tried to make him believe.

He felt as empty as a starless, moonless sky.

What would he do if he got a second chance?

What would he do if he didn't?

Chapter Thirteen

"Laurie! Laurie Dugan, for God's sake, answer me, girl!"

Stephan Polaski doggedly trudged up the front steps of the Palace for the sixth time in four hours. He sank abruptly to one broad white step and dropped his head into his hands. Where could she be? Molly would be beside herself by now, and surely Dugan was awake. He halfway expected to see his enraged friend appear any moment.

Patrick had been positive that she was coming here, but it was full dark now, and Stephan began contemplating what would happen if he was to arrive home without any news. All hell would break loose.

A low moan seemed to float to him on the sultry night breeze, and gooseflesh skittered up his spine. He stood with arms akimbo and tried to identify the shifting shadows around him.

"Who's there?" he demanded, moving into a fight-ready stance. "I'll stand for no monkey business, so be gone or prepare to meet my fists."

"Ste . . . phaaan?"

"Laurie?" His arms flew wide and his whole body whirled, trying to pinpoint the location of her voice. "Come here, my friend. I've been lookin' everywhere for you."

Not a sound

"Laurie!" This time Stephan's tone cut through the dark like a double-edged sword of anger and fear. Something was terribly wrong. He ran to the top of the stairs and sensed a ripple from a back corner.

"Help me. . . . "

Before Lauren could take another step, Stephan Polaski swept her up and held her safe in his arms. A random beam of moonlight illuminated her face, and he uttered a harsh, blunt curse.

"Aww, Laurie girl, what have they done to you?"

Thank God Molly was the first to see them coming.

Two things told her the truth of it even though the couple was still quite a ways off. One was the broad set and shape of her husband's shoulders, and the other was the ice-cold lump of women's intuition that settled low in her stomach. They were moving far too slowly. Molly knew Patrick would have to be prepared or too many questioning eyes would see what they should not see.

"Patrick?" she said quietly as she entered the murky room. He had obviously turned down the lamp before stretching out on his palette.

"Stephan?" he returned in a raw voice, rolling to his feet and heading for the door.

"Wait!"

That one word sunk like a spike, pinning him to the floor.

"We don't want an audience, Patrick," Molly cautioned, coming to stop before him and placing a restraining hand on his tensed forearm. "So, no matter what happens in the next few minutes, rein in that hot Irish temper!"

She lifted her palm and rubbed his back, as if he were a child in need of comfort. Dear God, what had Molly seen?

As Patrick's foot hit the bottom stair, he spotted them crossing the deserted street. Stephan was holding Laurie too close, unnaturally close. His first, glorious burst of relief began twisting in his veins. And then she stumbled . . . and a tiny whimper froze every nerve in his body.

"We're here, Laurie," he heard his friend murmur. "Let me carry you now."

Patrick materialized out of the shifting darkness, feeling like an apparition finally released from one hell only to find another waiting.

"Mine, Stephan." He held out his arms. "She's mine."

Patrick knew as he cradled Lauren's limp body that he had never carried anything so precious. With every creak of the stairs he felt the barriers he had built between them crumbling.

"In here." Molly waved, holding the flickering bedroom lamp in one hand.

The three of them stood in stunned silence as the light revealed the bruised and bloodied face.

"Merciful Mary, who did this to her?" Molly's sobbed question hung ominously in the stillness, and she tenderly began to unbutton Lauren's dirty, torn shirtwaist. "Oh, we've got to help her."

Patrick's hands closed over Molly's and stopped her. "I'll care for my wife. If you'll just bring me some water and . . ." His throat grew so thick with suppressed emotions, he could barely speak.

When Molly tried to protest Stephan gently circled her shoulders with his arm and led her to the door. Her watery eyes gleamed with a brief flare of anger until he whispered in her ear.

"If that was you lying there like Laurie, so hurt," he swallowed hard and rested his forehead against his sweet wife's, "I'd have to touch and care for every last inch of you to believe that you'd really be all right."

When her wet lips pressed against his Stephan knew she understood.

Patrick's hands were shaking so badly that he was having a devil of a time dealing with the tiny buttons running down the front of Laurie's ruined blouse. He had never been so angry and so afraid at the same time. Twice he had to stop and clench his hands into rigid fists to relieve the furious energy pulsing through him. Not for a prize thoroughbred would he lay one harsh finger on his angel.

Hell! He was a goner.

Move! Don't think.

As carefully as possible, Dugan sat on the bed, facing Laurie hip to hip, and slipped off her shoes and skirt. Reaching up gingerly under the lace, he peeled down her stockings and garters. With a brief ghost of a smile he registered that she wore only one petticoat, and re-membered the few times she had mumbled about men in the past controlling women with yards of cloth. The she-cat clearly pared it down as much as she could.

Of course he knew she wore no corset, but when he pulled away the slip and shirtwaist the sight of those tiny undergarments he teased her about left his mouth drier than the Great American Desert he'd read about.

Molly had placed a bleached muslin nightdress on the bed, and Patrick blindly reached for it. For both their sakes he draped it across her body. Even though she had been closer to him than any other living soul, he knew she was a modest little thing. Any minute her eyes might open, and he didn't want her to see the hunger blazing in his own. How could he explain it when he had taken the gift of her body and sent her away as if it meant nothing? And damn if he wasn't responsible for this beating, too. She must hate him!

"Uuuuuuuh . . ."

"I'm sorry, sweetheart," he whispered, carefully levering her back up off the bed. "I'd not hurt you, but I need to tend to your wounds."

Lauren's eyes fluttered open and looked straight into the face that she had vowed never to see again and yet had been her only hope as she had prayed fervently in the dark.

"It . . . was Bates . . . Patrick."

"I know, lass; hush now."

"No!" Lauren's breathless voice vibrated with effort. With a weak fist she latched onto his shirtfront. "He knows Stephan's name, and I'm afraid they'll find you and hurt all of . . ." Lauren shuddered. "I'm sorry, Patrick. I tried to make Stephan leave me, but he wouldn't." A deep sob racked her body and she trembled. "If he followed, I . . ."

"Don't fash yourself, love," Dugan crooned gently, rubbing her shoulders with hands that felt big and clumsy. "Stephan was very, very careful." There was no doubt in his mind that this woman must have passed through heaven on her way to the past. Even with bruises and blood coloring her tender flesh, her thoughts were only for them.

Delicately, he pressed her head to the spot where his neck and shoulder met, unpinning her poor ratty hairpiece and then running his fingers over and over through the short locks, comforting himself as much as her. The light, trusting sound of her sigh ruffling against his skin seeped into the fissures in his heart, fanning the tiny ember there. A faint, rich, rose perfume drifted around him, and unconsciously Patrick trailed his fingers down her neck.

Laurie gasped.

"What? What did I do?" Patrick moved back and began to search until he found the cause of her distress. With butterfly strokes he cleansed the angry welt on her neck, resting her forehead against his chest. As more and more of the blood was removed, he saw it for what it was: Teeth had punctured the skin.

He'd kill the bastard!

"He hurt me."

Patrick felt a burning sting in his nose and eyes. She must have been terrified.

"But I didn't freak out, Dugan," she said with a tiny burst of her old fire, lifting her head. "I got away."

The woman actually pulled her swollen cheek and lip into a cockeyed smile and proceeded to relate the details as he methodically tended her abused face. His fierce little she-cat still spoke in terms he couldn't always understand. He didn't think she could ever appear a freak, but he didn't need words to know that the telling was also healing. She knew she hadn't remained a victim.

"Now I understand why you were still a virgin. You modern women must not need men at all," he teased, trying to continue the distracting conversation.

Lauren wrenched back so quickly that her chest felt as if it had been stabbed. How could she have forgotten the humiliation she had endured at this man's hands? Unintentional though it may have been, it had caused a blow to equal the one Bates had given her. Illogically, she covered her heart with splayed fingers.

"Sweetheart, did that animal hurt you there?" Patrick asked, his voice grave with concern. He tugged on the thin cotton gown clutched in her fists, wondering why she was looking at him that way. When she reluctantly loosened her hold he sucked in a short strangled breath and swore. How could he have missed this? Already an ugly purple shadow was spreading up from the inside curves of her breasts.

Patrick tipped up her chin with a finger and looked directly into worried, pain-clouded pools of blue. Deliberately, he reached around her back and fumbled with the hooks of the outlandishly small garment she wore in place of a corset. For just a moment he felt her stiffen with resistance, and he ran his fingers lightly from her shoulders to her wrists, drawing away the flimsy thing.

"Sweet Jesus! I'll tear the man limb from limb!"

A hot rush of rage fanned his body into an inferno as he traced the discernable imprint of a huge fist defiling the vulnerable skin between Laurie's breasts. Patrick dropped his head and clenched her hands too hard. He knew it was too hard, but he couldn't let go. Because of him she had suffered, and merciful God—it suddenly struck him—maybe even more so.

Jerking his face to hers, he prayed silently. "Did Bates . . . force you, Laurie?" Her eyes darted away and his heart sank. She shifted her legs, and Dugan glanced down the length of her. Circling the two slim ankles he saw darkening marks and scratches. "No . . ." he bit out, twisting back to her nearly naked body and surrounding it with his own. "Tell me, angel."

Lauren felt the muscles in his back bunch and jump as he whispered the plea in her ear. One soft sideburn brushed against her cheek, and her hands smoothed over the coarse fabric of his shirt, comforting.

"No, Patrick." She paused and swallowed audibly. "He didn't . . . do that. I stopped him."

"Thank God, thank God," he murmured, pulling her on to his lap and wrapping his arms around her like a shield, raining gentle kisses down the uninjured side of her neck until she trembled in his arms. Patrick wished he could comfort her with passion but suspected her response was shock. One he could tend to and the other he dared do nothing about.

"Let's get you warmed up, lass." He let her go and carefully tugged the gown over her head, keeping her perched across his thighs. His needy hands smoothed the delicate cloth down to her hips and fluffed her honey-streaked hair into a halo around her face.

"I'm sorry for holdin' you so . . ." Patrick paused, silently cursing the urgent surge of desire he could not control.

"No, Patrick," Laurie assured him in husky, tired tones, bringing his hard palm up to cup her unblemished cheek. "Your touch makes me feel good, clean." Her gaze was straight and true. "It makes me forget how ugly . . . how ug . . ."

One shining tear rolled into the hollow of his hand, and before he thought he sipped it away and gently lay her flat on the bed. Molly's gown fell open to Laurie's waist, and Patrick shuddered at what she had endured and at what had nearly happened, and at what he had almost lost. With tightly leashed anger he twisted the wet cloth in the glazed basin until his knuckles turned white.

As he folded it into a compress, he silently measured Laurie's reaction. She'd said his touch was good, but would she object to this intimacy, especially after the way he'd treated her before?

He brushed the smocked bodice back to her shoulders and immediately noted the beating pulse at the base of her throat. He knew she watched him, absorbing every detail of her body through his eyes. Never once did she try to shield herself; by that choice she gave him the right of a true husband. She waited, totally revealed, for him to minister to her.

Can you understand what I'm trying to tell you?
Can you see what your trust means to me?

She uttered a small gasp at the sensation of the cool cloth on her fevered skin. It had been hot enough before from the bruise alone, but Dugan's rapt regard had turned up the heat. Lauren lowered her lashes to hide her intense reaction to his touch. Her body, however, could not keep the secret, and she knew by the tick in his jaw that he was affected too. It gave her hope. Wanting was not loving, but . . .

The man cared. Lauren could see it. Feel it. His every move in the last hour had confirmed it. Maybe he had been afraid the other night. Maybe he didn't think he could be loved or deserved to be loved after what his father and uncle had done to him. But he was loved, and she had almost three weeks to make him believe it. There was only one key left to open the time door, one last way to free him if he couldn't accept what she had to give; but there was no way for herself to escape a broken heart.

Patrick stood abruptly.

"You're not leaving, are you?" Her pride couldn't stop the question.

"No, lass, I'll be watchin' over you all night." His pride couldn't stop the answer. Patrick unashamedly stripped down to his underwear and snuffed out the lamp wick. From the small narrow window a stream of moonlight spilled into the room. With two long strides he reached Laurie's side and lifted away the now warm cloth. She scooted over, next to the wall, and looked up with wounded eyes.

"As long as there's breath in my body," Patrick promised, stretching out on the mattress, "that monster will never touch you again." He gently replaced the

253

refreshed balm and sealed his vow with a tender kiss on the rise of each discolored breast.

Sometime later Lauren lay in the dark, still awake and awash with feelings. As terrifying as her encounter with Bates had been, it had resulted in a second chance for her with Patrick. His hard, warm body tucked against her spoon fashion made her feel so safe. And she needed to feel that way tonight, because she had made a life-altering decision. Until the 31st she would love the man, no holds barred. No matter how he acted or reacted. She was willing to give up her life in the future or take him with her, if only they could be together.

But she needed something more to hang her hopes on, some feeling, some words that confirmed the connection she sensed between them. Lauren took a shallow breath and caught the familiar scent of Patrick's bay rum. She loved him so. Enough to expose her deepest insecurity so he would know he wasn't alone in fearing love; in needing love. Odd; born more than a hundred years apart and yet each missing the same thing. Into the still darkness she sent her quiet revelation.

"I know you will understand this, Patrick, and that's why I can tell you. Other than my parents and Aunt Lucy, no one has ever wanted me."

"Wha . . . t are you—what do you mean?" Dugan questioned, startled out of his thoughts of revenge.

"That's why I was a virgin. No one wanted me."

Her stark words cut through his distraction like a knife. Now he knew why she had drawn back and given him that look. How could he have done to Laurie what had been done so cruelly to him? He had taken and then proven he hadn't wanted her either.

But he did, God help him. He more than wanted her, and finally admitting it scared him spitless. Patrick could no longer deny that this link between himself and Laurie had gone way beyond just passion. Every little freckle, each short, spiky hair on her head, and even the paint rings around her eyes were precious, and tonight . . . so beautiful because they meant she was all right and here.

That was what mattered most.

Even though her encounter with Bates filled him with fury and horror, it had brought her back to him. And curse him for the selfish bastard he was, she'd missed the time door! Laurie couldn't leave! At least that obstacle was gone. And if he truly had the luck of the Irish, maybe she was carrying his baby already. A baby would tie them even closer, make her stay.

His hand slid down to cover her, low on her stomach. That knowledge gave Patrick the confidence to surrender a vulnerable piece of his feelings, leaving his small ember of hope more defenseless than it had been in years. He wasn't his father or his uncle, and he didn't want to live a wasted life. These past days with Laurie had shown him the truth of that. Perhaps now, after fourteen years, it was time to try and believe again.

"Maybe that's why you've come to me, Laurie." He pressed closer to her neck and back, holding his future in the palm of his hand. "Since the men in your time can't see the angel in you someone sent you to me." Very gently he nipped her earlobe, then soothed it with a suckling kiss. "Of all that has happened between us, lass, and all that will, never doubt that I want you!"

Lauren smiled very carefully. Wanting and caring weren't exactly loving, but lying there together in the Polaskis' hopeful, honeymoon bed, she felt as if her every dream of a real family, her own family, was finally within reach.

Thank you, Aunt Lucy!

* * *

Tap, tap tap . . . Tap tap tap . . .

Lauren stirred under the plump quilt and gradually surfaced from the deep sea of sleep. *The door. Yes, that's it.* She almost called to Patrick and then realized she was alone. Moving too fast, she tried to sit and moaned loudly.

"Laurie, love?" A sharp squeak proceeded Molly into the room. "I waited 'til I was so worried I just had to make sure you were still breathin'." Her faded blue day dress was covered with a white, yoke-style apron, and she carried a tray full of breakfast. "It's hours past noon, and you need to eat. These are the softest foods I could think of." She set the dishes on the simple table near the bed and reached out to help Lauren sit up, then stopped with a pitying little cry.

"Just how ghastly do I look, Molly?"

"It's the pain, love. It's your pain I'm feelin'. But eat now and you'll feel better."

Lauren was grateful that she basically only had to swallow the oatmeal. She hated feeling weak, so the agony in her jaw and chest would have to be tolerated. "Where's Patrick?" *Nuts!* She wasn't going to ask that right off the bat! Oh well, it's not like Molly didn't know how she felt. She took a careful bite of bread and jam.

"The man must have given me a list of do's and don'ts a mile long before he left here earlier." Molly gently settled on the bed, watching with scrunched-up eyes, as if estimating the damage. "He and Stephan were so furious about what happened to you that they both decided to go talk to Potter Palmer in person."

Lauren choked and pressed a fist against her chest.

"Now, don't fash yourself, love." Molly handed Laurie a cup of tea and sat down again. "That card Mrs. Palmer sent will get them in the high-and-mighty door, and they promised to be as cautious as mice."

"But Molly—"

The normally lighthearted raven-haired girl took her dear friend's hand and spoke solemnly. "Patrick is a man, and he must protect his woman. I could see it in those green eyes of his this mornin' as he watched you sleep. This is something he has to do. I know you're scared, but Stephan is along, keepin' close to his back." She gave a soft pat and smiled. "Isn't it grand to be loved so much?"

Lauren's heartbeat accelerated. Did Molly really see that?

"Now finish up and make yourself presentable," Molly said with a sly wink. "I've been told we're to expect a special visitor in the next hour or so."

Before Lauren could question her a very secretive Mrs. Polaski disappeared behind the pine door.

"Oh, mercy!" Lauren was shocked. The woman looking back at her from the small hand mirror would have been perfect for a part in any one of the *Halloween* horror movies. A swollen, purple-blue-green cheek distorted the right half of her face. Lauren could see the sickening colors snaking up under one eye. Make that both eyes. Oh, no! All last night Patrick had been looking at a beaten raccoon. The only thing missing now was a tube of bright red lipstick for her mouth currently the exact size of clown lips.

Lauren doggedly brushed her hair and repaired her smudged makeup. *Don't lose your nerve now, Sullivan! No,* her inner voice said. *Go all the way. Dugan you've become, and Dugan you want to stay!*

She inched her legs to the side of the bed and ran her fingers up the buttons on her fresh gown. Molly had helped her bathe and wash her hair, knowing intuitively that Lauren needed to feel completely clean.

With a soft groan, she crouched next to her bag and

replaced her toiletries. A quick spritz of her floral perfume and she'd done the best she could with what she had. How would Patrick act after last night? Did he realize she had to stay? Lauren propped herself up against the walnut headboard and rubbed the smooth wood of the honeymoon bed for luck.

"Laurie? You have a visitor."

Molly touched her shoulder and Lauren came instantly awake, one hand fluffing her hair and the other protectively covering her chipmunk cheek.

"Mrs. Dugan, I hope you'll forgive me for barging right in to your sick room, but I've heard so many glowing reports that I simply had to meet you."

The mysterious woman, dressed soberly in black, extended a small gloved hand.

"I'm Jane Addams of Hull House."

The Spinster Saint of Chicago. The original social worker. *Oh my gosh!*

In high school Lauren's favorite teacher had devoted three whole class periods to the impact this one lady had had on the moral conscience of America. What would Jane Addams think if she knew that in just a few short years her concept of "settlement houses" where the poor, the uneducated, the immigrant, could come for help and training, would spread across this country to every major city?

"It's an honor to meet you, ma'am," Lauren managed to respond through her awe-inspired daze.

"Now, none of that folderol, Lauren, if I may call you that. We are kindred spirits, I believe, and need not stand on formality." She sat on the chair Molly had unobtrusively brought in by the bed. "If you're up to it, I'd like to hear how you organized the women in this building. I couldn't believe my own eyes when I walked down the street."

Miss Addams' deep-set eyes sparkled and her dark, severely knotted hair never moved, no matter how vigorously she nodded. For the first time in her life Lauren really believed that much-touted statement, that one person could make all the difference. She was in such a person's presence.

The courage of these early women leaders just blew her away. In books the odds they faced were so—well, black and white, one-dimensional. But now, now that Lauren had really seen the fight they had been up against . . . wow!

For a good hour she revelled in the brilliance and caring personality of Jane Addams.

"As soon as you're up and about, Lauren, you must come for a visit to Hull House. I could use a woman with vision."

"Oh, Miss Addams," Lauren said, masking her regret with honest sincerity, "I can't think of anything I'd enjoy more."

"Well, then, I shall leave you, that our next meeting may come all the sooner. Mrs. Polaski has confided in me the story behind your injuries, and let me assure you that if there is anyone who can help you in this cause, it is Bertha Palmer. We're both working on the same problems, but from different ends, as it were."

Miss Addams stood, then moved a step closer to Lauren. "You can't imagine how much good you have done my heart. Sometimes it seems so overwhelming, the needs, you know."

She stared into space, as if seeing another scene entirely.

"And then," she said with renewed energy, "I'll hear of someone like you. Teaching our sisters. Helping them discover their own power. Thank you, my dear." She bent and pressed a feather-light buss to Lauren's bruised cheek.

"I hope you get those bounders. I'm sure it was one of Michael McDonald's henchmen who stole my purse on the opening day at the Fair. Come to me if there's anything I can do."

Before she reached the door, Lauren was compelled to speak. "Miss Addams, don't get discouraged, no matter what. Nothing you do will be in vain, truly."

With a nod and a beaming smile, Chicago's Spinster Saint was gone.

"It's my face, isn't it?"

Patrick stopped short at the sound of Laurie's voice. He'd been creeping into the room, along with the dawn, to check on her; hoping against hope that she'd stay asleep. After all he'd realized and revealed, two nights ago, he'd had to retreat and get his bearings before he found himself on his knees, begging her to make their marriage real.

Yesterday he'd finally admitted to himself that that was what he wanted more than anything, and that's exactly what had him running scared. Patrick had trained himself *not to want*, to avoid the kind of pain his father's cruel desertion and his uncle's rejection had inflicted, and years of control had been blown to hell. He'd taken a bit of time to come up with an approach that would salvage his pride if she didn't want what he wanted. . . .

I love you. Love me, too.

Did she mean it? Did he dare believe it?

"Well, I guess I should have expected it," Lauren sighed, pushing herself up against the pillows and smoothing her hair back from her tender face. It was hard to tell if the ache in her chest was from Bates's blow or Patrick's change of heart. "In the light of day it's pretty hard to take." She softly traced the puffy side of her mouth and grimaced. "But thanks for the try, Dugan. At the time the ego boost really helped." So much for her vow to go for it.

Lauren Ann, you are a world-class chicken!

Speak, ya great fool! The woman is stirrin' the wrong pot to a boil.

Patrick walked to her side and sat. Her false bravado wavered, and he knew she didn't believe that he had spoken the truth about wanting her. Of course, his staying away had helped that misconception right along. Why, in heaven's name, did he keep doing this?

"It looks like you had a run in of some kind, too." Laurie waved a hand toward his chin at the puzzled look Patrick gave her. "What happened?" She congratulated herself for the natural sound of her voice. Now if she could only get the man hovering so close to leave. Quickly.

"I ran into a Pole."

"Was it wood or metal?" Lauren knew she was losing her calm facade and starting to babble.

"Human!"

An awkward silence spun out between them until the sound became deafening.

Stop being such a coward!

Stop being such a coward!

"Nothin' to do with your face could change the way I feel about you, lass," Patrick blurted, lifting a hand to touch her and then dropping it back to his thigh. "In point of fact, Laurie," he took a deep breath, then forced that same needy hand roughly through his hair before delivering the whole truth. "One of the main reasons I've stayed away is because even though I know you're hurtin' bad, I want nothin' more than to crawl in this bed with you right now."

There, that should shock her speechless.

Lauren's breath caught in her throat at the look on his tired face. His thick auburn hair was damp, and she could smell the light scent of Molly's coconut oil soap drifting from his warm body. This was it. The moment to begin her campaign.

"Patrick Dugan, you silly man, that's exactly what I've been lying here dreaming of." She made herself go all the way and turn down the covers to spill across his lap.

Glory, glory, glory! Patrick felt the quickening in his body and fought the urge to tear off his clothes until he finished his proposal. This one would truly count.

"It seems to be time to talk about makin' this marriage a real one, then."

The poor man looked so solemn that for a moment Lauren did not compute the meaning of his words. A real marriage? The joy bubbled up so fast that she had to release a bit or she'd explode. "Oh?" She teased him outrageously. "Haven't we technically done that already?"

It was downright humiliating that this woman could make him blush. Patrick shot her a daunting glare and tried not to let his mind follow his body's lead and think further about that earth-shaking night.

He hated the fear that churned in his belly and fought for a casual tone. Believing in Lauren's love wasn't easy. He'd spent too much of his life shunning the very thought of love to risk too much too soon. The plan he'd come up with would give her an honorable commitment, but he'd not have to give his heart just yet.

"Since you missed the time door—I won't be able to claim you're dead. That leaves us back where we started; still legally married in the eyes of the Church and the law. We're . . . we're . . ."

"Stuck." A little more joy leaked away.

"Aye, stuck." Patrick stood, not noticing the subtle shift in Lauren's countenance, and paced to the window. Sitting on the squat bench he read again Molly's handiwork on the lemon yellow pillow.

Two hearts became one. Was that what he was really asking for? Was it even possible for him?

"I think we could deal very well together, lass, since you know I . . ." he turned back to face her and moved a step closer, "I want you, and you seem to want me." He dipped his head, indicating the bed she'd made welcome for him.

Lauren fixed her eyes on the shuttered look of longing in Patrick's expression. It was that look that was giving her hope. His words, devoid as they were of any truly deep emotion, were daunting, and she'd felt a twinge or two around her heart. Until she recognized the touch of fear in those green eyes she loved so well. And the strain in the strong, hard face framed with wavy russet hair that had grown a bit too long.

But it was the man's chin—his stubborn, Irish chin, with the shallow cleft making tiny, irregular jumps as he clenched and unclenched his jaw—that told her he was feeling much more than he'd given away with words. Lauren sensed a growing urgency he could barely control.

He sat again and took her hand.

"So we're agreed, then? You're here with me and that's unchangeable now."

The pressure on her fingers became uncomfortable. Somehow she knew that if her proud Irishman got even the vaguest idea that she could still leave him, he would never be saying this.

"I won't leave you, Patrick," she promised with total honesty. Her words seemed to galvanize him, and he continued.

"Too, our marriage can't be annulled because there might be a baby growin' inside you at this very moment; a baby who deserves the grand welcome you've talked so about—"

"Patrick," Laurie interrupted, struggling to shift her

hand in his until their fingers twined together. "If there is a baby already, I couldn't be happier. I've been alone most of my life, and I have so much to give that I can feel it bursting to get out." She watched his face intently, trying to read the impact of her words.

"So you accept me as a real husband then," Patrick said, almost as if speaking to himself, and spread his free hand wide over her cotton-covered stomach. "And all that I give you?"

The heat of his touch drove all the aches and twinges from Lauren's conscious awareness. She wanted to reassure him that she was his in the most elemental way there was. The difficulty he was having in accepting her promise was evident in his tone of voice and taut features. Only time would prove to him that she meant every word. Time and the physical closeness they had both been so deprived of.

Lauren swallowed to steady her voice and pulled her fingers free, lifting one hand to cup his cheek and resting the other on top of the hand Patrick held to her stomach, moving them in a slow circular motion.

"Yes, I want all you have to give me, Patrick."

He felt a sharp, sweet joy. This rare woman wanted him. His woman. His woman wanted him.

And he let himself believe it.

For most of his life he'd gone hungry; been starving for such sustaining emotion. Waited empty of everything but envy. Now it seemed to be materializing in his arms. Holy Mary! What had he ever done in his worthless life to deserve this? Ma must be havin' quite the profitable time on the other side of the pearly gates.

Patrick shucked all the other urgent concerns swirling around them along with his shirt and shoes. The news he and Stephan had gotten from Potter Palmer and the man's insistent invitation were forgotten in his need to get as close as . . . Bloody hell! No matter what Laurie asked, he knew her battered body wasn't ready to receive his in any more strenuous way than gentle holding; but that he would have. That much he had to have.

"Carefully, lass," he cautioned low in his throat as he stretched out beside her. Supple feminine arms tried to pull him down, and he hesitated.

"It's my face," she said again.

"Aye, Laurie," he answered, looking directly into her troubled eyes. Her uncertainty underscored his growing suspicion that someone had hurt her fragile self-perception very badly. He knew just how that felt.

"But not for the reason your silly woman's mind is fabricating." He quickly controlled the smile that her indignant gasp called up in him. "Your face and body need a few days to mend, sweetheart, or the closeness we want to share won't be what either one of us has in mind."

"But I nee . . ." Lauren froze on the word. She had told him once before that she needed him and had reached for all he would give. But such terrible heartbreak had followed; the memory swamped her again. Could she really trust him? Trust that his one concession, physical desire, would be enough?

Patrick was completely unaware of the strengthening sunlight driving the shadows from the room. Morning sounds drifting through thin walls filtered through his consciousness without causing a ripple. His entire being was focused on the uncertain woman next to him and the plea that had died in her throat.

He knew the words that would fix everything, but God help him, he couldn't form them with his lips; couldn't pull them up out of the jagged healing places in his heart. They would strip him completely bare, and he wasn't ready yet. He needed more time.

But I'll show you, darlin'. You won't ever have to fear askin' me for what you need. I'll never leave you with an empty heart and empty hands, as I was.

He caught her chin between his thumb and forefinger and tugged her face up to his.

"I need, too, Laurie," he assured her, marveling at the ease with which he admitted even that much. "I just don't want to hurt you."

"Then don't turn me away," she whispered, her heart in her eyes.

Chapter Fourteen

Ever so slowly, Patrick levered up on his elbow and tenderly placed his lips on hers. Moving as gently as a spring breeze against Laurie's swollen flesh, he sipped and kissed the hurt away until he felt her sigh against his mouth. Holy Mary, but he wanted to eat her alive! It took all his considerable willpower to hold back the fierce flood of desire she'd churned into crashing waves inside him.

Greedily, Lauren ran her fingers over Patrick's hair-roughened chest, from the base of his throat out to his shoulders and down to the waistband of his pants. She still couldn't believe that she could feel this way. It was wonderful and frustrating and so beautiful. Even looking like a Halloween mask, Patrick made her feel so beautiful.

The push of his tongue deep into her mouth triggered a rush of both pleasure and pain. He was right: It was too soon. But not yet . . . not yet. Swiftly, Lauren reached between their bodies and undid the buttons of her nightgown. Just a little closer.

Patrick tried to pull back and stop when he felt her movements, but he was lost. The first brush of her silky breasts against his chest and his entire body trembled from the effort of restraint.

"Saints preserve us, Laurie Ann. You're killin' me!"

The groaned words mouthed in the curve of her neck sent shivers racing up and down her spine. Everything in the world had narrowed to this one small room, this one small bed. And she loved him so much that the feeling translated itself into action, heedless of any physical discomfort.

Lauren set a string of sweet, wet kisses glistening along the ridge of Patrick's collarbone like a rope of precious jewels. She nuzzled her nose against the sensitive flesh just behind one ear and filled her lungs with the wonderful scent of warm man and soap.

Without conscious awareness her fingers stroked up his rippling back and burrowed deep into clean, damp hair, as precious as the spice it made her think of. Almost desperately she used her tongue and lips to taste that fragrant skin, to make him completely hers.

Like the tail of a lost kite snagged high in a wind tossed tree, Lauren felt caught in a storm of emotions; whipped to a frenzy of desire, love, hope, and fear.

Patrick had never imagined that wanting someone could feel like this. Laurie's touch brought both ecstasy and torment. She seemed to be trying to climb right into his skin with him. And damn if that wasn't just what he wanted, too. One more kiss, and then he'd stop. He pulled back from the drugging closeness of her trembling body and nearly dissolved at the tear-glazed expression in her eyes.

She tried to tug him onto her.

"Sweetheart." Patrick's voice was rough as raw cut

wood. "There's not a leprechaun in Ireland who'd be doubtin' what my one and only wish would be right this minute if I could get my hands on one of the little devils." He sifted a few fingers through Laurie's tangled hair and gently drew away one of her shaking arms from around his neck.

"I'm wishin' we had some fairy magic, lass, since neither of us has a great deal . . . of experience in this matter. . . ."

Patrick trailed off, not sure quite how to proceed.

"And although I pride myself on bein' a fast learner, for the life of me, darlin', I can't figure out how we could get to the . . . finish. Hell!" He stretched her out flat on the bed and held her curious gaze with his own as he placed a wide palm directly over her bruised skin and ribs. One firm push registered pain on her face.

"Ah, Laurie, I'm sorry," he murmured, replacing his hand with his mouth, trying to kiss away her discomfort. Patrick could feel her heart beating against his lips; could feel the tremors racking both of them. *Stop, ya fool. You're just makin' it worse!* He closed his eyes tight to keep the sight of her pebbled nipples from sending him over the edge.

Lauren felt Patrick's fiery breath explode in ragged bursts, searing a path from her breasts to her belly. The touch of his mouth was hot and healing, and as he lifted his head, she couldn't look away from the green flames.

"If we do much more, sweetheart, I'll not be able to stop. I'd hurt you, and then I'd . . . I'd be no better than that animal."

Laurie's gaze dropped to the center of his chest and a pink flush stained her sweet cheeks. "Now, none of that, my little she-cat." Patrick managed to grin, raising her chin with a knuckle. "Knowin' you want me as much as I want you is a mighty grand feelin', woman.

269

One I plan to act on as soon as you can tolerate a wee bit o' bouncin'.''

"Patrick Dugan!" Lauren couldn't hold in the laughter that bubbled with both embarrassment and anticipation.

"Patrick? Laurie?"

One brief knock was all the warning they got.

"Oh, faith and begorra! I'm sorry!" Molly Polaski stood in the doorway with her apron thrown over her face.

"What's the trouble . . . oh, ahem." Stephan smiled sheepishly.

Patrick sprang from the bed, dragging the quilt up over his wife in two seconds flat.

"We're sorry for the interruption," the big man said, watching Dugan shrug into his shirt, "but we've a bit of news, and Patrick, you need to be gettin' ready."

"What's happening, Dugan?" Laurie demanded in his ear, noting that his wide chest was carefully blocking her as she fumbled with her buttons.

"You're right, Stephan. I'm not thinkin' too clearly and I'm thankin' ya' for . . .''

"I know just how it is, me boyo." Stephan grinned again, and Patrick knew his friend was acknowledging his capitulation.

"Never you mind these two dunderheads, Laurie." Molly chuckled, sitting on the bed, her face still sporting a red tinge. "My da has come askin' for me and Stephan to stay with them for a few days." Tears sparkled in her eyes. "Isn't it wonderful?" She reached around Dugan for her friend's hands.

"Oh, Molly, I'm so happy for you." Yet, even as the words left her mouth, Lauren knew something wasn't quite right. Why would Molly's parents suddenly welcome them? It was such an about-face.

"And you and Patrick are goin' to have such a grand

time yourselves." She clasped her hands beneath her chin. "We'll have so much to tell each other in a few days."

Patrick felt a small tug as a fistful of his shirt tightened low on his back. The woman was far too knowing. He sent Stephan a silent message.

"That's enough, Molly. We've all got to be ready by twilight, so let's go speak to Greta about keepin' an eye on things here."

Lauren was up and awkwardly off the bed before Patrick shut the door. Just as she had done days ago at Mrs. Werner's, she began dressing, albeit slowly, under her nightgown.

"Is it hidin' we are then, Mr. Dugan?" she said, mimicking his Irish brogue.

Lauren opened her eyes with a sensuous stretch. The mouthwatering aroma of chocolate and cinnamon made her stomach growl, and she prepared to sit up. For two days she had been pampered like a princess. It should have been wonderful. However, as she elbowed her way up the goosedown pillows, she couldn't keep from frowning.

Patrick had been treating her like a china doll since she had hugged Molly and Stephan and said good-bye. Yes, she had been hurting; yes, she had spent a good part of the last two days sleeping. Sleeping alone. But it was all going to change. The bruises were fading and her ribs only ached a little. Not near enough to keep her from finishing what they had started four mornings ago.

Lauren swallowed the sweet hot chocolate and took a hungry bite of the spicy iced bun Patrick had left for her. Today was the day she was going to get that man right were she wanted him. Laughing with her; loving with her.

As Lauren threw back the pale peach satin comforter, she began humming softly to herself. No doubt the Irishman in question was out with the Palmers' horses. The first thing he'd done after tucking her into bed and leaving her under Bertha Palmer's watchful eye was to go to the stables.

They were actually staying in the stable master's cottage at the back of the castle's property. Bertha had the cozy little Tudor-style home filled with all kinds of luxuries, and her own cook brought them meals three times a day. Dugan hadn't known quite how to respond to the female half of the powerful Palmer couple. But Lauren had watched him with pride as he graciously thanked the queen of Chicago society with impeccable manners.

His mother had done a good job in the little time she'd had with him. Today Lauren was going to begin helping him remember other good things, replacing the bad memories with new, wonderful ones.

"Oh, Laurie," Dugan stammered as she entered the cheerful yellow-and-white kitchen. He set down his sloshing mug of coffee and got to his feet. "Should you be up so—"

"Patrick," Lauren interjected before he could start on a long lecture, "I'm fine. The swelling is gone from my face and the bruises are fading fast. My body needs to move now to work out the stiffness. It's not like I'm planning on entering the Olympics."

"The ancient Greeks would never have allowed women."

Lauren sauntered over to her amazingly intelligent, surprisingly polished, sometimes macho caveman and pressed an index finger into his chest until he sat. "I've got a news flash for you, buster. When the Olympics were in L.A. I happened to catch a historic retrospective, and for your information, in about one year ye old

Olympic games are going to become all the rage again. Be sure to catch the papers in the summer of 1900; women *will* be going for the gold.''

Patrick gazed up into her flashing blue eyes and felt the need he'd been suppressing for days shake his entire body. He barely even registered her fortune-telling. Laurie was so passionate about things. She was, in fact, such a fire in his blood that he'd been trying to keep something distant from her; something untouched. Because he still couldn't quite believe this was real, that it was going to last.

Oh, he was trying, but at the same time his need for her made him feel too vulnerable. But how did one stop a tornado, a hurricane? Maybe all he could do was hold on tight. That's what his ma told him to do when he found . . .

''I have to get out of this house for a bit, Dugan.'' She bent over, almost nose to nose with the silent man. ''I'm going stir crazy.''

''Now, Laurie, I've not seen you stir a thing. You've not had to cook at all here. But in any event, Mr. Palmer wants us to stay on the property for three more days. A number of his lawyers and a representative of the governor had a very interestin' meetin' with McDonald yesterday. But it'll take some time to convince the man to see it Mr. Palmer's way. We've got to stay out of sight and wait a wee bit longer.''

''Great!'' Lauren deadpanned with her hands on her hips. ''I mean, it's great about McDonald and all, but undercover work is just not what it's cracked up to be.''

''Well, woman,'' Patrick said with an odd look in his eye, ''don't you think you might be rushin' your fences with that opinion? You've not had enough experience to judge that yet, have you?

''Patrick Dugan, what in the world . . .'' Lauren stopped in midsentence when she got it. ''Good gosh,

I didn't mean under the *bed*covers!'' She grinned and began to chuckle. ''And it's not stirring crazy, either.'' She pantomimed with her hand and then ruffled her bangs with a laugh.

Lauren couldn't help but give one last toothy smile at the abashed look on Patrick's face. ''Okay,'' she relented, and vowed to stop teasing the poor bewildered man. ''Show me your treasures out in the stable, then.''

''How did you know?'' he asked, scraping his chair back from the round pedestal table. How did she always know what mattered most?

''Every time I've been awake to see you after you've been out in the stable you've seemed more calm, less stressed over this whole situation.''

''You've the right of it there, lass. I feel the str-stress, as you say, leavin' me when I care for Palmer's beauties.''

''You know, Patrick, it occurs to me that I might know another thing that could help with your stress.'' Lauren couldn't believe how brazen she was becoming. She was breaking her vow in under one minute. It just felt so delicious to be wanted; to want someone. She flirtatiously looked over her shoulder as she turned her back and sat on his lap.

Dugan didn't agree. His whole body became instantly rigid with—ah . . . stress.

''Wha-what are you doin', Laurie?''

''I need some help with my buttons. My poor bones can't take the stretch yet.'' She wickedly squirmed around on his thighs, arranging the skirt of the mauve day dress Bertha Palmer had given to her.

''This is not helping, woman!''

''Oh, no, Patrick.'' She tried to keep the laughter out of her voice but knew her eyes gave it away. ''This isn't it. My stress reducer will have to wait for tonight.''

Devil take her, Dugan thought as a cursed blush crept

up his neck. His new white shirt, sporting a fashionable turned-down collar—another gift from the Palmers—was cutting off his air. He reached up with a shaky hand to undo the top button. No way was the she-cat goin' to have the last laugh this time. Even as he formed his own teasing revenge Patrick acknowledged the deep sense of joy Laurie had brought into his life. *God, what would he do if he ever lost her?*

"Patrick?" She wiggled. "Buttons, please."

Her startled gasp was music to his ears. Each button called for yet another moist, suckling kiss, and Laurie's initial gasp became one low moan as he feasted on the silky, rose-smelling skin covering her spine. When he fastened the last pearl-shaped drop he deftly caught the flesh at the nape of her neck between his teeth and bit.

A shudder ran through her body and straight into his, just like the experiment he'd seen at the Electricity Building. Mr Edison's discovery wasn't the only current with incredible power.

"Pat . . ." Lauren swallowed with difficulty. "Patrick, I . . ."

He nuzzled the sensitive spot just behind her ear and felt her body melt against his. She wanted him as much as he wanted her, and it was more intoxicating than any spirits he'd ever imbibed. Her body was already his; Patrick's inherent male instinct told him so. With just three little words her heart could be also. But then his heart would be hers in return. Was he ready to trust that much? Slowly he ran his hands over her shoulders and tenderly cupped a breast in each palm.

"Patrick?" Lauren asked dreamily as her husband strummed her body to a fever pitch. "I don't think . . ." She licked her lips. "I don't think we need to wait 'til night after all."

When Laurie tried to twist around to face him Patrick crossed his arms over her chest and held her tight. The *stress* screaming through his body would have to wait to be eased. The angel on his lap deserved so much more than he'd given her their first time. She deserved to know the feelings in his heart, not just the feeling of his body.

"No, darlin', you were right." He inhaled a huge breath of air and set her away from him, rising on rubbery legs. The look in her eyes almost changed his mind, but he grabbed her hand and headed for the door. He needed a few hours to get ready, a few hours to prepare himself to surrender some harshly defended personal ground.

"Let's go see the horses."

"Are ya sure, boss?"

"There's not a damn thing we can do, Harry!" Mike McDonald stared down at the incriminating papers and lifted a shot of burning whiskey to his mouth. He needed something to dull the fury racing through his veins.

"If we don't call the dogs off that bastard mick right now, Palmer's going to send copies of this list to a number of important people on both sides of the law. Damn if the man didn't get the governor involved, too. Business will be shot to hell if I don't comply, not to mention the ladder climbers who'll be looking to shoot me in the back as well as the pocket."

"Ah, hell, Mike," Harry said, slumping down in the chair in front of the massive cherry desk. "No sense in losin' the money you've already got comin' to ya by tryin' to fight against Palmer and the governor." He leaned a heavy arm on the slick, polished surface and watched the emotions flick across his employer's face. McDonald hated admitting that someone else had more power than he did.

"I supposes you're right." Mike got to his feet and

paced to the window, which overlooked Clark Street. "You better get to Hansen immediately with this news, and then officially drop your charges. The captain told me that Bates had an encounter, shall we say, with the woman, and that he's been searching for her ever since. I don't know exactly what the dumb ox did"—he turned and nailed Harry with a ruthless look—"but Palmer's men warned me that if anything happens to either of the Dugans, the lid will blow sky high."

"Don't give it another thought, boss. I'll have it taken care of before we leave." Harry struggled to his feet and snagged his bowler off the hat tree. "No one will ever be the wiser, Mike. And just think about the money still to be made in the two months or so till the Fair closes."

An unholy light came to life in the eyes of the tall man dressed in formal black.

"You're exactly right, my friend." Michael Cassius McDonald sat back in his swing chair and lit an aromatic Cuban cigar. "And, when the Exposition is over, Palmer will likely forget all about his little charity project and this stir he's whipped up." He exhaled a plume of smoke and laughed. "Why, it wouldn't surprise me at all if sometime around Christmas the Dugans have an unfortunate, untraceable accident."

Lauren had never before seen such empathy and understanding between a human and an animal. She had certainly heard of people who possessed the gift of communicating by touch and tone of voice, but she hadn't witnessed the magic. For two hours she had watched Patrick brush and care for the big, beautiful horses that scared her just a bit.

The sum total of her horse acumen came from TV and a pony ride her parents had taken her on when she was eight. The little pony had been docile as a lamb, but her mom and dad had walked along with her, one on either side. . . . How could she have forgotten that sweet memory? As she took it out of a sealed place in her heart and embraced it fully, the love part of it was so big that the pain part of it wasn't difficult to bear.

Lauren shifted on the hay bale and brought up her knees to her chest, tucking her slippered feet under the mauve skirt. Would she ever be able to feel this way about Patrick's memories if setting him free would be the best thing for him? If he didn't love her and she had to leave him? In the last few days she'd been so sure she'd seen something more than just caring flickering in his eyes, but he'd never said the words. And so she hadn't either, hoping that it was the newness of it all that was holding him back.

Lauren wrapped her arms around her legs and followed the muscles rippling across his back with each long brush stroke over the mare's flank. She nonchalantly tipped her head to the side and let a tear roll away from her mascara. Flank: Patrick had taught her that. Patrick had taught her so many things.

Patrick Dugan didn't think he'd spent such a peaceful afternoon in years; surely not in the past months. How could he have accused Laurie of never keeping her mouth shut all those days ago? She had listened intently to every word he'd said about the horses, making him feel valued and important. Her big blue eyes and slightly puffy lips set his heart to pounding every time he looked at her for long.

What they had started four mornings ago and then heated up again in the kitchen never completely left his mind or his body. And blessed Saint Joseph, she was so willing; so welcoming. Tonight, tonight would be their real wedding night in more ways than one. He'd best get on with giving the gift he had once tossed back so cruelly in her face, sharing some of each other's world.

"I grew up in Ireland raisin' horses."

Lauren bit her lip to keep from smiling. The man was finally opening up! True, he couldn't have started with a more obvious fact, but she had made a career using her considerable patience in rooting out information. She sat completely still, watching Patrick's back.

"Until my ma died I'd always thought my life was set, you know? My uncle was a hard man, but I figured he wasn't about to turn the horse raisin' business over to me unless I proved myself." Patrick purposely kept his tone even and matter-of-fact as he lifted a hind foot and checked the iron shoe.

"But all along he knew he was never goin' to do that. And when he told me about my father I had to leave."

"How old were you?" Lauren asked smoothly, disguising the fierce, protective emotions rising in her.

"Well now, that was one of the blessin's my ma always told me to look for in the face of trouble. I was a big strappin' lad of fourteen who easily passed for older, and I could read and cipher. So, when I got to Dublin work wasn't as hard to come by."

Patrick finished with the chestnut mare and walked to the wash-up barrel without giving Laurie a glance. He needed a few more minutes . . .

"Come sit by me," she said.

He dried his hands before sitting on the bale, and barely kept himself from jumping when Laurie curled her fingers tight around his wrist.

"How did you get to America?"

"After five years in Dublin I knew I'd never . . ."

He stopped, and Lauren held her breath. She rubbed

279

her other hand up and down his bare forearm, praying he'd trust her.

Patrick rested a palm over her soothing hand and looked straight into her encouraging eyes. "I knew I'd never reach my dream of havin' my own horses and land stayin' there. So, I decided to come to the golden streets of America. It took me a few years to earn a grub stake and then a few more to work my way this far."

"Where are you trying to get to, Patrick?" Lauren spoke over the dull ache at the back of her throat. All she could see was the trail of lonely years stretching behind this man she loved. A journey he was never meant to make alone. Dream-building was so much better with someone to lean on occasionally; with someone to root for you; with someone in your corner.

Patrick pulled out of her hold and circled Laurie's shoulders with his arm. He cinched her body in snug against his and took a quick, deep breath. The soft fragrance of roses drifted up from her silky cap of curls, and he couldn't help but think that the smell of a clean stable and this woman were two of the best smells in the world.

"Up until a little more than three months ago I was workin' wherever I could and savin' my money to buy a ranch. I'm sick to death of livin' in crowded cities and almost never gettin' close to a horse." Patrick rested his chin on Laurie's fluffy hair, and he felt her arms steal around his waist. "Unfortunately, I discovered the dirty game bein' played at the Fair and, fool that I am, I just couldn't sit by and let another power-hungry man like my uncle dictate people's lives."

"But now, with the Palmers' help, everything should go back to normal, right?"

Patrick didn't want to worry Laurie, so he kept quiet. Potter Palmer felt sure that the problems were almost over; however, the actions of underhanded men were very hard to predict, even when their heads were in the noose. But for this small moment in time he felt safe and he wanted to savor it. Lauren wiggled her head free and tipped it back to look him in the eye.

"When will we be ready for the ranch?"

Patrick blinked and felt his mouth drop open. Not once in his adult life had he shared his dream. The place he had desperately needed to build in his head that nothing could destroy, that no one could take away. Never in his wildest imaginings had he seen a partner by his side.

"But my dream isn't yours, lass," he said, searching her open gaze. "I'll not force you another step in this marriage of ours."

"I'd say we're even on the force issue." Lauren got to her feet and tugged on his arm to make him follow her. If there had ever been a time to explain her dream to Patrick, it was now. They'd laughed and talked and just maybe he was ready to take another step toward trusting her.

"Come on, husband. Luckily for you, my dream goes hand in hand with that stress reducer I was talking about earlier."

Patrick could hear Laurie splashin' behind the closed door of the kitchen. By the time they'd gotten back to the cottage supper had been waiting, so his little wife had given him a saucy wink and said they should just go ahead and eat. Patrick didn't taste a bite of the fine pot roast. Before he knew it, she had him dragging in the hip bath, and he couldn't help but wonder if she was getting clean and sweet for him. That thought had him rushing out to the cold wash water in the stable to get clean and sweet for her.

Hell, he was nervous. The first time they'd made love

281

it had just happened. He'd been thinking of endings then, and now it was all about beginnings. He should tell Laurie that. Patrick got to his feet and paced around the white-enameled iron bed. Its decorative brass detailing winked in the lamplight that shimmered in waves over the satin comforter.

Mrs. Palmer was treating this like a honeymoon, he thought, running a hand over the cool fabric. The mattress wasn't a husk tick topped with cotton like the Polaskis had, either. Patrick took a little jump and bounced. This one had to be hair for sure, there wasn't a crackle to be heard. They hadn't even had a mattress last time. . . .

He scrambled to his feet, cursin' himself for acting like a child. Laurie had better enjoy all this elegance while she could. If she really stayed with him, it would be a long time before they had so much. Hell, the bedroom set alone must have cost better than fifteen dollars. Patrick walked to the dresser and rubbed a hand over his clean-shaven face. What had she left behind? he silently asked his reflection. Maybe it was time to find that out, too.

"Patrick, do you think you could dump the water?" Lauren called brightly as she walked from the short hall into the bedroom. With feigned casualness she rubbed the muslin toweling in her hand over her damp hair and stopped in front of the dresser mirror. Patrick grunted what she thought was an affirmative response and left.

Lauren quickly brushed her hair and fluffed it around her face. Man, what she'd give for a blow dryer and a curling iron. The plug-in kind! With deft, practiced strokes, she enhanced her pale lashes with color, pinched her cheeks, and glossed her trembling lips. She wanted to be beautiful for her husband.

Tonight she wanted to believe this was all for love; only for love. They had both done their share of forcing the relationship, but this could be the start of something different.

The snap of the back door sent her stomach into a spiraling nosedive. Lauren hurriedly sprayed a mist of perfume in the air and stepped into the moist essence. Mercy, but she was nervous.

Patrick stopped just inside the door and studied his wife. Her skin glowed in the candlelight. The lacy white nightdress she was wearing floated with the magic of fairy dust over the body he'd come to crave and need; over the soul he feared he would not be whole without. It looked as if some sensual baker had shaken tiny cinnamon sprinkles over the swell of Laurie's breasts, framed by the low-cut neck of her gown. This time he vowed to see her in the light and trace those angel kisses with his mouth.

"This is weird." It popped out before she could stop it.

Patrick smiled at his little she-cat's expression. It was against her nature to stand submissively waiting. She didn't play coy games, and it pleased him immensely.

"What's *weird* about a husband and wife makin' love, darlin'?" he volleyed back, equally direct.

"Let's just get to it, okay?" she pleaded, rushing to the bed and turning down the covers. Okay, so she still had a ways to go to perfect the role of the confident, teasing, sensuous woman in which she had briefly envisioned herself earlier today. It wasn't like Dugan had all that much to compare her to.

Laurie Ann sat perched on the bed like a bird ready to take flight. For some reason it made Patrick feel incredibly male to see this strong-willed female so unsure in this one intimate area. No doubt his suffragette-loving wife would call him that scum-sucking macho thing if she knew. Dugan smiled at that thought until his eyes crinkled.

God! She made him feel good. As he stepped closer to her, he pulled off his thick clean socks, tugged his undershirt over his head, and slipped off his black denims.

You're acting like a twit and the man knows it! It wasn't like she didn't know what was going to happen. She wasn't a virgin, after all. *Oh yeah, you're some experienced woman, all right!*

Lauren looked up at him just in time to catch his open, hungry smile. She burst into flame. The sight of Patrick's broad chest and powerful arms started a pulse pounding deep in her body, and the happiness that reflected in his smoldering green eyes took all the awkward uncertainty away.

She held out her arms, but he pulled her to her feet and flush against him. With long, strong strokes he ran his hands up her arms, over her shoulders, and down her back. Once, twice, three times. Just the way she had wished for him to touch her when she'd watched him with the horses. Then he circled her wrists and placed her arms high around his neck, lifting her to tiptoe.

"I'm thinkin' I know for a surety just what you had in mind to help with my *stress*," Patrick whispered against Laurie's lips. He pressed harder, gripping her soft, round bottom in his big hands and holding her mouth under his own. "What a thoughtful wife you are, lass," he murmured, licking the shiny, sweet lips brushing his, "to unselfishly help me so." His tongue slipped under her top lip and ran across smooth teeth. Laurie gasped and he plunged inside.

The hot, moist meeting of lips and tongues fed the pounding need surging through their veins. Lauren felt Patrick's grip shift as he picked her up off the floor and held her tight against the evidence of his powerful need. His mouth was fierce and tasted of spicy desire and more.

284

With his chest heaving, Patrick broke away and bent to push off the bottoms of his underwear. He never took his eyes off Laurie's flushed face. She smiled at him then, a healing, binding, all-trusting smile, and, reaching down to grasp her hem, she swept off the last barrier.

He ran one fingertip around the greenish bruise between her breasts.

"It's all right, Patrick. You won't hurt me."

Holy Mary, make me worthy. Don't let her ever regret what she's had to give up.

Even as the words poured through Patrick's mind, he determined to tie her to him so completely that she could never get free. Almost desperately, he pushed her back on the bed and covered her body with his own.

"I'm sorry, sweetheart," he breathed heavily, settling his legs between hers and cradling her head in his cupped hands. "I can't wait. I need you . . . need you," Patrick groaned hungrily, pressing his open mouth to hers. He reached down and ringed her ankle with shaking fingers and angled her leg up over his. "Next time . . . I promise more polish."

Lauren felt the heat of his kiss from the top of her head to the tips of her toes. His weight gave her a brief twinge, but no paltry ache would make her stop him. Her husband's husky plea shot straight through her heart, and she wrapped her whole body around his, shuddering as he filled her, body and soul.

Patrick stopped and lifted his eyes to the deep water blue of his love's. Pools of peace surrounded him; rushing waters of desire flooded his entire being. The promise he did not remember making days ago rang in the candlelit room.

"Now, wife, now . . . with my body I thee worship."

And he did . . . over and over until a wild, rippling power burst through the cathedral made of their joined flesh and took them to a place neither one had ever dreamed was possible.

Lauren raked her fingers through Patrick's damp hair as he rested bonelessly over her, his head tucked up under her chin. She felt her words of love pounding in time to their heartbeats. She slipped her arms across his back and held him tighter.

Patrick had still not said he loved her. This time, this time with things so different between them, she had hoped he would. But snuggled close in his arms, Lauren realized that, given his past and the small bit of honest affection he'd had and lost, it might take more time. Maybe her declarations would only pressure him.

Once again Lauren felt herself holding back the ocean of caring that longed to break free. Thank God, she could at least show him now, she thought, skimming her fingertips up his spine.

It wasn't until the squeak of the bed and the sound of their ragged breathing stopped that Dugan realized he'd been waiting to hear it. He felt it most definitely, lying in her arms, and so he resisted moving, even though he knew his weight could not be comfortable.

She was waiting, too, as she had the last time. And curse him for the coward he was, he could not say the words as he had planned. He couldn't say the very phrase he wanted her to speak. He couldn't tell her that he loved her.

Sweet Jesus, he loved her! What a fool he'd been to think he could hold anything back from this woman who pulled out every hidden need he had. Then it hit him again, like a fist: the panic that had followed so closely once before on the heels of this soul-deep satisfaction. Time. He just needed more time to trust. Soon he'd be able to give her every part of himself.

But what if he never could? What if it took too long? Would she leave him? Find another man who wasn't as twisted into knots? Oh, God! Doubt swamped him, and for a moment he was that young boy again, standing alone on the frightening streets of Dublin. The icy fingers of fear were as real as Laurie's inching up his spine. What could he give her right now? What?

Ah, the dream. Her dream.

Chapter Fifteen

Patrick flexed against her hold and rolled to his side. With a flick of his wrist he covered their cooling bodies with the cotton sheeting and determinedly tipped Laurie's face to his. He saw the brief flicker of uncertainty in her eyes.

Forgive me, love. I don't know what's wrong with me.

But he did. He was afraid to believe again; to give away all his defenses; to hope. If love left him again, it would kill him.

"Didn't you tell me this mornin', lass, that you had a dream, too. One that had somethin' to do with this . . . ah . . . stress reducer we've just enjoyed."

Lauren heard the forced lightness in Patrick's voice and decided to make this easy for him. The man couldn't really believe what they had yet, but she planned to convince him in a very tactile way. She understood. It hurt a little, but no way was she letting go.

Besides, her dream was a trump card in and of itself. This was a hand she had to play for both of their sakes.

"My dream doesn't really have anything to do with a place, like yours, Patrick," she said, keeping her voice steady and her gaze locked to his. "It has to do with being a part of a real family." She took his hand from her shoulder and placed it over her cloth-covered stomach.

"I have always wanted a baby," she whispered. "Now, your baby. The one you said could already be right in here." Lauren pressed his hand more firmly against her. "You need to know how I feel, Patrick, because I remember you saying this wasn't what you wanted."

Patrick reeled with the meaning of her words. He actually felt light-headed and sucked in a deep breath, only to feel even more unsettled as the scent of roses and their lovemaking filtered through his senses.

This he could give her. He wanted to give it because it would forge one of life's tightest bonds. But he'd not do it without being certain she knew what he was, what shame he carried. It scared the hell out of him, but it was best he know her feelings right now. He could only pray he'd survive her rejection.

"I never wanted a baby born like I was, Laurie. A bastard."

"So," she fumbled for the right way to handle his gut-wrenching confession, "does that mean that since our baby wouldn't be a . . . one, that it's okay with you?"

Patrick blinked. He'd watched her closely, and his illegitimacy hadn't even affected her.

"Sweetie," she patted his chest soothingly, very aware of the guarded look on his face, "in the future that whole issue isn't such a big deal. No one holds it against the innocent child. Society doesn't blame the baby for the parents' poor judgment.''

She spoke so simply, so honestly, that Patrick couldn't help but believe her. In Laurie's eyes he saw himself reflected for the first time without the cloak of shame with which his father had left him.

''The future sounds very promisin', lass,'' he admitted with a slight smile. ''Perhaps it's time I heard more.'' Laurie's squeal of delight rebounded off the walls of the small cottage and she rocketed into his arms.

''I can't believe it, Patrick.'' She laughed. ''This is so great!'' Maybe he hadn't actually said ''I love you,'' but this was nearly as good. At last he wanted to know about her world.

''Woman, please.'' He chuckled, flat on his back, teetering dangerously close to the edge of the bed. ''You're crushin' me with your enthusiasm.''

''Ooops, sorry about that,'' Laurie apologized, all the laughter immediately draining from her voice. ''I've always been just a little too much woman.''

Patrick stopped her as she tried to move off his body. ''Now, Laurie, lass, surely you can't believe after what we've just shared that I could want you more any other way.''

''Well,'' she said, ''in the future the waif look has been a big thing. Popular, you know? In. Real women are out.''

''Ah, thin. Very thin.''

''Some men think . . . well, you know the old saying: 'You can never be too rich or too thin.' '' Laurie tried to sit up. ''Let me get my bag.''

''You're wrong, sweetheart.'' Patrick rolled her to his side and levered up on an elbow. With two soft taps on her cheek, he held her gaze captive. ''That's one of our greatest problems now, in this time. Too few people are too rich, and there's goin' to be lots of trouble ahead for this country because of it. And darlin', I'll not ever look at a too-thin person and see beauty.'' He caught her chin in the notch between his thumb and forefinger and brought her nose to his.

''I see hunger, Laurie, and fear and desperation. I see mothers who give anythin' and everythin' away to feed their children.'' Dugan kissed the tip of her freckled nose. ''I want you, a woman strong in body and mind. Someone I can feel against me.'' In a flash he rolled her on top of him again.

''Who hurt you, lass? Who made you doubt yourself so?'' He held her shoulders and waited until she finally looked directly at him. ''I know somethin' about never bein' good enough, Laurie. I'll not have you feelin' that way with me.''

In a few terse sentences she haltingly recited the whole sorry story of her aborted romance with Jeff. After opening his deepest scar to her, how could she not return his trust?

''Well, darlin','' Patrick offered after she'd finished, relishing the feel of her body on his, ''I can't say as I'm unhappy that the fool couldn't make you feel like the wild, passionate woman that you are. . . . But I think we can find somethin' good comin' out of the bad, just like Ma taught me.'' He gently wove a hand through her tousled, honey-colored hair and caressed the back of her head with his fingertips. ''I think we understand each other better because of the hurt we've both carried.''

Lauren lowered her mouth to his and kissed him for all she was worth. Hoping she could speak past the tears thickening her voice, she said, ''Patrick Dugan, I am never letting you get away.'' And she kissed him again, until she could feel the flames rising in both of them.

''I'll not be goin' anywhere, woman,'' Patrick said, breathing hard. ''You've barely left me with the

strength to kiss you. Besides, who else would be willin'
to help me polish my new skills?''

Lauren had never laughed such a laugh, half silly and
half flame. It felt good all over.

''Wait, okay,'' she managed to gasp. ''Let's hold that
thought for just a bit. I want to show you my bag.''

In one smooth move, Patrick had her under his pulsing body. ''First the baby, lass, then the bag.''

Bloody hell. Patrick couldn't believe Laurie could
sleep so peacefully after the things she'd just told him.
He'd been so damn dazed that she'd finally gotten a
pad of paper out of her bag and drawn him pictures.
Music comin' out of a little boxlike thing. Television
and moving-picture stories. Airplanes flying up in the
sky. Faith, he supposed most of it was possible. Hadn't
he seen the seeds of it all right here in Chicago at the
Fair? Patrick raked his fingers through his unruly hair.

But men on the moon? He rubbed his hand down his
face. He couldn't think about it anymore.

Very slowly he eased Laurie's sleepy head off his
shoulder and slipped away from the warmth of her naked body. It was a mark of her trust that she hadn't
whipped on her nightdress. Patrick smiled in the dark.
For a man with very limited experience in pleasin' a
woman, he seemed to be doing at least that part right.
She was more comfortable with her body now because
he had proved to her that every inch of it pleased him.
Pleased him more than he had ever thought possible.

Patrick pulled on his drawers and headed for the
kitchen. He took a long drink of cool water from the
pump and dropped onto a chair at the table. Laurie's
world was a wonder. Women there could do much more
than they could now. God, but he wished his ma could
have had such choices. How different would their lives

have been? How truly different was Laurie's other life from his?

That she had given up more than he had ever imagined was ominously clear now. Damn, he'd wanted to know, but the knowledge was stoking his old battle with doubt and inadequacy. Patrick couldn't stop himself from asking if perhaps she was simply making the best of things here. After all, she was stuck. Maybe she'd decided this was the best way to make her dream come true.

Just before her eyes drooped shut she had explained how her time key worked the centennial numbers and all. She'd even shown him the article from the *Tribune*. There was no way back, not without an authentic printed date from the future.

But dammit! It was more than a matter of surviving here. He knew she felt something for him; she'd by heaven professed her love. But why hadn't she said the words again?

Patrick abruptly crawled into bed. With a little more strength then he'd intended, he pulled Laurie into his arms, and she moaned low in her throat. He would make her say the words again and again. He would give her a baby, too; lots of babies if she wanted. Hell, he'd give her everything he could, and hope she wouldn't regret all the riches she'd have to live without. Hope she'd not regret trading her world of wonders for a poor Irish bastard.

A poor, *selfish,* Irish bastard, for now he would never, ever let her go!

Three days later, Patrick had a big surprise for the anxious woman in his life, who was missin' her friends and tired of waiting for McDonald to be "nailed to the wall." Finally an expression that made sense! He bounded up the steps leading to the door of the cottage and hoped Potter Palmer's news would cheer Laurie up. Heaven knew he had worn himself out keeping her distracted.

A very male smile spread across his face. Too much more distraction like the kind in which they'd been indulging for the last few days and neither one of them would be able to walk. In this, at least, he knew he pleased her completely; this contentment was real.

Of course, the woman had done her share of distractin' him, and with more than her sweet body. She fairly swamped him with disbelief as on and off an incredible flow of information poured from her mouth. But at least now he knew that Mike Rowave wasn't a suitor he had to worry about.

Even the strain of waiting for McDonald's capitulation hadn't stopped the happiness steadily growing inside his healing heart. It was true, however, that once or twice his anxiety over Laurie's other life and all the luxuries she'd left behind had begun to eat away at his pride. She loved the Palmers' little cottage, and it was more than most folks like he and the Polaskis could ever hope to have.

Ah, but when he held her in his arms and she melted at his touch, all the other worries melted away too. She looked at him as if he were a dream come true, and he couldn't imagine living the rest of his life without her. Oddly enough, it felt as if they had always loved each other.

And it was such glory to have someone of his very own that Patrick had decided just a few minutes ago, after leaving Potter Palmer, that perhaps he was ready. Ready to give Laurie the promise of lasting love; the love his ma had told him was worth any price. In spite of all her disappointments she'd never stopped believing.

Now, at long last, Patrick Dugan was willing to believe too; that what he had to offer was worth all that Laurie had given up.

He paused for a moment with his hand on the door-knob and looked back over his shoulder. The day would be warm, but the sky was bright and blue and the best his time had to offer was waiting for them at the Fair. He'd show Laurie the amazing things there and somehow let her know that he'd work his fingers to the bone to make her life as beautiful as it had been.

"Laurie, darlin'?" he called. "I've got a surprise for you!" Two surprises really, but he'd give her the best one much, much later.

"Now, Patrick, honey," she said, waltzing into the kitchen with a little smirk on her face, "I've seen that surprise quite a bit lately and don't take this wrong, but it's hardly a novelty anymore."

Patrick couldn't believe his ears. A woman of his day would never say something like that. Oh, but his woman . . .

He burst into roaring laughter that whipped through the sunny kitchen. He laughed until tears came to his eyes and he dropped onto a chair, watching the giggles shaking their way out of his wanton little wife. She was, indeed, both a she-cat and an angel. Patrick lurched out of the chair and captured her, dragging her back onto his lap. They fell together like children, sharing the joy that comes so naturally when people share such close-ness.

"Quiet, now, you little hussy," he ordered gruffly, acting the part of a stern parent. "Hush, or you'll not be hearin' a thing from me."

"All right." Laurie nodded, desperately trying but failing to control herself.

"You've left me no choice, lass." He kissed her, bending her back over his arm until she had to hold on for dear life. Until all the energy filling the room from their laughter transformed into another emotion entirely.

"Oh-oh, darling," she whispered when he released her burning lips, "I think your surprise is showing." Laurie rocked just a bit on his lap so there was no mistaking her meaning.

"Woman!"

"Okay, geez! Can't a girl have a little fun?" She nuzzled her head up under his chin and circled his broad chest with her arms. *Mine! To hold, to touch, to love.*

"As a matter of fact, my saucy colleen, you are about to have a whole day of fun, courtesy of Mr. and Mrs. Potter Palmer."

"What?" Laurie's head shot up.

"McDonald has left the city as Nancy said, lass. It appears he already had a business trip scheduled, and the governor sent a message through Palmer, insisting he tie up all the loose ends here or his plans would have to be forcibly changed. The charges against me have been officially dropped, darlin'. McDonald won't be broken completely this time, but at least the black-mailing on the Midway will stop. We slowed him down, by God, and enough folks in the city will see his leave-takin' like a dog slinkin' away with his tail between his legs. That'll stay with the man for a long time."

"Oh, Patrick, love!" she whooped, swinging her arms around his neck. "This is the best, best news."

But the best news, really, was what she had called him.

"You heard me, Bates. It's official. We're to leave them completely alone."

Captain Hansen brushed either side of his mustache with the knuckle of an index finger to hide his anxiety. The big clod wasn't taking his orders as docilely as he had in the past, and it worried him. Brown had let him know in no uncertain terms that he would be held responsible if Jonas Bates caused problems.

"The woman ain't worth cow dung, Cap'n."

"I don't think you're listening to me, you idiot!" Hansen bellowed and slammed his fist down on his desk. He closed his eyes for a moment and took a deep breath, missing the feral gleam that flickered through the eyes of the apelike man before him.

"Michael McDonald will kill us, Bates," Hansen said slowly and distinctly, as if speaking to a dim-witted child. "If one hair on either of the Dugans' heads is harmed, we will be sunk to the bottom of Lake Michigan."

"A woman shouldn't get away with what she done, Cap'n. That one needs to be put in her place."

Captain Hansen soundlessly opened the drawer on the side of the desk and pulled out a gun. Deliberately he got to his feet and aimed it at point-blank range.

"You are the most stupid oaf I've ever had to work with, Bates. And I will not suffer just because you weren't man enough to subdue one small woman." With deadly precision he cocked the hammer.

"All right, Cap'n," Bates sniveled, holding up his hands like a surrendering criminal. "I ain't gonna do a thing. You can count on it."

A few hours later Jonas Bates stepped out of a shadow deep in the alley behind the police station. Captain Hansen had just finished his shift and was heading home. With a skill amazing in such a large man, Bates began to trail his boss.

He was tired of people saying he was stupid. Tired of people making him feel stupid. Captain Hansen ought not to have said what he had. He'd make the man beg for yellin' as he had done. Hell, he'd fix McDonald too. He'd get that list himself and sell it to the top bidder.

Then he'd just sit back and wait to see what happened to Mr. High-And-Mighty McDonald after they found what was left of Dugan's woman.

He'd make her beg, too, and then some.

Leave it to the Californians to display a knight made of prunes and a replica of the Liberty Bell formed from oranges. Lauren had to admire the off-beat creations they had seen in the sunshine state's exhibit. Patrick didn't understand her unladylike guffaw when she had commented on the kind of visionary it took to look at a flower or piece of fruit and see a masterpiece in it.

Not quite like Michelangelo and his marble, but it was comforting to know that even a hundred years in the past Californians had marched to a different drummer.

Potter Palmer had given them the all-clear and his wife had given them a day at the Fair.

Lauren had never seen Patrick like this. It was almost as if he was a salesman for his time. He rushed her from place to place, pointing out every possible wonder, and then flirted with her outrageously, as if he was trying to make up for all the years of lost fun in this one day. If ever a man deserved to let go it was Patrick Dugan, but Lauren was worried a little just the same. Something was wrong.

However, in the afternoon, as they walked through the White City, she forgot her concerns, basking in the sweet attention Patrick lavished on her. His arm was snug around her waist, which brought more than a few raised-eyebrow looks, and she saw a number of women—very reserved, 1895 women—discreetly eye her tall, broad-shouldered husband. He never noticed one of them. It felt wonderful to be envied.

To Lauren it seemed as if the love and emotion they had shared so privately the last few days had formed a bubble around them that outsiders could not penetrate. For this one day all the beauty and wonder surrounding them existed for their pleasure alone.

"Where do you want to go next, lass?" Patrick stopped in front of the commemorative Columbian fountain at the south end of the fairgrounds, far away from the Palace of Fine Arts.

"Let's take a gondola to the Midway."

"Good. I need to let the folks on the list know that McDonald won't be troublin' them anymore." He cupped her elbow firmly and maneuvered them through the crowds to the steps leading down to the canal. Patrick paid fifty cents for two half-trip tickets and then pulled Laurie snugly into his arms at the back end of the canoelike craft.

"Aw, darlin'," he nuzzled in her ear, "it seems that hours and hours have passed since I've had you this close to me."

"Patrick Dugan, watch those hands," Laurie ordered, trying to mean it. "You'll have some old woman fainting and falling headfirst into the water. Talk to me about some nonromantic subject."

He paused for a moment and felt the water-cooled breeze shifting through his hair. It helped in two ways; the refreshing gusts actually calmed his ardor a bit, and they made him think of something totally unromantic to tell Laurie, instead of the words he'd been holding back for hours.

"Did you know that they're callin' Chicago the Windy City?"

"I knew that was a nickname," she replied, swiveling around and angling sideways into his chest so she could see his face. "But I didn't know when it had originated."

"Well, sometime ago, when the powers-that-be began to plan this whole celebration, the folks in New

299

York announced that they wanted to host a grand party too. It wasn't long before the two cities started to boast and crow about which spot would be the best. Evidently, some newspaperman from the New York *Sun* didn't think a backwoods town in the wilds of Illinois could deliver on her promises, so he began referrin' to all the hot air blowin' around Chicago.''

"And the Windy City was born." Laurie grinned. "She's still called that in the future."

"Are people shocked by kissin' in public in 1995?"

"Not really," Laurie replied off-handedly, fussing with her green-and-white-stripped skirt and trying to figure out where Patrick was heading with this comment. It just wasn't like him. "I mean, a big, juicy liplock kind of thing with lots of body contact might not be accepted, but I suppose there are those who do it anyway.

"Have you seen such a kiss?"

"Sure."

He held her shoulders and turned her back around.

"Let's hurry then and go home soon, so you can show me."

The silky tone of his voice, followed by the silky drag of his tongue behind her ear had Lauren literally quaking in his arms.

"And if you do it very well," he added on a ragged sigh, "I just might have a surprise for you."

"Ste—phan!"

"Laurie? Patrick? Great day in the mornin', but I'm glad to see you both."

Dugan stood back and watched his personal tornado whip into action. In a swirl of green and white taffeta, Laurie flew into an enthusiastic embrace with an overwhelmed Stephan Polaski. The woman had a lot to learn about ladylike behavior, but he was pleased that she

300

liked the Polaskis so much. And yes, dammit, it made him feel more secure that she seemed so happy in his world.

"How's Molly? How's the baby? What's happening with her parents?" She stopped to reload and catch a quick breath. "Are you two okay? Have you heard about Patrick—"

"Laurie, honey," Dugan interrupted, prying her off his friend's neck, "if you don't let the man get some air, he'll not be able to tell you a thing."

Patrick held out his hand to Stephan and gave the Pole an enthusiastic greeting himself.

"Is it true?"

Patrick nodded.

"The news has been circulatin' since yesterday, but I was afraid to really believe it until I talked to you." Stephan clapped his friend on the shoulder and gave Laurie a wicked grin. "So, have you two been doin' anythin' interestin' since we saw you last?"

Lauren's memory flashed her a short, vivid picture of the position she and Patrick had been in when the Polaskis had walked in on them.

"Why, Stephan Polaski," Lauren scolded, her hands on her hips, as the man burst into laughter. "How indelicate to bring *that* up in polite conversation."

That stiff, pious response had Patrick choking along with his big blond friend.

Stephan signaled to another Ferris wheel worker and took a short break while Patrick filled him in on everything that had been happening. The Midway was busy, but they found an empty bench and sat down to talk.

"So, it's all over, then." Patrick knew Stephan had deliberately made his words sound like a statement, not a question. He was careful that Laurie, who sat between them, didn't see him return an uncertain shrug.

"When can I let Molly know you'll be comin' home?

The woman is bustin' at the seams, tryin' to hold in all she has to tell you, Laurie.''

Patrick got to his feet and held out his hand to his wife. ''We'll most likely be back tomorrow afternoon.'' Out of the corner of his eye he watched for Laurie's reaction and cursed himself for the coward he was. What was he hoping? That the Polaskis would make her return to the tenements easier? Damn. He should have prepared her.

''No! Not so soon?'' Lauren winked in an aside to Stephan. ''I hate to think of cooking again and doing the laundry. Of course, my day was getting hard to fill without these little tasks Molly and I love so. Why, my arms have lost nearly all that good water-hauling muscle tone and—'' She was stopped short by Patrick's hard squeeze on her elbow.

''Patrick,'' Lauren protested, shooting him a pointed look and pulling her elbow free before turning back to Stephan. ''Listen, Stephan, tell Molly I've had the greatest idea for a new Ladies League project. Bertha Palmer has agreed to talk to some of her friends and donate stuff they're not using anymore. You know? Like clothes and furniture, even knickknacks.'' Lauren glanced from one blank male face to the other, hoping to see approval and getting nothing but smooth granite.

''Laurie, wait. I—''

Patrick tried to interrupt her, but she waved him off and sidled closer to her Polish friend. He'd been on her side even before Patrick had.

''Will you please just be quiet for a minute, Dugan?'' Lauren raised her voice and continued, ''I want Stephan to get the facts straight so Molly can get going on this.'' Lauren winced as Patrick folded his arms and stepped back a pace.

''Come on, Patrick, don't be such a stick-in-the-mud.'' She tried a saucy smile, but he didn't crack.

"Well, Stephan, anyway, here's the deal. Wouldn't it be great if the ladies in the tenements could open their own little store and sell refurbished things? More money would help so much. Right? We could go to the papers and advertise, because former stuff of the rich and famous would be good quality and have celebrity status, too. It wouldn't cost much to start up, and Bertha said she'd even come down to the southside and—"

Lauren stopped the minute her husband grabbed the hand with which she was gesturing and tugged her to his side.

"I must apologize for my wife, Stephan." Patrick took a harsh breath and cinched Laurie in closer. He needed a moment to shake off the outright shock and disappointment he'd been dazed with. All this time he'd been thinking his unusual wife was adjusting to this time and in reality she still was hatching her wild schemes. Betrayal was an ugly word but an even uglier feeling.

"I'm not sure what to say, Laurie, girl," Stephan hedged, casting a quick glance at Patrick. "I suppose compared to how you've been livin' this past week the southside doesn't seem too hospitable." He shoved his hands into his pockets and shrugged. "I'm not sure folks would take to handouts from the Gold Coast, but . . ."

Lauren felt as if she'd just taken the wrong turn in a fun house. Moments ago everything looked normal, clear; now the world had turned upside down, and these men, who meant so much to her, saw only distortion.

"I think you're right, Stephan." Patrick made himself speak past the constriction in his throat in an attempt to salvage his pride—the pride that the woman he loved had just flayed by insulting his friend, his time. "I'm afraid these past days have made her forget how grateful she should be for all you've done for us and

303

what her husband can provide.''

Bloody hell! How could he have ever dreamed that what he could give her would be enough?

Lauren used her free hand then, reaching around her back and grabbing the bottom of Dugan's denim jacket. She scrunched up a wad of material and jerked on it to get his attention; to get him to look at her. When he did she wished she hadn't insisted.

"Wait, Patrick. Wait a minute. Don't make me the heavy here! I never meant this as an insult. You're just so old-fashioned sometimes. Why, it's done all over—''

Oh. My. Gosh. Lauren's stomach flip-flopped at the glare in Patrick's green eyes and the telling lift of one fine brow. She swung her head to Stephan and detected a little hurt and a lot of pity in the husky man's bewildered face. What had she been thinking to blurt out this modern idea like this?

"The strain's been hard on Laurie, Stephan. And as you can tell, she's been a might put out with me. I think tomorrow may not be the day we come back.''

Oh, please, please, Lauren cried silently.

What could she do? He was furious and had misunderstood her, and she'd been yelling, and his old-fashioned attitudes were painting the worst possible picture of this, and she couldn't turn, and he wouldn't look at her again. . . .

Lauren shifted in front of Patrick and used the bell of her skirts to camouflage the foot she backed right between his. The stiffening in his body signaled his reaction, and Lauren took a shaky breath of courage and leaned against him in tiny increments. He allowed it, and Lauren took another breath.

"Now, Dugan, Laurie does have a foreign, citified way of seein' things.''

This was awful. Stephan still wasn't sure whether

she'd insulted him, and the poor man was trying to be loyal to both of them.

"Please, Patrick, Stephan. Whatever it is you're thinking, I didn't mean it that way." She let go of the jacket and dropped her hand to Patrick's thigh, hidden by her dress, and patted him, hoping he'd know how sorry she was. He released Lauren instantly.

"I'm leavin', Laurie. If you want to stay, I'm sure Stephan will see you home."

"Patrick!"

"Now, now, you two," Stephan interjected purposefuly. "This has been a hard time for all of us. Everythin' will be back to normal soon, you'll see. Don't end your day this way. Come on, Laurie, how about a ride on this grand lady?"

Lauren looked away from her glowering husband and up at the huge monstrosity that reminded her of a giant steel spiderweb. She was completely bewildered by the last few minutes and felt as if she had stepped into a far more dangerous invisible web here on the ground.

The fame of the huge steel wheel filling the skyline had spread far and wide. Lauren knew that even in her time it would be quite a sight. Modern-day wheels usually topped out at around forty or forty-five feet. This one, Patrick had told her, rose to 264 feet, with not a high-tech tool or computerized safety system to its name.

Right now, with the way her beautiful day had just fallen apart, she wasn't about to take any more chances.

"In your dreams, Polaski!"

For the next hour Lauren held her peace while Patrick passed the good word to his comrades. The people were so obviously happy and relieved that her frustration lost its sharp edge, and she decided to wait until they got back to the cottage to set her hot-tempered Irishman straight.

After all, every couple had to make adjustments in their relationship. Considering the unusual circumstances involved in hers' and Patrick's, misunderstandings were to be expected. Nevertheless, it was disappointing that he had jumped so quickly, and so far, to the wrong conclusion.

Almost as if neither one dared to speak, they slowly worked their way past the Japanese Bizarre and the Irish Village, heading to the Illinois Central Train Station that would take them back to the Palmers' part of town. All the while, Lauren tried to catalog and freeze in her memory as many sights and sounds as possible. The amazing Chicago Midway Plaisance would delight and mystify for only a short time longer.

By the end of October the Great Columbian Exposition, the Chicago World's Fair, would be over. It added to Lauren's dejection to realize that, of the many hundreds of people flowing by her, only she knew that in little more than eleven months, nearly all the wonders around her would be burned to the ground.

In the waning heat of the August afternoon Lauren felt an unnatural chill. She rubbed her gloveless hands up and down the slick taffeta of her jacket. How was it that something so inspired and so amazing could fall to pieces so completely; that in the future few people would know it had ever been? But she had seen the magnificence of the wonders with her own eyes. Something this rare should have been stronger.

Lauren shuddered and backed under a festive awning, watching the long legs and the broad shoulders of her husband as he moved through the crowd, telling a man here and there the happy news. What they had was rare and amazing too. But it was fragile, and now it seemed they'd had their first major disagreement. It was a test of sorts: whether their love could balance their very different points of view.

The one thing she knew for sure was that without the magic of the Fair, she would never have found the time door back to Patrick. And suddenly, almost desperately, she felt compelled to have something tangible to remember it by.

Something that placed them both in the spot where the unbelievable had become reality. Something to remind her that the impossible wasn't always what it seemed to be. Something that wouldn't be destroyed.

She zeroed in on her solution just as Patrick returned to her side.

"I'm sorry for takin' so long with the hawkers, lass." Dugan tried to put an extra dollop of warmth in his stiff apology, for he'd seen the tired slump of Laurie's shoulders as he approached her waiting spot and sadness pleating little lines around her eyes. He couldn't ignore the closeness she'd been trying to regain when she'd rested her trembling body against his. That move had nearly been his undoing.

Her warmth and softness had warred with his feeling of betrayal, and he'd been keeping his distance since then—hating himself for feeling weak and less of a man because he wanted her to accept his life as willingly as she accepted his body. Maybe, just maybe, he'd misunderstood her.

"Patrick, let's have a sketch made of us."

"Aw, darlin', we can come back another day and have a special photograph taken."

"No!" Lauren gripped his arm, so lost in her need that she missed his reaction. "I want something today, in my hands. Don't worry; I've got money."

"All right, then, lass," Patrick said, unable to keep the icy chill from his voice. What would happen when she wanted something he couldn't give her? It didn't seem his love would be enough.

Just as well he hadn't offered it.

They sat side by side in the cottage's kitchen, sipping cool, tart lemonade and munching some candied popcorn Laurie had purchased. A barrier of silence sat between them, as solid as the pedestal table.

Yet Patrick, fool that he was, had a difficult time calling up the anger he'd felt earlier. Instead, it occurred to him that there had been a time when he hadn't thought Laurie particularly lovely. Now even fairy magic couldn't conjure a woman more moving than this one. His woman; sitting there wrapped up in her huge cotton tent of a nightdress.

He wondered again at his own blindness in the beginning. She had never seemed more beautiful than at this moment—and more distant. Nor more salvation and damnation both, draped in the same gown that also sent a clear message: Lace had been for making love.

A fanciful notion of loneliness, waiting for him just outside the cottage's stout oak door, suddenly popped into his head.

Was she really as dissatisfied as her speech at the Ferris wheel had indicated? Anything that smelled even faintly of betrayal threatened to start the whole ugly brew of rejection festering inside him again.

Bloody hell, man; don't be a fool. The woman sees things in a completely different light.

He grimaced, glancing at the coal oil lamp on the table, remembering the descriptions of electricity galore in her time; and her favorite colored Christmas lights. *Find out what's really goin' on in her mind. Listen, like you promised to long ago.*

"All right, Dugan. Enough of the silent treatment. What are you thinking?" Lauren blurted out.

She couldn't sit for one more minute and casually eat

Cracker Jacks. Trying to shove another bite down her constricted throat would probably choke her death. Her old-world husband might not be used to exposing his real emotions, but she would explode if she had to hold hers in any longer.

"I'm thinkin' I've never truly realized how much you've given up by stayin' here, lass." He lifted his hand quickly at her sharp inhalation. "And, too, I keep forgettin' that everything here is old-fashioned to you. But what you're forgettin', Laurie, is that it isn't to me. I suppose I've been foolish, tryin' to ignore the unhappiness this will always bring you."

Lauren kept her gaze lowered while she composed herself. This strong, sensitive man she loved read so much as criticism. She fidgeted with the cuffs of her cotton nightgown and then clasped her hands tight. This would not be the last time their differences would cause difficulties, and a lot was riding on how they resolved this.

"Patrick." Lauren lifted her face and looked straight into her Irishman's troubled eyes. "Most couples, even ones from the same time, argue sometimes, and disagree. They make up and argue again; that's normal. I was only trying to help, not hurt you. We both will have to be more patient, but that doesn't mean I'm unhappy here."

"Surely you're not expectin' me to believe there's nothing you'll miss," Patrick said cautiously. "I've been wonderin' these last hours, Laurie, just what have you been missin' the most, since you've been *stuck* here."

Oh, God, she thought with a stab of pain. *We're back to that. He's not hearing me.* How could she convince her macho throwback that he was twisting everything in his head into complicated little knots? Lauren felt as if she was stepping onto a minefield: one wrong move and all they were building would blow up.

"Oh, that's easy," she answered, forcing a false laugh into her voice. "Hot showers and Mexican food."

"What about cars and planes? What about wearin' pants and no underwear—"

"Dugan!"

"Hardly any underwear, then. What about your friends and radios and movies and medicine and . . . cookin'—"

"Patrick," she burst into his tirade and slid her hands across the polished wood to grab his. His broad shoulders were stiff, and beneath the open placket of his collarless blue shirt Lauren could see the ridged tendons in his neck standing out in sharp relief.

Is this what her harmless little plan to make money had triggered in his head? But, of course, she'd forgotten that it would only seem harmless to her. Stupid, stupid, stupid.

"None of that matters anymore." She laced their fingers together and squeezed. "I'm here and I'm not leaving. I'm not leaving and that's fine with me. Besides, the two things I miss the most are trivial and can be worked on. I'm sure of it."

"But if there was a way back . . . ?"

"No!" She hit the word too hard, but the memory of the brochure in her carpetbag suddenly loomed ominously in her mind. Patrick looked away. What was wrong? Maybe a little loving would reassure him. It would sure as heck reassure her. Suddenly, maybe because she was afraid of the distance this issue was creating between them, Lauren had to feel close to Patrick; had to see if he still wanted to be close to her.

"Come on, husband; let's go to bed so I can demonstrate that kiss you were asking me about this morning." She pulled her hands away and stood on shaky legs. Her stomach felt queasy, but she ignored it. Hadn't the man told her just last night that her body pleased him? Hadn't he shown her?

Laurie came to him with a saucy smile on her lips, but Patrick saw the uncertainty and confusion behind it. *Aw, sweetheart, what am I doing to you? Why can't I accept this as you have and make the best of it?* The physical pleasure between them was so good, and he needed her touch, her kiss, her sweet, welcoming body so desperately. Maybe he could make it enough for both of them.

Lauren snuggled onto Patrick's lap and rested her head on his muscled shoulder. Her lips were so close to the bare skin of his neck that she couldn't resist lavishing a few moist kisses there. She felt his shudder and sighed with relief, knowing he still wanted her. She needed to be the flexible one right now. It was up to her to take a small step back and fix things.

"You know, love, I don't think I'm going to have time for any big Ladies League projects anyway." Lauren raised her head as he straightened up abruptly. "I mean, you've been helping me with my dream so much that I'm sure I'll be doing babies really soon. In fact, I'm feeling guilty that it's just my dream on its way to coming true. So let's get started on yours."

Lost in the sensations zipping through him from the trail of her mouth and the weight of her body, Patrick didn't understand, at first, what she meant.

"I have some money, you know," she murmured next to his ear. "We can start shopping tomorrow for exactly what you want."

"Shopping?"

"I suppose that isn't the right term." She gave his earlobe a tiny nip. "What word would you use for finding the best ranch to buy?"

"What are you sayin', Laurie?" Patrick clenched her

311

upper arms and held her away from his chest.

"I want to help you . . . us."

The passion left his body as if he had been doused with a bucket of water. A hint of smoke and sizzle hung in the air for a moment and then was dead. What was she thinkin' now? That he couldn't provide a decent home for their baby?

"Did you decide this today when I told Stephan we'd be comin' back to the tenements soon?"

"Patrick Dugan, hold on a minute. You're doing it again—"

"It's hard to think of leavin' all this, isn't it?" Laurie's wounded expression made him feel as if a giant hand was squeezing his chest. "It's all right, lass. I see that it's somethin' you can't help." He sighed and let her go. His shoulders drooped. "I'm sorry I can't give you back the beautiful things you've lost, lass."

"Marriage is a partnership, Patrick Dugan, and I'm just trying to do my part!" she sputtered in disbelief, jumped off his lap. "First you completely misconstrue what I said at the Ferris wheel today and now you accuse me of being some feathered-brained woman only interested in the things you can give me. All right then, there are actually a number of things I want!"

Lauren took perverse satisfaction in seeing him flinch. Let him know how it feels when he realizes he's heard everything wrong. Maybe the big lug would understand her words better if she showed him with her body that no matter what, he couldn't push her away. She took a step toward him and pressed her legs against his iron-hard thigh until he looked up at her, lifting that one darn, infuriatingly sexy eyebrow.

"Yes, my stubborn husband, I do expect you to give me beautiful things. And you're right—I won't be happy unless I get every last one I have in mind. I think

I'll start by demanding that at least three have cinnamon hair and green-gray eyes!''

An urgent pounding at the front door shot Patrick to his feet, but he hesitated for a moment, as if trying to figure out what had just been said. Then, with a wary look on his face, he brushed past Lauren. Before she could follow him, he stuck his head around the corner, and she heard him speak in a remote, impersonal voice.

''Mr. Palmer wants me up at the castle. I'm not sure when I'll be back, so don't sit up.''

''Wait!'' She started to go to him and stopped.

''Lauren, I've got to go.''

Oh, God, he had called her Lauren; this was serious.

''Wait, please,'' she begged, all her bravado gone in an instant. I've . . . I've handled this wrong. I didn't mean to hurt you. . . . I didn't mean to make you mad. Let me explain so you understand. Let me . . .'' Her eyes stung with a rush of tears, and the sob in her throat made it almost impossible for her to speak.

''Please . . .'' She swallowed, trying to compose herself. ''Please come back and talk to me about this.'' Lauren's hands curled into such tight fists, she could feel the pulse of her breaking heart in them.

Dugan hesitated, silently cursing himself for the fool that he was. His love for her was tearing him apart, but could he bear not being enough again? Her eyes beseeched him; those desperate deep blue eyes. He nodded once and prayed he hadn't just agreed to his own annihilation.

''Mr. Dugan?''

At the sound of Bertha Palmer's cultured voice, Patrick froze, his hand on the servant's door. He pivoted slowly on one foot, very aware of his coarse black denims, his worn brown Brogans, and his unadorned working man's shirt. She was dressed to the nines in teal silk and sapphires.

"I made a promise to your wife concerning your safety, which my husband has just informed me will now take additional time to guarantee. Evidently there has been a problem."

Patrick narrowed his eyes and wondered if the gracious lady before him knew what the *problem* was. So he asked her.

"Potter has told me some papers were found on a body a short while ago, Mr. Dugan. They indicated that you and Lauren have been under surveillance. I suspect my husband called you up here to suggest you both would be best protected by taking a very quick and discreet trip out of the city."

She waited until Patrick nodded.

"Please do not take personal offense at this, Mr Dugan, but I find that men often forget the obvious needs of everyday life in the wake of a crisis."

The most powerful woman in Chicago stepped forward and extended an arm, gloved to the elbow for evening. When she opened her hand Patrick's knees nearly buckled. A roll of bills two inches thick uncoiled and filled her palm.

"Ma'am," he managed to get out, "I'll not accept this. We'll be fine. I can take care of my wife myself."

"Again, please do not take offense, but false pride is a very dangerous thing, Mr. Dugan. Particularly so at this time. It seems to be a common fault in men that is only aggravated by the blindness we women often exhibit in not acknowledging the power of it in the first place. This debt is owed to Lauren, as it seems that neither of your lives is out of danger yet."

Bertha Palmer extended the roll of bills once again, and Patrick could not refuse. How had this elegant woman pegged his flaw so quickly. The stubborn pride he used to cover his fear could, indeed, get them both killed.

"Lauren is the one to accept or reject. I'm sure you will understand that, not unlike most men, she was put in a situation that demanded she act independently on behalf of both of you."

A brief smile curved Bertha's rouged mouth at the snort he could not contain.

"I suspect your wife will expand your thinking most amazingly. After all, she is the one who contends that we are about to embark on the century of the woman."

Patrick left the Palmers' mansion like a zombie. The vicious trap he'd gotten tangled in had turned into a bloody nightmare. He squeezed the money in his hand. Mrs. Palmer was right; they would need this. Hell, in a roundabout way Laurie had come to the rescue again. Could he live with that, or would he rather they both die, as long as his foolish pride wasn't challenged?

Just two hours ago he had railed at his wife for wantin' to buy him a ranch, thinkin' it was terrible; now he only felt grateful for the means with which to protect her. Patrick paused at the door of the cottage. The night pressed around him, heavy with threat. He squared his shoulders and turned the knob.

His pride would be a small price to pay for her safety. For that matter, so would his life.

Chapter Sixteen

Patrick slipped off his shoes in the kitchen and tiptoed into the bedroom. Through a large window framed with white ruffled swags, the moonlight revealed the curled form of his wife. Soundlessly, he stepped close enough to watch her sleep. Close enough to smell the heady scent of roses. Close enough to hear the ragged breathing that follows tears and see a few dark trails on her cheeks.

With a sharp, painful twitch, Patrick's mouth curved up. He supposed men in the future were grateful they could always tell when their women had been crying.

He dropped onto the cane-bottomed chair in front of the window and bent forward, bracing his elbows on his knees. His hands and head dangled toward the floor, as if he no longer had the strength to hold them up. What was he going to do?

Captain James Hansen had been found brutally beaten to death and dumped in a downtown alley. His body had been found three hours ago by a drunk. Patrick was still mystified at how the incriminating papers in Hansen's coat pocket had made their way to an honest cop. It seemed Potter Palmer had had a hunch and days ago had arranged to have a man he knew personally be assigned as the captain's new assistant.

Although Palmer didn't have any information about the murderer, he had agreed to follow up on Patrick's chief suspect: Bates.

Patrick lifted his head, seeking her face. Bates had reason to hate them both. But Laurie . . . the man would never stop.

She had come to save him, giving up all she had, all she'd known, and by God, he wasn't going to let anything happen to her. He would die if anything or anyone took her from him. He loved her. Loved her more than his own life.

To hell with the money! To hell with her modern ideas clashing with his "old-fashioned" ones. She could organize anything she wanted. She could spend her money any damn way she wanted to, as long as she was safe. It was time he acted like a true man, not a strutting peacock.

Patrick rocked forward again and plunged his fingers deep in his hair, nearly ripping it out in frustration. He needed a plan or his little she-cat would get her back up and think she could fight this . . . like the last time. She'd go tearing off, trying to save him, and get herself killed or worse; Bates would do more than kill her if he got his sick, filthy hands on her.

What reason could he possibly give Laurie for leaving town so quickly that they couldn't stop and see Molly and Stephan first? Especially since he wanted her to continue thinking the danger was past. What in the world would she believe?

The thoughts running through his head agitated him

so much that he got to his feet and paced. In the pale light of the moon he saw Laurie's jacket and skirt trailing from an open dresser drawer.

Automatically he picked up the garments to drape them over the chair back. As quietly as possible he shook out the voluminous skirt only to hear a crackle of paper and the tinny clunks of coins hitting the wood floor. Lauren stirred and turned onto her side. Hell, the last thing he wanted to do was talk to the woman now— not feeling this close to the edge of losing control.

On his knees, Patrick scooped up the contents of the deep skirt pocket. At first he thought the paper was their Fair portrait, and he held it up to the window to be sure. He'd been so stricken at the time, after her insistent demand, that he hadn't really looked at it.

Patrick squinted at the print in disbelief. Bloody hell! In moments he was in the kitchen, staring at the blue page in his hand. The wavering lamplight clearly revealed the heart-stopping words:

Commemorative Exhibition of
The 1895 Chicago World's Fair
August 14, 1995 through August 31, 1995

All this time! All this time she had known she could leave! Why hadn't she said so? Why had she let him think she didn't have a choice?

The incriminating paper floated to the tabletop.

Did she realize that if he had known this key existed he would never have touched her again? Never made their marriage real?

Yes! Patrick was suddenly certain she did know, or she wouldn't have kept this secret. Laurie had willingly turned her back on her other life because she *wanted* to stay. She had willing left her showers and cars and malls and computers and ham . . . ah—hamburgers because she loved him. She loved him enough to stay when she didn't have too.

The truth of it filled his entire body with a jolt of pure joy, releasing a stinging burst behind his closed eyes. There had been a choice. She wasn't stuck after all.

Maybe, Patrick thought, as he got to his feet and slipped the folded paper into his back pocket, maybe they could make this work. He should never have doubted her love, even though his childhood had made him so slow to trust. But now—now that he knew how much she cared, the strange ideas she'd probably always have needn't threaten him at all. She really was just trying to help. From the beginning she'd been his angel of mercy.

Sweet Jesus, if she would just keep loving him for the next few days until he could explain. . . . If he could just keep her safe!

The small ember in his heart that had grown almost stone cold sputtered back to life.

There were many things he could not give his Laurie, many things he didn't have it in his power to do. But by the Saints he could and would protect her. He'd have to give her a part of the truth and then strong-arm her into compliance. The thought of acting the hard-hearted dictator made his gut clench.

Patrick pushed open the bedroom door, praying to God Almighty that Palmer's men could find Bates before she ran out of patience.

He stopped at the foot of the bed and debated his next move. Laurie would be furious and most likely hurt in the morning because he'd have to say harsh things to keep her safe. But tonight . . . Dammit! If everything blew up in his face . . . if he was left with no other option, he would have to send her back to the future, and this would be the last time . . .

He shucked his clothes in seconds and eased in beside his angel. Tonight he would love her as if the words already flowed easily and often between them. And if there was a power somewhere in the universe that cared—well then, maybe he would have the chance to hold her again. To explain his actions. If nothing else, he would always have this memory.

Lauren felt the silky slide of fabric up her legs. Vaguely she thought to surface, then remembered the heartache that hovered just out of reach. As long as she slept, didn't open her eyes, her subconscious could pretend Patrick's anger wasn't real.

Ohh, this was good. Dream hands were skimming over her body, weaving together countless threads of tingling awareness. Kisses followed. Soft suckling made her breasts achingly heavy; her neck arch; her mouth hang open; her eyes stare.

"Pa—trick?"

"Aye, angel."

"Am I awake?"

"At long last, woman." He covered her mouth with his, pulling her swollen lips inside to his waiting tongue.

"I'm sorry, Patrick," she whispered, running her hands over his back and holding him tight. "Please understand; I only want to help."

He kissed her again, trying to stop her talking, stop her thinking.

Lauren broke away from the desperate urgency that threatened to consume her.

"We're partners, Patrick. Don't you see? It's all I've ever wanted; someone to work with, someone to share with, someone to love."

He moved over her then, and Lauren knew she couldn't hold back the words any longer. He filled her until there was no more room to hide her feelings; until the walls holding back her love shattered and splintered, letting the emotional flood waters come.

"I love you, Patrick. I love you."

She didn't hear an echo.

This was going to be one hell of an awful day.

In the wee hours before dawn, after hearing the words he had been longing for, Patrick had kissed and stroked Laurie in a frenzy and then had taken her again, giving her the only beauty he had in his power to give. He had wanted to open his heart to her so badly at that moment that he'd bitten the inside of his cheek until he'd tasted blood to keep the confession unspoken.

His angel would never have believed his actions this morning if he had finally told her he loved her. Now he supposed that foolish misunderstanding they'd had at the Fair had been for the best, hurt and all. If not for that, he would have confessed the miracle of being loved and loving in return. And Laurie would never have listened when her life depended on it. It was terrible watching her stiff, controlled body moving around the cottage cleaning and packing, since he'd informed her they were leaving town for a few days, per Mr. Palmer's request. And on top of this, and his exhaustion and his worry, Patrick had had a bizarre dream that was still bothering him. He couldn't shake it.

He'd seen Laurie clear as day in a bright, white gown. At first he thought it was her nightdress, but then, as it shimmered in the sun, he knew it was different. She had turned to him with such a look of love and welcome on her face that he'd felt an ache at the back of his throat.

Suddenly others dressed in similar fashion had appeared around her, laughing and clapping, motioning for him to come. . . . Come join them. But he couldn't move. His feet felt heavy as lead. Laurie held out her hands to him, and he saw the glorious smile fading, the wet glimmer on her cheeks as the others pulled her away.

And then his feet were free! He could reach her still if he ran . . . if he ran . . . but he wouldn't go. Wouldn't move. Wouldn't follow her.

The last image that brought him abruptly awake was of Laurie walking alone between two huge carved doors that were slowly closing. To the side, Patrick saw a white-haired man behind a desk of gold, with his head in his hands.

Remembering a dream was very unusual for him. What did it mean?

Patrick stopped the unanswerable questions and cautiously entered the kitchen to pump a glass of water. Bloody hell, but acting the offended, prideful male wasn't as easy a part to play as it might have been four weeks ago, before he'd encountered a certain outspoken woman with a new way of looking at things.

''All right, Dugan.'' He froze at the tone of Laurie's voice. Her wounded silence was over; the she-cat was preparin' to pounce. Damn! Why couldn't the woman act in a predictable manner just this once? He should have thought of that! Now, dammit! What more would he have to do?

She marched across the kitchen dressed in her navy skirt and polka-dot shirtwaist; her bag in one hand, her gloves and hat in the other. Even her ratty hairpiece was back in place. It had taken Lauren an hour to get a hold of her anger and hurt and decide how to respond to Patrick's strange behavior. Now she was ready.

''What aren't you telling me?''

''What?''

''You heard me, Patrick Dugan,'' Lauren said, sitting at the table to hide her knocking knees. Something was very wrong, and she was deeply afraid of pushing her husband right now, but she had no choice. If the man was going to *stay* her husband, she had to know.

"I know I upset you yesterday with the secondhand store idea and the money and all. Frankly, Patrick, I forgot how it would sound to you. I mean," she paused and took a steadying breath, "I thought that we had kind of arrived at a new level of clo—closeness, you know, that it wouldn't be *such* big a deal to you. But now, with this order you've given me to pack and leave without even telling me why Palmer wants it or where we're going . . . Well, I want to be a partner, Dugan, not a lackey. Talk to me."

"This is *my time*, Laurie, and I'm tired of bein' judged by you and your future ways. I thought you were goin' to try to be a proper wife to me." Patrick winced at the hard edge in his voice. Thank heavens she had dropped her eyes and missed it. He leaned back against the sink and crossed his arms over his chest.

Lauren rolled her lips between her teeth to keep from crying and screaming at the same time. "I would really like to know how you can stand there, remembering the things you . . . I . . . *we* did last night and—" she locked her jaw until the sob died, "—treat me like I'm some wayward child in need of instruction."

"That's what a good husband does."

Ooooh! That self-righteous . . . "That isn't how Stephan treats Molly. It's not how it has to be. It's not how you are! Usually. So I repeat my earlier question." She stood and stepped around the pedestal table toward him. "What aren't you telling me?"

"Nothing. We're leaving; that's it."

"This it totally unreasonable, Patrick. If the danger is over, why are we leaving? Why can't I at least see Molly first? I want to meet with our Ladies League. I want to work with Jane Addams at Hull House." Lauren had advanced steadily until she was standing nose to nose with Patrick.

"If you *want* to stay my wife, you'll do as I say."

Holy Mary! What in God's name was he doin'? He was ruining everything. *Stop, Laurie darlin'. Stop.*

Lauren wrenched back as if he'd slapped her; as if she expected him to do it again.

"And if I don't?"

Her question shut out all sound, all light. Patrick was floundering like a drowning man, grasping for any leverage that might keep him afloat. Everything had gone cockeyed.

"As long as you're livin' in 1895, lass, you've not a prayer of gettin' a divorce."

"Ahh." Lauren sadly sighed and knotted her hands together at her waist. "We've come full circle, haven't we? Back to the beginning and my fatal mistake."

She looked up at him with an oddly tender and rueful expression that hurt as badly as any blow he had ever taken. The deep breath he drew in to hold off the pain only made it worse. Her own sweet scent, mingled with spring roses, formed an image from last night so sharply in his mind that he nearly broke. Soft, warm arms and legs enfolding him in the deepest embrace two bodies could share and 'I love you' whispered over and over again.

"No, I have to be honest, Patrick. Saving you wasn't a mistake. I'll never think of it that way. But falling in love with you . . . that, my boy'o, was a doozie." Lauren felt as if her body was no longer skin and bones, but fragile, brittle glass. As she walked to her bag on the floor next to the table, it occurred to her that the wrong move right now would shatter her.

"You're not by any chance lookin' for this?"

The flash of blue was all she needed to see; she closed her eyes to see no more. A long night of frantic worry and then lovemaking had not left her enough energy to deal well with complete devastation. Drawing on the last of her reserves, Lauren looked at Dugan and lifted an eyebrow.

"It fell out of your pocket. And it's probably for the best now . . ." Now that he'd ruined everything. Lost what he never deserved to have.

The fair, fragile brow climbed higher. Patrick had never felt so low.

"Since today's the 30th, I've a deal to make with you, lass."

Oh, God, the pain that familiar phrase caused.

"I'll give you your ticket home." He tapped the brochure with a finger. "If you'll do what I ask you 'til tomorrow, when I can take you to the Palace."

"Same song, second verse, huh, Dugan?" Why was she doing this? It was absolutely masochistic. *Don't you dare remember, you big doof. Don't you dare act as if you remember all the things we've said; as if it matters to you . . . don't you—*

"I'll not be singin', lass."

She sat down before she fell down. Tim—ber!

"All right, Dugan," Lauren uttered wearily. "You win. But I would like to ask one more question. I'm a fool for doing this, but as a professional researcher, and given this whole weird trip I've been on, I just can't leave without knowing."

It occurred to Lauren that she was speaking as if this had all been some kind of clinical experiment with cosmic powers. Cosmic powers gone crazy. *Yes, Aunt Lucy, Lauren thought, this is crazy. I jumped, all right. And fire hurts like hell.*

With all the courage she had left, Lauren sat up straight and looked him dead in the eye.

"Has there ever been a point in these last weeks when you've felt we've shared something—I don't

325

know—fated or destined? More than just the regular, or what I've heard is the regular, temporary type of thing . . . because, well . . . Later I know I'll wonder what your impressions were and there . . . there won't be anyone to ask, so . . ."

Lauren clenched her hands and knew she had finally lost it. Patrick was leaning against the dry sink, arms snug against his chest, watching her with dark, hooded eyes. His mouth was a thin, compressed line, and it nearly did Lauren in when she saw he wasn't going to answer. He clearly had no idea what she was talking about.

She was babbling, but she couldn't stop. In the back of her reeling mind she somehow had the impression that if she could just keep talking she wouldn't cry. And she absolutely could not cry.

"Not that I'm knocking what we've shared if you didn't feel anything, you know, extra." She pressed her mouth into a brief smile because it stopped the tiny tremors assaulting her lips. "No matter what, you've no doubt saved me from being the oldest virgin in America, and I think I'll do better at that whole thing now, when I get home."

Lauren choked back a sob, covering the sound with a vigorous cough. "And it was nice to learn with someone who knew almost as little as I did. There's so much stress about all of that in the future."

Patrick didn't think he was going to make it. His brave, beautiful woman was laying her pride at his feet and he, who had made so many mistakes because of his own, could not stop her pain. It nearly killed him to know that to save her life he would have to answer her brokenhearted plea with indifference.

The thought of her with any other man—past, present, or future—made him feel like chewing nails. He was already dying one agonizing inch at a time. Sweet, sweet memories of teasing laughter, hot, delicious loving, and baby-making washed over him. . . .

Please, God, if you can hear me, please let my Laurie have that dream if she still wants it.

"With or without any extras, I'll not soon be forgettin' the likes of you, Lauren Ann Sullivan."

Well. That was it, then.

Lauren locked her shoulders in place to keep them from dropping and exerted all her remaining will to form a neutral expression on her face and then get to her feet. She really did appreciate the way Patrick had of handling these horribly awkward moments between them. Very kind. Very polite. Very, very clear.

"Well, I—I think I'll go lie down for a while, then, since we won't be leaving the city now. Okay?" Lauren was proud of the level of cadence of her speech. Another few steps and she'd be safe.

Patrick had never seen anyone walk so precisely. It looked as if each move took her total concentration. Perhaps as much concentration as it was taking him to keep his shaking arms from reaching for her. He opened his mouth to speak and nothing came out. He had to swallow twice.

"I need to go up to the castle for a while." She nodded without turning around. "Try to get some sleep. . . . " The feminine body he was watching so intently swayed precariously for a moment, and he almost started forward.

"See you later," he barely heard before she disappeared behind the wall.

The moment she was hidden, Lauren sagged heavily against the closed bedroom door and slowly crumpled to the floor.

He only had the two names, but he wasn't worried.

Jonas Bates sat in a small work closet in the basement of the Cook County Jail and crudely copied the name and address of Stephan and Molly Polaski on a dirty piece of paper. Captain Hansen's police tablet had blood all over it.

As soon as he finished, he dropped the soiled sheets into a metal pail with some red-streaked rags and clicked on the lid. Bates snorted and laughed when he thought of how clever he was and how stupid the old cap'n had been. 'Course right before the end there the bastard had finally seen who was the boss. He begged real nice, but . . .

The only thing that would make Bates happier, at this moment, would be knowin' right where that pretty little lady was, and the list that would make him rich. He rubbed his hands together and was glad he'd asked Holmes about bringin' a guest to use one of his boarding rooms. That way he'd have lots of time to play some games, and it wouldn't make no difference how loud she screamed. In fact, Holmes probably had a room to take care of just that problem. He had all kinds of interestin' rooms.

Bates hauled himself up off the bench and yanked on a dark jacket and cap. He'd start watchin' the Polaski woman and see what turned up. The Palmers would be next.

The hulking man with the large lunch pail smiled now and again to folks passin' on the street. Most of the time though, he was too busy thinkin' to notice them. Instead, he was concentratin' on a picture in his head; a woman's blood dripping from his hands to form a pool around her lifeless body.

A loud knocking brought Lauren jerkingly awake. In those first, nether-worldish moments, as she lay trying to orient herself, a foreboding pressure filled her chest. What terrible thing had happened? For one more bliss-ful second she didn't remember; and then the memory came crashing into her awareness with the force of a tidal wave. Her stomach pitched and rolled as if she stood on the deck of a storm-tossed ship.

It was all over.

Yes, God help her. Now she remembered.

Standing on wobbly legs, Lauren held off the dizziness and tried to smooth her wrinkled skirt and tidy her hair. With a soft curse she tore the stupid hairpiece from her head and relished both that pain and the release that came from hurling the hideous thing against the wall. Feeling sick on top of everything else was just too much.

"Laurie? Laurie?"

The sweet sound of Molly's voice brought a swift rush of tears to her eyes and a victorious smile to her lips. Mr. Patrick Dugan could just go suck eggs. Women one; men zip! She was going to see Molly anyway. Lauren blotted away the telling moisture and pinched her cheeks. It was time to tell the story she'd concocted weeks ago.

"Molly!" she cried, throwing open the closed door. "It's so wonderful to see you! How are your parents? How's the baby?"

The two friends hugged like the sisters they'd become, and Molly began to answer Lauren's list of questions before they even sat down. Baby Polaski was doing fine. In fact, Molly thought she'd felt a tiny flutter just yesterday. Her parents—well, that had been a mite strange. At first she would have sworn that they weren't at all happy to have her and Stephan there. "And wasn't that just the ornery way to behave after they'd done the invitin'.

"But," Molly beamed, waving her hands expansively, "havin' to live so close together for a few days let them see for themselves what a fine man Stephan is. And things are a lot different now. Not perfect, but worlds better."

"I'm so happy for you, sweetie!" Lauren smiled, relieved to know that this hurt was on its way to healing. At least she could leave knowing Molly would have her family's support.

"I know showin' up here was jumpin' the gun a bit, Laurie, but when Stephan told me you weren't comin' back today I just couldn't wait another minute." Molly reached for her friend's hands and gave a squeeze. "Let's leave a note for Patrick and start lookin' for a place for you two right now."

Lauren took a deep breath and fixed on her face the most sincere look she could summon.

"Molly . . . I hate to tell you this . . . but I'm leaving Patrick."

"What? What nonsense is this, me girl?"

"Patrick can't accept my money, Molly." Lauren lowered her gaze to their clasped hands, unable to look into the eyes of her friend. "I can't be happy denying who and what I am. Can you understand that?" Lauren glanced up then, and the truth in her words touched them both.

"I can't ask him to accept what he . . . wasn't born to accept, Molly," she said, at last seeing clearly the insurmountable odds that fate had placed between them. "But please don't push Patrick out of your lives when I'm gone. Promise me!" She curled her fingers even tighter. "He needs you both, and your baby, Molly. Promise me you'll—" Lauren's voice faded and she fought for control. "Promise me you'll make him hold little Polaski Junior as often as you can."

"Fine, Laurie, but let's talk—"

"I've another promise to ask first," she interrupted. "Since I won't be here to become your baby's godmother," Lauren rushed on, hoping to get the bleak words out before her throat closed up, "I want you to accept this gift now." She pulled an envelope out of the pocket of her navy skirt. "This money is to help you and Stephan make the very best life you can for your child. For all your children. You might think about investing some of it in . . . well,'' she hesitated, ''some of the new inventions or discoveries at the Fair. Like electricity or the telephone or . . .''

''Laurie, no . . .''

''Please, Molly! Don't you do what Patrick's doing too.'' She twined her fingers around her friend's and tried again. ''This is the one tangible way I can leave my love behind. It will ease my own heart so much if you'll accept this part of me.

Molly could see the fragile hope behind the storm of sadness in Laurie's eyes; eyes the color of Lake Michigan on a cold winter day. But there was something else there too. Something that every drop of her ancient Celtic heritage recognized, only couldn't put a name to. Mystic magic beyond this world's ken.

''We'll pray for you every day and thank God for pickin' us to be a part of a miracle. Sure'n he sent us our own guardian angel.'' Molly reached out to brush away one lone tear that trailed down Laurie's cheek. ''Are you sure it has to be this way, love? Maybe if I talk to—''

''No, Molly. It won't do any good. Let's go for a walk around the grounds, okay?'' Lauren stood and tugged her too intuitive friend to her feet. If she didn't distract Molly quickly, the woman would have her wailing out the whole wretched story.

Later, after she was gone, and Molly read the letter tucked in with the money, Lauren hoped she'd understand and forgive—and maybe send word through Nancy Brown's journal.

''All right, lass, let's walk. But I'm not sayin' the talkin's finished.'' Arm in arm, the women walked down the gravel path toward the stables, both too filled with worry and sorrow to notice a large shadow disappearing into a black corner.

* * *

"Lau—rie, I'm hom-back." Patrick garbled the words, trying to disguise his revealing slip of the tongue. Hell! It didn't matter where they were; if Laurie was there it seemed like home. And where she wasn't . . . He couldn't even begin to think about that. Dugan wandered into the kitchen and braced himself to see the perfectly controlled smile she would offer him; to waste away a few more precious minutes from the small handful of their remaining hours.

"Laurie!"

Just as her absence was really sinking in, a round of staccato pops reverberated off the door. It was Stephan Polaski.

"I'm hopin' that look's not because my anxious little wife barged in on some last-minute, ah . . . plans?"

Patrick stepped back into the room without speaking.

"Where are they?" Stephan asked.

A horrible thought entered Patrick's churning mind.

"What is it, man?" Stephan demanded, shoving his friend down into a ladder-backed chair before he fell down.

As succinctly as possible under the conditions, Patrick told Stephan all he knew about Hansen's murder and Bates's involvement. "I've been up with Palmer for almost two hours, waitin' for reports from his men. I . . ." Dugan sent a fist slamming onto the table. "How long ago do you think it was when Molly—"

Both men heard a hollow thump against the door. They jumped to their feet at the same time, but Patrick turned the knob.

"Holy Mother of God, Stephan!" Molly crumpled into his arms.

It was a flurry of frantic minutes before either man could process a clear thought. Stephan had plucked his wife away from Patrick and dashed for the bed. After grabbing a bowl of water and a cloth Patrick had run right behind him. The back of his teeth were clamped together so fiercely, his entire jaw ached. Where was Laurie? Dear God in Heaven and all the saints, please let Molly wake up and tell him what had happened before his heart beat itself to death!

Patrick turned around abruptly when his stunned brain finally communicated to him exactly what he was seeing. Stephan was pulling off his wife's clothes as quickly and as gently as possible. The sight of his friend's big, trembling hands on the small, bare curve of Molly's stomach shocked him into action.

"Stephan, for God's sake! What's wrong with her? What can I do?"

"Ther—there seems to be only the one knot on her head. Look."

Patrick slowly swung about and kept his eyes fixed on the foot of the bed until he saw that Stephan had covered his wife with a sheet.

"See." The Pole tenderly bathed the purplish lump near his wife's temple. "I can't find another mark on her." His wide eyes revealed the inner battle he was fighting to keep his fear and anger at bay. Patrick knew only too well how hard that was.

"Molly? Molly, love? Can you hear me?"

"Ste—phan . . ." The soft voice grew steadily stronger. "Stephan, help me! Help!" Molly shot up off the bed like a sprung jack-in-the-box.

"Honey," he crooned, pulling her struggling body snug against his. "Honey, it's me. You're safe. You're safe."

The tears began to fall.

"A man . . . out by the stables." She sobbed and caught a ragged breath. "A big, horrible man took Laurie. Sh . . . she knew who he was because . . ." Stephan rocked Molly slowly, trying to ease her anguish. "She stepped in front of me and told me to run . . . but when

333

he . . .'' Molly turned her stricken eyes on Patrick, and the sorrow reflected there sliced through him like shards of broken glass.

"What, lass?" Patrick ground out.

"When he hit her I just couldn't leave. I tried to stop him, Paddy, but I wasn't strong enough." Molly's entire body began to quake so badly that her husband crawled into the center of the bed and gathered her up, sheet and all, onto his lap.

Patrick used every ounce of his remaining control to tenderly cup the cheek of his brave little friend. "I'll get her back, Molly. Don't worry yourself, now."

"Dugan!" Stephan ordered, when the Irishman lurched for the door. "Wait, wait and I'll go with you. I've a score to settle with that animal too!"

"No time." There was no energy left for argument. Everything was focused on Laurie. "I'll get word to you somehow."

Before the door shut he was running.

Harry Brown had gorged himself on the power of being in charge while McDonald was gone. The sleek surface of the mahogany desk felt like liquid glass beneath his rough fingertips. Ah, yes, this was what he'd had in mind years ago when he'd started working for Mike. Before his boss had come up in the world, so to speak. Harry had gotten his share of money, but he was tired of being the one to take care of all the dirty deals McDonald didn't want to touch anymore.

Maybe it was time he found a place where he could be the man in the fine suit sittin' behind a big desk all day. Maybe after the Fair he could leave and—

"Don't make a sound, Brown, or I swear to God it'll be your last." The rope cutting into his neck was growing tighter by the second. He couldn't turn around; he couldn't breath. Frantically, his fingers dug into his skin, trying to pull away the killing hemp. With a last desperate lunge, Harry hefted his bulk and managed to open the top desk drawer, reaching for protection, but the man behind him was too fast.

"You have two minutes to tell me where she is," Patrick growled, aiming the barrel of the small revolver at the sweat-covered forehead of Mike McDonald's righthand man. The bastard who'd gotten him thrown into jail in the first place.

"Du—Dugan, ya stupid Irish . . ." Harry paused to breathe and probe the ring of raw flesh around his neck. "What in the hell are you doin' here?"

"Where did you tell Bates to take her?" A tiny click boomed through the silent room.

"Oh, damn! Are you sayin' that moron Bates has the wh—"Harry almost swallowed his tongue when Dugan leveled his aim. "Does he have your wife?"

"Do you know what Potter Palmer will do if anything happens to her?" Patrick had distilled all the anger, despair, and fear tearing through his body into deadly calm. "Your boss will be lookin' for a scapegoat, Brown. But then, that shouldn't worry you, because if you don't give me the information I'm needin', you'll be dead anyway."

"I swear on my sister's life that I don't know where Bates is."

"He killed Hansen."

"Yes." He already had this troubling news to report when Mike got back. Did he want more?

"I'm out of patience, Brown. Tell me where he *could* be, then."

"With the kind of package he's carryin' and with what he's got in mind to do, Bates is probably down at Holmes's Castle." Harry paused, feelin' just a touch of satisfaction at the look on the face of the man who'd caused them so much trouble. His gun hand might still be steady as a rock, but Dugan was white as a sheet.

"The big oaf mentioned the place a time or two. You know, the big old boardinghouse down around Sixty-third and Wallace. The one with all the bay windows covered in sheet iron." Just thinkin' of his little wife in that place would age the man ten years.

"If she's hurt or . . . I'll be back for you, Brown!"

Patrick let all the rage roar out of his body through his right fist. The impact and moaning grunt from Harry Brown cleared his head and filled him with cold purpose.

Now for Bates!

ChapterSeventeen

Lauren had never been so terrified. Not afraid or scared; terrified! In the endless hours that had passed since Bates had taken her the knowledge that the man was truly mad had become increasingly more evident. Not even a spark of humanity remained within the demented shell.

At first Lauren had thought to escape, but the lumbering, slow-witted ox had fooled her. His threat to kick Molly in the stomach had taken all the options out of her hands and blown them away like chaff on the wind. The vicious blow to her friend's head had assured her that the man meant what he said. He had produced a black hat with a heavy veil and a long black cloak. The dark literally swallowed her up, and only his fingers clutched cruelly around her elbow gave her direction.

Each time she tried to lift her head and get a fix on her location Bates pressed the tip of a razor-sharp knife against the back of her neck. After a few pricks Lauren could feel a trickle of blood inching down her skin. She began to study the streets, the floor of the horse car, even the shoes around her. Anything that might give her a clue. She wouldn't let fear hold her hostage too.

But it was hopeless. She had no idea where she was. Bates had finally pushed her inside a building of some kind and thrown her into this windowless box of a room. Her hat and cloak were gone, but the blackness still surrounded her. A blackness so thick she couldn't see the hand in front of her face; so thick she could barely breathe.

Lauren pressed herself into a corner, as far away from the door as possible. She drew her knees up against her chest and pulled into a tight ball. Her eyes strained to see until they ached and she had to close them for relief. A nauseating blend of odors permeated the air, and Lauren felt that sick, dizzy sensation she had experienced earlier. She fought to calm her roiling stomach, but the strange, almost sweet, burning scent, mingled with a harsh chemical taint of acid or lye, made it very difficult.

As horrible as her flight with Bates had been, this was infinitely worse. Because now her poor fear-numbed brain was starting to think. What had happened to Molly? Oh, God, please let her baby be all right! What was Patrick doing? How would he ever find her? Was he even looking? Lauren knew she couldn't let the terror clawing away inside of her escape. The evil she sensed around her would feed and grow stronger on her hysteria, until she, too, went mad.

"Patrick," she whispered into the void, "I love you. I need you so. . . . " The words of love seemed to make the oily air in the room writhe, and Lauren shuddered, clenching her arms more securely around her bent legs.

She dropped her head to her raised knees and silently let the tears fall. Her only solace came from the memories she began to replay in her mind.

Patrick ran as if the hounds of hell were snapping at his heels. He ran until his heart felt as if it would surely burst, and still he kept going. Even after he'd gotten on the train to take him to Sixty-third Street he could not sit but moved steadily through the cars to get closer to his destination. The look on his face must have been deadly, for even the conductor didn't interfere.

The day had just slipped away into darkness when he located Holmes's Castle. Once, about two months before, he'd heard an unbelievable rumor about this boardinghouse whose nickname mocked the Palmer's mansion. It seemed an out-of-town family had rented a room there while they were vacationing at the Fair. Only, according to a worker passing along the story, the family never returned home. Some brother or cousin had come looking for them, but there wasn't a trace to be found. It was as if they had gone in and had never come out.

Standing in the shadows, Dugan knew with sick dread that something evil was happening in that house. He fought down his killing fury and horror and tried to formulate a plan—something that would keep them alive if he got caught. If Bates was as greedy as he was demented, maybe the promise of McDonald's list would control him. Patrick flexed his taut shoulders and shook out his cramped hands. He hadn't even been aware of his numb fists hanging at his sides.

Every second she was trapped in there could be bringing unspeakable agony, but dammit to hell, he had to wait a bit longer. The night needed to settle into its accustomed pattern, and then he could sneak inside.

When Patrick estimated it to be about midnight he crept silently to the back door. Not a soul had entered or left. Not a sound had been heard. The sheet iron did a very effective job of blocking out the light.

How would he ever find her? A weak light from one coal-oil lamp barely illuminated the first hall he came to. Door after door lined either side. If the structure proved to be the same on the upper floors, Patrick estimated there to be well over seventy rooms. But this area, less desirable because it was near the kitchen, seemed deserted. A sudden sharp, biting chill sliced up his spine, and he turned to start his search in the basement. Room by room, top to bottom, he'd not leave one hellish inch—good God! What was that awful smell?

Patrick cautiously pushed open the rough-hewn door at the bottom of the descending stairs. The rotten, acrid stench was so vile, he nearly wretched. Swiftly he pinched off the air to his nose and tried to shake away the dizziness. Most of the room was shrouded in deep shades of black, but the eerie glow of light from the upper floor outlined a few large objects, as if drawn with a heavy piece of charcoal.

With measured steps Patrick moved closer. A big rectangular, tablelike apparatus made of wood gradually took shape. What . . . ? Dugan had seen some callous and cruel, almost inhuman things in his day—in his own life—but sweet Jesus! He swallowed hard to force back the bile surging up his throat. At either end of the table were manacles. Patrick had a nauseating suspicion that the dark, blotchy wood beneath those iron rings had been stained that way with blood.

Lost for a moment in this waking nightmare, he backed up without thinking, trying to escape the truth of what was going on here. With an involuntary grunt he smacked into a huge metal vat. What looked to be innocent water shimmered with the motion his jarring had caused. The smell alone told him that this vat held not one drop of innocence. A hot tingle on his arm confirmed his worst suspicions: Acid.

Patrick Dugan began to pray as he had not since the night his mother had died. *Laurie!* he raged silently. *Help me find her, God! Ma!*

He ran up the stairs and straight into the gun of Jonas Bates.

The resounding crack of the door against the wall wrenched Lauren to screaming consciousness. Like a small animal trying to burrow away from danger, she pressed so hard into her corner that she hurt.

"Got two buckets here, little lady," Bates cackled, his huge frame outlined with a pale glow from the dim hall gaslight. "One's water to drink and one's for the water you make. Hope you can tell the difference in the dark." His wheezing laughter stopped abruptly. "I was gonna play with ya now, girl, but we've got an unexpected guest."

The monster bent for a moment, and Lauren's light-sensitive eyes shut automatically. Something heavy rolled and thumped against one of the walls.

"You better be useful and keep it alive or you'll be mighty sorry."

"Wait!" Lauren made herself speak. She couldn't allow her fear to control her even more than Bates already did. "I can get money. I can—"

"Are you sayin' you want to give ol' Bates somethin' right now?"

Silence.

"Not yet, huh? Well, I can wait." The solid, impenetrable door began to close, sealing her inside a living tomb. "Best be quiet, though. You'll want it to sleep as long as you can."

* * *

341

Every inch of Lauren's body was in agony. Her muscles had passed the point of no return about an hour ago. With any luck she might faint from the fast, shallow breaths she was taking in an effort to keep her presence a secret from whoever—or whatever—was in the room with her.

Lauren had tried, at first, to make her logical mind send her scared-stiff body over to check *it* out. But she couldn't bring herself to leave the security of her corner, the solid feel of the walls snug against her back. Somehow her traumatized thoughts convinced her that if she ventured out into the blackness, she would drown. It would swallow her up.

At the first moan Lauren nearly plowed her feet through the floor. The sound pounded in her ears until she bit her tongue to keep from crying out. It was awake! She licked her parched lips and tried to stop breathing.

"Oooooh, bloody hell . . ." The last slurred words groaned from the far side of the room actually seemed to stop the beating in her chest.

"Patrick?"

"Laurie? Holy Mary! Lass, is it you?"

Lauren pushed off from the wall and used her arms to stroke into the blackness. She heard shifting grunts and the slide of fabric over wood. The blood surging through her body was rushing to all the cramped, protesting muscles, and she gritted her teeth against the stinging burn.

She found his leg first and started the sobbing second.

Patrick literally felt Lauren crawl up his body and collapse in his arms. By the time her face reached his she was wracked with tears and raining them down his neck. He wasn't surprised to feel his cheeks grow wet too. Slowly, gently, Dugan began to run his hands over Laurie, letting them be his eyes.

"Oh, Patrick," she sobbed. "You should never have come for me, but I'm so glad you did."

"Aw, Laurie, my darlin', I've died a thousand deaths in the last few hours. Come here, woman," he rasped, scooting back against a wall and arranging her more comfortably on his lap.

"But, Patrick, this is all wrong," Lauren insisted in a watery voice. "Bates might kill us both now, and I've failed then. Failed you and Aunt Lucy and who knows what else—"

Patrick carefully drew his wife's trembling body even closer, close enough to feel the hectic thudding of her heart. "Laurie, hush now, and listen to me. If there's one thing I've learned for certain since you dropped into my life, it's that miracles really do happen. We can't fail unless we give up, darlin', and we're not about to do that.

"But, sweetheart . . ." He hesitated for only a moment, preparing himself for her answer; preparing himself to give her whatever comfort she might need. "I need to know what the bastard's said, and . . ." He lightly rested a hand on either of her cheeks and brought her lips to his for a tender kiss. "I need to know what he's done to you."

Lauren snuggled her head under Patrick's chin and slid her hands up his back to hook on his strong shoulders. She turned her face until her lips brushed the beating pulse point at the base of his throat and took one deep, quivering breath, comforted by the smell of her man and bay rum. It would be best for both of them right now to minimize the trauma of the last few hours.

"He's added a few more bruises to my collection, but compared to what he could have done—what he's threatened to do—I'm all right." As Lauren spoke, the truth of her words gave her strength. She had survived without going crazy. In fact, now that she wasn't in this alone anger was starting to take the place of fear. "Mostly the psycho's terrorized me by keeping me locked up in the dark.

"What about you?" she asked, lifting her fingers to trace the planes of his face. Patrick tried to shift away from her touch. "Okay, Dugan, it's your turn. What is it?" Lauren's roaming hands stopped at the sticky feel of blood near his mouth.

"He hit me a bit, too, but not as bad as before." Patrick felt her scramble off his lap. "Wait! Where are you goin'?"

"I'm finally going to get some practical use out of this blasted petticoat." The sound of tearing cloth followed her feigned bravado. Lauren crawled toward the buckets, patting her way one hand span at a time. "This is the only advantage I can see in hauling all this underwear along everywhere."

"Hurry back here, woman. I don't want you out of my reach."

Dugan lay still in this unlikely haven and savored Laurie's touch. Just as in the beginning, she was caring for him. Careful, probing fingers soothed his abused flesh and washed away his pain with a cool cloth. Even after what she had endured, after all the things she *hadn't* told him, still this woman thought of him first. Guilt cut him to ribbons.

"Forgive me, lass, for not keepin' my vow. I didn't stop that bastard from hurtin' you again. Hell, it's my fault you're here."

"What?" Lauren sat back on her heels.

"Palmer told me last night that someone murdered Captain Hansen." Patrick paused when her warmth left him. No less then he deserved. "Remember when you asked me what I was keepin' from you?"

"Yes."

"Well, I suspected that Bates might come lookin' for us, but . . ."

"You wanted to protect me, right?"

"Aye, lassie."

"Convince me to leave you at any cost, right?"

"Yes," he said, without realizing what he was admitting. "I can see now that I was treatin' you like a child. You're a strong woman, and I should have trusted you, planned with you. Then when he—"

The inky darkness of the room gave him no warning of her movement until her mouth met his just a bit off center.

"Do you mean it, Patrick Dugan? Do you really accept my differences? That I want to be your partner?" She kissed him again. "Tell me," she urged, forgetting the danger surrounding them, forgetting everything else but the love she had for this proud man who'd had so little of it in his life. "Tell me the real reason you were sending me away."

All the fears that had been pounding through his body for hours had pummeled the walls around his heart to dust. The feel of Laurie, alive and nestled close to him, was all that mattered; all he needed. And hell itself be damned but for as long as he had her, he would glory in the feelings between them! Ma was right: True love was worth whatever the cost, and he would gladly pay.

Patrick reached for Laurie in the dark and stretched her out beside him. He rolled up on an elbow, cradling her head in the bend of his arm, and ran his other hand down her side, scooting her closer until they touched each other from head to toe. Because she would not be able to see his face, his body had to tell her.

With my body I thee worship.

Dugan circled one small, sturdy wrist and carried her open palm to the back of his neck. He pressed it there

345

and then possessively rested one heavy leg over hers, skirts and all.

"I want you to *feel* what I'm sayin' down to your bones, my fair and fine colleen." He found her other hand, lying between her breasts, and couldn't stop himself from gently caressing each soft mound before placing her fingers low on his jaw.

"The truth of it is, me darlin' wife," Patrick whispered against her lips, his voice as thick with emotion as it was with the lilt of Ireland, "I feel as if I have loved you forever, been wandering my whole life looking for you."

He took her hand from his cheek and pressed it over his heart. "Years ago, after seeing my ma's broken heart, I . . . I guess I stopped believin' it would ever come for me; stopped hopin'. And I'm thinkin' now that only you . . ." Blindly he found her trembling lips with his. ". . . Only you, with all the rare and different things about you, could have reached right inside me like you did. And I've nothin' but me own stubborn pride to blame for the fight I've waged to keep my love from you."

"Well, I'm warning you now, husband, that I'll never let you take it back," Lauren vowed with a husky catch in her voice and rubbed her hand pressed over his heart in a tiny circle. "We can really do this, Patrick, can't we? I mean, a hundred years couldn't keep us apart, right? Together we're strong enough to handle anything."

She slipped her arms up around his neck and pulled his chest down to rest on hers. "But first we gotta get out of here, partner."

Lauren could feel him holding back, but this time she wasn't letting the man get away with it. She was going to lovingly, forcefully, show him how a partnership worked. Her fingers at the back of his neck wove deeply into the thick cinnamon hair she couldn't see.

"I love you more than I ever thought possible, Patrick Dugan. I know your old-world male gallantry is having a hard time giving in to my future-world female assertiveness. But please trust me. Let me help you get us out of this mess." As she spoke she felt his body stiffen, relax, and stiffen again.

"I love you," she whispered once more and kissed him, feeling the tingly scrape of his whiskers and the puffy rise at the corner of his mouth. "I love you and I've wasted too much time hiding it. I could have been gone already, Patrick! Don't you see, no matter what happens I know you love me and you know I love you. It's a miracle I don't want to take for granted for a moment, not even under these circumstances."

Mercy, Lauren wished she could see his face—those smoky eyes that could conceal so much. How would they look shining with unrestrained love? Well, if she couldn't see the love, feeling it would do just fine. Patrick had been so careful with her, but now she needed more; needed to give more. Something to drive away the demons of fear. Something to hang on to.

The touch of Laurie's mouth, still sweet with the words of love, was the most delicious thing Patrick had ever tasted. This was a woman like no other: his woman. Ignoring the sting of his swollen lip, he sent his tongue into the honeyed cavern of her mouth, coaxing her to a dueling response.

As gently as possible, he tugged her onto her side and slid his free hand down her back until he cupped the soft curve of her bottom and pressed her closer to his straining body, wishing he could give them both the completion they craved. But this was not the time or place. A few more sweeping strokes and he withdrew, dragging the rough tip of his tongue over the satiny lips he could not get enough of.

"No more, love," he murmured hoarsely. "I can't share something as sacred as our love in this evil place. We've got to clear our heads, partner, and decide what to do. I need to tell you the story I've spun for Bates." At Laurie's whimper of protest he hugged her. "We've all the rest of our lives, darlin'. A little more time won't make a difference."

For just a moment Lauren felt the icy void close in on her again, as it had before Patrick's arms had circled her in the darkness. An ominous sense of foreboding swept through her at his words, but she shut the feeling out of her mind. They had planning to do.

A few hours later Lauren stirred at Patrick's side. They had moved back to her corner, a better defensive position, her husband had claimed. At his insistence they had both tried to get some sleep, and, amazingly enough, in the safe harbor of each other's arms they were able to.

"Feelin' better, love?"

His lips moved at her temple, leaving a tender kiss there. The words soothed the aches and pains in her body.

"Hearing you call me love makes all sorts of things feel very, very good." Lauren sighed, wishing she could forget what lay ahead.

"Woman, if you knew what your wanton ways did to me, you'd not be sayin' such things here and now."

For one precious moment they held each other in the dark, reveling in the love they now openly acknowledged.

"When will he come?"

"Could be any time now." Patrick sat up and leaned back against the wall, stretching out his long legs straight in front of him. "It's most likely about nine o'clock. Bates said we'd leave after the Fair had shut down for the night. Forcin' him to break into the Palace is the best hope we have that someone will catch him."

"So," Lauren scooted up beside her husband and rested her cheek on his shoulder, "if we play along with the man, assuring him of all the money McDonald will pay for the original copy of the list, it should guarantee us a certain degree of safety. At least until he actually has the papers in his disgusting hands." Lauren shuddered.

"That's when all hell could break loose, lass." He slipped his arm around her back. "Once we leave here, you must watch me. If any opportunity arises, we'll have to act quickly."

"We'll run, right?"

"Yes. I've the money I told you about from Mrs. Palmer stashed in your bag back at the cottage. We'll be fine once we leave the city."

"But later we can come back?"

Patrick pulled her onto his lap and pressed her head to the hollow beneath his chin. There was an option he hadn't discussed: one that made him feel gut-punched, but one that she had to know. Just in case.

"Okay, Dugan." Lauren tried to sound playfully gruff. He was acting very strange. Even though by all accounts she should still be terrified, the very fact that they were together pushed the fear away. "I know you can't tell me *when* we can come back. But sometime in the future we will be able to see Molly and Stephan again?"

Patrick ran his hand up her spine and wrapped his fingers around the nape of her neck.

"Ooooh, ou—" Lauren stopped abruptly, remembering that she hadn't mentioned this injury.

"What did he do here, lass?"

Patrick's voice was as hard as steel. He ran a gentle fingertip around the puffy wound and traced a crusty path that went under her blouse. The joy of having Laurie in his arms had dulled reality too much. The bastard who had them was a monster. Unless they were very, very lucky, Bates would kill him without a qualm and make his sweet wife beg to die as quickly.

Dear God, help me make her see what must be done!

"I'm fine, Patrick. Please don't make a big deal out of it." She shifted a bit on his hard thighs and rubbed her palm over the burgeoning whiskers covering his taut jaw. "Please, love, it's over and done. Tell me about Molly and Stephan."

"Lauren?"

Oh, oh. "Yes?"

"Do you believe me when I tell you that I've never wanted anythin' more than to live the next fifty years or so with you?"

"Ye-s."

"Do you believe that if somethin' were to happen to you, all the joy, all the color in my life, would be gone?"

"Yes . . . because I would feel the same way."

"Then on the love that we have for one another I'm askin' for your promise, wife. A vow that I must have in order to do what we must when Bates comes."

Lauren sat up and placed her hands on his shoulders, wishing she could see his face. Wishing she could keep his next words from coming.

"If there's no other way, no other choice," he paused to steady his voice and take a harsh breath, "if Bates tries to kill us in the Palace, you must go back."

"Back where?" Lauren stubbornly refused to understand him.

"To the future, my angel."

She shoved against him and scrambled up off his lap. "No!" She backed into the blackness, trying to escape. "No, I won't leave you!"

"Laurie, can you see me?"

"Wha—? You know I can't."

"Are you afraid right this minute?"

"No . . . no, not really. I'm angry because—"

"Why aren't you afraid, love?"

His voice held such aching sadness that Lauren felt her eyes fill with tears.

"I . . . I—" Oh, God, she knew what he was trying to make her see. "I know you're still here."

"If the moment comes, Laurie, as it very well might, I must have your promise that you will do what has to be done to live." Patrick swallowed hard, pressing his back to the wall. "If I had at least the comfort of knowing you were still alive, even in another dimension, I believe I could stand the pain. But if you were to die before my eyes, when I had the power to save you . . . That, my precious wife, I could not stand for even one day."

"Don't ask this, Patrick! Please!" Already the darkness between them felt like miles. What would it be like when it was years?

He heard the desolation in her plea, but he had to continue. There were two more cards to play.

"Lauren?"

"Yes?" The word wavered with tears.

"Could you have left me in the jail?"

"Never! They were hurting you! I would have done anything, *anything*, to get you out."

"You must know, darlin', that the most horrible consequence of this night, the one that fills me with the worst fear and despair I have ever known, worse than all that happened in my childhood, is that Bates kills me and still has you."

"Patrick . . ." Lauren couldn't hold against his raw anguish. "Love, love, please . . ." she cried, stumbling

351

forward and dropping to her knees, searching for him in the darkness.

At the first brush of her hand he scooped her up, crushing her shaking body to his chest, burying his face against her smooth neck and breathing in the sweet, faint scent of roses.

Their kiss was a terrible thing. Tongues thick with unshed tears tangled and clung. Greedy hands ran wildly over the precious bodies that might soon be out of reach forever. Neither one knew whose tears they felt, but seeking, hungry mouths sipped them all away. And after the flashfire had exploded and burnt itself to embers he asked again for her promise.

Lauren lay wilted across his lap like a day-old wild-flower ripped out by the roots. She heard Patrick's question and knew the answer she had to give, but the words felt like razors slicing her throat. In her moment of hesitation he burrowed a hand between their bodies and cupped the heart of her through her skirts. The heal of his palm pressed over her womb.

"If there's a chance that you've a part of me in here, love," Patrick said, low and rough, cradling her in the circle of his arm and flexing his hand, as if trying to feel their baby, "you *must* give me your promise."

Lauren felt tears running into her hair. "You have it, Patrick. I swear." She touched her lips to his.

The sigh she heard came from the bottom of his soul. Through her fingertips she could feel the tension leaving his beautiful, strong body. "Of course, I have a promise to ask of you too." She sniffed and lifted a corner of her skirt to wipe away the mascara trails that surely would be streaked everywhere.

"Lauren . . ." he warned, not daring to guess what she would say.

"I want some baby insurance, husband."

At first she knew her request did not compute. But

the man was too sharp. Even without seeing his face, she could tell the moment he understood what she wanted. The tension was back, fairly humming under his skin.

"Sweetheart, I told you this isn't—"

"Patrick . . . please!" She swiveled around, straddling his hips, and pressed her hands to his cheeks. "Please, love, give me something to live for if I have to leave you."

This was a need that couldn't be denied. Yet, even as he swept her skirts back over her legs and moved the fragile cotton barrier aside, Patrick kept her covered and protected should the worst happen and Bates barge in. He felt the loving slide of her fingers through his hair and her soft kiss just behind his ear. Time! Mother of God, but the time was almost gone; would that he had hours and hours to show her all she meant to him. Someday . . .

"Patrick," she whispered, sipping at his torn lip and then soothing it with her tongue as she had wanted to so many days ago. "Make love to me. Make us a baby."

His slow possession filled her with the bittersweet wonder of their love. For a moment she would close out all the pain around her and engrave this sensation on her heart.

Patrick noted her questioning movement and stopped too. He ran his fingers from her shoulders across her collarbones to the buttons at her neck and deftly undid them halfway. The soft rounding curves beneath his hands urged his body to break free, but he held back for a minute more.

Lauren felt the paper slide between her breast and her bra. She knew without words that this was the brochure that could take her far away from the man she loved. She felt the soft brush of Patrick's sideburn

353

against her chest as he lowered his head and pressed his lips to the skin that lay over her heart.

When the buttons were closed he kissed her as tenderly as he'd ever done, and then slowly, relentlessly, drove the darkness from the room.

Much later Patrick realized he'd been wrong. Just around them, in that one spot, he'd found holy ground.

"Now, mick, where do we go from here?"

Bates jammed his gun once again into Laurie's ribs, and Patrick saw the suffering register on her face. The man hadn't taken the weapon from her side since they'd left the horror house. It had surprised and then infuriated him that the sadistic oaf was smart enough to use a cab and not the train. Although the trip to the fairgrounds took longer, there had been no opportunities for escape.

The only person who could have helped was their very disinterested driver, but Bates paid him and sent him off immediately after their arrival. Patrick knew then that their captor had no intention of letting them live.

There was only one thing to do—but could he make Laurie understand?

"I'll shoot her if ya don't tell me where that list is right quick." Bates held Laurie in a fierce grip and dragged her toward the stairs leading to the rotunda.

"If you harm one hair on my wife's head, you'll not get a word out of me." Patrick brazenly folded his arms across his chest, trying to get a rise out of the mountain of dehumanized flesh. "I'll be more than happy to follow her to the grave—"

"No! Patrick, don't—" Lauren gasped as the animal tightened his stranglehold around her neck.

"Let my wife go or I'll not tell you a blessed thing."

Some measure of the Irishman's fearless honesty got

through to Bates and confused him. Nobody ever chose death willingly. It made no sense, and it was taking too much time. He wanted out of the spooky building filled with gewgaws and hodgepodge.

"Get over here, then, ya bastard!"

Bates viciously shoved Lauren down to her knees at the bottom of the steps. She lurched out of his reach while Patrick walked toward them. Not for a moment did he take his eyes from hers. The message he was sending was the one she had vowed to obey, though it killed her to see it.

"The time has come then. . . . " Dugan gave her a slight smile that grew larger and sweeter in his emerald eyes. He turned to Bates and gestured toward the top of the staircase. "Up there is where I've hidden the list. Where I'd hide anything of great importance." Lauren remained rooted to the floor, not quite sure what he wanted her to know.

"I can get lots of money, Bates." She tried once again. "Let us go and we'll vanish."

"Your whore is as big a fool as all women before her, mick." Bates swung his gun in her direction and pretended to pull the trigger. "You two are gonna vanish, all right. Off the face of the earth."

"You heard him, Lauren Ann," Patrick said firmly. "Get ready!"

"Yeah, stupid woman! Get ready to breathe your last—"

Patrick launched himself forward with all the strength left in his body. He collided into Bates's gun arm and threw them both off balance on the stairs.

"Run, Laurie, run!" he yelled, struggling to turn the brawny arm.

Lauren staggered to her feet and stumbled up the steps. With trembling hands she tore open her buttons and grasped the paper hidden there. At the top she looked back at the man she loved. A bullet whizzed past her head.

"No!" She heard him scream and then, "Laurie, go!"

The pounding up the staircase sent her running into the dark rotunda, the brochure clutched in her hand. All at once two shadowy shapes crashed onto the floor behind her, knocking over a display stand.

Lauren saw Patrick's frantic scan of the area while he tried to hold Bates down. She was about to move to help him when everything went double, and a strange, dizzy feeling swamped her traumatized body. The objects around her began to dissolve and she lifted her hands in panic, only to see her fingers, holding the centennial brochure, fading into nothing.

"Patrick!" she screamed, straining for one last glimpse. "I love you!"

A gunshot that sounded as loud as a cannon pierced the swirling images and Lauren saw a body fall.

Then she saw no more.

Chapter Eighteen

The minute Lauren opened her eyes the recollection of what had happened drove the air from her lungs like a hammer blow to the chest. She struggled to her elbows and then pushed up to her feet. The faint flow of emergency lighting made the rotunda of the Museum of Science and Industry heartbreakingly identifiable.

Patrick! What had happened? She bent nearly in two on a crashing wave of nausea as tears rolled down her cheeks. *Oh God, don't let him be dead!* Lauren sniffed and swiped at her face with the backs of her hands. When a cool stream of air-conditioning blew across her damp face she knew it must be time for the maintenance crew to start work. And, destroyed life or not, she had better get out of sight if she didn't want to find herself answering a barrage of questions that she couldn't—wouldn't—answer.

Just as she put her rubbery legs into motion, Patrick's voice echoed in her head. Once, Lauren would have thought that impossible, but never again. If there was any chance, any chance at all, she was taking it. *Aunt Lucy, please help!* She stopped, closed her burning eyes, and listened more intently.

Up there is where I've hidden the list. Where I'd hide anything of great importance.

She couldn't make herself leave the mezzanine without checking for the crack way up on the back of Patrick's column. With her last bit of energy, Lauren strained her shaking fingertips to feel for the small opening. What were the chances that it would still be there, a hundred years later? Just as a shooting cramp knotted across her shoulders, she brushed over something barely protruding from what felt like a painted-over rift.

A few long minutes later Lauren swiped her sleeve over her damp forehead and gently placed the small folded piece of heavy paper deep in her skirt pocket. If it was from . . . Patrick, she absolutely could not look at it now without crumbling into a million tiny pieces.

Very slowly, Lauren made her way down to the bathroom in which she had changed weeks ago. The only thing she would let her battered mind think about was getting back to the hotel and Nancy Brown's journal. Any answers she'd hoped to find just might be there.

One by one she closed and barricaded the doors to her heart and her memories, huddling in a corner to wait for morning.

Dear Lauren, I think this will be my only entry. Harry and I are leaving Chicago in two weeks at the close of the Fair. Winter is starting to rear its cold, harsh head, and so many people are out of work and hungry. It seems the bright days of summer were just an illusion. Underneath, everything is rotten. I don't know much, but you told me to record news of your husband if I heard any.

Harry was in trouble with the police and his boss when both Captain Hansen and Officer Bates turned up dead around the end of August. He's been very nervous since then because no one has seen either you or Patrick. Mr. McDonald was furious, and Mr. Palmer has men over at the saloon all the time. I think that's why Harry wants to leave. The Tribune *did a big story on your husband's innocence and is asking for any information on your whereabouts. I hope you two are all right and out of the city. It's going to be a terrible winter.*

Good luck,
Nancy Brown

Dear Laurie,
I've not much time to write. Stephan would be having himself a fit if he knew I was in Harry Brown's house right this very minute. I've no idea why the Good Lord chose you for this trial, my dear friend, but I've too much Irish blood in me veins to doubt the possibility. Besides, Laurie, I know you'd never lie to me about somethin' like this. Rest your mind about us at least. I'm as big as a house and the baby is fine. Stephan had a touch of that male chauvanism you talked about when I showed him the money, but now he understands.

I've got me a wonderful plan of how to use some of that very gift. I hope, sister of my heart, that if I'm successful, somewhere in the future you'll find a bit of me there. Think chocolate!

Now, about your stubborn Irishman. We've only seen him once and it's taken me until now, near the end of October, to find a way to get to Nancy. It seems he tried to give Stephan some money too. Patrick feels it's best to stay out of sight even though he's been proven innocent. McDonald has mighty long arms, and he doesn't want anything to happen to us.

He's missing you so, Laurie. I could see it in his eyes. I'm not wanting to hurt you with this, but I want you to know that wherever you are, your man is grieving for you and loves you so much that I've been worried he'd not stay on this earth long. Stephan found out he's working on the snow gangs. What with the terrible snows we-'ve been having, it's hard, brutal work, but Patrick told him it's the only way he can get tired enough to sleep.

I warned him you'd be mighty unhappy if he worked himself to death, and he gave me the strangest look. He smiled just once, as though he had the King of the Leprechauns under lock and key. "I've only got to stay alive for three months, Molly." We haven't seen him since. I'm prayin' like a brand-new convert, Laurie. Begging that a special saint takes your case straight to Mother Mary for divine intervention.

Well, I must go. Nancy Brown has been right sweet about all of this. I can't help agreeing with so much you said while you were here. We women seem to see straight to the heart of things, by-passing so much that has the men up in arms. By the way, our League is busting at the seams. The ladies wish you were here, but they're moving ahead. Jane Addams asked after you, too, and was disappointed to hear you'd left.

We'll none of us forget you, my best of friends. I miss you and love you. Thank you for coming into all our lives.

Love,
Molly

P.S. How do you like the names Lauren Kath-
leen and Stephan Patrick? Sweet heaven, but I
wish you could be here!

Lauren's head felt as if it was going to explode. For
three days she'd been grieving in her hotel room, reading Nancy's journal over and over. She would never
doubt miracles again, because her hunch weeks ago had
been correct. New messages, written in the past she'd
shared, had appeared in the old Brown journal and sent
her on a frantic trip to the historical society to read all
the related history she could find.

It had taken until the second day for her to gather the
courage to open the fragile paper she'd retrieved from
the column in the Museum of Science and Industry.
Patrick's note had literally brought her to her knees on
the soft mauve carpet in her room. The crying had
started then; she had cried so much that she hadn't been
able to keep down more than a bite of food since then.

She was weak, wrung out, sick, depressed, afraid, and
lonely. So achingly lonely that she hurt deep in her
bones. As a man condemned to die at midnight might
compulsively check his watch, Lauren couldn't stop
herself from picking up the thick, yellowed paper that
represented both heaven and hell; all that had been and
all that she was terrified to hope for.

Pushing back her limp, dirty hair, she toed a few
books out of the way and burrowed into the tangled
bedding. She had the words memorized, but the scrawl
of Patrick's actual handwriting was the only tangible
evidence that he had really existed. One dim light illuminated the closed room, and Lauren easily ignored
the rumbling of her stomach because of the pain in her
heart.

My dearest wife,

I'm praying that somehow, one day, you'll have this in your hands. Right now it's the only thing keeping me from jumping in the lake. I think of you nearly every minute of the day, lass, and I dream of you so at night that I—Well, I'm supposing you know how I feel.

Just as you disappeared before my eyes, Bates was shot in our struggle and died. I went to Potter Palmer, and all the legal things were taken care of. But I'm not taking a chance that anything will happen to me. I'm laying low, lass. McDonald is not a man to take lightly, and I'm not giving him the least little opportunity to find me.

I've your bag with me, love. It alone has kept me from losing my mind. Whenever I feel you becoming too much the dream, I can open it and touch a part of you; a part of your world. I'll guard its secrets, my little she-cat, so don't you worry.

I found our only hope in the bag, Laurie. Your automobile license, your birthday! An artifact with printed dates of importance! The numbers better damn well open the door! Please be in the rotunda if you can. I'm livin' for this day, love.

But if it doesn't work, I'll not have you crying the rest of your life away. The time we had together was worth it, sweetheart. Thank you for teaching this stubborn Irishman to trust again, to love again.

And I want you to know, Lauren Ann Sullivan Dugan, that not a one of your modern ways would ever keep me from being with you; from loving you with my whole foolishly prideful heart. Because of you, I know I'm not at all like my father or my uncle.

As long as there's a breath in my body, I'll not

*stop trying to get to you. My love will never hold you
down or hold you back and, God willing, if He gives
us the chance, we can work everything out.*

*I carry the card next to my heart. It never
leaves me. The thought of holding you in my arms
again is all—all—God, Lauren, I love you. Be
there. Be there.*

Patrick

*P.S. I was such a fool that day at the Fair.
Men, money, and pride are a crack-brained combination. Forgive me. Faith, but I would have
wasted away without your beautiful image to hold
in my hands. Maybe mine will comfort you until
my body can. Is there a baby?*

Lauren lay flat on her back, letting the tears dribble
through her hair and onto the sheets. She held the charcoal sketch of Patrick above her head. He had ripped
their picture in half and sent his love along with his
face. And she was so grateful. He couldn't have left
anything dearer.

How was she going to endure the wait? It would be
three and a half long months until her birthday. If she
lived them like this, she would be a physical wreck and
probably institutionalized. She drew her hands over the
rumpled bedding and covered her stomach with her
palms. This behavior had to end right now! If there was
a baby, and she'd been sick enough for it to be a possibility, it was high time she started taking care of them
both.

Lauren hated to leave the city she and Patrick had
shared, albeit a hundred years ago, but it was time to
go home. She had to eat and work and live one day at
a time until she could come back for him. On weak
legs, she headed for the shower and even felt a tiny
spark of anticipation. She could get ready for him to

come to the future just like she'd gotten ready to go to the past.

Horse breeding and ranch living jumped to the top of her research list. She was going to play this out to the very last card and hold nothing back, just as Aunt Lucy had told her. Whatever happened, she knew Patrick loved her; there wasn't anything that could take that knowledge away from her. It made her strong. Lauren turned on the hot water and started making a mental list.

Patrick thought the days would never pass. From dawn 'til past dark he worked with the snow-removal gangs and tried to remain invisible. Just another man down on his luck, surviving any way he could. They shoveled ten back-breaking hours a day to earn one meal and lodgings for the night. But he had it better than so many that winter. Every morning he saw policemen carrying away babies abandoned in the streets, some of them dead. Folks were starving. Oh, he still had the money from Bertha Palmer, but Patrick felt it was Laurie's. He would only use it if things got truly desperate.

Stephan had tried to make him come for Thanksgiving, but Patrick gently refused. It hurt too much to be with the Polaskis and not see Laurie there. He'd rather work himself to mind-numbing exhaustion; if he ever rested with the energy to think, the despair became unbearable.

Now, at long last, he only had a week to go. He sat with his back to the wall in the far corner of the large communal room that housed the snow gangs. Makeshift cots ringed the open area, and a number of dirty, hungry men tried to sleep. Patrick could almost smell the desperation along with the sweat. The musty odors of unwashed clothes and unwashed bodies couldn't stop him from dreaming of fragrant roses and satin-smooth skin.

He closed his eyes, trying to conjure the feel of Laurie's welcoming body closing around his.

The sharp burst of heat warmed him from the inside out, and Dugan quirked his mouth in a rueful smile. *There's no point startin' the fire, me boyo, with nothin' to dose the flame.* He forced the fantasy from his mind and pulled Laurie's driving card from the protective spot inside his undershirt.

Bloody hell, but it got to him every time. Seein' her so real; the colors and all. Her honey-streaked hair, her deep blue eyes, the cinnamon sprinkle across her cute little nose, and those sweet, berry pink lips curved into a breath-stealing smile. Had there ever been born a woman more tempting, more beautiful, more perfect for him? Patrick felt the blood pumping thickly through his body.

The numbers on which he was pinning his entire future were printed in the top left corner: Expires birthday 12-15-1995.

"Hey thar, fella, what's that ya got?" The grasping hand came out of nowhere and latched onto the card in Dugan's hand. Hell! He'd been so far gone that he hadn't kept up his guard. Many of the men around him would kill him for the carpetbag alone.

"Just take your hands off, me friend," Patrick drawled in a heavy brogue, belying the tension coiled inside him like a snake ready to strike. His grip tightened, and he felt the other man's pull against his. He would rather lose his life than lose the only hope of getting back to Laurie.

"Just want to take a look at them colors, mister."

"No—"

The rip echoed like thunder in Patrick's ears; he felt his flesh tear away along with the heavy, coated paper. The filthy bastard ran before he could even get to his feet. Dugan surged up and then slumped against the rough wall. He couldn't believe his eyes. The corner

365

was gone. The top of Laurie's head was gone. The last number of the year was gone. Now it read: expires birthday 12-15-1995.

Not a man in the dismal room slept through Patrick's roar of rage.

Lauren forced herself to sit on the bench and watch the parking lot slowly empty. It was the second Saturday in December, and shopping had definitely taken precedence over museum-going. She was glad of that. The fewer people, the fewer spectators to her breakdown. It was cold, and the manicured layer of snow on the ground gave everything that Christmas card look. Luckily the skies were clear, and bundled up as she was, she felt warm enough.

It was so odd to see the Palace like this. A parking lot and high-rise buildings where the state houses had been. No Midway; no laughing tourists in turn-of-the-century dress. Lauren sniffed back the tears that had been threatening since she'd gotten on the plane two days ago. The changes in Jackson Park had been almost as big a shock as the weather. It made Patrick seem so far away—impossibly far away.

She wiggled a gloved hand deep in her parka's side pocket and pulled out the one and only kind of food for which she had an uncontrollable craving. An uncontrollable craving that had started three months ago, right after the throw-up phase had passed. Lauren juggled the small cellophane bag with one hand and rested the other on the small round bulge barely discernable under all her padding.

The first smooth glide of her tongue across the chocolate drops in her mouth brought with it the rich flavor of comfort and bittersweet memories. She and Patrick and Molly and Stephan toasting with chocolate chip cookies; the baby shower; making love for the first time. Lauren's eyes felt heavy and hot from the exquisite agony those memories called up.

She spread out the empty bag flat over her stomach and smiled in spite of her tremendous anxiety. Four weeks after returning to California, Lauren had known she couldn't deny her morning sickness any longer. She'd been working like a possessed soul, trying to discover how to go about creating an identity for someone who had no records when another urgent trip to the bathroom convinced her to get a pregnancy test.

Carrying that little box to the checkout register had been one of the loneliest moments she had faced since she'd been flung back to the future. It would have been so wonderful to have had Patrick with her, kissing her, laughing with happiness. And just when Lauren felt all her control about to be washed away on a sea of tears, she saw them. Stacks and stacks of small bags on sale for holiday baking.

Molly's Morsels! Lauren had literally trembled from head to toe, handling the bag as if it was a live grenade. *Since 1896* was printed boldly under the drawing of a certain Irish Gibson girl. And on the back was a recipe and a note from the president of the company, John Patrick Polaski.

To this day she didn't know how she had made it out of that store and back to her condo. When her little stick turned pink, she didn't feel nearly as alone with Molly's image in her hands.

With a quick tug, Lauren pulled her knit cap lower on her ears and checked the new backpack at her side. *Time to gut it up, Mrs. Dugan, and get in there.* How could she be dragging her feet like this? Except for the precious life growing under her heart, waiting and planning for this day had been her whole focus. She shifted forward and determinedly grabbed the bag packed with a man's long winter coat and hat, then started walking to the entrance.

Although Lauren had gone over this repeatedly until both her head and her heart ached, she still had no idea how it worked, how to make it work. A huge wave of fear broke over her as the warm air from inside the museum streamed around her body. With a yank her hat was gone and she trudged up the stairs, fluffing her hair and shrugging off the down jacket.

A careful scan of the rotunda confirmed that it was deserted. The coast was clear. Lauren's heart hitched at her memory of Patrick and that phrase. She moved back to the spot against the wall where she had collapsed so long ago. Then, after placing her things on the floor, she smoothed the soft, amethyst maternity sweater over her stretchy jeans and folded her arms tight, trying to control her wild emotions.

Not once had she allowed herself to contemplate what would happen should this day go wrong. Her un-flagging optimism was like a talisman. But now . . . what would she do if . . . ? *Oh, baby mine,* she thought, closing her eyes and shaping her hands over the tiny life that had kept hers going. *If only Daddy . . .*

With no warning, a biting chill whipped into the room and the very air began to smell of frost and lingering smoke. In a panic, Lauren opened her eyes and squinted through the unnatural, gray gloom that had filtered into the rotunda. It took a minute for her brain to verify what her heart knew instinctively. *It was happening!* Patrick! Patrick!

"Patrick?" The actual sound finally burst from her aching throat. Lauren stepped forward into the grainy mist and saw a shape huddled in a corner. All around that area the color had drained from the objects. The images were shaded with tones of gray, as if they weren't quite real, not fully materialized. The cold in the room took Lauren's breath away. Hoarse with fear, she spoke again.

"Patrick, love, I'm here. Where are you? Please come to me. . . . Please!"

The obscure shape began to shift and take form, until turning, it was revealed to be a man. Her man! Patrick Dugan!

"Laurie?" His voice was weak and frightenly distant, as if it were still too many years away.

"Patrick!" Lauren demanded, fighting down the dread twisting her into knots. "What's wrong? I can see you," she took a few jerky steps toward him, reaching out her hands, "but I . . . I . . ."

"Aww, darlin'," he sighed faintly. "My prayers have been answered. I'll never doubt the powers of Heaven again, for here you are, lass," he waved a hand sheathed with a ragged glove in her direction, "my very own angel come at last."

"Patrick," Lauren cried, moving until she was stopped at the fuzzy line of demarcation between reality and ghostly mist. One side, rich and vibrant with the colors and objects from 1995, and the other, the muted, toneless images of a hundred years ago. It was almost as if he were trapped in some kind of limbo.

"Tell me why you're not completely here! What do we have to do?"

"I had what we needed, sweetheart." She could see the weary lines of grief marking his tortured face. He shrugged and lifted her old carpetbag, setting it between his feet. "I tore this bag apart, lookin' for a key to get to you. The day I found it, I started wantin' to live again."

The smile on his too-thin face was painful to see. It was hell on earth to be this close and not be able to hold him, feel his arms tight around her.

"But your license got torn and . . . now it seems I can't come all the way. Sweet Jesus, but you're beautiful."

Patrick lifted his wavery hands, as if to touch her, and the colorless eyes that bored into hers were filled

369

with such agony and such desperation. . . . Oh, God. Lauren had seen that look once before, and she felt fear such as she had never known.

"I'm dead to you, lass, and there's not a thing we can do." He, too, tried to press through the eerie barrier and groaned in frustration. "Tell me quick, are you well? Will you be all right? Promise me, love." Patrick straightened completely and fisted his hands at his sides. "Lauren Ann Dugan, promise me you'll not wither up—"

"No! No! Do you hear me?" Lauren threw back her head and screamed. "This is not going to happen to us again!"

The fury burning in her veins completely incinerated rational thought. She had no idea why she was saying these things, but deep down, on some undefinable level, she knew the truth.

"You are not dead, Patrick Dugan," she cried. "And I am not going to wither up. In fact, I am going to blossom." She dropped her hands to the curve of her belly and watched his gaze follow.

"Holy Mary!" he whispered.

"This is your baby in here, Patrick, yours and mine. How can you be dead when it's your seed filling me with life? How can you be dead when I feel part of you moving and growing in me?"

The wonder on his face was transforming.

Patrick's eyes slowly traveled from the soft mound of his child to the wet, fierce eyes of his wife, his love. Some tingling force seemed to snap and writhe around him. It was almost as if he could feel him-self . . . becoming.

With a mighty surge of concentration he opened his hands, spread his fingers wide, and pushed them pain-fully through the barrier. He clenched his teeth and leaned into the effort with all his strength.

"Nothing . . . nothing will keep us apart this time,

love,'' he ground out as his gray fingers reached the edge of Lauren's sweater.

They both watched it happen. They both felt it happen.

At the first touch of Patrick's hands over their baby, life began to flow, freely and unchecked. All that was long dead, long past, melted away. Color and light rushed into the void, and Patrick Dugan sank warm and real into his wife's joyous arms.

''Laurie, are you sleepin', love?

''Mmmm . . . no.''

''What are you doin' then?''

''I'm feeling.''

''What?''

Lauren lifted her head from her husband's shoulder and ran her fingers lightly through the crinkly russet hair covering his chest. Only the festive lights from a small tabletop Christmas tree glowed in the warm hotel room, illuminating the remains of a Mexican feast.

It had taken all their combined strength to get the overcoat on Patrick and get them both out of the museum and into a cab. And it was probably for the best that his first view of a modern city had been blunted by exhaustion.

''I'm memorizing this moment. Feeling you . . . our baby . . . happiness.'' She lifted up on an elbow and leaned closer to nuzzle the tender spot behind his ear.

Patrick tugged on her chin so he could look into her eyes. ''What happened to us?''

''I don't think we'll ever know completely, love.'' Lauren pressed a lingering kiss on his mouth. ''I'm just grateful that somebody, somewhere, brought us together.''

''I'd not be surprised if my ma and your Aunt Lucy had a hand in this.''

She smiled and nodded, rubbing her nose against his. ''I'm glad you're a man who's open to unusual possibilities. You're going to need a flexible outlook for the next little while.''

''I've read the history book you had in your bag, lass,'' Patrick murmured, trailing a string of kisses across her jaw. ''I'm sure there'll be much to learn, but I've got you and our baby. More than enough reason to love this new time I've been given.'' He boldly fitted one hand to her bare breast and then slid it down her body until it brushed over her silky, rounded stomach.

''Faith, but all that I've seen so far has been wondrous beyond belief. I like your favorite food. . . . I like your colored lights. . . . And most of all, I like your showers.'' He rolled fully on top of her and took a long, loving taste of the sweet welcome waiting between her parted lips.

''Aw . . . darlin', to have you close to me again like this—to feel every inch of your skin next to mine . . .'' He nudged her legs apart and moved forward, sending the power of his love deep into the haven he'd thought eternally lost.

Lauren's joyous tears washed away all the months of loneliness and fear. The strength of Patrick's arms fueled the fire that burned so bright between them, the flame that would never die. She looked deep into his shining eyes and he into hers.

''We'll have . . . each other . . . forever now,'' Lauren whispered in breathless gasps.

''That and more, my angel,'' Patrick vowed, his needy mouth moving with love and passion over hers. ''For such as us, even longer than forever. . . .''

Epilogue

"Tell me truthfully, Patrick, how much do you think it will hurt?"

Patrick couldn't look away from the serious eyes of his white-gowned wife, sitting nervously on the hospital bed.

"You were right next to me in class, Laurie," he said with a mix of tenderness and humor. "You know as much as I do. But *truthfully*, I think that what you imagine will always be worse."

"Is that supposed to make me feel better?" she shot back, and Patrick smiled. It must be a crazy, hormonal surge giving her the odd feeling that they had played this scene before.

Seven hours and ten minutes later, after his mother had quite vocally assured his father that even her wildest imagination could not match what she'd just been through, redheaded, red-faced Patrick Stephan Dugan was born. Caught in the arms of a man who had not believed that fathers-to-be were actually encouraged and trained to do this until he had attended his first Lamaze class. Talk about culture shock!

Lauren watched her husband with such love and pride. He had handled it all like a much younger man; a hundred years younger, to be exact. Oh, it was still a challenge to fit in and adapt, but Patrick had come so far in the last months, it was amazing. When something really threw him for a loop, their ranch in central California provided a laid-back, low-tech sanctuary from the fast-paced 1990s.

They had found a comfortable way to balance both their worlds, and their love had flourished along with Patrick's horses. Gradually his reputation as a breeder was starting to grow, and thanks to the money he'd saved from Bertha Palmer, finances weren't a worry. The collectors Lauren had contacted had been ecstatic at the number and quality of the antique bills.

Lauren settled back against the pillows with a sigh of sleepy contentment as the amber glow of the May sunset gilded the objects in her room. Her dearest dream had come true. The love, the family Aunt Lucy had told her to reach for was only ever a kiss away.

Patrick held his son as if he were made of fragile china. The small ember of hope he had hidden for so long burned bright within him now, stoked by the love and acceptance Laurie had brought to him across time. Never again need he fear that it would all be taken away or turn to ashes. Between the three of them they were generating enough fuel to last a lifetime. And this was just the beginning.

He walked carefully to sit beside his beautiful wife, still a wanton mix of priss and she-cat. With a luscious melding of lips and tongues he told her again how much she pleased him, how much her love meant.

"So, my sweet angel, when will you be willin' to go through all this again?"

Lauren looked up from the precious bundle on her lap and into the glowing eyes of her husband. "Patrick, darlin'," she drawled, reaching up to sift her fingers through his still surprising blown-dry hair, "I know that you've gotten into this baby thing in a big way, but really, that is not the question to ask right now. Everyone says mothers forget the pain of childbirth, but I think I need to give it a few more days before I even contemplate getting back into this particular saddle."

"I suppose we can wait for little Molly Ann then...."

"Hey, Dugan," she teased wickedly. "Cheer up! With the scientific strides they're making almost daily, who knows—maybe you could do it next time."

For just a moment she had him. His sexy eyebrows jumped up to the middle of his forehead and he opened his mouth as if to ask her if it was possible. And then he laughed. Wrapping her up in his arms and his love, they both laughed until wee Stephan cried.

"No matter what the world learns in the next years, my sassy lass," he murmured against her smiling lips, "making babies is one old-fashioned custom I'll not be changin'."

Following a quiet tap, the ornate ivory door swung open. A small man with a round, anxious face rushed toward the single occupant in the long hall.

"Counselor," he gasped, puffing great gulps of rarified air, "I was told the correction has finally been made."

Behind the gold desk topped with luminous marble, the imposing counselor nodded and directed the recorder to sit.

"This has weighed on you for a long time, hasn't it, Tomas?"

"It had never happened before, nor has it happened since. What was I to think, but that somehow I caused it. And with that one insistent woman always asking . . . I . . ." He twisted his hands together and continued. "Well, since that transport, I have not been able to forget the looks on their faces. Please tell me if it is true."

"It was no one's fault, Tomas. It happened just as it was planned."

"What?"

"It was their test."

"But I have never heard of it being done that way."

"You know that all of earth life is a test. We've been there, remember? These two are very special, and sometimes, when the example will influence many, an unusual trial is given."

"But is that fair?"

"When they have finished their span you ask them if they could have learned so much any other way." The tall man stood and gestured to a mural halfway down the hall. "Now, every person on earth who comes in contact with them will feel what they share, and believe it is possible. And then my friend . . ." he said, coming to stand before the huge picture that had become an opaque screen, ". . . the hope will grow inside those people also."

"I see."

And the small recorder did see. The two faces that had haunted him for so long grew large and brilliant before his eyes. The force they radiated was awesome. It came only to those with the will to overcome anything required.

It was the timeless power of love.

Author's Note

Friends:

Finding this extra bit of insight at the end of a book has always been one of my favorite parts to read. Now, I discover, it's also one of my favorite parts to write.

What was real? The Chicago World's Fair and the sights and sounds I've described were most definitely real: the Cracker Jacks, the Ferris wheel and even young F.D.R.'s visit. I am still amazed that, considering my love of history, an event of this significance came as a total surprise. Needless to say, my imagination took off and I built my first book around it.

My facts are as accurate as the information I researched and I must thank the helpful people at the Chicago Museum of Science and Industry, who answered so many questions. I did make a few structural changes in the museum for my story, but it is truly the only remaining building of the great World Exposition of 1893. Yes, friends, the Fair was in 1893. It just took me a bit longer to get Patrick and Lauren there.

Michael Cassius McDonald was indeed a major crime figure of the time, although his actions in *Longer Than Forever* are my own manipulations. Also, unbelievably, the existence of the Holmes horror house is historical fact. The man they called Doc Holmes was tried in a court of law in 1895. His various torture rooms were real.

Last but not least, I simply had to include the origins of the chocolate chip cookie, one of our country's favorites. It was just plain fun. If you have any other questions, I love to hear from fellow readers. You can write to me, with a SASE if you'd like a response, in care of Leisure Books.

SPECIAL SNEAK PREVIEW FOLLOWS!

Madeline Baker writing as Amanda Ashley

Cursed by the darkness, he searches through the ages for the redeeming light, the one woman who can save him. An angel of purity and light, she fears the handsome stranger whose eyes promise endless ecstasy even while his mouth whispers dark secrets. They are two people longing for fulfillment, yearning for a love like no other. Alone, they will face a desolate destiny. Together, they will share undying passion, defy eternity, and embrace the night.

He walked the streets for hours after he left the orphanage, his thoughts filled with Sara, her fragile beauty, her sweet innocence, her unwavering trust. She had accepted him into her life without question, and the knowledge cut him to the quick. He did not like deceiving her, hiding the dark secret of what he was, nor did he like to think about how badly she would be hurt when his nighttime visits ceased, as they surely must.

He had loved her from the moment he first saw her, but always from a distance, worshiping her as the moon might worship the sun, basking in her heat, her light, but wisely staying away lest he be burned.

And foolishly, he had strayed too close. He had soothed her tears, held her in his arms, and now he was paying the price. He was burning, like a moth drawn to a flame. Burning with need. With desire. With an unholy lust, not for her body, but for the very essence of her life.

It sickened him that he should want her that way, that he could even consider such a despicable thing. And yet he could think of little else. Ah, to hold her in his arms, to feel his body become one with hers as he drank of her sweetness. . . .

For a moment, he closed his eyes and let himself imagine it, and then he swore a long vile oath filled with pain and longing.

Hands clenched, he turned down a dark street, his self-anger turning to loathing, and the loathing to rage. He felt the need to kill, to strike out, to make someone else suffer as he was suffering.

Pity the poor mortal who next crossed his path, he thought. Then he gave himself over to the hunger pounding through him.

She woke covered with perspiration, Gabriel's name on her lips. Shivering, she drew the covers up to her chin.

It had only been a dream. Only a dream.

She spoke the words aloud, finding comfort in the sound of her own voice. A distant bell chimed the hour. Four o'clock.

Gradually, her breathing returned to normal. Only a dream, she said again, but it had been so real. She had felt the cold breath of the night, smelled the rank odor of fear rising from the body of the faceless man cowering in the shadows. She had sensed a deep anger, a wild uncontrollable evil personified by a being in a flowing black cloak. Even now, she could feel his anguish, his loneliness, the alienation that cut him off from the rest of humanity.

It had all been so clear in the dream, but now it made no sense. No sense at all.

With a slight shake of her head, she snuggled deeper

under the covers and closed her eyes.

It was just a dream, nothing more.

Sunk in the depths of despair, Gabriel prowled the deserted abbey. What had happened to his self-control? Not for centuries had he taken enough blood to kill, only enough to assuage the pain of the hunger, to ease his unholy thirst.

A low groan rose in his throat. Sara had happened. He wanted her and he couldn't have her. Somehow, his desire and his frustration had gotten tangled up with his lust for blood.

It couldn't happen again. It had taken him centuries to learn to control the hunger, to give himself the illusion that he was more man than monster.

Had he been able, he would have prayed for forgiveness, but he had forfeited the right to divine intervention long ago.

"Where will we go tonight?"

Gabriel stared at her. She'd been waiting for him again, clothed in her new dress, her eyes bright with anticipation. Her goodness drew him, soothed him, calmed his dark side even as her beauty, her innocence, teased his desire.

He stared at the pulse throbbing in her throat. "Go?"

Sara nodded.

With an effort, he lifted his gaze to her face. "Where would you like to go?"

"I don't suppose you have a horse?"

"A horse?"

"I've always wanted to ride."

He bowed from the waist. "Whatever you wish, mi-lady," he said. "I'll not be gone long."

It was like having found a magic wand, Sara mused as she waited for him to return. She had only to voice her desire, and he produced it.

Twenty minutes later, she was seated before him on a prancing black stallion. It was a beautiful animal, tall and muscular, with a flowing mane and tail.

She leaned forward to stroke the stallion's neck. His coat felt like velvet beneath her hand. "What's his name?"

"Necromancer," Gabriel replied, pride and affection evident in his tone.

"Necromancer? What does it mean?"

"One who communicates with the spirits of the dead."

Sara glanced at him over her shoulder. "That seems an odd name for a horse."

"Odd, perhaps," Gabriel replied cryptically, "but fitting."

"Fitting? In what way?"

"Do you want to ride, Sara, or spend the night asking foolish questions?"

She pouted prettily for a moment and then grinned at him. "Ride!"

A word from Gabriel and they were cantering through the dark night, heading into the countryside.

"Faster," Sara urged.

"You're not afraid?"

"Not with you."

"You should be afraid, Sara Jayne," he muttered under his breath, "especially with me."

He squeezed the stallion's flanks with his knees and the horse shot forward, his powerful hooves skimming across the ground.

Sara shrieked with delight as they raced through the darkness. This was power, she thought, the surging body of the horse, the man's strong arm wrapped securely around her waist. The wind whipped through her hair, stinging her cheeks and making her eyes water, but she only threw back her head and laughed.

"Faster!" she cried, reveling in the sense of freedom that surged within her.

Hedges and trees and sleeping farmhouses passed by in a blur. Once, they jumped a four-foot hedge, and she felt as if she were flying. Sounds and scents blended together: the chirping of crickets, the bark of a dog, the smell of damp earth and lathered horseflesh, and over all the touch of Gabriel's breath upon her cheek, the steadying strength of his arm around her waist.

Gabriel let the horse run until the animal's sides were heaving and covered with foamy lather, and then he drew back on the reins, gently but firmly, and the stallion slowed, then stopped.

"That was wonderful!" Sara exclaimed.

She turned to face him, and in the bright light of the moon, he saw that her cheeks were flushed, her lips parted, her eyes shining like the sun.

How beautiful she was! His Sara, so full of life. What cruel fate had decreed that she should be bound to a wheelchair? She was a vivacious girl on the brink of womanhood. She should be clothed in silks and satins, surrounded by gallant young men.

Dismounting, he lifted her from the back of the horse. Carrying her across the damp grass, he sat down on a large boulder, settling her in his lap.

"Thank you, Gabriel," she murmured.

"It was my pleasure, milady."

"Hardly that," she replied with a saucy grin. "I'm sure ladies don't ride pell-mell through the dark astride a big black devil horse."

"No," he said, his gray eyes glinting with amusement, "they don't."

"Have you known many ladies?"

"A few." He stroked her cheek with his forefinger, his touch as light as thistledown.

"And were they accomplished and beautiful?"

Gabriel nodded. "But none so beautiful as you."

She basked in his words, in the silent affirmation she read in his eyes.

"Who are you, Gabriel?" she asked, her voice soft and dreamy. "Are you man or magician?"

"Neither."

"But still my angel?"

"Always, *cara*."

With a sigh, she rested her head against his shoulder and closed her eyes. How wonderful, to sit here in the dark of night with his arms around her. She could almost forget that she was crippled. Almost.

She lost all track of time as she sat there, secure in his arms. She heard the chirp of crickets, the sighing of the wind through the trees, the pounding of Gabriel's heart beneath her cheek.

Her breath caught in her throat as she felt the touch of his hand in her hair and then the brush of his lips.

Abruptly, he stood up. Before she quite knew what was happening, she was on the horse's back and Gabriel was swinging up behind her. He moved with the lithe grace of a cat vaulting a fence.

She sensed a change in him, a tension she didn't understand. A moment later, his arm was locked around her waist and they were riding through the night.

She leaned back against him, braced against the solid wall of his chest. She felt his arm tighten around her, felt his breath on her cheek.

Pleasure surged through her at his touch and she placed her hand over his forearm, drawing his arm more securely around her, tacitly telling him that she enjoyed his nearness.

She thought she heard a gasp, as if he was in pain, but she shook the notion aside, telling herself it was probably just the wind crying through the trees.

386

Too soon, they were back at the orphanage.

"You'll come tomorrow?" she asked as he settled her in her bed, covering her as if she were a child.

"Tomorrow," he promised. "Sleep well, *cara.*"

"Dream of me," she murmured.

With a nod, he turned away. Dream of her, he thought. If only he could!

"Where would you like to go tonight?" Gabriel asked the following evening.

"I don't care, so long as it's with you."

Moments later, he was carrying her along a pathway in the park across from the orphanage.

Sara marveled that he held her so effortlessly, that it felt so right to be carried in his arms. She rested her head on his shoulder, content. A faint breeze played hide and seek with the leaves of the trees. A lover's moon hung low in the sky. The air was fragrant with night blooming flowers, but it was Gabriel's scent that rose all around her—warm and musky, reminiscent of aged wine and expensive cologne.

He moved lightly along the pathway, his footsteps making hardly a sound. When they came to a stone bench near a quiet pool, he sat down, placing her on the bench beside him.

It was a lovely place, a fairy place. Elegant ferns, tall and lacy, grew in wild profusion near the pool. In the distance, she heard the questioning hoot of an owl.

"What did you do all day?" she asked, turning to look at him.

Gabriel shrugged. "Nothing to speak of. And you?"

"I read to the children. Sister Mary Josepha has been giving me more and more responsibility."

"And does that make you happy?"

"Yes. I've grown very fond of my little charges. They so need to be loved. To be touched. I had never realized how important it was, to be held, until—'' A faint flush stained her cheeks. ''Until you held me. There's such comfort in the touch of a human hand.''

Gabriel grunted softly. Human, indeed, he thought bleakly.

Sara smiled. ''They seem to like me, the children. I don't know why.''

But he knew why. She had so much love to give, and no outlet for it.

''I hate to think of all the time I wasted wallowing in self-pity,'' Sara remarked. ''I spent so much time sitting in my room, sulking because I couldn't walk, when I could have been helping the children, loving them.'' She glanced up at Gabriel. ''They're so easy to love.''

''So are you.'' He had not meant to speak the words aloud, but they slipped out. ''I mean, it must be easy for the children to love you. You have so much to give.''

She smiled, but it was a sad kind of smile. ''Perhaps that's because no one else wants it.''

''Sara—''

''It's all right. Maybe that's why I was put here, to comfort the little lost lambs that no one else wants.''

I want you. The words thundered in his mind, in his heart, in his soul.

Abruptly, he stood up and moved away from the bench. He couldn't sit beside her, feel her warmth, hear the blood humming in her veins, sense the sadness dragging at her heart, and not touch her, take her.

He stared into the depths of the dark pool, the water as black as the emptiness of his soul. He'd been alone for so long, yearning for someone who would share his life, needing someone to see him for what he was and love him anyway.

A low groan rose in his throat as the centuries of

388

loneliness wrapped around him.

"Gabriel?" Her voice called out to him, soft, warm, caring.

With a cry, he whirled around and knelt at her feet. Hesitantly, he took her hands in his.

"Sara, can you pretend I'm one of the children? Can you hold me, and comfort me, just for tonight?"

"I don't understand."

"Don't ask questions, *cara*. Please just hold me. Touch me."

She gazed down at him, into the fathomless depths of his dark gray eyes, and the loneliness she saw there pierced her heart. Tears stung her eyes as she reached for him.

He buried his face in her lap, ashamed of the need that he could no longer deny. And then he felt her hand stroke his hair, light as a summer breeze. Ah, the touch of a human hand, warm, fragile, pulsing with life.

Time ceased to have meaning as he knelt there, his head cradled in her lap, her hand moving in his hair, caressing his nape, feathering across his cheek. No wonder the children loved her. There was tranquility in her touch, serenity in her hand. A sense of peace settled over him, stilling his hunger. He felt the tension drain out of him, to be replaced with a nearly forgotten sense of calm. It was a feeling as close to forgiveness as he would ever know.

After a time, he lifted his head. Slightly embarrassed, he gazed up at her, but there was no censure in her eyes, no disdain, only a wealth of understanding.

"Why are you so alone, my angel?" she asked quietly.

"I have always been alone," he replied, and even now, when he was nearer to peace of spirit than he had been for centuries, he was aware of the vast gulf that separated him, not only from Sara, but from all of humanity as well.

Gently, she cupped his cheek with her hand. "Is there no one to love you then?"

"No one."

"I would love you, Gabriel."

"No!"

Stricken by the force of his denial, she let her hand fall into her lap. "Is the thought of my love so revolting?"

"No, don't ever think that." He sat back on his heels, wishing that he could sit at her feet forever, that he could spend the rest of his existence worshiping her beauty, the generosity of her spirit. "I'm not worthy of you, *cara*. I would not have you waste your love on me."

"Why, Gabriel? What have you done that you feel unworthy of love?"

Filled with the guilt of a thousand lifetimes, he closed his eyes and his mind filled with an image of blood. Rivers of blood. Oceans of death. Centuries of killing, of bloodletting. Damned. The Dark Gift had given him eternal life—and eternal damnation.

Thinking to frighten her away, he let her look deep into his eyes, knowing that what she saw within his soul would speak more eloquently than words.

He clenched his hands, waiting for the compassion in her eyes to turn to revulsion. But it didn't happen.

She gazed down at his upturned face for an endless moment, and then he felt the touch of her hand in his hair.

"My poor angel," she whispered. "Can't you tell me what it is that haunts you so?"

He shook his head, unable to speak past the lump in his throat.

"Gabriel." His name, nothing more, and then she leaned forward and kissed him.

It was no more than a feathering of her lips across his, but it exploded through him like concentrated sunlight. Hotter than a midsummer day, brighter than lightening, it burned through him and for a moment he felt whole again. Clean again.

Humbled to the core of his being, he bowed his head so she couldn't see his tears.

"I will love you, Gabriel," she said, still stroking his hair. "I can't help myself."

"Sara—"

"You don't have to love me back," she said quickly. "I just wanted you to know that you're not alone anymore."

A long shuddering sigh coursed through him, and then he took her hands in his, holding them tightly, feeling the heat of her blood, the pulse of her heart. Gently, he kissed her fingertips, and then, gaining his feet, he swung her into his arms.

"It's late," he said, his voice thick with the tide of emotions roiling within him. "We should go before you catch a chill."

"You're not angry?"

"No, *cara*."

How could he be angry with her? She was light and life, hope and innocence. He was tempted to fall to his knees and beg her forgiveness for his whole miserable existence.

But he couldn't burden her with the knowledge of what he was. He couldn't tarnish her love with the truth.

It was near dawn when they reached the orphanage. Once he had her settled in bed, he knelt beside her. "Thank you, Sara."

She turned on her side, a slight smile lifting the corners of her mouth as she took his hand in hers. "For what?"

"For your sweetness. For your words of love. I'll treasure them always."

"Gabriel." The smile faded from her lips. "You're not trying to tell me goodbye are you?"

He stared down at their joined hands: hers small and pale and fragile, pulsing with the energy of life, his large and cold, indelibly stained with blood and death.

If he had a shred of honor left, he would tell her good-bye and never see her again.

But then, even when he had been a mortal man, he'd always had trouble doing the honorable thing when it conflicted with something he wanted. And he wanted— no, needed—Sara. Needed her as he'd never needed anything else in his accursed life. And perhaps, in a way, she needed him. And even if it wasn't so, it eased his conscience to think it true.

"Gabriel?"

"No, *cara*, I'm not planning to tell you good-bye. Not now. Not ever."

The sweet relief in her eyes stabbed him to the heart. And he, cold, selfish monster that he was, was glad of it. Right or wrong, he couldn't let her go.

"Till tomorrow then?" she said, smiling once more.

"Till tomorrow, *cara mia*," he murmured. And for all the tomorrows of your life.

SHADOW LOVER

Lori Handeland

"A powerhouse of a story...one you don't want to miss!"
—*Rendezvous*

Devastated by the loss of her brother, Rachel Taylor vows to avenge his death. And after three long years, only one unforeseen problem will make her well-laid plans go awry: She is falling under the seductive spell of the man she blames for her pain and suffering.

The victim of a horrible accident, Michael Gabriel hides away from all save his most trusted friends. Yet the talented singer can't deny his growing attraction for Rachel—or his fear that secrets from his past may destroy her life.

Night after night, Michael and Rachel draw closer, unleashing long-suppressed passion. But someone will stop at nothing—not even murder—to come between them and keep Rachel from the love that can heal her heart.

_52010-9 $4.99 US/$5.99 CAN

CHARLIE AND THE ANGEL

LORI HANDELAND

On the run from his past, Charlie Coltrain never plans on rescuing a young nun in the desert. Charlie tells himself he wants only the money she offers him to take her to the convent. But hiding away such shimmering beauty is a sin he couldn't abide, and he yearns to send her to heaven with his forbidden touch.

Hoping to find happiness, Angelina Reyes is ready to follow her calling and dedicate her life to the Church. But the first soul she finds that needs saving belongs to a gunslinger wanted by the law, not the Lord. Determined to help Charlie at any cost, Angelina discovers that he is far more than a mere man—he is her mission, her temptation, her greatest love.

_3776-9 $4.99 US/$5.99 CAN

Futuristic Romance

Love in another time, another place.

Don't miss these breathtaking futuristic romances set on faraway worlds where passion is the lifeblood of every man and woman.

Circle of Light by Nancy Cane. When attorney Sarina Bretton is whisked to worlds she never imagined possible, she finds herself wanting to explore new realms of desire with the virile stranger who has abducted her. Besieged by enemies, and bedeviled by her love for Teir Reylock, Sarina vows that before a vapor cannon puts her asunder she will surrender to the seasoned warrior and his promise of throbbing ecstasy.

_51949-6 $4.99 US/$5.99 CAN

Paradise City by Sherrilyn Kenyon. Fleeing her past, Alix signs on as the engineer aboard Devyn Kell's spaceship. Soon they are outrunning the authorities and heading toward Paradise City, where even assassins aren't safe. But Alix doesn't know what real danger is until Devyn's burning kiss awakens her to a forbidden taste of heaven.

_51969-0 $4.99 US/$5.99 CAN

An Angel's Touch

Forever Angels

TRANA MAE SIMMONS

Tess Foster is convinced she has someone watching over her. The thoroughly modern woman has everything: a brilliant career, a rich fiance, and a glamorous life. But when her boyfriend demands she sign a prenuptial agreement, Tess thinks she's lost her happiness forever. Then her guardian angel sneezes and sends the woman of the nineties back to another era: the 1890s.

At first, Tess can't believe her senses. After all, no real man can be as handsome as the cowboy who rescues her from the Oklahoma wilderness. And Tess has never tasted sweeter ecstasy than she finds in Stone Chisum's kisses. But before she will surrender to a marriage made in heaven, Tess has to make sure that her bumbling guardian angel doesn't sneeze again—and ruin her second chance at love.

_52021-4 $4.99 US/$5.99 CAN

MOUNTAIN MAGIC — TRANA MAE SIMMONS

"Readers will remember Trana Mae Simmons's historical romances long after the last page has been read."
—Michalann Perry

Caitlyn O'Shaunessy is a born survivor. Orphaned at a young age, raised by a kindly old trapper, she fights hard to bury her demons as she ekes out an existence in the unforgiving wilds of the Rocky Mountains. But while she has faced down harsh elements and hostile Indians, she has never met anyone like the blue-eyed stranger who steals her heart and forever changes her world.

Jonathan Clay travels out West to ease the pain of betrayal and heartache he has left behind at his Virginia home. But when a game of chance lands him a feisty beauty with a sharp tongue, Jonathan is left with more than he bargains for. Caitlyn is the most independent, muleheaded woman on the frontier, and her innocent touch arouses a desire like none he has ever known.

_3835-8 $4.99 US/$6.99 CAN

An Angel's Touch

D.J.'s Angel
LORI HANDELAND

D.J. Halloran doesn't believe in love. She's just seen too much heartache—in her work as a police officer and in her own life. And she vowed a long time ago never to let anyone get close enough to hurt her, even if that someone is the very captivating, very handsome Chris McCall.

But D.J. also has an angel—a special guardian determined, at any cost, to teach D.J. the magic of love. So try as she might to resist Chris's many charms, D.J. knows she is in for an even tougher battle because of her exasperating heavenly companion's persistent faith in the power of love.

_52050-8 $5.99 US/$7.99 CAN

Dorchester Publishing Co., Inc.
65 Commerce Road
Stamford, CT 06902

SECOND CHANCE
LORI HANDELAND

Second Chance is a small Missouri town where the people believe that anyone who has done wrong deserves another shot. All the condemned man needs is someone to take responsibility for him. And that someone will never be Katherine Logan. With a bad marriage behind her, and the bank note on her horse ranch coming due, the young widow has neither the time nor the inclination to save a low-down bandit.

But the sight of the most wickedly tempting male ever to put his head through a noose changes her mind real quick. Although the townsfolk say Jake Banner will as soon shoot Katherine as change his outlaw ways, she won't listen. Deep within Jake's emerald eyes lie secrets that intrigue Katherine, daring her to give him a second chance at life—and herself a second chance at love.

_51966-6 $4.99 US/$5.99 CAN